NUCLEUS

Copyright © 2020 Aaron Hughes

ISBN: 978-1-925952-94-0
Published by Vivid Publishing
A division of Fontaine Publishing Group
P.O. Box 948, Fremantle
Western Australia 6959
www.vividpublishing.com.au

 A catalogue record for this
book is available from the
National Library of Australia

NUCLEUS

THE VIOLENT SCIENCE

AARON HUGHES

Hey Warren?

'Yeah?'

Would you tell me the story?

'Which story?'

Don't act like that, your story.

'Oh, that one, right. Eh, I don't know. It's pretty long'

It's not like we're going anywhere.

'I suppose not, no'

So, let's hear it already, I want to know why it is exactly that they call you the most influential person in history.

'Is that what they call me, is it?'

Look we have nothing but time. I'd like to hear about your travels is all.

'Why?'

Fine, we can sit here in silence if you prefer, it's all the same to me.

'Where would I even begin?'

Well from the beginning would be nice.

'Well, I was seventeen and didn't really have anything to care about. You know, to be honest I think I was afraid'

What did you have to be afraid of?

'It's not what I had, it's what I didn't have. I was so afraid of dying without anything mattering'

Well I don't think that's an issue anymore, now there's probably not a single person on this Earth who doesn't know your name.

'Probably not no, but back then I was just background noise, and I remember the exact day that started to change'

Was that the day when-

'Hey do you want to hear the story from me or not?'

My apologies, I'm listening, I understand if you need time to gather your thoughts.

'No, I remember it like it was yesterday'

———————————————

I
Sociability

I let my eyes wander around the room, washing only over the jars of beasts that never came to be. Ms Gwendolyn Harper's Year Twelve Advanced Biological Science, classroom number nine, right before lunch on a Thursday. The sides and back walls of classroom number nine are lined with shelves full of jars of preserved animals, all notable for one reason or another, and all collected by her on her own travels, as she'll quickly tell anyone who will listen. The entire front wall from the ceiling to the floor is covered in one ancient blackboard, it's had the same food webs and evolutionary trees drawn on it every year for every class since long before any of us existed. In front of the board lies Harper's desk, which she uses as more display space for her morbid collectibles. It also holds a fish tank full of pond scum and tadpoles currently on the cusp of frog-hood. The room always smells old, but not in a bad way. Not stale, but well-travelled. Not like it's dying, but like it has stories to tell.

The cavity in between all the chaos is filled with smaller desks, the habitat for us, the students. Two rows across and four rows deep for a whopping grand total of eight students taking this class, all thirsty for science, tantalised with the promise of a good university followed by a prestigious career. Eight is actually an unusually large number of university hopefuls in one grade for such a small town, or so we're told, I wouldn't know what it's like anywhere else. I couldn't tell you much about most of these people beyond their names. I sit on the left in the furthest back row, next to a girl named Ava. She's on her phone under her desk with one hand while trying to scrawl notes with the other. I've actually known her for a long time, we've always shared classes since we were five, but I'm only just realising that she's left handed, I can tell by the notes scribbled on the back of her right hand. I guess you do learn something new every day. Her long blonde hair trickling and piling onto the desk as she looks down, covering her notebook. I don't have people to text, but I sit here in the back for the same reason she probably does, to get away with not paying attention.

I direct my gaze past her and out the open window to my right, a portal hidden behind the familiar shelves and bordered with chipped paint and spider webs. Beyond the jars and behind the glass, the grey clouds linger above as far as I can see. A floorboard under me creaks, causing me to look up. I see Elliot ahead of me, with a foot on his desk and a pen in his mouth, not a care in the world. His dark hair styled meticulously, the same way it has been ever since he moved to this town. His immaculate jacket worth more than all my clothes combined. Proud and wild at heart, full of an explosive loathing to things that don't go his way. For now, the beast swings back on his chair peacefully.

Elliot Young and I are the only two students in this room who are unconcerned with the all-important, future-deciding exam tomorrow morning. Both confident in our own abilities, both unaffected by what anyone else thinks, but that's where our similarities end. I work hard, I study every spare minute I find in the day, I've never seen him toil for anything in his life. A challenge or a struggle would feel so foreign to such a brat. But I don't spend all that time studying because I want to compete with him, to be honest I don't know why I do it, it's just what the teachers say to do.

I tune in to Ms Harper's voice, just to make sure I haven't missed anything actually important. She's supposed to be going over the exam structure, but she's been spinning this tangential story about how she got bitten by this snake once. Gwendolyn Harper, an ecologist by trade. Barely thirty, and already been to more countries than most people can even name. In class, she chooses to wear a lab coat all the time, with the sleeves rolled up and her ash brown hair tied back, as if she would start a dangerous experiment at any time. She's a fun and caring teacher, with a way of encouraging her students without even trying. Which makes me feel bad for zoning out and daydreaming so often, but I make up for the lost time by always reading ahead in the syllabus later. It's an unusual system I know, but it works for me, and it affords me time in the days to let my mind wander.

Hearing Harper's tale about almost dying makes me look to my left at the coiled snake in its jar. It looks peaceful, neatly twisted around itself, suspended in its safe vessel. Two metres long according to its label, its cream underbelly transitions into its jet black dorsal scales, only the most perceptive could notice, that it's eyes are actually open. I stare into them.

'What would you say, Warren?'

Shit.

6

'Daydreaming again?' tuts Ms Harper, one hand on a hip, the other on her counter beside the tadpole tank.

'I'm sorry, I wasn't listening' I reply, my voice breaks.

Everybody shares a snicker, no one louder than Elliot.

'I can see that' Harper quips, she turns her attention from me to the whole class, 'You guys, I know this our last class of the semester but I'm sure I don't need to remind you that the exam is *tomorrow*, so let's use the time we have efficiently yeah?'

'We're trying but you keep distracting us by talking about getting bitten by snakes' Elliot says, as he slips his hands into his jacket pockets.

The class, save for me, erupts with laughter. I'm not one to suck up to the teacher, but I feel bad for Harper, she's trying her eccentric best, but even she cracks a smile.

'Oh, you're just so funny Mr Young!' she claps sarcastically, 'And so clever, for mocking the person who is in control of your grades on the last day of the semester'

Everyone laughs even harder and I join in this time, I see Elliot's ears become red. Harper quickly settles the class down. He doesn't like being pushed back.

'What I asked Mr Avery was, "What would you consider the most important adaptation for animals that evolution has ever produced?" Now, there are no wrong answers, highly subjective here, but I do have one in mind. Any takers?'

I immediately get to thinking about this riddle. Elliot removes his foot from his desk and lets his chair swing him forward back into a proper posture. He's thinking too. I cycle through my knowledge in my mind, determined to win. The development of eyes? No, extremely helpful but there are always the other senses. The ability of flight? No, again, useful but species have been successful without it.

'I'm loving the concentration you guys'

Harper beams proudly in this direction, now stepping out from her desk to pace the room. It's impossible to tell whether she was looking at me or Elliot.

'A very similar question *may* be on your exam so if you can think outside the box here you could *potentially* bump up your final grade' she laughs as she wanders down between the two rows.

The mention of bumping up their grades gets everyone else excited, even Ava pockets her phone and starts flipping through her notes. As everyone else joins me and Elliot, I briefly consider symbiosis, I'm tempted to throw my hand up but I pause, is there anything more important than even that? As the rest of the class scours the room with their eyes for hints or rummages through their books, Elliot and I are calm, both deep in thought. Ms Harper is at the back of the room now leaning on a shelf behind Ava and I. As I stare forward in thought, Elliot begins to turn. Time seems to slow, Elliot and I lock eyes as he extends his hand, the petty, unspoken challenge set for us filling the air with our spite. He smiles at me as his arm straightens and his wrist flicks his hand upright. Harper crosses her arms and raises her eyebrows.

'Ah yes Elliot?'

'Mimicry' Elliot states, strong and confident.

'Interesting answer. Elaborate?' Harper chews at her top lip.

'To avoid predation, to camouflage as a piece of landscape or another animal entirely is an unrivalled adaptation. In my opinion' he concludes.

Wow, he sure is trying hard. Harper brings her hands together and then up to her mouth.

'That's…Not bad' she says.

I see Elliot's eyes widen and his nostrils flare. As I watch his face fill with rage, I see the snake in the corner of my eye and face it once again.

'Camouflage is a fascinating thing without doubt, I've seen it in many species in my time, but there's something else that gives some creatures the edge over others'

Elliot begins to argue his point but I tune him out and survey the creatures in their jars. There's a certain uniformity to them. All floating in the same way, preserved in the same solution, all posed in the same way, with their most striking features facing the glass for us to study. Each one dead, alone in its jar. Alone. Separate. I've got it now.

'Sociability' I say aloud without meaning to.

He faces me and I face him. I see his teeth clench and his cheeks redden, I realise now that I've interrupted him. We usually don't have much to do with each other, I roll my eyes whenever his hubris rears its ugly head, and he barely acknowledges that I exist. Harper breaks our spell.

'What was it you said Warren?' she wags an index finger at me as if she can't stay still.

'I'm sorry, I didn't mean to cut you off, but I just thought of social behaviour, that's pretty important, right?'

Harper rubs her hands together in excitement.

'That's what I was waiting for! You see, in this humble biologist's opinion, life's greatest adaptation isn't a body part or a poison or even a special skill at all really. No no, it's behaviour, working together, raise offspring, hunt, gather, watch for predators. Once you all get out into the field you'll see that species capable of this, are the ones that have fared the best over our crazy evolutionary journey. Look at us, it's only because we're social creatures that we could form a society at all, right? If we all insisted on working alone, we couldn't assign some people to prepare food while others create shelter. We would all need to be proficient in everything, and with that, there would be nothing unique about any of us."

Every one of us stares at Ms Harper, in awe of her insight, even Elliot, who might have just experienced the first defeat of his life. Perhaps he's

been humbled. Our teacher composes herself, checks the time and begins to conclude the lesson.

'I'm sorry I got carried away like that, I know that's out of character for me' she laughs.

Almost everyone groans at her sarcasm. Not him.

'So, I hope you all took something on board from this one. We're out of time, I will see you at the exam, but if we don't get a chance to speak, good luck tomorrow and enjoy your holiday everybody. I'm proud of you all'

'Fucking loser' Elliot hisses at me, his eyes narrowed.

I get it, I do. I can understand why this would frustrate him so much. The bell rings as if on cue, and he turns forward and begins collecting his things.

'Oh, another thing!' Harper calls, 'I want you to be careful, over the break, okay? In light of recent events... Just take care'

Elliot rises with everyone else and begins to file out of the room. Harper stands by the door and sees everyone out, congratulating them on a great semester and wishing them good luck one more time. I'm still seated.

'Surely you aren't hanging around again Warren?' Harper asks, moving over from the door and sitting back at her desk.

'As long as that's okay' I say, 'I'd like to do some more study'

'You were in here this morning studying... And again at recess... And I have a feeling you'll be studying at home tonight too'

She rests her head on her fists at her desk, and waits for me to argue, but I don't.

'You work far too hard, you need to spend time letting the information convert from short term to long term memory'

'Is that a real thing?' I ask.

'Warren listen, I wrote the exam myself and I can tell you, at the level you're at, you'll do absolutely fine'

I bow my head and blush, as she says this. She says it like having good grades is something to be proud of. Instead of good grades, could I instead have evolved sociability?

'I'm not going to stop you, just remember to spend time on other things. Besides, the Sun is out for once, you should enjoy it!'

'What? No, it-' I start to say, but when I look at the window to confirm, the light fills into my eyes.

The sun now piercing the grey sky and filling the school outside with its rays.

'Told you' Harper smiles, 'Go on get out of here, and don't forget to eat'

'You're right Ms Harper, thank you' I say to her, nodding, still shocked that the Sun has made an appearance.

I collect my things and rise, leaving my desk and meandering over to the door, locking eyes with the snake on my way past.

'Oh, and I'm sorry for interrupting before. Elliot, I mean' I say.

She waves it away with her hand.

'Don't lose sleep over it Warren, it won't kill him' she smiles, and I smile back.

'Okay, and thank you again for the semester, I think I learned a lot' I add lamely and simply.

I'd like to tell her how talented of a teacher she is but I'm not outspoken enough for that sort of thing.

'You've met the quota for learning I'd say, go and enjoy your holidays' she nods at the door.

'I'll try'

We wave at one another and I step out the door. I think of what she said about not losing sleep about interrupting Elliot. I can tell that he will.

II
Chew the Fat

I spill out into the hallway and see the students of Southway High School filling the courtyard, capitalising on the unusual amount of sunlight. Corridors of classrooms line the central quad on all sides, fencing in the verdant, dewy grass as it glistens in the fresh sunshine. The grass speckled with shady oak trees, neatly boxed in by brick squares, and tables that are all at maximum capacity. Elliot sits on the central most tabletop, his friends on the seats surrounding. While they chatter amongst each other, he leans back on one palm, and holds a large crimson apple in his other, chin up and eyes closed, looking smug as he basks.

A crackle begins over the intercom, Principal McGovern speaks, booming as the sound bounces around the corridors. He was in the army or something, and tends to use that experience to command attention as though we're soldiers.

'Ahem. Hello students, I would just like to take this opportunity to wish our students finishing their exams tomorrow the best of luck, and everyone a safe and happy semester break'

I hear that in University you can just watch your lectures online and put them on at triple speed. When McGovern rambles like this, I wish I could do that in real life. But not this time, because he has more to say.

'I am sure you are all aware of Mr Mayhew's disappearance last month, it has been brought to my attention that another person reportedly did not return to their home last night. More information will likely be on the radio tonight. So, to all of you, I just ask you to keep safe and take care of one another. Thank you for your time'

The speakers sputter silent as the principal signs off, the courtyard comes alive with new discussion. The other week, Bert Mayhew, local old coot, just vanished into thin air. The couple from the next farm over went to check on him, they said they hadn't seen him drive into town for a while. When they got there he was gone, no sign of a struggle and no valuables stolen. I didn't know him or anything, I don't think many people did, but it was a big thing on the local radio news, The Chatter as

13

insufferable as it is to listen to. Now apparently another person has gone missing? I don't know if I think there's much to it, it's just the way it goes, isn't it? Sometimes people just wander off and get lost?

I search for somewhere to sit. All the tables orbiting Elliot's are occupied and the grass too wet, I make my way over to a vacant oak on the fringe of the grass, place my bag on the mossy bricks and sit down beside it. I know one of the bricks here is unattached, so I make sure to not rest my bag on that one, I know this because I sit here often. I remove from my backpack a pizza slice from work last night, along with my copy of *Mechanisms of Evolution*. I skim through it for some time while I eat, but I know this textbook inside out. I've read it all the way through a dozen times, but I keep it held in front of my face so I can peer over towards Elliot's group, Ava is there, arms crossed, phone in hand, tapping her foot impatiently. I know who she is waiting for.

'Yo'

My heart skips a beat. The figure walks up from behind me, gently running a hand along a low hanging oak branch as he passes.

'Hey Danny' calls Elliot, and my stomach drops.

'Hey guys' Dan says to the group.

Ava jumps to her feet and throws her arms around his neck. He picks her up and spins her around, then gives her a long kiss and places her back on the ground.

'So, Danny where are you hiding these people that you kidnapped?' Elliot jokes.

Everyone shares a pained grimace at his dark jest. Ava begins playing with her hair.

'Man, that's not cool' Dan tells him firmly, 'So last day huh?'

'Yep, I can't wait to get out of here, you'll think of me in Barcelona while you're all here in the hole of the Earth, won't you?' Elliot says, slicking his hair back.

'We will, don't worry' Dan says through the most forced of smiles, seemingly speaking for everyone there.

He covers his eyes with his hand and looks up at the sky.

'But I don't know, the weather here might not be too bad at all'

'Yeah right, I'll tell you all about some nice weather when I get back next semester'

Elliot rolls the apple around in his hands.

'But if the weather here finally improves, are you finally going to throw a party at your place when I get back?' he continues.

Their group cheers loudly in agreement, Dan hushes them immediately.

'No. No parties at my place. I've told you a thousand times' he says defensively.

'Come on Dan, I thought we were mates?'

'No parties at my house. Ever' he says with finality.

Elliot looks at him with envy at the way he commands their crowd. Dan sits down next to Ava and she puts her hand in his, he stares off vaguely and grasps it unenthusiastically. I watch him, wondering if maybe he feels the same as me in a way. Even after all this time.

I remember being six years old and starting my first year of school. I remember looking at my feet a lot, and when I absolutely had to speak to someone, I would look past them, too ashamed to make eye contact. At the end of the first day of school, a day I had spent in terror, this older boy, whose name we later found out to be Kevin, bumped into me and knocked me down when I was trying to make my way out of the school. His elbow colliding with my cheek, threw me backwards. He towered over me, he must have been nine or ten.

'What's wrong with your eyes? Can't you see out of them?' Kevin had said.

Maybe he genuinely thought I was blind because of the way my eyes look, but I thought he was just being a bully. I wanted to explain to him but my voice refused to work, tears forming, threatening to slide down my swelling cheek.

'Can you even talk?' he barked as he took a step closer.

I closed my eyes and braced as hard as I could, but another voice called to him.

'Hey!'

And when I opened my eyes, a kid I had seen in my class stood between Kevin and I, staring him down despite being about two feet shorter. I recognised him from my class, he was a restless boy, he seemed unable to keep still. He was skinny and tanned, jet black hair, with a slightly upturned, mousy nose. The sleeves of his school uniform rolled all the way up to his shoulders. I could see his arms and legs were covered in scratches and bruises. I thought he looked cool as hell.

'What's wrong with you?' he asked Kevin.

'What's wrong with your friend's eyes?' Kevin jeered back.

Kevin had begun to laugh, impressed by his own joke, when this little kid punched him in the face so hard he staggered backwards, tripped and fell just as I had. There had already been several onlookers watching when Kevin bumped me, but when Kevin hit the ground the calls for "fight!" were rabid. Kevin looked from my saviour to me and back again, before scrambling to his feet, nursing his elbow which he must have landed on. He felt the blood from his nose reach his lip, wiped it and looked at his red hand in horror before running away. The crowd laughed at Kevin's defeat, then began to dissipate and the boy helped me to my feet. I remember he had warm, amber eyes.

'Are you okay?' he said to me.

'Yes' I stammered, still crying.

'You're not bleeding, maybe you'll have a black eye though maybe' he said, studying my face, 'Wait, your eyes do work, right?'

'Yes, they work normally' I laughed, 'I have heterochromia, which means my eyes are different colours'

He looked at each of my eyes, taking in the Nordic blue of my right, then the deep jungle green of my left, and back again.

'Did it hurt?' he asked, still surveying me.

'It didn't happen to me, I've just always had it, it's special' I told him proudly, I touched my cheek and grimaced, then I wiped my eyes into my shirt.

When I stopped he was beaming at me, a hand outstretched to shake.

'I think it makes you look cool, my name is Daniel'

I shook his hand and smiled back.

'My name is Warren'

That next day we found out that Kevin had a broken nose and Daniel was suspended for a week. But I waited for that week to end and from the moment he returned, we were inseparable. Every day, both in and out of school, we spent by each other side. He lived on a farm out of town, we'd spend endless hours fishing and exploring in the summer, he was really into archery, it was just something he always had a knack for, he even won a few state competitions. I'd show him books and movies and video games that we'd read, watch and play from when the sun went down and then came back up again. I'd help him in school and he'd help me talk to people. We were each other's biggest fan and most trusted confidant. I remember I was the only one he told that he had a crush on Ava. We were about thirteen, when we began high school and study was becoming increasingly important to me, while he remained carefree. I was pulled in by reality, determined to study hard and keep my grades strong, he was determined to enjoy the youth we still had, and when Elliot moved to town, he was exactly what Dan wanted. He was loud and fun, and made people listen, I was quiet and didn't want any attention. And so it went, nobody's fault, we didn't fight or hate each other, we just grew apart.

I stare longingly at their group, I've always wanted a chance to talk to Daniel one more time, but you never see him away from Elliot.

'Oi' that sharp voice of Elliot snaps me back to the present.

I blink, and realise I've been staring for so long while I reminisced, Elliot is waving a hand at me to get my attention. I close my book and shake myself awake.

'What is your deal Fuck Eyes?' he spits at me, he stands up and throws his apple from one hand to the other.

'Elliot just chill' pleads Dan.

'Why should I? No, I want to know. What's your damage?' he says, turning back to me.

I seize up. Elliot's eyes are full of wild rage, like my existence is crossing a boundary for him.

'Dude come on he's just trying to eat, you need to calm down' Dan says softly to him, then rises, standing tall.

He places a hand on Elliot's arm but he violently jerks away.

'Why do you have to defend him?' Elliot says irritably, his voice now loud enough to have garnered attention of onlookers.

Unmoved by Dan's peacemaking attempt, Elliot brings his arm back, apple in hand, I can feel what he's doing. I reflexively raise the textbook to shield my face. His apple collides with my textbook with a surprisingly loud thud, before bouncing off and dropping to the grass by my feet. I hear gasps from other people, a few surprised laughs. I can't look up yet, so I peek down at the apple. Its skin torn and flattened with a bruise on the side that connected. I grant myself an instant to process what happened, and then I take the book from in front of my face.

I see Elliot taking a step towards me, face as red as his apple, and pride just as bruised. Dan one step behind, attempting to stop him. Ava covers her mouth with her palm. Everyone on the edge of their seat, all eyes in the courtyard on the three of us.

'What was that? What is going on out here?'

Principal McGovern's resonant voice halts both of them, he must have been walking past. With a head like a cinderblock and a spine so straight he mustn't be able to tie his own shoes, he steps out from the hallway and hustles over. His white dress shirt creases and he stomps over to Elliot, his glasses flaring in the sunshine. He stands right in front of them, to tower over and intimidate. Elliot's wrath begins to leave his expression, hiding back away within him, replaced with a nervous surrender. Dan is calm, he looks past our principal at me, and then to Elliot, and then to McGovern.

'You boys throwing shit in my school?' McGovern says to them, it's not a question.

'N-No' Stammers Elliot, his audacity completely missing in action now.

'Don't lie to me, I heard the noise. You think that makes you tough?'

All three of them turn to look back at me.

'No sir' Elliot mumbles.

'Then why did you do it Mr Young?' McGovern bobs down slightly to get up in his face.

'No, I threw it' Dan says. Everyone looks at him surprised.

Me, Elliot and McGovern must all share the same expression.

'*You* did it? But you and Mr Avery... Why?' he trails off.

'I just thought it would be funny, I guess. Sorry' Dan nods.

From what I remember, Dan never really responded well to authority, and McGovern doesn't seem to really be buying it. He looks at the both of us in disbelief, then puts his stoic persona back on.

'Right, well you will be sorry, Mr Steele. You will be staying behind after school today. Library. Until five. Understand? And you're lucky it's the last day of the semester because I'd keep you back every day for a week if I could'

'That's fair' Dan nods up at him.

'Good. Now get your act together' He booms, then he spins around to address the courtyard as a whole, 'I hope you will all remember, we treat one another with respect, this will be the last instance of bullying, fighting, assaulting, anything at all, in my school is that clear?'

Everyone mumbles in agreement. I just stare at Dan, who's looking down defeated now. Why would he do that?

'Warren?' McGovern kneels down next to me, 'I asked if you were alright? You're red in the face'

I can see Elliot breathing deeply, relieved. He must be forcing Dan take the blame. They must have a deal. He must be paying him, his family has plenty of money.

'Yeah I'm fine. The apple only hit my textbook here so…' I tap the book's hard cover.

'Ah well that's lucky then' McGovern nods, 'It's a shame, you guys used to be such good mates, I remember. Anyway, don't let him get to you, just worry about your final exam okay?'

'Sir?'

'Yes?'

'May I use the library after school? To study?' I ask.

I have to know why.

'I mean, sure but, he'll be there and-'

'I don't mind, I'd just like to do some last-minute study before work tonight, is that okay?'

'Then sure, it's good to see such a hardworking young lad' he places a hand on my shoulder, 'I'll be in my office after school anyway so I'll come and check on you'

'Thanks' I say, my teeth starting to clench, annoyed at being babied.

'Righto, well if everything is in order, I'll be on my way. Good luck lad!' he smiles, then salutes and wanders back into the corridor and shuffles away.

Elliot and Dan are back at their table, Elliot back on his throne and Dan sitting elbows on knees.

'Hey man you're the best, you know I'll bring you back something sick from Spain' Elliot ruffles Dan's hair, catching his attention.

'It's all good, you're welcome'

'No, I mean it, I really will bring you back something awesome'

And that's it. They don't speak any more of it. Elliot goes back to bragging about his family holiday to Spain, the rest of them looking up at him, listening intently. I feel something new. I usually feel bored, unsatisfied, even lonely. But now I feel hate for Elliot forming inside. Not for the apple, but for making Dan take his punishment. His ever-present arrogance is usually something I can wade through, but now I'm drowning in it. I watch Daniel force a thin smile as his friends chatter around him, and I can't help but wonder if he needs saving this time.

The rest of the day passes uneventfully. I spend my two afternoon classes, English and Chemistry, thinking of explanations for why Dan would throw himself in the line of fire the way he did. The exams for these classes are already behind us, having been done earlier this week, so we're just being told what to expect next semester. Maybe Elliot is blackmailing him into being his servant? Or has he been brainwashed somehow? I know that isn't true, Elliot may be an ingrate, but he took Dan from me fair and square.

I don't have any classes with Dan, and haven't for a few years now, he opted for more hands-on classes like metalwork, and as much physical education as they would let him take. Life placed on this more academic path. I have every class with Elliot this semester though, and he seems to have forgotten about our incident by the afternoon. These classes don't capture me anywhere near as much as biology does. Words and atoms push and pull one another, but I think life has a sense of unity. Cells working together to keep a body alive, bodies coexisting to keep the ecosystem balanced. I don't know, maybe I'm too young yet to really get it. I still devote copious amounts of time to studying these subjects too of course, university entrance is counting on it. With plenty of spare time and nothing else to do, my grades have been in excellent health for as long as I can remember, which is good, I guess. At this age, it's the only measurement we're given to tell if your life is on track.

When the final bell rings everyone frenzies out of their classrooms and flows through the corridors to the school gates like salmon heading upstream. I hear people from my class say goodbye to Elliot and wish him a safe and happy holiday, and I can't help but notice he doesn't thank any of them. I walk against the current, picking the gaps between excited students, making for the library at the bottom end of the school grounds. By the time I get there, the sea of students has evaporated as quickly as it appeared, leaving the school feeling lonely as I look back.

I enter the library, not even the librarian, Mrs Sage is here. Usually she floats around after hours, eager to help vigilant students locate a book, I guess she's gone home to enjoy her holidays too. I'm instantly struck by the signature musty odour of old books, I take a deep breath in through my nose and savour it, countless adventures all held within this one room. The bookshelves begin just past her desk, taking up the majority of the library, which I think must be one of the older buildings in the school, judging by the peeling of the eggshell coloured paint on the walls, which I suspect was once a perfect white. The long desks, reserved for group projects, quiet study and detentions, lie beyond these bookshelves, hidden away in the recesses of the library. Lightly running my fingers over the cold wood, I pass by towards the desks. Four of them, usually spread out to allow students to sit separately if they wish, are now arranged in a line, joined at their long sides, forming one long table. All the chairs stacked in the corner, I guess Mrs Sage really did pack up for the holidays. But she's kind of old, I hope she didn't try to move all these tables and chairs by herself. And that's when I see Dan, sitting on the last chair, at the part of the long table closest to the back corner, spinning a pencil around his thumb.

We nod politely but awkwardly at each other then look away. The teenage years together that we lost seem to have followed me into the library. I sit down at the opposite corner, as far away from him as I could geometrically be. I pull out my books but don't open any, instead I discreetly watch my old friend, using them as cover. He can spin the pencil and catch it again, he's practised that a lot. He doesn't even have a piece of paper in front of him. He looks around the room longingly, as though he's lost, but not trying to find anything either. It's as though he's expecting the empty room to do something. I'm about to give up and actually do some reading when his pencil spirals out of his hand and patters as it runs across the desk, shattering the silence. He throws a hand over the pencil, muffling it, then he looks up and around to make sure no one is here to see. He catches me looking out the corner of his eye, it's too late for me to try to look away.

His eyes have a certain duality to them, not in the literal way that my eyes do, they're both warm and yet burnt out, somehow full with both an optimism and a burden. Old copper pennies eaten by rust, being held in the light of the warmest flame. He flashes a handsome, closed-mouth smile, I try to return one. It mustn't be very good because he laughs.

'I'm sorry if it was annoying, you should have told me to stop' he says.

'No not at all' I reply, 'I'm not even really studying'

It feels surreal in a way, having to dance around small talk with someone who you once knew better than yourself.

'Why are you here then, if you're not studying?' he cocks his head sceptically.

Shit.

'Well I mean, I am studying, a bit, I'm just… Letting the information convert into my long-term memory' I say.

'Is that really a thing?' he asks.

'According to Ms Harper, the biology teacher anyway'

Dan rubs his knuckle against his strong jaw.

'Oh yeah, Elliot says she makes things up a lot though'

'Maybe she does' I say dejectedly, 'I've got work at five thirty anyway so I thought I'd hang out here and kill time'

'Where do you work?'

'Wanda and Rhonda's, you know the Pizza place in town?'

'Yeah, I know the one' his eyes light up, 'Do you get free pizza?'

'As much as I can eat'

'Damn, I should get a job there' he laughs

I laugh with him, that would be pretty cool. Our laughter fizzles out and an awkward silence begins to form.

'So, do your folks still live in town?' he asks, breaking the tension.

A simple question, a way of admitting that we have so much catching up to do.

'Yeah same place, you still on the farm?'

'Sure am, not much has changed out there' he sighs.

'Hey, that old man who went missing, didn't he live out that way?' I ask.

'Eh, sort of, I've never met him. I wouldn't even know which place was his'

'What do you think about that?' I ask, 'Those people'

'I don't think there's exactly a conspiracy behind it. Old dude goes for a walk, gets lost or gets bitten by a snake or whatever. I hope they find him soon though. Poor guy'

'I think the same thing' I say, 'No conspiracy unfortunately'

Although, it's Winter, snakes wouldn't be out yet, and it's two people now...

24

'Still into archery?' I ask instead of arguing.

Dan blinks, surprised.

'You still remember that?' he asks in disbelief

'Of course, it's all you used to talk about'

His smile changes. More open mouthed, more genuine.

'I don't compete anymore, got slack with practicing' he says.

'Got a girlfriend you mean? No time for arrows after that' I poke.

He laughs and nods slowly. His voice seems to loosen, it actually feels like I know the person across from me again.

'You remember that time in scouts, on camp?' I ask, 'When that kid, Greg, said no one was better than him at archery?'

He strokes his chin.

'Shit, I had forgot about Greg! The only way that kid beat anyone at archery is if he accidentally killed his opponents with his shocking aim'

We both laugh for a minute straight.

'Mind like a steel trap Warren, you always have been like that' Dan says, once we've calmed down.

'You think so?'

'Yeah, you're good at seeing things and remembering them, and I don't just mean with learning' he gestures at my books, 'Perceptive! No that isn't the word, observant? I'm trying to say, you're good at taking everything in'

'Thanks man' I say, my heart the fullest it's been since I can remember.

He gets up out of his seat, picks it up and walks it around and sits next to me.

> 'Like today, I swear you could see that apple coming before it happened and BAM!' he makes the noise and slams a fist into his open palm, 'That was awesome'

> 'Yeah… Just reflex I guess'

Neither of us seem to know what to say next and the mood becomes uncomfortable again.

> 'I really am sorry about that, about Elliot today'

I gulp. Now's the time to ask him. It's now or never.

> 'Why did you do that for him?' I spit it out.

> 'What?' he asks puzzled.

> 'Why would you take the blame for someone who wouldn't do the same for you? He didn't even say thank you'

Dan looks away for a moment, then returns to me.

> 'Do I need a reason?'

I blink at him, perplexedly.

> 'It doesn't matter to me if they'd do the same or not. I offered to move the tables and chairs for Mrs Sage. She's old and weak, she isn't stacking any chairs anytime soon, does that mean I shouldn't have done it? Because she couldn't do the same for me?'

This feels like a lecture I wouldn't want to fast forward through.

> 'If someone needs help, I help them' he finishes.

I pause to take in what he just said. Is it really that simple? No blackmail, no brainwashing?

'The same reason I broke that kid's nose when he made fun of your eyes. Shit, I don't even care if they're grateful or not' he adds.

I'm taken aback by his answer. But when I look back it was always there in him, the burning drive to help people.

'I was thinking about that earlier actually' I laugh, 'But Elliot? Him? He doesn't need help, he can pay for his own mistake'

Dan just shrugs.

'I knew he had his exam tomorrow, he should be allowed to focus on that, and not have to worry about a detention. I could either sit around at home or sit around here, makes no difference to me'

'He could have studied during detention, you didn't have to punish yourself for him' I say.

'Well, then you'd be speaking with him now and not me' he gets up and stretches.

He always did hate to sit static, always had to be moving or doing something athletic. Climbing or running or anything to not be still and stagnant.

'Or did you only stay after school because you knew I'd be here and you wanted to chew the fat?' he asks jokingly.

He knows, I wouldn't trust him in the lab, but Daniel Steele is far from dumb.

'I don't know Dan' I sigh, 'What can I say, I was intrigued'

'*Intrigued?*' he asks with a raised brow.

'I just couldn't believe it, but now that I think about it, it's totally something you would do. But I just had to know. I'm sorry' I say, embarrassed.

'You know lots about science and blocking apples, Warren but you don't know much about people do you?' he laughs.

Not wrong.

'Well since you came, I'll try to explain myself. I guess I just feel like…' he sits back down, 'If I can help people out whenever I can, even if it's only something tiny, then I should just do it you know?'

'Well what if you helped someone do something bad?' I counter.

He thinks about this one, and then decides to shrug.

'Alright fair point, I wouldn't help anyone kill or steal, but just about everything else is fair game. If I make someone's day just a tiny bit easier, at least that's doing something, something good. It feels like it's a purpose, I don't know'

My ears prick up when they hear mention of having a purpose.

'I understand what you mean' I tell him.

'You do?'

'Well I think so, it's like with all this study' I hold up a book, 'I only study so hard because I feel like that's *my* purpose. I just…'

'Want something more?' we finish at the same time.

It feels like a weight lifts from my being, finally able to reveal these thoughts to someone else, allowing me to bring my shoulders back. Confident.

'Well unfortunately for us, not much happens around here' I continue.

'And that's putting it generously' he laughs.

'If I study hard and focus on that, maybe that's my best chance of getting out of here and doing something exciting' I say.

'Mate you sound just like Ava' he rolls his eyes, 'You want to do something exciting that badly huh?'

'Well, I mean yeah. I don't know' I reply, stunned, 'Doesn't everyone want excitement?'

'Eh, not me' he shakes his head slightly, unimpressed, 'I'm happy enough just taking things as they come. I just want to hang out with my Ava, practise archery, have fun, and help people where I can. That's purpose enough for me'

I replay what he said ten times in my mind. Being content is contrary to me in every way. The larrikin to my scholar.

'You know what? I think that's pretty cool' I manage to say eventually.

'Huh? What is?' he asks.

'Being able to just take things as they come. I wish I could be like that' I admit.

He just laughs it off.

'Well Warren, if you can't learn to take things as they come, life might knock you around a bit. But I do think it's possible to be too laidback. To be honest Warren, I was always a bit jealous of your grit'

'What grit? Growing up I was always jealous of you!' I say in disbelief.

'You know how to chase after something. The whole study thing, even if you only do it because you think it's your only ticket out of here. That's something, it's ambition. I think that's why Elliot can't stand you, no offence' he laughs.

I'm about to ask what he means by that, when the library door groans open. Dan and I panic, he shuffles away to make it look like we haven't been talking and laughing and learning this entire time. Footsteps grow louder until McGovern emerges from the bookshelves.

'It's past five lads' He looks at his watch, and then nods over his broad shoulder towards the door, 'Make yourselves scarce already'

I pack away my books and Dan collects his single pencil. We stand and walk past McGovern, who then follows, escorting us out.

'I hope you learned something this afternoon' he says.

'I did' we say together.

Dan and I look at each other, unclear of who he was talking to. Outside of the library, McGovern chastises Dan for throwing things at others and wishes me good luck on the exam again. It feels like that's all people have said to me today. As our principal walks away, either back to his office or to his car, I don't know, Dan and I walk down the corridor in the opposite direction.

'That went quick, don't you reckon?' Dan says.

He stomps unnecessarily loudly, enjoying the thunder of his feet echoing through the empty school.

'Yeah it did, what are you doing now?' I ask.

'Driving home' he says.

I swear I see him struggle not to pout.

'Do you need a lift to work?' he asks.

'No that's okay' I say, not ready to impose, 'Wait, you have a car?'

'Well my folks let me use the ute, you know the old red one?'

'No way! You got the farm ute? I used to think that thing was badass!' I laugh.

'So did I, until I had to drive it, piece of shit. Nah, I'm not complaining, it gets me from A to B. You sure you don't want to experience my driving?'

'Nah I want to make it to work alive, thanks' I say, stirring him up.

We continue out to the front of the school, where the Steele family's beaten up, burnt red ute is parked out the front. Scratches in the paint are filled in with orange dust from the gravel.

'You recognise this old beast?' Dan gestures grandly at the vehicle.

'Wow do your folks hate you or something?' I joke.

Dan breaks his stride for a second, then hoists himself up into the driver's seat.

'Last chance for that lift' he sing-songs.

'Another time, a day when it's raining' I shake my head.

'There's plenty of those'

He starts the car with his fingers crossed, the engine sputters to life and a puff of black smoke is spat from the exhaust pipe.

'She lives!' I cry, holding my arms out like a mad scientist who just created life.

We both laugh.

'Hey Warren?' Dan says from the window.

'Yeah?'

'Your heterochromia is just about the most unique thing in this whole town'

I chuckle dumbly, I didn't expect him to remember what it was called.

'I'll uh, see you around sometime then?' he says.

'See you around' I wave.

And he chokes away down the road in his struggling car, leaving me in the smoke. I watch until he's well out of view. I grin from ear to ear and start walking to work before I'm late.

III
Humdrum

My shoes slap enthusiastically at the pavement of Southway's main street, my phone tells me it's five fifteen so most of the shops in our tiny town have closed their doors for the day. The buildings come in two colours, grey and light grey but no one seems to mind. I suppose the locals don't mind the humdrum, they know what they want and where to buy it and don't need their eyes caught, but tourists passing through wouldn't exactly be blown away. By no means a village, the place is a decent size and has everything you could ever need to stay alive, but the isolation comes from just knowing that the next closest town is one hundred and eighty four whole kilometres away, leaving only two options: Get out, or get ready to watch your life start dwindling. My two bosses always joke that the only people who come here must be trying to hide away from the rest of the world, but I had no say where I was born, I didn't choose to be hidden here. Right now though, with nothing open and no people to walk the streets, it feels spooky. I think of the disappearances.

I pass the post office and wave at Mrs Mabel the owner, it's a Thursday afternoon so she's wiping down the windows before she goes home. I guess she does it on Thursdays so she doesn't have to on Friday afternoon. She's worked there ever since I can remember, but then again, I've never known anyone in Southway who's changed their career path. Timber was once a massive industry decades ago with mills all over the place, but they were lost to the times and left us with small owned businesses that must be struggling to stay afloat. Locals like to throw around the word "quaint", but I think what they mean to say is "stagnant".

Let's see, what else happens on Thursdays? Honestly not a lot. I rack my brain but Thursdays are an especially unexciting day for Southway. I'll be able to see Mr Abernathy, who owns the shoe shop, watching sport on the TV in the back room because he leaves the door open. He does that every evening of the week, I don't know why, most people just go to the pub after work. I get closer to the shoe shop, only to be surprised to see the TV and lights off, no sign of Mr Abernathy at all. Huh, maybe he did go to the pub after all.

As I continue down the main strip, I make my turn onto Collins Street, a dilapidated lane off of main street, a graveyard for the many run-down businesses that failed to stand against the tide, and a shortcut I often take. I see something very much alive today though, a stack of cardboard boxes on the footpath, huh. The type of thing I imagine you'd see in an office's archive room or something. I had completely forgotten about that downstairs lot, its last stint that I remember was as a gym that no one ever used. For a time before that, it had been a sports and hunting equipment shop that Dan had dragged me down into a few times, but it's been years since anyone has been game enough to touch that place now.

I imagine they're filled with boring official papers and forms. I wonder what the tower of boxes is doing out on the street when a lanky, hunched man in a lab coat emerges from downstairs and skulks over to the boxes, picks up the top one, and pivots. I steal a flash of his face as he turns his body. His aquiline nose barely able to hold his thin, glasses to his deep-set eyes. His irises a strident, icy blue, focused and unaware of me and everything else, hidden away in his own mind. He must be in his late sixties, going by the long, silver hair he has slicked back and tucked behind his ears. It creeps down his temples into an unruly, white stubble. It looks like he hasn't slept in a week. His lab coat sweeps up off the footpath as he twirls and disappears, lugging his boxes down the stairs. I'm mesmerised, is this man a scientist? I want to hang around, wait for him to re-emerge to collect his next load of boxes. But I can't bring myself to annoy him like that. I think about the ease with which Dan would be able to strike up a conversation with this stranger, but not me.

So instead, I keep my pace, set to pass by long before he comes back up, but I do steal a peek at the remaining boxes. Four left, all tightly closed revealing nothing about his secrets. I turn to look down the stairs. I had completely forgotten about this downstairs chamber. The enigmatic, downward staircase in-between the old Chinese restaurant and the derelict sewing supply shop. I think it used to be a costume hire down there many years ago, but no one has paid mind to this section of town in a long time, you'd have to be mad to set up shop here. Well perhaps he's a mad scientist. I brisk through the rest of the short street before making my final turn onto Unity Street, home to Wanda and Rhonda's Pizza. Before turning the corner, I take one look back, but the remaining boxes have been already whisked away down below.

Work shouldn't be too busy, on Thursday there's only usually about a dozen orders, give or take. I'm grateful for this, I'm hoping to get home at a decent time to cram in some more study before tomorrow morning.

I don't really have set hours, they just send me home when things have died down. The door clangs open as I enter, the heat of the kitchen and smell of the grease hit me like a train, my body having been out in the cool, clean Autumn air.

'Hello' I wave, making my way past the counter and into the back to get changed.

'Hey Warren' Wanda and Rhonda both reply simultaneously.

Wanda is putting some pizza bases into the oven while Rhonda scribbles down something beside the cash register. I go to the back room, pull my work shirt from my backpack and throw it on. I try to neaten my wavy hair as best I can and then go to join my bosses out in the shop. They're both leaning against the bench in the kitchen donning their aprons already. Older ladies, Wanda is shorter and stockier with wiry blonde hair she keeps tied back. Rhonda is the ganglier of the two, with straight, burgundy, not subtly dyed hair and a skeletal face. Rhonda mostly handles the front counter and deliveries when we get them, which is deceptively often for such a small town. I have asked Rhonda about this, she jokes that it's because the bachelors know she'll be delivering.

As for me, I just help out with whatever needs doing, sometimes I help cook, sometimes I'm doing dishes, that sort of thing, though Wanda and Rhonda always say they can't wait for me to get my driver's license so I can do the deliveries. The three-employee system we have here always seemed strange to me, I think the place is doing well enough to hire more. The two of them have been friends since they were teenagers, from some city I can't remember the name of. They were dating men that were best friends, and apparently bonded over their similar names. While their relationships fizzled out, they remained friends for all these years, before deciding to move here to enjoy the country and go into the food business. They're very kind and helpful women, and they love to crack jokes, which is good since it's just the three of us and I'm no stand-up comedian. They don't run a very tight ship and business isn't exactly booming, a lot of the time they brew up coffee and we just sit around out the back drinking it and the two of them have a smoke. Sometimes they get caught up in their old stories and leave me on the sideline, free to daydream.

'Oh yeah Warren, we have news' Rhonda says.

'Pay rise?' I ask.

'I said news, not a miracle' Rhonda laughs, 'We're taking on a new employee, a young boy, Lucas'

'That's cool, what's he going to do?'

'He's going to help me in the kitchen' Wanda says, 'His family has just moved here and he's an aspiring chef'

'And, we have a favour' Wanda says, 'When he came in to apply this morning, he seems very shy, even more shy than you were when you started. We want you to make him feel welcome'

'Sure thing, I'll do my best' I say, excited at the thought of having someone new to talk to at work.

'We appreciate that, he starts tomorrow night' Wanda says.

The front door opens, the familiar old man and woman hobble up to the counter, regular customers.

'Just the usual tonight Philippa?' Rhonda asks them.

'Yes please, one of these days I'll get him to agree to try something different' smiles the woman.

Rhonda explodes with laughter. Every Thursday this retired couple dine in and share a margarita, and every Thursday she makes that same joke.

'Warren, get that base out of the oven' calls Wanda.

And with that, the night is underway.

When eight comes around, and the slow stream of customers has dried up completely, we're sipping our coffee out the back of the shop in one of Southway's many alleys.

'So, did you guys hear that someone else went missing?' I ask.

'Oh yeah' Rhonda says, 'Some old lady'

'Was it one of you guys?'

'Watch it boy!' Wanda laughs, 'Besides, she's the old one!'

We both laugh at Rhonda and she gives us both the middle finger in response. She takes out a cigarette and passes it to her friend before lighting one for herself.

'But no, it was a local woman, so I heard anyway' she says once we've calmed down.

'You hear everything that goes on around here' I say.

'That's the magic of talking to so many customers' she takes a mock bow.

'Jesus, Ms Congeniality over here' Wanda rolls her eyes at her friend.

'Since you hear everything, do you know the guy who owns that downstairs shop now?'

They both stare at me like I've just confessed to murder.

'On Collins?' asks Rhonda.

She taps her cigarette, sending ash fluttering into the gutter, her hands clanking as she does so. She always wears an excessive amount of jewellery on both hands, rings and bangles of silver, gold or any alloy in between that she likes the look of, no concern for theme or colour. Wanda always tells her that she'd be no good at sneaking up on someone.

'Yeah that's the place' I nod.

Their cigarettes glow in the cold.

'Kid, no one's touched that place for nearly ten years'

'I'm serious, some smart looking old guy was moving boxes down there today'

'Well, he better not be opening a pizza place, we're goners if we have to compete with a smart person' Wanda says.

Her and Rhonda are in conniptions.

'You should get out of here Warren' Wanda says after they've gotten hold of themselves.

'You sure you don't want me to do those dishes?' I point inside.

'Nah go on get out of here, sick of looking at you' Rhonda says.

'Your exams are finishing soon, aren't they?' Wanda takes back over.

'Last one tomorrow I say.

'Tip the rest of that coffee out then, get plenty of sleep' she smiles.

They're rough, but they care. I tip my coffee into the gutter. I retrieve my school bag from the staff room and the ladies wish me luck as I take my leave. The cold air biting at my face and arms, exposed to the evening chill as I make the walk home. Mum or Dad probably would pick me up if I called and asked, but I prefer to be away from them, to spare myself the interrogation about how school is going. The lampposts' light is spread thin through the fog of the night, guiding my way to Fourteen King Street, where the three of us live. I wipe my feet and enter the front door. My mother Judith sits at the kitchen table, doing a Sudoku, while my father, Kenneth is in the lounge room watching the rugby. They're honest and hardworking, I like to think that's how they raised me, they don't seem to mind the humdrum of this place, but I find it suffocating.

'Hey' I call, removing my shoes and placing them by the door.

'Hey love, how was work?' Mum asks, not looking up.

'The usual' I say.

'Ready for tomorrow mate?' shouts Dad from the other room.

'I think so Dad' I reply, 'I'm actually going to go and do a bit more study tonight so, I might head to bed'

'I thought you'd come home after school before work, what did you do?' Mum asks.

'I stayed behind at the library, to study'

'Oh, okay love, I'm glad you're keeping up with your study. I left some pasta aside for you, in the oven'

I thank mum and scoop myself a bowl of pasta. It's cold and simple, and frankly not very nice, it's a lazy dish that they often make when I have work and won't be home. I hug both of them before heading to my room. I close the door, throw my bag down on my unmade bed, and hit the power button on my computer, all in one motion. Time to study, I pull the textbooks from my bag and let them drop onto my computer desk. The slab of books bounces slightly, *Mechanisms of Evolution* slides towards the edge of the desk, without looking, I throw my hand out and catch it before it can hit the ground.

It's all reflex, I'm mesmerised by something else. The computer lighting up with life, my wallpaper takes my breath away, just like it does every single time. A triangular mountain stabbing its snowy tip up through the clouds and looking down at the photographer's camera. It's tucked behind a crystal-clear lake, creating a reflection of the mountain that meets the real thing at their bases and invert to make a diamond in the heart of my screen. I don't know who took this photo, I don't even know where on the globe it is. In a way, I don't think I want to know, there's enough places on this Earth that I'll never get to see, I'm no Elliot Young. Sure, it's fun to dream, I think I'm better off not knowing what I'm missing out on. Even so, I chose to set it as my background, and every day after school I sit down to study and get caught staring at it for an eternity, and it hurts me.

Sitting down at the desk and still in my work shirt, I flip open *Mechanisms of Evolution* to a random page. It's one about gene codominance and how black and brown fur colour are both dominant over blonde in Labradors. I don't care about codominance this evening, and I don't care about any lakeside mountains either, my mind runs back over the day. Elliot, Dan and the mystery man, all dance in my head while I close my eyes.

I'm jolted awake when I hear a car on our street stop and the engine shut off, I fell asleep at my desk. The computer has gone into sleep mode leaving me in almost complete darkness. I look out my window to see the familiar beaten up, red ute parked in the fog across the street on the curb. The hairs on the back of my neck stand up. I see him in the driver's seat, the car's interior light raining down onto his head. I flick my bedroom light on catching Dan's eye. He looks at me from over the road and waves. I wave back, then look at the time, ten fifty-eight. Dan steps out of his car and crosses the road without looking, he dons a dark hoodie with his hands in its pockets. As he approaches my window, I slide it open to welcome him.

'Daniel?'

'Warren' he nods.

'What are you doing here?' I ask.

'Well, I felt bad about this afternoon. I know you have the exam in the morning, and I feel like I kept you from studying at the library'

'I was never going to do any study in the library dude. Anyway, get in here it's freezing'

We both make our way to opposite sides of the front door, I open it for him and we quietly make my way to my bedroom. Sneaking through the house as to not wake up my parents. Dan sits himself down on my bed, while I sit in the office chair.

'So, you want to help me study because you feel bad?' I ask sceptically, 'It's too late, I have to be up in the morning'

He looks down at his hands sheepishly as he picks his fingernails.

'I do feel bad Warren' he says.

'Don't, I told you, I didn't even plan to study in the library, I just wanted to talk to you'

'No not that, I feel bad about everything' he says.

'What do you mean?'

'With us, I mean... I...' his voice trembles, he drops his hands down to his sides, 'You were my best friend and I abandoned you. I let you down'

He looks right at me, with eyes beginning to fill. In this moment, I think about what it means to be there for somebody, and how much it means to him to be helpful. I extend my fist for him to bump.

'You're here now, aren't you?'

He bumps the fist and nods.

'And you still remembered where I live after all this time?'

'As if I'd forget, I practically used to live here' he looks around my room.

He laughs and slides himself off the bed and onto the floor. He sits with his knees up and his arms resting on them.

'How are you feeling about tomorrow anyway? You ready?' he asks, looking up at me.

I shrug back.

'I've done all I can at this point anyway'

'What will be, will be?'

'That's right' I agree.

Dan points up at me and winks.

'I see you're learning quickly, you did say today that you wanted to take things as they come a bit more'

That reminds me of what he said in the library about Elliot, before McGovern interrupted.

'Anyway, if you're not studying, is it cool if I sleep here tonight? I'll clear out early, or I can drive you to school if you want?'

'You never had to ask to stay here before, why start now?' I laugh, 'You take the bed I'll sleep on the floor'

I stand up from the office chair.

'Absolutely not' Dan lays down stubbornly, rooting himself to the floor, 'You need a good sleep, I'm all good down here'

'Alright fine' I say, stepping over him and sliding into the bed, 'But you have to take the pillow'

I throw the pillow up, so that it arcs, hopefully landing on his head. It lands beside him.

'D-five, miss' he tuts, then throws the pillow back, 'And it's all yours, I've got this hoodie'

He takes it off, rolls it up into a rough pillow shape and slides it under his head. I'm about to offer him the blanket when he reads my mind.

'Don't even try to give me the blanket either, it's warm as hell in here'

'Wow, how did you know I was about to say that?'

'It's just who you are my friend'

I feel the smile flourish across my face when he says "friend".

'You didn't need to come all the way into town tonight Dan, you could have just come to school to see me before the exam. Why the rush?'

He stays silent, I sit up, raising my head just enough to see over the edge of my bed. He lays on his side, facing away from me.

'I just felt like it' he finally says.

'Well, you're always welcome here'

'It's late Warren' he says, I hear him exhale, 'You should get some sleep'

IV
Vitriol

'Rise and shine'

Dan shakes me awake, I blink the sleep out of my eyes and sit up.

'What time is it?' I yawn.

'Five past' he says.

'Five past seven?'

'Five past five'

'What the hell did you wake me up for?' I rub my eyes.

'Why? What time do you usually get up?' he asks.

'I don't know, seven, seven thirty. School isn't far away'

'Oh right' he says, 'Well my body clock doesn't let me sleep in too late, maybe getting up a bit earlier will help you in the exam'

'How do you figure that?'

'Uh, more time for your mind to... wake up?' he stumbles through his sentence and I laugh at him.

   I finally sit up, still rubbing sleep from my eyes. Out the window there's still nothing but fog and no sign of the Sun. Dan turns on the light in my room and I have to blink away, but once I can see again, I realise he has *Mechanisms* in his hands.

'This is the one, right?' he asks.

'Yeah'

'And you've read the whole thing?'

'Heaps of times'

'So, if I ask you any questions about it you'll know the answer?'

'Is this what you woke me up for?' I ask.

'First question!'

He flips through the meat of the tome and stops on a page at random.

'Okay... So, a type of... Shit... Symbiotic relationship where one species benefits and the other is unaffected is known as...?'

I can't help but humour him, he's a good friend.

'Commensalism' I say.

'Not bad Avery' he nods once he's checked the word.

This goes on until the sun finally rises and lifts the fog away. It's around the same time that Dan has run out of words he can pronounce, and he's grown frustrated that he wasn't able to trip me up even once.

'That's incredible' he sighs.

'Harper based the syllabus around that textbook, so it always just made sense to me that if you can memorise what's in that book, then you can't not ace the class'

Dan gets up off the ground to stretch.

'Well I should be charging for my efforts I reckon' he groans.

'What happened to waking the mind up?'

'The real question, is what are you cooking me for breakfast?' he asks, throwing on his hoodie.

As we leave my room I hear the radio humming from the kitchen. Mum is hunched over the stove, producing a hearty looking breakfast. On the table is a bowl of scrambled egg, and another bowl of avocado, two pieces of toast and two hash browns. I suspect that she's made this much fuss to wish me luck on my exam. I appreciate it, I do, but at the same time I can't help but look at it and think of the teenage years wasted buried in textbooks. Between the bacon sizzling in the pan and the drone from the radio, I don't think mum has even heard us come to the doorway.

'Hey mum' I say

'Morning Mrs Avery' says Dan.

Mum quickly whirls around and looks at him in disbelief when she hears a second voice.

'My God, Daniel Steele that isn't you' she gasps.

'It has been a while, hasn't it?' he laughs.

Mum abandons the stove and runs over to us, she embraces Dan in a hug. At first, he's shocked, last time he was here he was just a rascally little boy, but now he towers over her when he hugs her back.

'How many years has it been? Oh my God I need to cook more food!' she says, flustered, then she scurries back to the stove, shoving two pieces of bread into the toaster on her way past.

'We must have just missed Dad then?' I say as we sit down at the table.

'Only by about ten minutes' she says, 'Do you boys want some tea? Coffee?'

'Coffee please' Dan and I say together.

'Trying to wake yourself up for your exam huh? You boys better not have been up all night' she laughs, 'God it's like you're kids again, when did you even get here Daniel?'

'Uh, I was in town late last night and I needed somewhere to stay, I hope this was okay'

'Don't be stupid Daniel! Of course it's okay'

'Mum!' I say.

Dan laughs.

'Warren I'm just saying, he doesn't need to worry about that sort of thing, he is always welcome here, he's family' mum says.

I see Dan gulp and his lip threatens to tremble. He quickly regains his composure.

'That means a lot to me Mrs Avery, thank you. I'm sorry I haven't come around in ages'

'I thought you guys must have just had a fight, I'm glad you're still friends' she says.

Dan and I look at each other and smile. The bread re-emerges, transformed into toast. Mum whisks the toast over to Daniel and gives us the go-ahead to begin eating. As we shovel down the food greedily, something on the radio catches mum's ear and she turns it up. Dan and I stop eating to listen.

'That's right Sophie, yes Southway Police have announced the disappearance of fifty-three-year-old, Joy Abernathy this morning. We are told that Mrs Abernathy was visiting a friend out of town two days ago when she failed to return. Her husband, George Abernathy was unavailable for interview, it is understood that he is assisting with the investigation. Mrs Abernathy was heading westward out of town, notably through the same area where Bert Mayhew also went missing only last month, however, police are treating the disappearances as unrelated at this time. Back over to you Soph'

'Oh God' Mum says, turning the volume down.

'I walked past the shoe shop before work yesterday, Mr Abernathy wasn't there, I thought it was weird'

'I hope Joy is okay, and George must be worried sick' Mum says.

'Do you think it's connected to that other guy?' Dan asks.

'I hope not' says Mum, 'Isn't that out your area Daniel?'

'Kind of, the Mayhew guy lived sort of close, I guess'

'You promise me you'll be careful!'

'I will Mrs Avery' he smiles.

We finish our meal and I get my things ready for the exam while Dan sits around and talks to mum in the kitchen. I grab my pens and calculator from my desk and change out of my work uniform and into a t-shirt, I pick what I think is the coolest looking one. After shoving everything into my backpack, I join them in the kitchen.

'Ready to go?' I ask.

'Oh, Warren wear a jacket, look at the weather!' mum says pointing out the kitchen window.

The early sunshine of yesterday afternoon has been taken from the Southway sky, and swallowed up by the grisly cloud cover we all know and love. Dan gets up from the table and goes to my room.

'They said on the radio it was meant to be sunny all week, huh' Mum notes, 'Dan can you make sure he takes a jacket!'

I roll my eyes behind her but Dan soon returns with a coat from my room. It's a thick, brown leather one that Dad got me for my sixteenth birthday.

'This one is cool' Dan says, studying the jacket as he holds it up.

'It is very handsome, Warren never wears it though' Mum says.

'Why not? I think it looks cool as hell' Dan asks me.

'Alright, I'll wear the jacket' I take it from Dan and slip it on,

'Can we get going now?' I say, starting to become embarrassed by the two of them fussing over me.

'Thank you for the hospitality Mrs Avery, really, tell Ken I said hello'

'Not a problem Daniel, now you come back soon' Mum says, pulling us in and hugging us together, 'Good luck today Warren'

She escorts us out the front and watches us climb into Dan's car. Specks of rain are starting to dot the windscreen, Mum stays under the front porch to avoid the drizzle. Dan manages to get the ute to start and we wave to my mum as we drive towards the school, he almost immediately has to flicks the wipers on to combat the thickening rain.

'You're very lucky' he says.

'How's that? I have an exam in twenty minutes'

'Your mum, she's so lovely'

'She was happy to see you hey?'

'Yeah she... sure was' he sighs.

'What's wrong? I ask.

He looks at me quickly.

'I feel bad, for your folks' he says, 'They always showed me so much hospitality, and one day I just didn't come back'

'Water under the bridge' I tell him, 'Anyway, it's like you never left, you just got way taller'

He nods his head side to side, unconvinced.

'So, you really think Mayhew and Abernathy are connected?' I ask, trying to take his mind off it.

'Yeah I do. Come on Warren you're smart, nothing has ever happened in this town, and suddenly two people go missing in the same area? It's too coincidental'

'What are you thinking? Serial killer? Vampire? Grizzly bear?' I joke.

We arrive at the school car park, it's small but barely anyone is here so Dan is able to snag a parking space right near the hall where the exam is. He's right, nothing ever happens, and when something finally does, I'm just going to lie down and take it at face value? No, I won't.

'Maybe we should go and find out' I say.

'Find out what?'

He knows exactly what I'm talking about, but his voice tells me that he doubts my sincerity.

'What happened to those people. If you think there's murder most foul at play, after the exam let's go for a look and see if we find anything'

'You're not serious' he looks away from me.

'Sure am. Come on it will be like the old days, us getting lost out there'

'We never went hunting for missing people when we were kids Warren'

I brush my jaw, wondering how to convince him, he's always been very straight-laced.

'You really do want that excitement don't you mate?' he sighs.

I nod, trying to hide the excitement that I've convinced him.

'Alright, I'll go along with it. We won't find anything, but for old time's sake. I'll pick you up after this' he points at the school, 'But forget about it for now, you've gotta focus'

We bail out of the ute and walk from the car park towards the hall. Dan melodramatically rubs my shoulders, like I'm a boxer going into the ring.

'You got this champ, go get 'em' he jumps up and down behind me, hands still on my shoulders.

His energy is infectious, its pull impossible to escape from. I shadowbox down the hallway, Dan laughing behind me, ruffling my hair into my eyes.

'I'm ready coach, let me at 'em' I laugh out loud, surprised to be having so much fun.

We arrive at the hall, everyone sits or stands butted up against the wall, all desperate to escape the rain. The glum atmosphere shattered by me and Dan rocketing around the corner laughing. My classmates stare at us like we've just killed someone. Ava ignores me but stares at Dan completely mortified. She moves over to us and Dan hugs her, I let the two of them embrace and step aside to give them a chance to talk. Elliot slinks towards us, bumping two other students out of his way. His eyes narrow and he throws his scarf around his neck in a huff. That unmistakable privileged smirk fades away.

'What is this? he hisses.

'Hey Elliot, ready for the exam?' Dan replies casually.

'You're just hanging out with Fuck Eyes now?'

Dan doesn't say anything, he just stares Elliot down. Elliot drops his hands to his sides and shakes his head. He starts to turn away, as though having to look at us any longer would make him gag.

'Did you even check on him? Did you even ask about the detention that he got for you?' I spit, causing Elliot to turn around.

'You speaking out of turn *again* Fuck Eyes?'

Elliot grabs me by the shirt and I grab his scarf reflexively. Dan, quick as light, steps around me and thrusts his hands between us and drives us apart.

'Hey!' McGovern howls, sticking his head outside the door to the hall.

He must be overlooking the exam.

'You three again? Steele why are you even here? You causing more trouble?'

'No' I protest, Dan's hand still on my chest, 'We're all good out here'

'Yeah, everything is under control here' Elliot says slyly, looking me in the eye as he does.

'Alright then, glad to see you boys have made amends. It's time, sit down and no talking once you enter the hall'

Elliot fixes his scarf, and after ascertaining that the deep blue strip of wool isn't injured, he storms inside, Dan nods at me and pats my shoulder and gently pushes me in, I want to ask him what he plans to do for the next few hours but I'm inside the hall before I can form the words. Ms Harper and Mr McGovern are here to supervise the exam, keep track of time, make sure no one cheats, that sort of thing. A whiteboard has been wheeled in, and *Year 12 Advanced Biological Science* has been written on it.

The eight desks are arranged in one line running up and down the middle of the hall, probably to make it impossible to cheat off the person next to you. The other seven seats are already filled, the only one left for me is the fourth one back. A quiet but clever boy, William, is immediately behind me and Elliot is behind him. I take the seat and the exam paper is handed out by McGovern while we are read the rules by Harper. These rules are identical to the ones we had last year in year eleven. Three hours, no cheating, no talking, no looking around, no leaving, no using anything apart from a 2B pencil.

'You may begin, good luck everyone'

And for the next three hours, I shade in multiple choice bubbles and I scribble down definitions. I draw diagrams to show how DNA replicates and I fill in the table of the different barriers that lead to speciation. The time goes quick, but my mind works even quicker. I blaze through every question in my path with ease. The final question, the essay question reads, "*Discuss the advantages of animal species exhibiting the capacity for sociability, using examples from your studies*". I smile and start writing.

McGovern instructs everyone to place their pencils down. It's eleven, our three hours already long gone. Harper collects everyone's paper, I smile at her as she takes mine. I feel pride in what I wrote and confidence in my answers. When all have been collected, we are released outside. The drizzle persisting, everyone franticly covers their heads as they dart to the car park, the luckiest to be picked up by their parents. Elliot slinks away, hands in his pockets.

'Elliot' I call out to him.

He stops walking and turns around. I catch up to him and the two of us stand in the drizzle.

'Look, I don't know what you have against me, but I don't hold anything against you. I think we just got off on the wrong foot and Dan and I go way back, I-'

'You know he just feels sorry for you, right?' he interrupts, 'Which is more than you deserve'

'What have I even done to you?' I plead.

His eyes widen and his pupils contract like a snake's.

'Why can't the three of us be friends?' I swallow hard and extend a hand to shake.

I can feel the vitriol seeping from his pores, simply existing in his proximity is almost overwhelming. I've always known Elliot to be cocky and arrogant, but in this moment, it feels like he's capable of a ferocity I could have never imagined. His jaw locked and his breathing now short and rapid, he knocks my hand away with the back of his own, then steps forward to lean in close to my face.

'Why can't the three of us be friends Warren?' he breathes, 'Because you make me sick, people who don't know their place. He's such a bleeding heart, and maybe the two of you deserve one another'

He moves his face away from mine and turns away from the hall, he's on his merry way to Europe. I stand completely immobile until a strong hand rests on my shoulder and shakes me back to reality.

'What did he have to say?' Dan asks.

'Not much' I lie.

'Well don't worry about it, he's off to Greece or wherever it was now'

'Spain' I correct him, although that's only what I overheard yesterday.

'Lucky him, come on' Dan sighs, and starts walking to the car park.

'We still finding out what happened to those people?' I ask, catching up to him.

'You're insane'

'Come on!' I nudge him with my elbow, 'Schools out! You wouldn't let me walk home in the rain, would you?'

'Fine, but I'm only going along with this because I'm...' he trails off, 'Glad to be hanging out with you again'

'I don't think we'll find anything honestly, but imagine if we did'

'We aren't going to mysteriously disappear are we Warren?'

'No promises' I laugh.

We arrive at the car park and stand together in the thin rain, at the end of my eyelashes I can see the mist starting to collect. I blink it away.

'You know what Dan?' I say.

He nods at me to continue.

'A few days ago, I probably wouldn't have minded just disappearing'

'Huh?' he looks confused.

'Christ, I don't mean like that! Just, I don't know, vanishing, going away'

He thinks about this a moment before squinting at me.

'I know what you mean, I think' he nods.

We hop into Big Red once more. And for the first time in years, I'm going to my best friend's house.

V

Set in Stone

It takes about twenty minutes for us to reach the Steele family farm, as far west as the roads will let you go, the Southway streets replaced with long winding gravel roads leading us out of town. The farm is exactly as I remember it, the rustic homestead in the centre, surrounded by paddocks of livestock, eventually bleeding into thick bush that stretches out for miles in all directions. Out east was where Mayhew lived, is he still out there somewhere beyond the trees?

We pull up at the house and Dan welcomes me in, stepping aside for me at the front door like an usher. Visually, it's exactly as I remember, every piece of furniture exactly where I remember it last, but the sensation I get is completely different. This doesn't feel like the place I spent half my time in as a child. It isn't a horrible feeling, this isn't like in the horror movies where the characters say the house feels haunted but still go inside, it just feels…empty. I sweep the thought away, it's probably just because no one else is home.

'Make yourself at home Warren' he says, 'You know where my room is, I'm sure'

I know exactly where it is, the room where we had spent countless summer nights staying up until the sunrise playing video games and watching shitty B grade movies we'd rent from the video shop in town. Gone are the toys and posters, replaced with more sensible, mature furniture pieces and a fresh white coat of paint on the walls and ceiling, the only part of the house that looks like it's evolved over these lost years. A double bed shoved away in the corner of the room with a nightstand by its side, a wardrobe on the wall opposite the bed, archery gear kept neatly in the corner beside it.

'Different than it probably was when you were last here' he says.

On his nightstand, his archery trophies are still proudly displayed, I count about a dozen different little gilded men pulling their bows back, and not a speck of dust sits on any of them. My eyes naturally then search for the archery gear, a large and heavy but simple looking bow stands upright in a holder, three quivers full of different sorts of arrows strung on the wall beside it by little hooks in the wall.

'Deadly stuff' I say, nodding at the bow.

'Only if you're a rabbit or a kangaroo' he laughs.

The simplicity of the bow fascinates me, growing up Dan would watch archery competitions and the bows they wielded always had scopes and sights and more strings that a guitar. This one looks like he could be borrowing it from Robin Hood.

'Is this like an older style or something?' I ask.

Dan laughs.

'It's just not what I imagined a modern bow to be like is all, this isn't the same one you had growing up, is it?'

'No, I outgrew that one quicker than I could shoot it' he laughs, 'You're thinking of compound bows, the ones that look more... Complicated, this one is a recurve'

'What's the difference?'

'The difference is I prefer recurves' he says picking it up, 'More traditional I guess, harder to use, physically I mean, but if you work hard that isn't a problem'

I don't think the physical strain would impact his preference much at all, the guy has more upper body strength than most adults I've seen.

'It looks nice anyway, where did you get it?'

'A gift' he says quickly.

'You hunt much anymore?'

'Eh not anymore, I'd hunt and skin a rabbit or maybe a kangaroo and mum would make this stew, she hasn't done it for a while though'

57

'How rusty are you?'

'Not at all' he scoffs, 'It's just like riding a bike mate, something you never forget'

He moves over to the bow and picks it up, feeling its weight in his hands.

'We should go sometime' he says, 'You know, in the summer when the weather gets hotter'

'I'd like that' I say.

Back on the nightstand, hidden in the trophies, is a small but thick paperback book, *The Pursuit of Adventure* by Maximillian Murphy.

'I didn't know you were such an avid reader' I say, picking the book up.

'I'm not, I just like this guy, that's his autobiography' Dan says.

'Who is he?'

'Maximillian Murphy, he's an explorer'

'An explorer? Is he from the sixteen hundreds?' I laugh.

'No, you idiot, he's like, a modern-day explorer. He's climbed Everest four times'

'Four times? Does he forget things up there or something? What does he actually do?' I ask.

'Everything, mostly helping scientists do field research and stuff. He goes all over the world, and he puts together a crew of experts and people he knows, and they film their adventures' he explains with fire in his eyes.

'Sounds like he lives the dream, when did you become such a fan of his?'

'A while ago, I've seen all his documentaries, he's actually in Australia right now'

I'd never say that I've seen him so giddy before.

'He is? Huh, you should go looking for him' I say.

'Yeah he's here for some geology thing. I wish I could meet him one day, but he's out in the wilderness somewhere, you'd never find him'

'One day you'll meet him my friend' I put the book back down in its place.

'One day' he agrees, 'Speaking of finding people, are we really doing this? Think about it'

I don't answer, deep down I know it's insane, that I'm disregarding the sheer impossibility of two seventeen year olds being the ones to solve this town's biggest mystery, and only seeing the accomplishment we'd feel if we did. I imagine the ecstasy Mr Abernathy would feel to see his wife again, Mr Mayhew's relief to be found and led back to safety. To finally do something worthwhile. His features soften as we stare each other down, I think understands.

'Okay, let's do this' he nods.

'Yes!' I punch at the air.

'Alright let's eat something quick and make a move'

'You bringing that?' I gesture at the bow, still in his hand.

'No' he states firmly, 'We won't need it, we're just doing a bit of...'

'Reconnaissance?'

'That's the one, shit you know a lot of words'

He places the bow back and grabs a jacket of his own from the wardrobe to replace his hoodie. As he opens the closet I see a plethora of other outdoor gear in the bottom below his clothes. Lamps, axes, shovels, tents, all manner of equipment one would need for survival. It's weird to think that someone so outdoorsy would hide this stuff away in their cupboard. Before he shuts the doors, I spy a machete laying down at the bottom, it's worn, gunmetal blade hilted by a rubber looking orange grip.

'What about that thing? The machete' I ask

'What about it?'

'Should we bring it? For like, trees?' I say, waving my arms and pretending to slash.

It must look awkward because Dan visibly cringes.

'Sure, you can bring it if you like' he picks it up and passes it to me, handle first.

I take it in my right hand and swing it softly to get a feel for its bulk. It feels meaty, the blade is only thin and the tip is rounded, not practical to stab with, but the heft it carries makes a part of me feel like a knight in medieval times.

In the kitchen, he slaps together two peanut butter sandwiches, and fills up two bottles with water, throwing one of each to me. I can't help but notice that the pantry was almost empty. In the car and on the move, we agree to head out east, park near the trees and head in on foot. Dan finds us a point of entry where the plant limbs are less thick and tangled underneath the heavy canopy, the sun struggling to break through to us.

'This was your idea, after you' he says.

I take the machete in hand and begin to hack through the ferns. I lead Dan in, flailing the blade at the brush in our path.

'So, a new guy is starting at work tonight' I say, after we've walked some fair distance.

'Who?'

'Not sure, they said his name was Lucas, he wants to be a chef and he's new in town'

'Poor bastard coming here. How old is he, did they say?' he asks.

'About our age I assume, they want me to make him feel welcome, whatever that means'

'How are you gonna do that?' he asks.

I hadn't thought that far ahead, my lack of a response says enough.

'Try talking to him tonight. It might be hard but I'm sure he'd appreciate it, being new in town, especially *this* town, must be hard' he says compassionately.

'Yeah sure' I grunt, slashing at a particularly stubborn vine, 'I can do that'

'You should relax your wrist a bit, be a bit more fluid you know?' he rolls his wrist around, demonstrating.

I take his advice on board and loosen my arm. My slashes immediately become more refined, dispatching any thick undergrowth that obscures our path.

'Look at this little swashbuckler go!' laughs Dan, as I make sound effects while I slice.

We hike for about an hour and a half, me clearing a path, like I'm some sort of an adventurer, Dan laughing and singing close behind. It's slow going, stopping often to adjust course slightly when we reach an impasse, but I'm in no hurry. I feel nostalgic, taken back in time to when there were no worries aside from getting lost, no growing apart from friends and no making enemies you didn't even want. The problem with nostalgia is that you can't tell if you want it to end or not, but in this moment while it's happening, I think it's enough to just enjoy it.

'Hey Warren?' Dan calls after a while of silence.

'What's up?'

'Thanks for speaking up to Elliot today, even if it almost ended in blows'

Deserving each other, that's what Elliot had said. I turn away from him and start kicking around the area around us.

'Not sure how much good it did' I say, 'Hey! Check this out'

The trees have thinned and we've come to a small clearing. About ten metres in diameter, with large boulders scattered around, quartz coated in mosses from years of being untouched. Long, verdant grass feels up past my ankles, water creeping in through my shoes at this point. One large tree grows in the centre of the field, a willow or something. Its branches droop down low, bald of leaves in the back end of Autumn. Half a million raindrops cling to its wooden fingers, light refracting from every single one as they cling in their cohesion, magical.

'Not a bad spot hey?' I say.

Dan is already investigating the rocks, looking for the best one to sit on.

'Bloody oath, I can't believe we never found this place growing up, did we ever venture out this way?' he asks, having selected his rock.

We both look around in awe at the beauty.

'No, I'd remember this' I breathe.

I find a rock of my own and rest the machete against it, tip down in the grass. I take a seat and bring my knees up to finally get my feet out of the wet foliage.

'How are we doing?' I ask, 'I mean, do you think we're getting close? To like, anything?'

'If I knew how close we were to anything Warren, I'd be leading the way' he laughs.

I get up, and start studying the shrub around us. In all directions, the trees eventually thicken back up, aside from the path I cut for us of course. I walk around the circumference of the meadow.

'Anything Detective?' Dan calls out.

'No, I-' as I look over at him, I see his rock from the other side.

A thin strip has been sliced in the moss, revealing the stone underneath. As though another stone has brushed up against it.

'Did you do that dude?' I point. He cranes his neck over to look at it.

'No, why?'

'It's unnatural, someone did that'

'As if anybody else has ever been here'

We stare at each other, I can feel the chills.

'Or some*thing*'

'What do you mean?' he laughs.

I move over to investigate with him, he peels the moss away, and the newly exposed surface has a thin, but unexpectedly deep, slice into the rock itself, as though some Greek God has run a knife across it.

'What the hell' I breathe.

'Look!'

Dan points out that the grass has been trodden on beside the scratched boulder. The stamped grass makes a path leading to the trees on the opposite side to the way we came in.

'Recent you reckon?'

'Has to be'

'Someone was here then'

We follow to wear the trail leads, all the way up to where the trees thicken, it looks like something has forced its way through. Something much larger than any person could be.

'Dude' Dan whispers.

He's bending down, pointing at a low, sharp branch, caked in a red crusty substance.

'Is it blood?' I ask.

'I think so'

'Holy shit' I hold my head.

'Let's keep it calm? Someone was running and got caught on this branch and cut themselves?'

'So why were they running? What about the rock?' I point at it, 'A person couldn't have done that'

His face full with worry, he looks from the flattened grass to the bloody branch to the scratched stone.

'Okay so what are we dealing with here? Do you think somebody was *chased* through and they sliced their leg while running?'

'Whatever came through this way, I think it was bigger than a human, and the rock... I don't know'

'Someone could have had a weapon and scratched the rock with it?'

'I... It... It just looks like, whatever did this-' I stutter, the fear taking over.

'What? You really think some monster did this? The blood is probably from a kangaroo or a... A wild pig or something'

Of course, I hadn't thought of that! There are so many wild animals around the town, feral cats and wild boars, I've even heard that there are deer around, they have sharp horns, right? That must be what it is.

'You're right, must have just been a big animal' I laugh nervously.

He stares at the mossy gouge in the stone, I don't think he's really convinced himself.

'We should get out of here. It's-'

We're interrupted before I can finish. A low howl erupts through the trees, sending the cockatoos flying in all directions. It curdles in the air, making my hairs stand on end. It's coming from further east, further past this meadow, in the direction of the blood-soaked stick.

'What the fuck?'

'Go back, go back!' Dan says, expressionless.

Another shriek, closer than the last, its echoes carry in the wind and blend with the first's. We spin on our heels and hightail it away from the meadow, scooping up the machete on my way past. Dan is far more athletic than me, but he throws me on ahead first.

'Go, go!'

We sprint through the path I had carved for us. My ragged breathing, rustling strides and pounding heart drown out any more roars there might have been. I don't hack at the trees, I just let their thorns tear into my skin as I weave past, slicing my exposed flesh on my hands and face. We both trip several times, each of us pulling the other to their feet and hurling them ahead, never looking back. Adrenaline flowing through our bodies, we get back to the car, rip the doors open and Dan has the car started before we even close them. We're soaked and gasping for breath, but we're safe.

'We're okay, we're okay' I mumble, petrified, I try to calm myself down.

'What was that?' Dan breathes, equally as shocked.

'I don't want to find out, let's just get back to the house'

'No seriously, what the fuck was that?'

'I don't know!'

He doesn't ask again, and I don't try to explain again, he just drives us in silence while we hope that there isn't anything behind us. At the house and satisfied that there isn't, I can finally stop looking over my shoulder. His mother is home.

'Jesus Christ' he groans.

We calm ourselves, and wipe away the blood from the scratches on our faces the best we can. Dan tells me to just leave the machete in his car and he'll put it back later. Inside, Dan's mother sits at the kitchen table with a cup of coffee. No steam wafts from the mug, and dried streaks have spilled down the side and congealed on the table in a ring around the base. She stares out the window.

'Hey' Dan says.

'Oh, hello' she says languorously.

It seems that we've startled her from a daydream, jostled her awake just enough for a response but nothing more. She doesn't turn to look at us.

'Warren's here, you remember Warren, right?' he says.

'Warren?' she finally turns her head, 'Oh, Warren, yeah. Hello'

Dan definitely inherited her nose and eyes, though she has light brown, shoulder length hair, much lighter than his. I can't even remember what his dad's hair was like.

'How have you been Mrs Steele?' I say.

'Just fine' she says softly, 'Thank you'

A small girl appears from the lounge room, she hides coyly around the doorframe to look at me. She has dark, uncombed hair, the same tone as

Dan's, and wears a school uniform even though school has been done for hours. It takes me a moment to put the pieces together. Dan's parents had a daughter when Dan and I were about ten, and we had grown apart by the time she was three, so I never interacted with her.

'Hey Izzy' Dan says to her, bobbing down to her level, a massive smile on his face, 'How was school?'

'Good' she says shyly, still looking at me.

Dan laughs and places a caring hand on her back, and encourages her into the kitchen.

'You probably don't remember him, but this is my friend Warren, he used to be here a lot. Warren, you remember Isabelle?'

No, I actually didn't.

'Hi Isabelle' I squat down to her level as Dan did, 'You were only a baby when I last saw you!'

I use that over-the-top enthusiastic voice people use to talk to kids. She turns bright red and laughs, covering her mouth, embarrassed. I smile. Dan lifts her up and spins her around.

'Come on' he says, 'Let's go and get that hair brushed, I'll be back in a sec Warren'

I'm left with Dan's mother, still gazing out the window absentmindedly towards the trees, her untouched cup of weak coffee starting to smell stale. I sit next to her, the scraping of the chair as I pull it out wakes her, she blinks away the glazed sheen of her eyes. I wonder how long it will be before his dad gets home.

'So, what, um, what are you doing with yourself Warren?'

'Looking to go to university' I say, 'Right now I'm working at the pizza place in town, just until I finish school'

'Oh, that's good, you know I wish Daniel had a job' she closes her eyes, 'What are you going to study?'

'Science, I guess'

'Well what do you want to be?'

I take some time to think, but I'm at a loss. The thought of *being* something, I hate it, it has a certain finality to it. Talking about hypothetically study and degrees is okay because it comes with flexibility, nothing is set in stone, it's all eventual and distant, but when you're asked about *being*, answering feels like a life sentence.

'Much better huh?' Dan coos, returning to the room with his sister, her hair now neatened.

I'm saved from this conversation by the Steele siblings.

'Warren, you want to get going?' Dan points at the dusty clock above the stove, 'Four thirty'

'Yeah good idea, I've got to go, I have work soon' I explain.

'Okay, take care' Dan's mother says.

Isabelle follows us to the door like a lost puppy, begging us not to leave her.

'I'll only be gone a minute Izzy, I have to take Warren home' Dan assures her.

'And I'll be back soon' I wave, and she seems to cheer up.

We sit in silence as we rumble down the long winding driveway and beyond into town, both shaken by what we saw and heard. I also worry about Dan's mother, she didn't seem to be fully aware, but I'm unsure of how to ask him about it. Before I get a chance, we're at my house.

'Warren?' he says.

'Yeah?'

He's going to ask about that sound again.

'We should exchange mobile numbers, we haven't done it yet'

'Oh right, sure' I hand him my phone and he starts to enter his number.

I'll do it then, we can't dance around it forever.

'So, what do we do? Who do we tell?' I say.

He knows what I'm talking about, he runs his tongue over his teeth and thinks.

'Look right now, you have work to worry about, and you promised to try with this new kid remember?'

'Oh yeah, can't say it was exactly at the forefront of mind right now' I jibe.

'Well it is now. I'll drive you, go get ready, I'll wait here'

I run inside, greet mum and dad quickly, they ask about the exam, but I brush them off and get changed for work, and fly back out the door. I want to ask Dan to drive past where I saw the man with the lab coat, but Dan speaks first.

'So, got any plans for the holidays?'

'Work, I guess, try not to go missing'

'Jesus Warren, come on, you're free! Alright sure, you have work at night but what about during the day?'

'Why? Elliot's out of the country and you need someone to hang out with?'

'Hey you know that isn't it' he snaps, 'I just mean it works out well, you have work in the evenings, and I have certain *boyfriend duties*'

He gestures suggestively.

'But if we've both got nothing on during the day, want to go fishing or something?'

'No more searching for missing people though' I say.

'No way, I say we just forget that happened'

'Somehow I don't think I'll be able to'

'Yeah same' he laughs, 'Wait until Elliot hears about this'

My heart breaks a little. As terrifying as it was, I imagined our adventure today would be a memory that stayed between the two of us. Dan can tell how crestfallen I am by this.

'You really, really don't get along, do you?' he asks.

I think about what he said to me earlier.

'I mean, I think he's a bit of a dickhead, but I don't have a real problem with him, it's all him. I don't know, maybe he's just evil'

Dan's pupils dilate.

'He's not really like that you know? He's just... overdramatic, trust me. But, if you don't think we should tell him, then I won't tell him, I promise'

'So, who *do* we tell?' I ask again.

He thinks about this, and so do I.

'The Police?' he suggests.

'It's close to your house, we should at least tell your parents first' I add.

Dan exhales.

'Actually Warren, it's just *parent* these days'

It takes me a moment, but then I see, it makes sense and I feel embarrassed.

'I'm… Sorry to hear' I say, it's all I can think of.

Dan looks at me and smiles, although it's weak.

'He didn't die, he just doesn't live here anymore'

'Do you know where he's gone?'

With a faraway look, he shakes his head.

'It's not the sort of thing I worry about'

'So, it's the three of you then?'

He nods.

'Wait, does that mean you take care of the whole farm, yourself?'

He nods again.

'But it'll be great dude, hanging out again, I could even introduce you to some people?' he says before I can ask anything else.

I respect his desire to not want to talk about it further, but I can't believe how much responsibility he must have at home. A bleeding heart, that's what Elliot had called him isn't it?

'Sounds good' I say, forcing a smile.

We arrive at the restaurant, the sun on the cusp of retreating for the night. The neon signs of Wanda and Rhonda's aglow, but the *Closed* sign yet to be spun around.

'Wait come back' Dan calls to me from the driver's window.

'What?'

'You got...' he gestures at his own face, then whispers like it's a sin, 'Blood'

He licks his thumb and wipes it over a scratch on my jaw, I didn't know there was a scratch there until now.

'Man, that's so gross'

'Alright, remember to really try with this new kid' he ignores it.

'I'll do you proud Commander' I salute.

'I know you will' he laughs, I'll make a social butterfly out of you yet Warren Avery!'

VI

Lucas

The weather has cleared up since this afternoon, the tangerine sunset watches over Unity Street, glowing up the evening, with no one out and about to enjoy it. The stench of the grease fills my nose in an instant as I enter Wanda and Rhonda's, the tables freshly wiped and the floor recently swept, unusual, I normally do that, and then I hear the humming from the kitchen. It's not from a popular song, it's a melancholy tune with no clear direction or pattern, but it's beautiful, in its own way. Does listening to humming count as eavesdropping? I check that the scratches on my face aren't still bleeding by using my reflection in the window. The ladies are out the back, having a coffee and a cigarette before we open, I assume. We're good, it's time to make Dan proud.

'You've been here one night and you've already done more than I ever have since I started here'

The young man is hunched over the sink, his hands plunged into the water, scrubbing violently at a pizza tray. My pile of dishes that I didn't do last night still rests on the sink, but an even bigger pile is already spotless, drip-drying on the dish rack. He's been working hard. He stops when he hears me, wipes his hands on the apron he's wearing, the same kind that Wanda wears in the kitchen. As he turns to face me, he flicks his hair to the side, undulating, shadowy hair that threatens to spill down over his eyes if he doesn't keep it in place. He's quite a skinny boy, but he has a round, happy face, he looks a bit younger than me.

'Oh, uh, yeah, well I just wanted to make a good impression' he says, his voice chirpy but wavering.

He's caught off guard by my different coloured eyes. It's always funny when people see me for the first time and try not to stare. Unfortunately, it doesn't happen often, since everyone around town know me by now.

'Heterochromia' I point up at my face, laughing, letting him know I take no offense.

'Oh, I'm sorry to hear that' he says, empathy charging into his expression.

'I don't mind, it's like an inbuilt conversation starter, did they offer you coffee?' I point at the back door.

'They did, I don't drink it though'

He seems very meek and mild, I wonder if this is how I seemed to Dan. I make my way over to the sink and grab a tea towel, I start drying the cutlery in the rack.

'Well, you better learn to like it, it's just so busy here all the time you need a pick me up' I say sarcastically.

He laughs, revealing a huge, open mouthed smile and beautiful teeth. I smile too.

'Warren Avery' I extend a hand.

'Lucas Kawamura' he dries his hands on his apron again and we shake.

He seems relieved for some reason, Rhonda probably told him that I was completely different for a laugh.

'Let me help you out Lucas, these are my dishes from last night anyway' I sink my hands into the warm water beside him.

Rhonda and Wanda come through the back door laughing, coffee cups in hand.

'Oh, Warren you're here' says Rhonda.

'And I see you've met Lucas' adds Wanda.

We both nod.

'Alright well it's Friday night so you know what that means, I'll be on deliveries, Warren you take the counter and wait the tables,

Lucas I want you helping Wanda in the kitchen' Rhonda dishes out the commands.

The ladies start flying around the place getting things in order

'If the dishes start piling up, and there's no customers, you boys are on that'

'You got it' I say, giving her a thumbs-up.

'Beautiful' Wanda says, 'Lucas, do you want to do the honours and open the door?'

'Me? I…' he freezes.

'Go on, it's a tradition, I had to do it the night I started. Besides, they don't pay you if you don't do it' I say, trying my best to ease him in.

The look on his face tells me that he believes me, but when the bosses start to howl in the back, he finally loosens up.

'Okay, yeah, I'll do it' he grins.

He hops down to the front and flips the sign around, I give him the thumbs up. Showtime.

Friday nights usually are quite unpredictable, the other nights I can predict the customers, what they'll order, and when they'll show up within about five minutes either side. But once the weekend ticks over, we get any combination of families with hysterical kids, twenty-something couples, stoned teenagers and everything in between. Tonight, is no exception, for hours I dart between the counter and the tables, taking orders and giving change. Bringing out pizzas and cutlery, being told by irritable middle-aged couples how I'm pouring their drinks wrong. I feel like I got the short end of the stick here, having to do so much legwork, but even under the pressure, I look over to Lucas whenever I get the chance to make sure he's coping. Beads of sweat form on his forehead and roll down his temples, each taking the same moist, tracks left by the ones that fell before.

While Wanda knows the routine inside and out, he frantically dances around the kitchen, almost slipping over at times, but as manic as his movement might be, the way he prepares food is absolutely mesmerising. No one pizza slice has any more or any less topping than any other slice under his watch. Not once does he allow a stove of pasta sauce to congeal to the sides of the pot. He doesn't even let a shred of cheese escape onto the bench or the floor. Once the chaos subsides, everyone in Southway fed and gone on their way, the four of us take a collective breath, Lucas finally wipes away his sweat.

'You did good Lucas' Wanda says, patting him on the back.

'I did?' he asks, surprised.

'Better than good' I add, 'Everyone was saying how good the food was'

His eyes light up and his cheeks raise.

'Wow, thanks you guys' he's unable to hide his happiness and relief.

'Can you boys get started on those dishes? Christ, I need a smoke' Rhonda laughs, 'You guys want coffee?'

'Yes please' I call back.

'Yes please' Lucas softly copies.

Rhonda looks back to make sure she heard him right, then nods and gives me a thin smile. I crack my knuckles and we get started on the pile of dishes that sits higher than us both. Wanda pours us both a coffee.

'I gave you a few sugars love, I can tell you don't drink too much coffee' she laughs.

'Can you really tell?'

'Yeah' I nod, 'They have witch powers'

She scowls at me and sets the coffee down next to the sink for us. We thank her, before she slips outside to join Rhonda, leaving the two of us to resume scrubbing.

'So… How many sugars do you have Warren?' he asks.

'None' I lift a soapy hand and make a zero with the thumb and index finger.

'Don't you think it's bitter without sugar?'

'I used to, but I drank so much to stay up late studying that I guess I just got used to the taste'

'Studying?'

'I'm in my last year of school, had my last exam of the semester today actually'

'Wow, you must be really smart! Are you going to be a scientist? Or a doctor?' Lucas gawks.

'You know, I was asked earlier today, and I have no idea' I say, looking up at the light overhead.

'No idea? Like at all? Come on, you must have something in mind'

'I don't know, and ecologist or something, something that gets me out of here. What about you? You want to become a chef I hear?'

'Well, yeah kind of'

'You really know what you're doing, have you had formal training?'

He stops scrubbing the bowl he's currently working on, I stop too. The sink hisses as the suds fizzle away and laughter muffles against the back door, but otherwise the restaurant is noiseless.

'My dad he… He's a chef, he taught me'

'Wow' I say, impressed, 'Does he have a restaurant?'

Lucas starts scrubbing again, harder this time.

'No, he doesn't anymore' he says, his teeth slightly clenched.

This is a touchy subject for him, I feel guilty for bringing it up, this is just like Dan and his dad, I'm no good at this talking thing, perhaps I should eat my lunch alone with my books.

'You just moved here hey?' I ask, trying to change the subject.

'Yep, a couple of weeks ago' he says, pleased to talk about something else, 'I'm starting school next semester, year ten'

That puts him at fifteen or sixteen, only a year or two younger than me.

'Well, I hope you don't expect too much excitement here Lucas' I laugh.

'I don't mind it, the small town, it's a nice change from where I'm from'

'Where's that?'

'Melbourne'

'I hear the food scene is insane, I hope you brought some flair over with you, this town needs it'

He can't help but laugh, he has to raise the back of his wrist to cover his mouth.

'Yeah, I'm not going to lie, I wasn't impressed when I got here'

I think about the apple, the library, the exam, Elliot, Dan's house, the meadow, the blood and the roar.

'You know what Lucas, I take it back, thinking about the day I had today, this town can be plenty exciting'

'What happened?'

I hesitate. I wonder if he even knows about the disappearances, I don't think I should be the one to tell him, not here and now at least.

'Uh nothing, just hung out with my friend, played some video games, you know?' I spin my lie.

Finishing the plate that I'm working on, I slot it into the rack and dry my hands to take a sip of coffee. Lucas follows suit, but immediately grimaces when the taste touched his mouth and I can't help but laugh at his reaction.

'What games do you play?' he shakes his head at the bitterness, 'There's this computer game I like, it's a bit of an older one, it's my favourite game ever actually, Monster Masher, you have to track down monsters and work out a way to defeat them'

I'm glad he kept talking, I don't think I could have named a current video game, we used to play frequently Dan and I, but that like many things was left behind. Lucas turns a sunny pink in the face, instantly embarrassed by what he's said.

'Ugh, yeah I know it's lame, I play quite a lot of games'

'Are there Werewolves and Vampires in Monster Masher?' I ask.

I can't get a confident read on him just yet, I've only known him for a few hours but it's like he was expecting me to ridicule him. I make sure he sees me smiling, ensuring him it's alright.

'No vampires, but there are werewolves, but they're an easy monster really, I'm up to this one, it's called the Mother Dragon, and I just can't beat it. Been stuck on it since we were still in Melbourne' he sighs.

It's like hearing Dan talk about bows and that explorer guy, or Elliot talk about himself, there's just something about hearing people talk about what they're passionate about.

'I have a computer? Does this game have two-player mode?' I ask.

His striking, wide smile shows itself again.

'You have a PC?'

'Sure do, I actually got the job here because I wanted to save up to buy one, I only ever use it to study though' I laugh.

'It does have multiplayer, we could play online together, I mean, if you want to get it'

'Sure, it's school holidays now, I'll help you slay your dragon' I present a fist for him to bump.

He scoffs.

'Warren if you can beat the Mother Dragon I'll follow you until the ends of the Earth' he bumps the fist.

Rhonda enters from the back, bringing in her and Wanda's mugs.

'Jesus, do you guys actually do anything around here?' she gestures at the remaining dishes.

Lucas panics, places his coffee cup down and throws his hands back into the water. Rhonda laughs at him.

'I'm only pulling your leg love, you guys did great tonight. I know starting on a Friday night may have been a bit hectic for you, go on get out of here, I've got this mess' she drops her mug into the sink.

'Thank you, Miss' Lucas says.

We're gathering our things when Wanda appears in the doorway, breathing cigarette smoke out into the drizzle.

'Have fun walking home in that' she laughs, 'We'll get a uniform made for you, what size are you?'

'Just a small' he says.

'Small, got it' she writes on the back of her hand, then throws the pen away 'Warren show him the deal make yourselves a pizza if you want, and get out of here. Lucas Kullick, welcome to the team' Wanda beams.

Kullick? Did Wanda really mess up his name?

Outside the restaurant Lucas explains that he lives on the complete opposite side of town to me, so we'll have to walk home in separate directions. He pulls out a woollen hat from his bag. It's red and grey, it's the kind that has the flaps that cover your ears and the tassels that hang down from them. He wrenches it over his head and has to shove his hair up underneath it, tufts still sticking out.

'I'll see you next time we have work' he says sheepishly.

'Or you can see me online, I think I might pick up that game tomorrow, it sounds fun'

'You will?'

'Sure, I'll give you my number, text me your username or whatever it is'

He hands me his phone and I plant my number in his contacts.

'Do you want to hang out sometime Lucas? You know, before school starts, I could show you around?'

'Maybe sometime, but I don't know' he quickly takes his phone back, 'I'm, I'm sorry'

I can tell this boy is hiding something. Not something sinister, he radiates too much innocence for that, but I can't shake the feeling that there's more to him than cooking and video games.

'But I am keen to play, I've never had anyone to play with before' he adds.

'No stress, whatever works best for you'

'Warren, you can just call me Luke'

'Okay then, you did good tonight, Luke'

81

VII
The Mother

'What are we doing here again?' Dan asks, picking up a game case and flipping it over to read the back.

'Looking for computer games, one called Monster Masher' I scour the shelves.

We're at Mick's Electronics, the only chance you'd have in Southway to find anything technology related from the current century. It's a small, grimy shop and of course we're the only people here on a Saturday morning. We're searching up the back, where all the games are arranged to form an overwhelming wall of plastic cases. There's so many kinds for different consoles we're already lost in the colourful titles.

'Sounds kind of dumb to me, they really don't make games like the ones we used to play. What was the one where you were like a soldier or whatever?' he puts the game back down, 'Now that one was good'

'This guy Luke, he's really cool. He's real shy but he loves this game, and he's never had anyone to play two-player with. What are you on about anyway? Didn't you want me to try to befriend him?'

'Okay chill out' he holds his hands up, mock surrendering, 'I'm just saying you better not spend your entire holidays working and playing video games inside, we're going fishing tomorrow, remember?'

'I just feel bad for Luke, he just moved here, and it sounds like he's never had many friends at all'

'Warren Avery: Man of the People' Dan bows low to me as he announces my new title.

'Dude shut up'

'Okay jokes aside, I'm sure he'll appreciate it'

'Can I help you fellas with anything?' a nasal voice sneers behind me.

Mick himself has made his way over, a short man with a large belly, he spins a set of keys around on his plump index finger. He looks at us from behind the thick, round lenses of his spectacles.

'We're looking for some game called Monster Masher' Dan says.

Mick laughs so hard he snorts. He calms himself and strokes his thin, wispy beard.

'Why? That game was terrible, even for its time. A four out of ten at best'

'You sure know how to make a sale' Dan says dryly.

'Do you have it?' I ask.

'Yes, I have it, of course I have it' he straightens his glasses.

He pushes past us to the shelf and bends down with great difficulty. He thinks for a moment and picks Monster Masher from behind another game. Dan rolls his eyes. Mick takes the game and we follow him back to the counter.

'Seventy' he says.

'Jesus Christ is the disc made of gold or something?' Dan says.

'Are you kids just wasting my time?' Mick says, growing tired of Dan's cheek.

'No, I'll take it please' I say.

I pay the seventy dollars, thank Mick, although I'm not sure what for exactly, and leave the shop, Dan going out of his way to stare daggers at him on the way out. It's a sunny weekend in Southway, people are out and about on the main street, chatting with one another and trying not to jinx it and bring the rain back.

'What a dickhead' Dan says, probably too loudly.

'Were games always this expensive? Even when we played them as kids? Makes me grateful whenever I got one for a birthday or Christmas' I say, studying the game as we walk.

The case looks like a Hollywood action movie, a man with a giant battle axe is fighting a giant dinosaur type creature.

'I sure hope it's worth the seventy bucks' Dan says.

'I guess seventy isn't too bad'

'That's a tank of fuel'

'Hey that reminds me actually, I've been wondering, and I'm sorry if this is too personal, but how do you get the money for fuel? You know, without a job'

Dan skips a breath, caught off guard. He looks at me and then sighs, ready to open up.

'It's just the deal I've got with my mum'

'The deal?' I ask.

We've reached the park, it's a massive block just down the street from the town centre, it's mostly just a grassed with plenty of space for folks to kick a ball or walk their dogs. Thick, willowy trees form a border around the whole thing, blocking the outside view completely with their leaves, young people often use this to their advantage and get drunk in here away from the prying eyes. An entrance in the trees on either side of the park, each where a brick paths winds inward and meets each other at a rusty and dented playground in the middle. Dan moves towards a nearby bench and we sit.

'My mum feeds me, lets me live at home, and pays for my fuel. That's it. In return, I keep the farm ticking, look after the sheep. She wants to sell it soon, move away from this place'

I wonder, food, shelter and fuel, is that really it?

'You have other stuff though, arrows and stuff, that book? She must buy you stuff' I say instead.

He covers his eyes in shame, as if he needs to hide from the world.

'Dude, what is it?' I place a hand on his shoulder.

'Elliot, he gives me money, sometimes'

A rage builds within me, I imagine the same kind that Elliot feels when he remembers that I exist. It courses through my veins until it fills every cell in my body, looking for pores to escape from.

'Is that it then? Because you owe him?'

'No, god no' he says, 'He *is* my friend, I look out for him and he looks out for me. He doesn't expect to be paid back or anything. He's just a good bloke, that's why I can't believe he's so cruel to you'

'He doesn't ask for it back because money isn't a problem for the Youngs. Do you think he'd be so generous with his money if his parents didn't give it all to him?'

His breathing slows. He thinks hard about that.

'I know he's your friend, and I don't want you to have to choose a side or anything like that, but just don't let him shame you into being his lap dog okay? It's fine to accept gifts from the prick. Hell, I'd be taking his money if he offered, he can afford to give old Fuck Eyes seventy bucks'

It makes him laugh, and that's worth way more than seventy bucks to me.

'Don't lose sleep over it, it won't kill him' I quote Harper.

He throws his arms around me. When he finally pulls away, his face is burning red but he's quick to recover.

'Come on, let's go see if this game really is a four out of ten' he says.

He pulls me up and we make our way back to my house. We went into town on foot since it was such a nice day, and as always, I analyse the downstairs place where the old man took those boxes when we pass it. No sign of him, nobody else even throws the hidden basement a glance. I'm starting to wonder if that was even real at all.

'You okay?' Dan asks.

'Yeah of course, why?'

'You always look at that place when we pass it, how come?'

'It doesn't matter, I just thought I saw something new opening there once'

'A new nest of rats maybe, but that's about all' he laughs, 'No one's been in there for years'

'Yeah, that's what my bosses said' I keep looking down the stairs.

'So, you gonna tell your friend you got the game?'

'I'll do it now' I say.

I tap away, I've barely hit send when my phone lights up again, his response almost immediate.

Cool, keen to play?

Yeah, just heading home now

See you online

On the way to my house, Dan challenges me to not step on the cracks in the footpath, and when you live in a regional town, such a challenge proves difficult with so many ancient, fractured slabs. As we awkwardly march on, Dan pulls the leaves off all the trees we pass by and throws them into the wind, watching them dance behind us. Instead I watch him, I want to speak up and ask him about his dad, but right now he's truly happy, and I can't bring myself to steal that from him. Neither of my folks are home, they went to some farmer's market or something out of town.

'Is it alright if I make some food?' Dan asks.

'Yeah dude go crazy' I say, making my way to my room.

'Thanks mate' he calls back, judging by the echo, he's already inside the pantry.

I plop myself into my office chair and insert the game into my computer. It takes a while to load up, and it has to download some internet update or something, Jesus when did games get so complicated? Dan enters my room with a plate full of crackers with cheese. Half of the crackers are broken, and the pieces of cheese he's sliced from the block are of vastly varying size and shape. Actually, I'm pretty sure he pulled some of these apart with his fingers.

'Holy shit I'd hate to see you in the kitchen' I say, taking one of them and eating it.

'Fuhk hoff' he says through a mouthful.

The game finally finishes updating and the starts up.

'What took you so long?'

'Had to download something or whatever'

'Far out, you wouldn't want to be in a hurry'

I laugh and put the headphones on. Dan rolls his eyes and eats the last cracker.

'I can use it to talk to Luke' I explain, tapping the microphone piece.

'Fuckin' nerd' Dan jeers, he pats my head and gets up to get more food, 'That reminds me, we've gotta get you a haircut soon too'

'Hey what's wrong with my hair?' I ask, but he's already back in the kitchen.

The music on the game's menu is loud and epic, the type of music you imagine playing over a Viking battle or a castle siege in a movie. "MONSTER MASHER" is plastered on my computer screen in big, red, block letters. I quickly make up a username and password to log in and begin the adventure. It's confusing, when I played computer games as a kid they were so simple, but I locate the option to add friends and punch in Luke's username. The option to "Join Game" appears under him, he must be online waiting. I click join and we're together in another menu.

'Hey Luke I'm in, well I think so anyway' I laugh.

No answer. Dan comes back into the room with a toasted sandwich.

'You become a knight of the magical realm or whatever yet?'

'Eat your damn sandwich. I signed up and joined Luke but I don't think it's working. Hello? Luke?'

I wait a moment, then take the headset off and rest it on the desk.

'Hey seriously though, what's wrong with my hair?' I ask Dan.

Before he can answer, we hear the sound of a man yelling, followed by the slamming of a door and then footsteps. It's coming from the headset. Dan and I look at each other with suspicion.

'*Shit*' Luke's voice comes through softly. Rustling follows, he must be putting on his headset, '*Can you hear this Warren?*'

His voice is louder and clearer now. Dan nods at me to put the headset on.

'Hey Luke, yeah I'm here. Are you okay?'

'*Yes, what do you mean?*' he says irritably, catching me off guard, he seemed so friendly last night. If I didn't recognise the voice I'd think I'm talking to somebody different.

'Nothing I think your microphone was spazzing out, ready to get this Mother Dragon?'

Luke laughs down the line, I can visualise his huge, innocent smile even though we're on opposite sides of town.

'There's no way you can beat that yet, I can't even beat it and I basically live in this game'

'Come on let me see what's so hard about it, if anything I can distract it for you'

'Alright sure, we're gonna die though I'm telling you. You'll have the beginner equipment and abilities, oh what the hell, let's show you what it's about'

He does something on his end and loads us into his mission. Next thing I know, I'm in a clearing. My first thought is back to the meadow Dan and I found yesterday, this is far more European though. It's lightly snowing, the powder collecting on the emerald needles of the surrounding pine trees. Towering over them are giant mountains, bigger than anything I've ever seen. I spin my character around, I'm in awe.

'This game looks insane!' I gush.

I look over at Dan, laying down on my bed eating his toast, judging by his wide eyes, he's impressed too.

'I love it, makes me want to go on a big adventure' Luke says, *'Really takes you into another world huh'*

I know exactly what he means, I'm fired up and ready to go, hungry for adventure.

'Okay watch me. So, you can attack, dodge, jump and roll' he demonstrates as he lists them.

His character has flash, sturdy looking gunmetal armour that covers him head to toe, and wields a battle axe that's even taller than him. I finally take time to look at my character. He has basic looking leather armour, he must be very cold. My only weapon is a small, unintimidating looking dagger.

'Aw man I don't even get a helmet!' I say.

'Your guy sucks!' Dan laughs at me.

Luke laughs, he must have heard Dan.

'Yeah to be honest your guy does suck. You won't be able to do much damage or dodge or roll very far, but the more you level up the better you get, see?'

'Okay I get it' I slash and stab the air.

'Alright, follow me, I've tried this so many times I know exactly where the dragon is. It should say the controls on the screen in the corner if you get stuck'

Luke leads us away from our starting point like he's my barbarian tour guide. He weaves us through the labyrinth of trees, there are small creatures in the snowy forest with us but Luke says to ignore them. I practice the manoeuvres Luke showed me, my poor, rookie character diving and rolling around on the forest floor like a maniac. I don't say anything for fear that Dan will call me a nerd, but this game is blowing my mind. It makes me want to pack up and run far, far from Southway, take charge of my life and have an adventure. We emerge from the trees at the base of the mountains that at first seemed so far away.

'That didn't take us long' I say.

'Not when you've found and memorised the fastest way' he says.

His burly character starts climbing the mountain, and I make my frail avatar follow, once I work out how to climb, that is. We ascend high above the clouds, I climb so slow and have to rest often, making Luke wait for me. He insists that as I level up it will be easier, and that his guy can climb the whole mountain without stopping now. We reach the icy summit, a broad plateau, with several large rocks strewn around towards the edges, placed there to hide behind or climb on I assume. The Mother Dragon sits in its nest watching us. As big as real-life truck compared to us, with cyan scales that blend almost perfectly it into the ice and snow. Fog expels from its massive nostrils with each of its heavy breaths, leathery eyelids sliding closed and then open over it purple eyes as it blinks.

'It's about to attack, try not to die I guess'

As if on cue, the beast stands up and roars, spreading its wings and swinging its long, spear-like tail. I flinch and jump in my office chair at the noise. Dan laughs, then gets up to sit closer to the screen to spectate.

Luke charges at the dragon, swings his axe at its snout. It connects, blood sprays out of the wound.

'He's got some moves' Dan says, getting absorbed into the game with us.

I position myself safely behind a rock, and watch the master at work. The dragon tries to head-butt Luke, but he rolls backwards dodging it. They pace around one another, exchanging blows and bites for a while, I notice the Mother Dragon has a health bar at the top of the screen, it's almost down to around three quarters. The dragon roars again and flaps its wings, whipping up a storm of ice and stone at Luke, blowing him back into a boulder. It follows up by charging straight at him. He leaps to the side, the dragon slams into the rock before it can adjust its charge. Luke has set himself right beside it's throat.

'Yes!'

'Get 'em Lukey!' Dan cheers.

He readies a powerful looking attack as Dan and I shout, a mighty downward of the axe onto the nape of the monster's neck. Before it can land, the dragon's tail whips around at Luke, interrupting his attack. It wraps its thin tail around his torso and hurls him through the sky, his body entering the clouds without returning.

'*No! So close*' Luke laments.

Dan and I groan. But then the dragon starts to crawl in my direction. Luke laughs.

'*Good luck my friend, I'm watching you now*'

It doesn't take long to find my hiding place. I run away frantically, trying to remember the controls. The dragon chases, closing fast, just as it's about to snap me in its maw, I dodge away with fractions of a second to spare.

'*Wow*' Luke says, impressed.

The Mother Dragon pecks at me with its snout but I dodge again. And again, and again, I tussle with the beast for longer than Luke managed to survive. Dan's started chanting my name, Luke is anxiously trying to give me a million pieces of advice at once. I drown them out and survey the plateau as I evade, there's nothing but the rocks to work with. I can see why even Luke struggles with this mission, it's so barren here compared to what else I've seen of this world. I decide to build off of Luke's strategy, I line myself against a rock, and wait until the last moment as the dragon rams forward with its skull to crush my weak character against the stone. But instead of dodging to the side, I roll right underneath the dragon's belly and hind legs. I'm going to cut off its tail.

'Go go go!' my friends scream, even Dan the realist is tangled up in the hype.

I use the strongest attack I have access to on the base of the tail, a pathetic slice with this flimsy dagger that leaves a pathetic scratch on the dragon's hide. I look at its health bar for answers, but it hasn't changed at all. The dragon bucks me with its powerful back leg, killing me instantly.

"MISSION FAILED" the game announces.

'No!' all three of us moan at once.

I slap my knee in frustration, Dan dramatically collapses on the bed.

'Close though! I thought that was a good idea!' I say, once the adrenaline fades.

'It wasn't really close, but it was a good idea' Luke tells me, *'You have really good reflexes Warren, it took me ages to dodge like that. One hit was always going to kill you, I can't believe you survived for so long'*

'It's just pressing the buttons' I tell him.

Dan stands up, checking his phone.

'Alright mate it's getting late I'm going to go around to Ava's place' he presents a fist to me.

'Okay Dan no worries' I bump his fist as he's about to leave.

'But!' he spins on his heels and suddenly points at me, 'Fishing. Tomorrow. Do not forget'

'I'll be waiting'

'Sweet I'll pick you up, I've got plenty of gear' he brings his face in close to talk into the microphone, 'I'm out of here, nice to meet you Lukey'

'Nice to meet you too… Uh, Dan' Luke laughs, *'Can I call you Dan'*

'Yes Lukey, you can call me Dan. Have fun you guys' he waves on his way out.

I hear his vehicle start up and roll away down the street.

'He likes you I think'

'You think?' Luke sounds shocked.

'He does, I hope you can meet him one day'

'Maybe. One day maybe yeah' he mutters.

'You keen to keep playing?'

'Sure, I'm free all day, let's fight something easier though, I'll help you level up a bit first'

'Thank God' I say.

'I appreciate you getting this game to play it with me. And for being kind to me when you didn't even know me. You're a good friend, thank you'

'Don't even mention it' I laugh, 'You just watch though, one day I'm going to be the best monster slayer you've ever seen'

VIII
Red and Blue

That's how my Winter Holidays go. During the day, I hang out with
Dan, if it's raining we stay in at my house lazing around, enjoying each
other's company. He shows me all the Maximillian Murphy
documentaries, I have to admit the guy is pretty cool, he's in his fifties,
which I was surprised by. I try smoking weed for the first time with Dan,
it's pretty cool, it made me cough a lot but everything was so funny. Dan
doesn't do it often, but he says it calms him down and cheers him up, I
can't fault him for that. He tells me how Elliot smokes it a lot, and we
both laugh when he tells me how Elliot pays over three times what is the
normal price. Sometimes when the rain holds itself back, we spend the
days in Southway. Dan eventually does convince me to get that haircut,
coming to my rescue and "saving me from the mop", as he put it. I was
self-conscious about it at first, but Dan assured me it was cool, and sure
enough, I grow to love it. He introduces me properly to Ava, she says she
can't believe how different I am outside of school, whatever that means.
She said she wants to introduce me to one of her friends, I'm not too sure
about that. Initially I didn't want to be around the both of them for fear
of intruding, but they never let me feel that way. They're so in love, I'm
very happy for the both of them.

Whenever we get an especially benevolent bout of weather, we spend
our time out at his farm. He picks archery back up, although it's like he
never put it down, the finesse and the focus he possesses with the bow
are beguiling. We spend time with Isabelle, we let her tag along with what
we're doing, when it isn't too dangerous of course. He drives like a lunatic
on the dirt roads, I'm sure we almost crash every other day because of
Dan trying to skid for longer and longer, flick up more and more gravel.
We explore the area around his family property, steering clear of that
meadow of course, we vow never to go East again. There's one day where
we find a deep stream and both agree to jump in, despite the south west
Winter's bite. I slice my leg on a sharp, hidden stick and we both have a
cold for a week for our troubles. Life is good.

When the night comes, Dan and I go our separate ways. He spends time
with Ava and I spend time with Luke. I get to see more of his culinary
talent each night at work, as Wanda assigns him more and more

responsibilities for more complex dishes once she realises the goldmine they hit by finding him. He often sweats profusely in the kitchen, but no matter how hot it gets, he refuses to change into something with short sleeves, some sort of superstition, or perhaps it just keeps spitting oil from burning his arms.

Some nights, when it's especially busy, the ladies get the both of us to wait the tables, I think talking to the customers helps Luke let his guard down a bit. We have a lot of time to talk, just the two of us, so naturally we learn a lot about each other. His mother moved to Melbourne from Japan, she got a job at a restaurant that his father owned. They fell in love, got married, had him, and then gave up the restaurant to move over west, tired of the city. He tells me about how he wants to go to Japan one day and see where his mother grew up, and meet her side of his family, once he's become a chef of course. He speaks a little bit of Japanese, if Wanda and Rhonda are outside smoking and we have nothing else to do he teaches me some words. Although I'm not very good at it, he always at least gets a laugh and tells me to stick to science. Eventually, he does acquire the taste for coffee, in fact I think he's a bit addicted to it. I tell him all about Elliot and Dan and the apple, and how the latter must feel torn between us.

After work is done, we play Monster Masher together. Luke has an aversion to doing anything in real life apart from work, it's a shame since I'd love for him and Dan to meet, but I don't want to pressure him into anything. I sink myself into the game in my spare time, seeing new areas of its gorgeous world, rising through the ranks, coming up with strategies that he says he never thought could work. Luke is even a little bit envious when I catch up to his level, but ultimately, he's grateful for the team mate. As the weeks go on it reaches the point where even the strongest battles in the game are a joke to us, and we mostly just play the game to talk to each other. Sometimes if we have ten minutes to kill before work we'll quickly slay a Mother Dragon.

Until the day before school returns. It's a Sunday evening and we don't have work. Wanda and Rhonda sometimes do this, if they can handle things, to avoid having to pay us Sunday wages. I'm buried into the office chair at my computer, headset on, Luke on the other end of the line, we've just slain a Griffon.

'That one was pretty quick' he says through his microphone.

'Might be a personal best even' I laugh.

My phone buzzes on the desk beside my keyboard. It's a text from Dan.

lets do something tonight before school starts im coming to get you

This could mean anything, should I be concerned?

'Hey Luke I've gotta bail, Dan's coming to get me he wants to do something, to commemorate the end of the holidays I guess'

Oh, hey that's alright, I hope you have fun'

'Knowing him, it will be' I laugh.

'Hey Warren?'

'What's up?'

Tomorrow, at school' he says quietly, he clears his throat, *'Do you want to meet up at lunch?'*

'Of course, it's about time you met…'

I trail off, it only just now dawning on me that Elliot will be back.

'You're worried about Dan and Elliot, aren't you?' he asks caringly.

'Yeah. I dunno, I hadn't even thought about Elliot for weeks now, but now that he's back, Dan will probably want to see him. I just kind of assumed the two of us would stay friends, but now, I don't know what's going to happen'

'Well' Luke says, *'It sounds like you should talk to him about it when you see him'*

I hear Dan screech to a halt out the front.

'He's here now, thank you O Wise One'

'See you later' Luke laughs.

I turn my game off and place my headset down on the desk, I grab my jacket and head out.

'I'm going out with Dan, I'll be home later' I call to mum and dad who are watching the news.

'Just don't be late, don't forget you have school tomorrow' Dad says.

'I won't, love you' I say, hanging my head.

I hop into the passenger seat.

'Alright, what's our mission boss? I swear if we're going looking for missing people again...'

'Hey, hey! That was your idea if I recall correctly' he wags a finger at me, 'Besides, it's been weeks since then, no one else has disappeared but they haven't found the old guy or the woman, I think the case might be cold'

'Do you think we should tell the police about that blood?' I ask.

He shakes his head and starts the car.

'I can't send anyone out there after what we heard Warren' he says solemnly.

I suppose I can't say I disagree.

'Come on' he says, reversing out of my driveway.

'What are we doing?'

'Driving. Fast'

He takes the highway leading north out of town. It's poorly lit out this way, the streetlights end at the town border, a large archway over the road, so it's up to the moon's weak beams to light our way. Hey, at least it isn't raining. We accelerate faster and faster still, the highway is straight, so I'm not worried. All of a sudden Dan pulls the hand brake. The back wheels snake to their own rhythm, Dan laughs as he struggles to keep us under control. Eventually, we straighten up and I can stop bracing and clinging onto the dashboard for dear life.

'Holy shit dude, at least tell me first' I find myself genuinely annoyed and he notices it.

'Sorry' he raps his fingers on the steering wheel, 'Ugh it's just school goes back tomorrow and I'm so bummed. I know I said I didn't need any excitement but after hanging out with you all break, going back to classes is going to be so lame'

'Yeah I feel you dude'

'Exam results tomorrow though, excited?' he sings.

I shrug. We speed up, even more this time. I wonder who will get a higher biology grade out of Elliot and I. I'm not sure why I care, but I really hope it's me.

'I haven't been thinking about it, I'm sure they'll be fine'

'What's on your mind?' he asks.

Red and blue flickers in the mirror catch my eye, and immediately afterwards the police siren's wail drills out into the night. They alternate behind us, red and then blue, red again and then blue again. I track them so carefully to see if there is a brief instant where neither colour flashes, but there isn't. It seems that one colour waits until its partner is there before it takes its short rest.

'Shit' Dan says, closing his eyes in frustration for a second before pulling over onto the gravel.

The police car follows suit, and an officer starts to make his way over to the driver's window. Dan takes a deep breath. Once he gets closer, I have a clearer view of him in the mirror, he has an oily head of slicked back hair, and stubble that's shaven in such a way that it forms a point to make his jaw look squarer. He looks kind of like a smug gnome, but he's very muscular and intimidating in the police uniform. My heart bashes against my ribs, I've never had a run in with the police before.

'It's okay Warren' Dan says, just in time before the cop knocks on his window, signalling him to wind it down.

'How are you tonight boys?' he taunts, his mouth twisting into a grin.

They always tell you to trust the police, but I already don't like this guy. He's unable to hide his delight with having found somebody speeding.

'Not bad officer, how are you?' Dan says dryly.

'Do you know why I've pulled you over this evening?'

'Was I going a little bit quick back there?' Dan asks, sarcastically.

His voice never quivering, even now. Dan was never one to back down, and this greasy prick can't make him start.

'You were going very quick back there' the officer smiles.

'How quick?' Dan asks, rising to the challenge. I want to tell him to cool down.

'Well, the speed limit is one hundred and ten here, and I clocked you going one hundred and thirty-eight. Actually, I'll round it up to an even one forty, since you're so proud of it'

'What the fuck? You can't-' Dan protests.

And for the first time ever, I hear the confidence leave his voice.

'Which, means...' the cop, interrupts, 'You were found exceeding the speed limit by over twenty-nine kilometres per hour. Which will be six demerit points and an eight hundred dollar fine tonight'

'You can't' is all Dan can say.

'License please' the cop slides a demanding hand inside the car in front of Dan's face.

'Please, don't' Dan looks up at him with tears in his eyes.

'Ah you know what? Don't worry about it' he takes his hand back and waves it away.

For a moment Dan sighs, I see the relief beginning to fill his body. But then the cop opens his mouth again.

'I've got your number plate already that's all I need really' he starts scribbling on a pad.

He passes Dan the slip and the tears start falling when he sees that it's official.

'Twenty-eight days. Enjoy the rest of your night lads' he laughs as he turns back to his car.

He digs his fingers into the paper and his teeth grind together.

'Don't you have missing people to be looking for?' Dan spits at him.

He turns back around. I put a hand on Dan's shoulder, a silent request to ease up and hold his tongue here.

'I know your family mate. You're nothing. That's why your mum hates you, and that's why your dad ran as far away from you as he could get'

'Shut the fuck up' Dan lashes out.

He grabs the door handle, but thinking quickly, I hold him back.

'You know what, I hope you can't pay up you little shit, because I'd really like to see you again'

'Don't worry we'll pay it' I say staring the cop down.

He didn't bother to tell us his name but his badge says "Sergeant Dillon".

'I don't know who *you* are, but if you keep hanging around with this delinquent I'm sure we'll get to know each other soon. Get out of my sight' he peers at me.

I can tell he's making an effort to memorise my face, if that's the case, he can go for it, I refuse to look away. He walks away for good this time, gets back in his car and drives back South, leaving us to sit in silence long after he's gone and Dan to stare at the fine in the dim interior light of this timeworn ute of his. He grips it tight in disbelief, his strong fingers scrunching the paper.

'What a fucking joke' I finally say, 'He can't just bump up the speed like that, what was he even doing out here on a Sunday night anyway?'

Dan punches the side of the door in his wrath, catching me off guard, it sounds like it hurt. Before he leans over the steering wheel and sobs into his crossed arms. My heart aches to see my friend like this.

'I'm sorry Dan, I should have been keeping an eye out'

'No' he states, wiping his face, 'No, this was my own fault, my idea'

A car heading our way flies into view, it's blinding high-beams making us both shield our eyes. It flies past, much faster than we were ever going.

'I'm so fucked'

'What do you mean?'

'I'm fucking gone, Mum is going to throw me out' his voice breaks.

'Hey, hey!' I calm him, 'She doesn't have to know, and the car's in your name now'

'Where the fuck am I gonna pull eight hundred dollars from?' he blubbers, 'I'll... I'll have to beg Elliot, I-'

Fuck no you won't.

'I'll give you the money' I tell him.

He blinks at me.

'Take the money from me, I've got eight hundred'

101

'No' he starts.

'I don't wait tables every night for fun' I laugh, 'I get paid to do it believe it or not, let me help you with this'

'No Warren, that's your money, I'm not taking it"

'You should know me, what do I need money for? I don't buy expensive clothes, I don't travel the world. Not like your other friend' I laugh, 'They pay me in cash anyway so it's just sitting around. I can always make more, I get paid this week anyway'

His golden eyes seem to round off, the rest of his features look softer too. He throws his arms around me.

'Thank you' he says, relenting.

'It's all good man, get that shit paid tomorrow' I pat his back.

He releases me from his embrace, leans back over and starts the car once more, taking us back to town.

'I'll pay you back for this Warren, I mean it'

'Don't even worry about that, I'm not going to hunt you down and break your kneecaps'

'You couldn't even if you tried' he laughs, his tears already dried up.

'You're my brother Warren'

'You're my brother too Dan'

We drive all the way back, sensibly this time, not saying a word the entire rest of the way, we don't need to. Until we reach my house.

'You want to stay here tonight?' I offer.

'No thanks, I've got to go and do something'

'Go home soon man, don't let Officer Friendly see you again'

'It won't take long'

'Alright well, I'll see you at school tomorrow hey? To give you that cash?'

'Bloody oath you'll see me' Dan smiles

In the end, I didn't need to ask him what will happen tomorrow. This evening we've solidified that the two of us were there for each other, and nothing more needed to be said about it.

IX
Contact

The Southway High courtyard is jam-packed with chattering students, itching to discuss their holidays and exam results during lunchtime. All the ones I've got back so far have been quite good, well above average scores for Maths, English and Chemistry, perfect results for getting a job to pay bills until I die. This semester I have Biology immediately after lunch on Monday, so I wait nervously under my tree, the same one I was under when Elliot threw that fateful apple at my skull.

Elliot has made his grand entrance already this morning, sporting new clothes and a dark tan from the Spanish sun. For someone who spent six weeks in paradise he's terribly petulant, maybe he's disappointed that no one kissed his feet on his way in. He and Dan have reunited, they sit and gossip with their troupe right now. The sun heavy on Elliot's back, his cronies talking over one another, all desperate to be the next one allowed to ask him a question about Spain. A distracted Dan doesn't sit at Elliot's side, he's instead detached from their discussion, engrossed in his phone and not Elliot's epic tales from around the globe. I wonder what he's doing.

'Warren?' says a voice from behind me.

Luke appears, sporting a brand-new, uncreased Southway school uniform, the first time I've seen him in anything except our work clothes. The school uniform is "recommended" but not "compulsory" so barely anyone wears it, which drives the patriotic McGovern up the walls. He hates seeing people out of uniform but being the only school in town, there's no real reason to enforce the label on us kids.

'Hey' I shake his hand and he sits down beside me, 'How's your first day so far?'

'It's…okay' he sighs and sits down beside me.

'Hey it may not be like the citadel you went to back in Melbourne, but at least this isn't big enough to get lost in'

'Yeah that's a bonus' he laughs.

'You're not nervous?' I ask.

'A bit yeah, I had cooking all this morning, I've made a good impression, I think'

'You're a better cook than anyone here, I bet'

Luke just grunts reluctantly in agreement. I point over at Elliot's group.

'You see that guy? Sitting on the bench' I ask. Luke leans in close to me to see exactly where I'm pointing.

'The one who looks like he thinks he's the greatest thing to happen to the Earth? Yeah, couldn't miss him'

'Well that's Elliot' I explain.

'Right' he nods, 'Looks exactly like I imagined'

'I was sitting right here when he threw the apple at me that day.

'Jesus, I wouldn't want to get on his bad side'

'He's nothing but bad sides' I laugh.

'So, which one is Dan anyway?' Luke asks.

'Oh, right I forgot you haven't seen each other, Dan is-'

'Holy shit!' Dan exclaims from across the courtyard.

He throws his hands in the air in triumph and jumps to his feet, a proud smile wrapping around his face.

'That one' I finish.

Elliot and his disciples stare Dan down, he must have interrupted, a grave sin as I would know. Elliot rolls his eyes at him.

'What is it?' he says, utterly unimpressed.

I can tell that he isn't asking why Dan is so excited, he's asking why he dared cut him off. Dan doesn't even acknowledge him though, he starts making his way over towards us, I can almost hear Elliot's teeth grinding together.

'Guess what!' Dan says, it looks like he's about to explode if he doesn't tell me.

'No idea' I say.

'I'll see you at work tonight'

'You got a job? At Wanda and Rhonda's? When?'

'I sure did' he says, radiating with pride, 'Last night, after I dropped you off I went in to see them. They were just smoking out the back, but once I told them I had my own vehicle they seemed like they'd really consider it, you know? And I just got the text then'

He holds his phone up for us to read.

Daniel we have decided to take you on as a delivery driver. you start tonight at six. we look forward to seeing you cheers Rhonda

Rhonda has horrendous grammar, even by text standards, but now isn't the time, I'm delighted for my friend.

'Dude that's awesome, we're gonna be working together!'

'I told you, I'd pay you back' he nods.

Luke stands up, infected with our second-hand jubilation.

'Is this Lukey?' he asks, pointing at him.

'It sure is' I say.

The two finally face to face, Dan towers over Luke by almost a full foot.

'Hello' Luke waves.

'We're all gonna be working together!' Dan shouts.

He wraps his arms around Luke's waist and lifts him up. He places Luke back down and grabs one of us under each of his arms. Everyone else in the school must be looking at us like we're mad, but I couldn't care less, I hope Luke wasn't worried about being embarrassed because I think Dan's just burnt that bridge for him. I check, and he's smiling too. The bell rings out and Dan grounds himself. I get the money for the fine out of my backpack and palm it to Dan, he insists we angle it so our bodies hide the money from Elliot's sight. Dan thanks me and hugs me again. Luke stares at the wad of notes, stunned.

'Long story, we'll tell you tonight, I've gotta, you know, get back to Ava, but I want to hear all about your grades tonight Warren. Nice to meet you Luke' he says, introducing himself properly, with a handshake this time.

'Still keen for this afternoon?' I ask.

'This afternoon? Shit! I was meant to spend tonight with Ava' the gears hard at work in his mind, 'Okay, I'll have to spend this afternoon with her, Warren I'm sorry'

'Hey don't be stupid, I understand, I can walk'

'But! I'll see both of you at six. I can't wait'

He points at us and then turns back to his other group, but Elliot is already behind him, and for whatever reason, he doesn't seem livid anymore, he's serene.

'I leave you alone for a few weeks and you start getting chummy with the losers huh? Like a disease you've come into contact with. I thought you understood what we talked about this morning, I guess not' Elliot says, revolted.

'Jesus what the hell was that outburst?' Ava laughs.

'Starting a job tonight, at six. But how about we hang out after school instead?' he asks.

Ava shakes her head in embarrassment.

'Sure, whatever' she says.

'Cool, I'll see you then' he kisses her, and she unenthusiastically reciprocates.

We all head towards classroom number nine in a loose group until Dan departs from them and Luke parts ways with me.

'See you!' they both call out from down the corridor.

Ava and Elliot push past me rudely as we approach the classroom.

'You feel good about yourself now Fuck Eyes? You guys have fun together over the holidays?' he sneers.

'Actually, we did' I say, surprising him and Ava.

That day, I had never meant to speak out of turn to him, my brain just had the word and said it out loud, but this time I'm deliberately spiteful, I want a reaction, I want to see him get angry. I don't think he talks to people who aren't his yes-men very often, he doesn't like it at all.

'Who do you think you are?' he hisses, 'What gives you the right?'

We grab each other's collars at the same time. Our first clash before the exam was quick and I was clumsy, but this time we match, I don't want to beg for us all to get along this time.

'Your friend Danny's not here to interfere this time' he smiles sadistically, with a fist loaded and aimed at my face.

'Okay, okay, enough!' Harper calls, pushing past Ava and placing a calmative hand on each of our fists, 'The two of you need to keep your rivalry strictly *academic*, do I make myself clear?'

We both nod, not taking our eyes off each other. I can tell Harper isn't used to having to deal with things like this.

'Be better than this' she says, though I'm not sure who to.

We step inside together.

'I'm warning you, I never lose Warren' Elliot says calmly.

This is the first instance he's ever used my name, fitting, the time has come for these results. Harper slides the door behind us closed and turns to the class enthusiastically, she seems to have tanned up a bit over the holidays too, I wonder what adventure she went on over the break. I survey the room for new trinkets she might have picked up. As I take my usual seat behind Elliot I look at the serpent in its jar, unmoved, the layer of dust coating it has grown even thicker. Nothing has changed here.

'Before anything else' Harper begins, 'I'd like to welcome you all back, I hope you had a fantastic break, and are revitalised and rejuvenated, ready for semester two' she waves her hands as though she's warding off an evil aura.

She picks up a stack of papers and drops them back on the desk loudly, causing everyone to become alert. I even see Elliot ahead of me flinch harder than anyone else.

'I'm sure this is what you've all been waiting on' Harper says, patting the pile of exam papers gently, 'For the most part, I'm very impressed'

She seems more serious than usual. She looks around at all of us, her eyes sifting through her eight pupils, but I swear her eyes dwell on me for a second longer. My heart beats faster.

'The class average was about seventy one percent, however that was the average with one person's results removed. Including that score would have skewed the results too far and made the average inaccurate'

Was it me? I can tell that it was me. How was my score so low? Did I forget to fill in my name or something so I just got a zero? No, I triple checked all that stuff, I always do. I feel like I'm about to throw up.

'In any case, here are your exams back' Harper leaps up from her desk and begins handing the papers out.

She works her way down the room towards me at the back. As everybody gets their result they gasp and squeal with glee.

'Ninety-three huh?' Elliot scoffs loudly so everyone can hear, dropping his paper on his desk.

'Yes, Mr Young your result was exceptional. You should be very proud of yourself, you must have studied very hard' Harper says.

'Eh, about the same as my other classes' he says matter-of-factly.

I'm crushed. It isn't fair. I wanted to beat him so bad, but I wasn't good enough. Why is it that he gets to go to Europe and then comes back to crush me with the grades, and all I do is study, work in this shit town that I'll never leave? I'm about to choke back tears. I want to let out some rage. I want to slash like I slashed my way through to that meadow. I want to slay every Mother Dragon out there. I want to grab Elliot and ask him why it's his God-given right to be spoon-fed everything he could ever want. I subdue my anger, clench my jaw and close my eyes, waiting for Harper to drop my exam down on the desk. I wait and wait but it doesn't come. I look up at her standing over me, she has my exam in her hand, it's the last one.

'I need to see you after class Warren'

And my world collapses.

I zone out for the entire hour. I think I'm in some sort of shock. Harper leaves me be, she doesn't call on me for any questions, she must know how devastated I am. A zero, hell even a ten or a twenty, on a year twelve exam would destroy any chance of being accepted into a university. My hopes of escape, my chance at being worth anything, and getting out of this place. The one thing I thought I could do, robbed from me. Dan, Luke, all the fun I had, all the joy I felt over the last few weeks evaporates away, burnt to a crisp by my failure. The hour passes, and everyone else leaves the room to head back to their homes. Harper stands by the door, closes it once everyone is well out of earshot, and calls me to the front. I stand in front of her desk, she looks down at me as though I'm on trial.

'How hard did you study for this Warren?' she asks.

'Not enough, apparently' I laugh weakly.

If I don't laugh, I'll cry.

'You did put in quite a lot of effort last semester, didn't you? Although I seem to catch you daydreaming quite often, you spend quite some time studying and getting ahead of the syllabus in your own time, correct?'

My eyes widen in my skull. Is she going to offer to bump up the grade to pass me? She seems so stern right now though, either way, I won't beg.

'I did work hard' I say, 'But listen Ms Harper, I don't want you to round my grade up or anything, I'll take what I earned'

She eyes me up for what feels like an eternity, and then Gwendolyn Harper smiles.

'Round your grade *up*?' she asks.

She's been clutching my paper to her chest this whole time, finally she drops it in front of me. My grade sits etched onto the front page of the exam booklet, three digits in bright crimson ink, right next to my name. One hundred percent. My mouth falls open.

'I... I don't understand' I stammer.

'Well yeah neither did we' Harper leans back, in her chair 'I looked over it again and again. I couldn't believe it, but there was nothing to fault you on, nowhere I could take a mark away. I saw Principal McGovern about it and he was certain you'd cheated. We even watched the security camera footage from the hall to make sure you didn't have notes or your phone or anything like that. I tried to tell him how hard you work, I even personally vouched for you and said you'd never cheat'

'I...' I'm unable to speak.

'So, Principal McGovern asked me to make you sweat over it for a bit, he said that if we did that you'd break and admit that you cheated' she shrugs, 'Looks like he was wrong'

'When you said you removed one grade from the average... I thought I'd failed'

'Pleasantly surprised?' she cocks an eyebrow.

'I almost had a heart attack!' I say.

'I'm sorry Warren, the principal made me do it. I didn't think I could, wow I'd make an awful interrogator'

'What happens now?' I ask.

'Well, now you can go home and take a breath, I suppose'

We smile at each other.

'You earned this Warren. Congratulations'

Everyone else is long gone when I leave the classroom, with no one to watch out for, I read over my exam paper while I walk. I do make eye contact with McGovern through his office window as I walk out of the school grounds, he nods sternly at me. The sun sheens down gently on Southway today, Winter in its final days and the springtime ready to settle in for the coming months. I can still notice the fresh, earthy smell of rain, I take a deep breath, cherishing it before the smell of the grass and pollen takes its place. Main street is eerily peaceful, it's only three in the afternoon but there's hardly anyone walking around. A month or two ago I could list everything that happens here on a Monday afternoon, but I've long since abandoned keeping track of that sort of thing. My life is slowly getting way too interesting to worry about that.

I keep my head buried in my exam for the most part, only looking up when I pass the shoe shop to see if Mr Abernathy is back at work. He isn't. There's been no more information about the missing people announced, Mum has been studying the paper and listening to The Chatter every day but I don't have much hope for them. Something collides with me suddenly, knocking me back. The weight of my backpack pulls me to the ground, hurting my shoulder. The exam flies up into the air, the pages separating from each other and raining down around me. I've walked into somebody, they've fallen down too. I sit up and rub my shoulder.

'I'm sorry, I wasn't watching where I was going, are you okay?' I ask.

The person sits up. Long silver hair falls over his face, he quickly runs his fingers through it and tucks the stray curls behind his ears. It's the old man with the lab coat.

'Disrespectful worm!' he scolds, placing his glasses back on his nose.

'I'm sorry Sir, are-'

'Is this yours?' he cuts me off.

His glasses now in place, he's staring at one of the exam pages that's landed on the ground between us. It's the cover page, with my name and grade facing up.

'Yeah, yes that's mine' I say.

He doesn't look at me at all, he starts collecting the pages, reading through my answers. I feel uneasy, I want to ask him to stop. But then I realise, this scientist might be impressed with my exam. Maybe he could recommend me for a job once I graduate. I'm practically bouncing up and down at the thought.

'One hundred' he says, 'The estimated number of years before all life will be unsustainable'

What the fuck?

'I'm sorry?' I say out loud.

'You must study quite hard, or cheat quite well' he says accusatively.

'My teacher thought the same thing' I laugh nervously, 'But no, I didn't cheat'

'This is very impressive, you enjoy the life sciences?' he asks.

He has a very slight accent but I'm not well-travelled enough to say where from. It's European, I think.

'I do, Sir'

'Why?' he asks, immediately.

I'm stumped. Most people will ask why you study, because they expect you to say what career you want, but barely anyone asks if you *enjoy* what you study, and even less people than that ask *why*. This man is obviously clever, I can tell, I want to show respect and try to present myself as professionally as possible.

'It's the way of the future, I guess' I announce.

'You really believe that, boy?' he laughs to himself.

He finally looks away from the paper and we make eye contact for the first time.

'Oh, heterochromia iridium' he says, intrigued 'Even for the condition, that's a rare combination of colours'

I feel uneasy around this man, he's seemed very eccentric but straightforward, but when he gets off topic like this, it's like talking to two people.

'Sorry, yes. So, you think that's where the careers are? You going to work in a big lab and make your boss a lot of money?' he sounds flustered now.

'To be honest Sir, I haven't thought that far ahead, I just want to be able to leave this place and do something meaningful for the world'

His blue eyes widen, revealing exactly how bloodshot they are, it looks like he hasn't slept in a week. He gets to his feet with some exertion, I can't blame him considering how old he looks, the sun beats down on his back, when he turns his head slightly to one side, some light refracting through his glasses, causing me to squint away from the brightness. He chuckles.

'It's funny, I came here because I didn't want to find anyone, but here you are, why am I tested like this?' he talks to himself.

I stand up too, he's much taller than me, even taller than Dan, but this man is skeletally thin, the sleeves of his lab coat are rolled up past his bony elbows, but his reedy arms aren't able to keep them from rolling back down.

'Locke Dawson' he announces, 'I do have several titles but they don't matter'

'Warren Avery'

I wonder what his titles are? He's definitely a professor, or maybe a doctor?

'It's nice to meet you. I saw you, it was a while ago now, you were taking boxes down some stairs' I say, hoping he'll reveal more.

'Ah yes that was some weeks ago now wasn't it, I was just setting up then'

'Setting up what?' I ask.

He looks around, making sure nobody is within earshot.

'My new lab of sorts' he whispers.

My fingers twitch at my side. A lab? There's no way Southway, Western Australia, dirty back pocket of the Earth, is getting a laboratory.

'Your *new* lab?' I ask. Why does he need a new lab? And why here of all places?

'Yes, I was forced to move on I'm afraid' he says with a heavy exhale.

'Did you lose funding or something?' I ask.

This might be prying too far, too soon. He clears his throat.

'I'm more of a freelance scientist, I suppose'

'What brings you here? I ask.

He crosses his arms and leans on the wall of the building we're in front of. I notice his fingernails have been bitten so far down they've been bleeding, he quickly conceals them.

'Do you think the universe pulls some strings sometimes? Decides the things we must do for us?'

I think of playing Monster Masher with Lucas so he'd have his first friend in a strange new town. I think of giving Dan the money so his mother wouldn't find out about the fine. That wasn't the universe or destiny. That was me. That was me trying to do something with purpose.

'Not really, to be honest. I think our time is ours to do with what we think is right' I tell Locke Dawson.

He unfolds his arms and then nods approvingly.

'Do you have a lot of spare time? To sit around and think about things like that'

'I study... As you can probably imagine. But I work too, at the pizza place, with my two friends. I like spending time with them too'

'Then I don't suppose you have time to work for me as well?'

'Work, for you?!'

'To be honest Mr Avery, I don't talk to many people, and I've only entertained this conversation because of your grade. Good God, I was never open to taking on an assistant but-'

'I'll do it' I interrupt without thinking.

He presses his hands together and holds them up to his mouth to think.

'The project I'm working on...' he begins, 'Is concerned with the preservation of planet Earth and its sustainability. You'd have to be ready for that, and not get overwhelmed easily'

'I have what it takes' I state.

He breathes very heavily though his nose.

> 'I'm not sure that you do, I don't know if anyone does, but I need another set of hands. I'd need some time to get things ready for you. Yes okay, okay, this time next week, where you saw those boxes' he mutters.

> 'Thank you! I know the place' I go to shake his hand.

But he won't take it, he just looks at it and wrinkles his nose, he turns almost feral with no notice.

> 'This work is serious, and you will take it seriously. It's for the very future of the planet you see. I came to this place as to not be… interrupted. The risk that I'm taking on you is enormous, but I need the extra hands' he flexes his own, then buries them in his lab coat pockets.

His fingers crack when he stretches them out, telling of how the years have taxed him and left him feeble.

> 'Tifteen hundred' hc sighs.

> 'I'm sorry?'

What is he on about?

> 'Fifteen hundred' he repeats, 'That's roughly how many acres of the Amazon rainforest were just destroyed'

> 'Today?' I ask.

> 'No, since we've been speaking' he sighs again.

Surely that's not correct? That's more land than I've seen in my whole life.

> 'That's… a lot'

'It is, but it's nothing compared to how many species go extinct every single day' he sighs, 'This planet needs saving Warren, are you the one to help me do it?'

My eyes flash.

'I will Sir' I nod up at him.

'Wonderful, I'll be seeing you this time next week Warren' he says before walking away.

He's slowly hobbling down his stairs, when I call out to him.

'Excuse me Locke?'

'Yes?'

'How many species go extinct every day?' I ask.

'Estimates vary' he calls back up, 'Extinctions are natural though, we just need to carefully direct them. I'll see you in one week'

By the time I hear the door at the bottom click closed, I'm smiling from ear to ear. Work with both Luke and Dan starting tonight, my two real friends, I got under Elliot's skin, I got the highest grade possible on the exam for my favourite class, and by some sort of miracle, I made contact with a great scientist and he wants to take me on as an assistant, and on nothing less than a project to save the planet. I skip through town, unable to contain my excitement, this is fulfilment, I found it. Although, I can't help but think about how strange he is though, I'm desperate to know more about his plans. It's like he was in two minds the entire time, both calculated and hot-blooded, I already know I'm going to remember Locke Dawson for the rest of my life.

X
Three

I arrive at Wanda and Rhonda's Pizza ten minutes early for work, but even then, Dan and his car have beaten me here. I've decided I'm not going to tell Dan and Luke about Locke Dawson until after next week and I actually start working for him. He stands at the door, impatiently tapping his foot, like he's wished the door open and it hasn't come true. I'm not used to seeing him so eager, Christ, I think he's even combed his hair. I decide not to stir him up about it, I'm proud.

'I think they're closed' I say, pointing at the *CLOSED* sign.

'Do the jokes come naturally or do you have to practice?' he retorts.

We both laugh.

'How are you feeling?' I ask.

'Keen to get you that money back' he says.

'There's no rush, you paid the fine then?'

'Sure did, and didn't even have to see Sergeant Dickhead there either, it's-'

Dan is cut off by a car screeching to a halt right on front of us, I didn't hear it coming, unusual for something like that to sneak past me. The sleek and smart white sedan's front bumper comes so close to Dan's set of wheels I can almost see the rust starting to spread onto it.

'Oi! Are you high?' Dan calls to the driver, its tinted windows so dark we can't even see them.

The passenger door opens and Luke is thrown out onto the footpath. I catch a glimpse of a hulking, muscular man with long, tied-back hair in the driver's seat, one hand on the wheel, the other on the gear stick, he's chewing on gum like a pig eating its slop. He's even more beefy than the Sergeant, although I get the impression that this man's physique is for show, while the Sergeant's sort of came with the job.

'Thanks, dad' Luke says.

So, this is the chef, all the way from the east coast? I can't help but think about how little resemblance they share, judging from the side of his face, he's almost paler than me. He looks at Dan, their eyes locked like nothing in the world could separate them. Shit, I hope Dan doesn't start anything.

'You'll be okay to walk home tonight' the man tells Luke, while declining to look at him.

Dan refuses to relent, and eventually, Luke's dad drives away.

'Hey guys' Luke says quietly.

'Hey Luke' I say.

'Where are the bosses?' Luke asks.

'I'm actually not sure, everything is locked, Dan's been waiting longer that me, right Dan?'

'That's your dad?' Dan asks, apathetically.

'Dan' I scold before he can start.

'What? I just thought-'

'That he would be Japanese? Yeah no' Luke cuts him off.

I look to Dan when he doesn't respond, he's busy gazing out the direction Luke's dad had driven.

'Just don't hold it against him. Please' Luke begs Dan, 'We were just in a hurry and he's not used to driving these small-town streets yet. I know he feels bad for almost hitting your car'

'No harm done' Dan says sardonically 'How was that exam result Warren?'

'Oh yeah, come on tell us!' Luke says.

'It was good' I tell my friends, I don't want to brag.

They look at each other and then back at me. Maybe they wouldn't think I'm bragging. Maybe having friends means you're allowed to be proud of yourself.

'Good?' Dan probes, '*Just* good?'

'Okay better than good' I smile, unable to contain it.

'Better than Elliot?' Luke asks.

I wait a while.

'Yeah, better than Elliot'

Luke cheers, Dan looks uneasy at the mention of Elliot.

'Did he tell you about his grade?' I ask Dan.

'No, actually he hasn't messaged me this afternoon' he answers.

'From what you've told me, it sounds like he deserves to be taken down a notch, congratulations my friend' Luke goes

'Bloody oath he deserves it! But he doesn't even know yet, our teacher only gave me my result after everyone else had left' I say, 'I can't wait to tell him, he's going to be so pissed!'

'Hey listen' Dan says frankly, 'I think it would be best if you don't let him find out'

'What? Why?' I ask flippantly.

Dan rubs his temple and then pinches the bridge of his nose, annoyed.

'This afternoon Ava told me about you and Elliot today. I don't know if I'm seeing him through a new set of eyes, or maybe he just changed since last semester, but after speaking to him today... I don't think he's someone that you want to cross'

'You might be just seeing him for what he is now, but it's not new, and I'm not afraid of him'

'No, Warren. I mean, I don't think he's someone that *you* want to cross'

Luke and I look at each other and then back at Dan, in the street, the wind squalls behind us.

'What's that supposed to mean?' I ask.

'I think he could be dangerous, maybe. It might be better to just leave him be'

Where did this coward come from?

'Dan, what did he say to you this morning?'

He doesn't answer right away, he taps his fingers on his head. The stress is visible now, Dan audibly groans.

'I just need more time to convince Ava about him, and then we can just...slowly pull away from him without him snapping' Dan assures us, although I think he's trying to assure himself the most.

'What are you talking about? What did he say?!' I repeat.

Dan pulls at his own hair in frustration.

'You want to know what he said? He said he could make you disappear if he wanted!'

I blink at Dan. He blinks at me, tears forming in his eyes and his lip trying its hardest not to falter, but it's like its caught in this wind.

'Wh... What does that mean?' I splutter.

122

'I don't know' Dan sits down on the footpath and leans against the door.

'You're not saying it was him?'

He stares up at me. I know him too well.

'That's insane' I tell him.

'When he was out of the country, no one else went missing' he raises his voice slightly.

'It's not him Dan' I raise my voice back.

'You thought it was a fucking werewolf Warren! Now you're trying to talk to me like I'm crazy?' he shouts.

'Did you not hear what I heard that day? That was him roaring out in the forest, was it?'

Screaming over each other in the empty street, we must look crazy to Luke.

'Listen! Listen, you guys hear that?' Luke waves us quiet.

A different car squeals around the corner and speeds towards us.

'Now what?' I ask.

'Warren, promise me you won't provoke Elliot, just in case. I'll convince Ava that he's bad news and then we'll distance ourselves from him. No bad blood, he won't snap' he says quickly as the car approaches us.

'Alright, I promise, but I hope you know what you're doing Dan'

'Isn't that Wanda?' Luke squints at the car.

It screeches to a halt in the middle of the road, and Wanda rolls down her window. She's a mess, her hair is especially wiry, this is the first time

I'm seeing her without it tied back. Has she been crying? She throws me the keys to the shop, and I catch them against my chest.

'You're in charge Warren' she says hoarsely, she's definitely been crying.

'What's happening Wanda?' I ask.

'I just need you to handle things for tonight. Just for tonight, it's… Fuck'

She leans out the window and sobs, Luke approaches her and rests his hand on her forearm.

'I can't get hold of Rhonda, I haven't heard from her since Saturday night. I need to go to her house and find her… I need to make sure…' she croaks.

'It's okay' Luke tells her.

'Don't worry about things here, I'll look after it' I say, stepping forward.

'Thank you boys' she nods, 'You're good kids'

She leaves us standing outside the shop, I know exactly what Dan's going to say.

'I thought they lived together? I hope she's okay' Luke says, returning to us.

Dan and I stare at each other in terror.

'Okay let's not assume the worst, it's been weeks since those two people went missing, surely this isn't related'

'It's the same day that he came back' Dan breathes.

'What is going on? What are you guys talking about?' Luke asks.

I fill Luke in on the two disappearances, Dan refuses to contribute at all the conversation.

'What does Elliot have to do with those two people? Did he have a problem with them?' Luke asks.

'He probably never saw either of them in his life' I assure them.

'Does he know that you work here Warren?' Dan says softly, still on the ground.

'I'm not even entertaining this thought Dan' I roll my eyes.

'Then why the fuck, did he say he could make you disappear, the same day that your boss goes missing?' he strains, voiced raised again.

'If he could make me disappear then I would have disappeared already' I snap.

Dan gets to his feet but Luke steps in between us before he can keep going.

'For right now' Luke says gently, 'We need to run this place for them'

The two of us look at each other over his head and nod, agreeing how rash we're both being, two boys fighting over nothing. We're both confused, well at least I know I am.

'Right' Dan nods.

'Yeah, no need to freak out yet, let's get to work' I spin the keys on my finger, then unlock the door.

I'm not convinced though, simply putting on a brave face, we have to get to work, and I'm already feeling the pressure of being at the helm. I call orders back to Luke as he toils away furiously in the kitchen, I lend a hand when I can to help alleviate his stress. It's funny, he prepares food so effortlessly, pizzas and pastas must be child's play for him, yet he always concentrates so hard it must give him a migraine, like he's afraid of making a mistake. Dan takes care of deliveries, and when there's no deliveries to take, he helps me wait tables. He isn't very good at waiting tables but he tries his best, I can tell how hard it is for him to speak formally, but his determination to do well shines through.

It feels good managing the three of us, I feel like a leader. But I guess Wanda only trusted me with the shop because I've been here the longest, the least bad option to leave in charge of your restaurant. The stream of customers gradually dries up, and I decide we should give the place a good scrub for when Wanda, and hopefully Rhonda, return.

'I think that went okay don't you guys reckon?' I ask as I mop the floor.

'Hell yeah' Dan says, he and Luke scrubbing the kitchen benches together.

'I'm glad I got to just stay back here, I couldn't manage all three of us' Luke says.

'Yeah Warren, nice work mate' Dan nods in agreement.

'Did I do alright?' I ask, to which they both give me two thumbs up.

Once everything is spotless, Luke decides to brew us all up some coffee before we go home, Dan and I wait patiently outside for him. The two of us got pretty heated out the front, I feel bad for losing my temper, but he shouldn't suggest that somebody we know is the cause of two, no, possibly three, people going missing, even if that person is as despicable as Elliot Young.

'What do you think? Working here?' I ask him.

'Well, not exactly a normal night to start, but it was alright' he says.

'No, normally we have two extra sets of hands, it'll be less crazy when the ladies get back'

He sports a slanted smile and knitted brows.

'You really think she's coming back?' Dan says softly, I guess he doesn't want Luke to hear.

'Of course she's coming back, what the fuck Dan?!' I hiss.

'Listen, I'm hoping for the best too, but if Rhonda is gone then-'

'She's not *gone*' I bark, 'She's fine okay?'

'When Wanda parked that car tonight I saw it on your face, you were thinking it too' he says with plenty of blithe.

'Yeah and then I thought about it logically, and she's going to be okay'

'You didn't answer me earlier, does Elliot know you work here? Because if he does-'

'Jesus Dan we're not on this again' I rub my temple.

'Yes, we are on this Warren'

'How is a seventeen-year-old making people disappear?'

He leans back on the crate he's sitting on, ready to speak without the venom.

'Okay, I've been thinking about it, and…Cult'

'A cult?' I ask in disbelief, 'Are you pulling the piss?'

'Don't give me that Warren, it all adds up. He's from a powerful family, they're always travelling all over the world, and he said he could make someone disappear, that's like textbook cult behaviour'

'Alright, even if I pretend that isn't the dumbest thing I've ever heard, what do you want me to do? Go to the cops and report it as a threat?'

'No!' he sizzles, 'That's the opposite of what I'm saying to do. Do *nothing*. At all. Don't even interact with Elliot until I find out for sure about him'

I feel bad already for calling his theory dumb, it's better than anything I've got. As long as he's being safe, I guess I have no problems with him keeping an eye on Elliot. I guess a cult isn't too crazy in the grand scheme of things, I've read about cults that sacrifice people out in the wilderness to Gods or devils. The roar.

'What are you guys whispering about?'

Luke joins us, he expertly carries all three coffees at once, one in each hand and one balancing delicately on his wrist.

'Nothing, thanks man' I say, Luke hands me my coffee.

'Cheers Lukey' Dan clears his throat.

'So, you never told me what grade did you get on the exam to top that Elliot guy?' Luke asks, sitting down next to Dan.

'Yeah tell us' Dan sips his mug, 'Shit this is a nice coffee mate'

Dan pats Luke on the back, Luke smiles wide and proud. I look at them, my two friends, they never would have interacted in a million years, and yet they've come together over me.

'Hundred percent' I say.

Earlier I was ecstatic to tell them, but the evening and its news has soured the joy I had felt this afternoon, until now I had even forgotten about Locke Dawson.

'You what?' says Luke.

Dan chokes on his coffee.

'That's right' I smile.

'No way dude!'

'Keep it between us though' I say, looking at Dan, 'In the unlikely event that Elliot is as dangerous as you think he is, we don't want to set him off'

'Thank you, just don't challenge him, at least until we can be sure he isn't a threat'

He's always been practical, never jumping the gun without reason, but when he's sure about something, and thinks there's something he can do, well then, he just can't sit idly by. For him to want to be so passive, he must genuinely believe Elliot is a risk, and he must be worried for the people around him.

'What did your parents say?' Luke asks.

I hadn't even been home to tell them about it, and the day has been far too eventful for a text message. I imagine running in the front door, exam in hand, holding it up proudly to mum, I bet she'd say, "Were all your other subjects that high?"

'We have to celebrate' Dan punches his open palm.

'How?'

'Free this weekend? You should both come out to my place for some camping and fishing'

'I've never been camping before' Luke frets.

'Oh yeah I forgot you were a city slicker Lukey, it's alright, Warren was useless too but I made an outdoorsman out of him this holidays'

'Depending on what happens, you know here' I say, shutting down Dan's elation.

'What do you mean?'

'The three of us may all need to work, depending on... You know'

It's a grim subject, and I hate to bring the spirits down like this, but Dan seems to only be looking for the cause, but not the effect. Three people have vanished without a trace, coincidentally only during times that Elliot Young has been around, and Dan refuses to look at anything else. I'll amuse his theory for now since he has his bleeding heart so set on it, but has he thought about anything else? The whole town knows *what* is happening, and Dan thinks he's worked out *who*, but has anybody at all even thought about *why*? Or... *How*?

XI
Of the Fittest

But it turns out that we don't have work that night, I don't know if we'll ever have work again. Rhonda Lewis was declared missing the next day, and the Southway Police began investigating. The arrow tears through the air, the dim light from the campfire illuminating its tip. It pierces the pinecone, plucking it from the tree before rocketing onward and implanting itself into the tree trunk, pinecone still intact.

'I got it, didn't I?' Dan calls from his assigned position.

'That must be eighty metres away' I say from beside our campfire.

He walks over to the fire, bow in hand and quiver on his back, he places them down next to his sleeping bag and holds his hands up to the flames, taking in the warmth. It's Saturday night, out on Dan's family farm, and the three of us are celebrating my "Hundred" as we've come to call it. His mum was out in the morning, so we spent that time keeping an eye on Isabelle until she got home, we mostly just watched cartoons. Then, when Faye returned, we just had to convince an enthusiastic Isabelle not to follow us when we ventured out into the wild. We're out east, careful as always to stay as far away from where Dan and I heard that roar. The day was spent setting up camp, Dan and I have a sort of system we worked out over the holidays, we'd find a good tree for firewood, and then take turns hacking away at it with an axe, swapping when one got tired.

We introduced Luke into the rotation, although he isn't physically strong, he sure makes up for it in vigour, he sweated profusely as he hacked, just as he does when he cooks. We ended up with plenty of firewood, and enjoy a large campfire as the fruit of our labour. I showed Luke a nearby river where Dan and I always have luck fishing, Luke is much better at this than chopping wood. While we reeled in trout after trout, Dan took his bow out hoping for a rabbit to stew, and although we're treading into the Springtime, he says he didn't see any animals out at all. I wonder why that is.

'Wow, that was badass. You really are as good as Warren says' Luke says, impressed.

'He's been doing it for over ten years so you'd hope he'd be half decent by now' I laugh.

'Shut up Warren' Dan grabs me in a headlock.

I writhe around to escape, and tackle him to the ground.

'Listen!' Luke fiddles with our tiny handheld transistor radio beside him and turns the volume up.

We stop strangling each other and look up, our feet are dangerously close to the coals. I help Dan sit up and we dust ourselves off.

'Good evening Southway, this is Sophie Martin with your seven o' clock news recap. Local police once again, refused to comment on the search for local small business owner Rhonda Lewis. Our own Jim Brandt approached Sergeant Charles, affectionately known to most as "Chuck", Dillon, and Jim, he wasn't very talkative you say?

'That's right Soph, yes when I attempted to interview Chuck he declined to make an official statement on behalf of Southway police and, at first, I was shocked because I've known Chuck since we were knee high to a grasshopper and I can't remember a time he shut up! Ha ha! But not only that, it shows a complete lack of confidence in him and his officers, and quite frankly, it brings into question the competency of our police'

'I agree completely Jim, of course it's possible that Sergeant Dillion didn't comment for other reasons, but when you're dealing with three people, vanishing without a trace, people have the right to know what you're doing to find them. I mean for God's sake people are starting to panic around town, everyone is desperate for a clue, at least'

'Absolutely, now while he didn't make a statement on anything specific, he was able to tell me that he is having some new officers imported from interstate to help with the investigation'

'Can we turn this shit off?' I ask, 'I'm glad Wanda refused an interview with those clowns'

Luke spins the volume dial all the way off for me.

'Yeah, they're the worst, fucking media parasites' Dan slams a fist on his sleeping bag.

I've been trying to not think about it all week, instead choosing to bury my head in the proverbial sand and spend my time theorising what Locke Dawson's world changing project is, I'll find out after this weekend. It's a flimsy distraction, deep down I'm realising that three is too much to be a coincidence.

'Please, the master requests absolute silence while he works' Luke lightens the mood.

He's working some culinary magic on the trout we caught, he brought a whole bag of spices and herbs, and what I'm pretty sure are sesame seeds, certainly covering all bases. Using the tray of Dan's ute as a kitchen bench, he operates carefully, only stopping occasionally to keep his long hair sneaking out from under his woollen hat.

'Hey you could always give me a hand here' he says.

'I don't think that's a good idea' Dan laughs, dragging a log closer and sitting down on it.

'Yeah you stay there, I don't want food poisoning'

'Hilarious' Dan laughs as he pokes the coals with a stick.

'I'm just kidding anyway' Luke returns to the fish, 'This is like, my thing'

'Your *thing*?' I ask.

'Well yeah, cooking is my thing, just like how being smart is your thing' he explains.

'What's my thing?' Dan asks far too keenly.

'Probably being cool' Luke says, he finishes preparing the fish and brings it over to us.

The fillets sit in a foil parcel, Luke lets us take a peek before covering them for cooking. The fillets look like they've been prepared by a master, the specks of flavour from Luke's bag of tricks makes our mouths water. It's been marinated in something, I think, can fish even be marinated?

'Don't take this the wrong way, but what is it?' Dan asks, looking over it like a seagull.

He folds the foil over the fish and then takes Dan's stick from him. He scrapes some red coals from the fire off to the side, moulds them into a nest shape, and tucks the parcel in, covering it afterwards.

'Hopefully, it will be baked rainbow trout' Luke puts his hands on his hips once he's satisfied with their placement.

'See, he doesn't even need a kitchen he's just that good' I say.

'I hope you know what you're doing, it looked so good' Dan watches it carefully.

'I admit this is… different to what I usually have to work with but I hope I made it work'

He sits between us and gives Dan his stick back for now. Is being smart really my thing? Is that all I have going for me? I'd rather be known for something else.

'Am I really that cool?' Dan asks.

'Yep' Luke and I say together.

'Really? I just don't see it' he stokes the fire, careful to not disturb the fish, 'Have you seen the car I drive?'

'The… Rustmobile over there?' I say, struggling to come up with a funnier name.

Even though I didn't think much of the nickname, they both howl like wolves with laughter.

'Far out that's a good one, that's what we're calling it from now on' Luke wipes his eyes, 'But yeah Dan, people in my grade talk about how cool you are, these girls in my cooking class, they-'

'Jesus are you serious?' he groans, and pulls the stick from the flames.

It's tip red hot, and angry looking, he rams it back into the fire.

'I don't think it's something you have a say in' I add, 'You're just… Well cool'

'Well I don't want to be cool. I don't want anyone gushing over me, I just want-'

'To help people, I know' I finish for him.

Dan nods at me. Luke looks between us.

'Did I miss something?' he asks.

'I think helping people is Dan's thing' I say.

Dan's warm eyes flicker even brighter than the campfire.

'I like that a lot more' he smiles.

Luke picks up the stick and pries open the foil to inspect the fish. He shakes his head, rotates it and nestles it back in the coals.

'Give me a different thing too' I announce.

'Hey you can't just change your thing, there's lots of paperwork involved, very complicated process' Luke laughs.

'I don't want to just be smart'

'Well what do you want?' Dan asks.

'I want to not waste my life' I say.

They both look at me like I've confessed to murder. Was that too serious?

'So, you want to leave Southway, is what you're saying' Dan says, turning back to the fire.

I remember our conversation in the library, so much has changed.

'Not necessarily, I mean I used to dream of leaving here, graduation couldn't come quick enough. But to be honest, I wouldn't mind sticking around'

They look at me again, not in disbelief this time. Dan springs up and moves over to my left and sits back down, putting me in the middle now.

'Isn't he just a big old sweetheart Lukey, he'll miss us too much when he's a big scientist'

Dan puts his arm around me.

'Dude fuck off, forget I said anything' I shove him away, humiliated.

'I agree' Luke says.

'Huh?' Dan cocks an eyebrow at him.

'Well I always wanted to become a chef, and then move to Japan, to see where my mum comes from, you know? And I always wanted to do it as soon as possible, but now, I don't know, what's the rush? It can wait for a while, it's not going anywhere'

In a lot of ways, I relate to Luke more than anyone else. I've known Dan for much longer sure, but he and I have always been rather star-crossed, Luke and I are on the same page.

'Fish is probably ready anyway' he announces.

He levers it off the coals with the stick and onto the cool ground away from the fire. As he peels back the hot foil quickly with his fingers, I'm instantly enveloped in the peppery flavour. Dan leaps up and ruffles both of our heads, messing up my hair and putting Luke's hat on a funny angle.

136

'Don't worry about me, I don't have any plans to leave soon, I like hanging out with you two as well, I guess' he says.

He retrieves the paper plates we bought from the… Rustmobile and throws us one each before sitting back down.

'And I really do mean that' he adds.

Luke arranges the fish on the plates and adds the finishing touches with his meticulous grace and presentation, it's like he's on one of those cooking shows and one stray dollop of mayonnaise could mean elimination for him. Dan forgot to get plastic cutlery, so we're about to pick at it with our fingers. It's succulent, as amazing as I've come to expect from Luke, even more impressive considering it was cooked in tin foil. It's funny, I've only known him for a couple of months, but I already feel like I've grown up with him. He watches us chew like starved animals, while he eats carefully and gracefully, like he's dining with royalty, like he doesn't know otherwise. But most importantly, he looks proud.

'I gotta say Lukey, you really should be charging us for this' Dan picks his teeth with a thin bone.

'You know I wouldn't ask you guys for money'

'Yeah, please don't actually charge us, I couldn't afford it' Dan flicks the bone into the fire.

'What's in it?' I ask.

'Heaps of things' he shrugs.

'So, when can we expect you to invite us over for a full meal?' Dan asks with his mouth full.

'I wouldn't be able to do anything like this at home'

'How come?' I ask.

'Dad doesn't let me use the good ingredients myself'

'Wait, how do you have these then?'

'Well, they're kept locked up, but locks can be picked' he smiles.

Dan can't believe it.

'*You* know how to pick a lock?' he asks Luke.

'Yeah' he says.

'That's badass, maybe being cool is *your* thing'

'You can do it with a knife, all you have to do is poke it into where the door and frame meet' he makes the angles with his hands, 'and then move the knife left to right until it's catches on that… thing, the part that goes into the frame'

'You little burglar you' Dan laughs, 'Anyway I was just pulling the piss, you don't have to invite us over'

'No' Luke says, 'I will, soon'

I look up from my fish, all this time I've known him, Luke has been anxious about even seeing me outside of work hours, could he really be ready to invite us into his home?

'You'd do that? For us?' I ask.

'Yes' he nods, steeling himself.

Dan and I look at each other and smile, the two of us having helped this frightened boy relax.

'Well how could we say no to that' I say.

'If your parents are chefs, you must have a massive kitchen' Dan wonders.

'Sometime soon okay?' Luke smiles, 'I'm sorry, that I haven't yet, it's been rude of me'

'Don't stress' Dan says.

'Hey you guys?' Luke says, quieter now.

He looks down at his thumbs, playing with the bones in his wrists.

'Yeah?'

Luke just shakes his head with regret now, deciding he's said too much.

'Don't worry, it's crazy'

'Let's hear it' Dan insists, they lock gazes, and Dan's warm eyes burn through Luke's inhibitions.

'Okay well, it's true I want to be a chef. I do, more than anything. But, I feel... guilty for it' he admits, cryptically.

'I don't get it' I say.

'Neither, why would you feel bad?' Dan asks.

With the cords in his neck rigid and pronounced, he stares into the fire.

'Because it's what my dad wants'

'So?' I say.

'Huh?' Luke looks almost offended.

'So what if it's what your dad wants? As long as it's what you want'

'It's... more complicated than that'

He's leaning in so close to the fire that the pom poms on the tassels of his hat are almost dipping in the flames. The heat evaporates his tears almost immediately after the leave his eyes.

'Does he ever hit you?' Dan asks, after being silent for some time.

'Dan!' I scold.

'What? Come on Warren don't pretend you didn't think he seemed like a prick too'

'He's a perfectionist. Real loud, and controlling as well, I guess'

Luke leans in closer to the flames and Dan puts his head down, the skin bunching around his eyes.

'It's no secret that me and your dad didn't get off on the right foot, but I shouldn't have assumed that, I'm sorry'

'Don't stress' Luke copies him from a moment ago, 'You're right to not like him, he is a bit of a…Dickhead'

Dan instantly begins to laugh, not out of tactlessness, at how unnatural the word "dickhead" sounds coming from Luke's mouth. I don't think I've ever heard him swear about anything, not even the most difficult Monster Masher missions or the most taxing nights in the shop.

'Hey, if you ever want to stay somewhere else, just come over' I tell him.

'Thanks Warren, your parents must be cool' Luke can't change the subject fast enough.

'They are' Dan says, 'I show up unannounced all the time and they don't mind'

'It's different if you live with them' I say.

'How?' Dan says.

'Hey don't get me wrong, they don't hit me, they don't yell at me, they're perfectly great. It just feels like, as long as my grades are up that's all they care about. They never ask about work or what we did on the weekend, fuck, I could go missing next and I bet they'd be disappointed that I'd miss school the next day'

I realise that I've spilled a lot. Luke and Dan both hold their hands on their knees. I feel selfish. Shit, of the three of us, I have the least to complain about. But once I got talking, it was like I learned something about myself.

140

'I didn't mean all that, sorry guys, I don't mean to whinge'

'Trust me' Dan unrolls his sleeping bag and lays down on it, 'They're not like that, they just want you to be successful, but if it bothers you, just talk to them and they'd understand. Ken and Judy are the best, you don't know how lucky you are to have them'

'What about you?' Luke says to him.

'What about me?'

'Well, if we're talking about parents' Luke goes on.

Dan sighs up to the stars, asking them for help navigating this conversation. I don't interfere, if he doesn't want to talk about it, then he won't.

'My mother though, she does fuck all around here sure, but it's daddy dearest that pisses me off'

Dan kicks back on his sleeping bag, trying to act as though he couldn't care less, but I know the situation with his dad troubles him deeply.

'What happened to him?' Luke asks.

'My sister happened' he says.

Oh?

'What do you mean?' Luke asks. He shouldn't dig deeper, but he asks out of innocent curiosity.

'They didn't...' Dan makes an exaggerated mouth shape as he selects his words carefully, 'exactly *want* her'

'Oh' Luke shuts his mouth quickly.

'I don't think they ever loved each other, and one failure of a kid wouldn't have helped that. When she came along I think it was the breaking point, and when Izzy was about three and I was about thirteen he just took off one day. Abandoned all three of us. You know what the last thing I remember him saying to me was?'

'What did he say?' I ask quietly.

'He said, "Don't end up like me", and I think about that every day'

'I'm sorry to hear about all that, it would have been hard, I can't even imagine' Luke says.

'I'm just glad Izzy was too young to really understand. But yeah it got me'

Suddenly, everything about the way Daniel Steele is makes more sense to me.

'I don't think you ended up like him. You'd never abandon anybody' Luke tells him, 'I mean, I haven't known you for long but I don't think you'd run away like that'

'Thanks mate, that means a lot to me'

Luke smiles across at him through the flames.

'Alright I've got one for you' Dan claps his hands, 'What's the worst fight you've been in?'

'That guy, Kevin, I guess, if you can even call that a fight' I laugh.

'Fuck no that doesn't count! You must have a… less one-sided fight under your belt Warren? I can't remember you ever hitting anyone growing up'

'I've never been in one either' says Luke.

'Jesus Christ, you guys are gonna die with no scars!'

I don't need to be reminded about my nice, safe, beige existence thank you Daniel.

'I don't believe in violence' Luke says.

142

'What do you mean you don't believe in it' laughs Dan, 'I'm pretty sure violence exists in the world'

'I mean, I don't believe in spreading more violence, because there's enough in the world'

Dan looks through the fire at him on the other side, questioning his sanity with his eyes.

'Everyone says that, until they're in a situation where violence is the only answer'

Luke looks back at him, I wouldn't call it hostile, but to me right now, their many differences are all the more obvious.

'There's never just one answer, but have you ever been in a situation where violence was the problem?'

I never expected the two of them to clash like this. They're two very different people no doubt, the two coming together over me, but the heat from the friction between them is almost knocking me over.

'I wonder what Kevin is up to these days' I ask, keen to talk about anything else.

Dan immediately curbs his argument for me.

'I actually sold weed to him a few times, but he's moved away now'

Dan rolls over to his backpack.

'Speaking of…'

He pulls out a beaten-up metal tin, and some rolling papers. He opens the tin and gives us a flash of the ground green leaves, the smell makes Luke grimace away from it.

'Warren knows I don't do this often, but we've just talked about some heavy shit, need to chill out'

I'm just glad I could get the two of them to not take that conversation any further. Violence, Jesus, it sucks but it happens sometimes, how are the three of us meant to know what to make of it?

'Fire it up my friend' I say, 'I'm in'

'Lukey?' Dan shoots him a look, 'Would you care to partake?'

'I... I'm not sure' he looks at Dan's fingers crafting the joint as though he's defusing a bomb.

'Don't do it if you don't want' I say.

'Yeah no pressure' Dan adds.

'Why? What's it like?' Luke asks.

'Yeah, this drug addict got me to try it'

'Fuck off' Dan laughs.

'Alright sure, I'll have a go'

The joint hangs from Dan's lip precariously. He produces a lighter from the bag, it's one of those metal ones that flip open, he strikes the flint and a small flame spouts.

'Then watch and learn'

Before I know it, we're all laying down on our sleeping bags, in a formation so that our heads are all together in the middle, and our legs run out in different directions. Slurring our words and talking about who knows what while we look up at the stars together.

'So, could evolution give me wings if I wanted Warren?' Luke asks me.

For what feels like hours now, they've both been asking me biology questions, you ace one exam and suddenly everyone wants a lecture.

'Evolution doesn't really care what anything wants, it just... You know what fuck it, you can evolve into anything you want mate'

'Fuck yeah' he says, hiding his thrill under his breath.

'Would definitely help with survival of the... Uh, shit'

I've forgotten the word, in this moment it won't come to me.

'Of the fittest, isn't it? Dan asks.

'Yeah, of the fittest' I nod up at the stars, 'That's the one'

'Oi how did we set this up without anyone falling in the fire? It's so... triangular' Luke asks.

'Always analysing the situation Warren Avery' Dan murmurs, 'Always analysing'

Dan points to his own eyes for some reason, then passes the glowing joint to Luke, who in turn brings it to his mouth to take a drag.

'Dan mate, you're so burnt, that was Luke who just said that'

'Wow' Luke peeps, his voice suddenly becoming very high.

Dan and I burst out laughing.

'Alright you guys I'm serious right now, you guys need to help me get a haircut, later'

He takes his hat off and throws it weakly. It lands on my chest, after floating in the air.

'I don't think I can do it right now, maybe later' Dan waves him away.

'Oi watch this, get ready to laugh' I say.

I lift Luke's hat and put it over my head, and pull it down over my eyes. They wail with laughter until they're both coughing, and then their coughing makes me laugh until I start coughing. I love these guys. Eventually we calm down enough to talk.

'One time while I was stoned with Elliot, you know what he told me? He told me he's afraid of not being good enough, and even though I'm pretty sure he's a murderer, I think I'm afraid of that too' Dan slurs.

'Same' Luke and I answer.

'You know what I think?' I say, 'I think, we're all just afraid... of being afraid'

'That's so true, fuck you're clever!' Dan slaps at his sleeping bag.

'That and my dad' Luke says.

'Yeah, and wasting my life' I add.

'And not being there for people' Dan finishes.

We all let out a collective sigh, a unanimous, unspoken signal of ready to doze off. Life is good, I sure have spent a lot of time complaining about it, but it's good. I'm about to slip into a dream when Luke talks one more time.

'No but seriously, can you guys help me get a haircut later?'

XII

Root and Stem

I wore my best jacket to school today, the one Dan said was cool, I imagine Mr Dawson will give me a lab coat, or maybe today will just be more of an induction to the lab. I waltz through town towards the lab, I hope he hasn't forgotten that today is the day. I arrive at the steps, creeping down into the dark, ending in a doorway. He's inside, I can tell by the light morphing around his shadow in the light coming from the grimy window. Looks like he didn't bother to clean the place, filthy or not, I knock on the door.

'Mr Dawson? It's Warren, you wanted to meet this afternoon'

He's right at the door in a flash, his frame blocking the light.

'Please place your phone inside your bag and leave it outside the door. You have my word that it won't be stolen' his muffled voice instructs.

I understand, he doesn't want me to take photos of his data and then send it to someone else, I could be a spy for all he knows. I do as he asked, and when he's satisfied, he unlocks the door. I can tell by the scraping sound that it's a heavy, sliding bolt lock.

'Welcome Warren' he pulls me inside by my collar, and closes the door behind me.

He doesn't slide the lock back in though.

'Wow' I exhale.

The room is deceptively small, it should be as big as the two shops above combined. I don't know if I'd call this a fully-fledged lab though, it's bare bones to say the least, but then I remember the only other laboratory I've ever seen is at Southway High, and I realise this place is in my top two. Chemistry equipment is scattered around the benches to one side, although it's not clean, it doesn't look like it's been used recently either. One corner has three old school computers set up, all of them are in use,

the retro style green on black writing you see when the hackers are digging into the code in the movies, but I make an effort not to be nosy as to what's on the screens. I'm sure I'll be shown all this business in due time. The boxes I saw out on the street are now opposite the computers, along with dozens more, filled to the point of overflow with papers and files stacked roof high. I can see all of this only in the buzzing, dim light, courtesy of a single bulb that hangs delicately from the ceiling's midpoint. Apart from all that, it's empty space, weird.

What's even weirder still, is that between the corner with the computers, and the corner with the boxes, hangs a dirty, brown curtain, strewn across the back wall. I don't know what to make of the place, it's not much, hell it's barely anything at all, but it reminds me of hard work, and I'm sure Locke didn't exactly have a lot to work with. He's done well, I think the place is a testament to his skill.

'I did what I could with the place' he puts his hands in his lab coat pockets.

'I'm impressed' I say.

'Apologies for the lack of furniture'

I hadn't even noticed yet but he's right, there's no chairs at all.

'I don't mind' I tell him.

'Now Warren I hate to ask grunt work of you right out of the gate, but could you stack those boxes as far into the corner as they will go for me? These old joints have reached their limits for the while, I'm afraid'

'Of course, I've got it, these ones here?' I point.

'Yes, my boy thank-you, just stack them in the corner as high as you can. I want to keep the floor space as clear as possible'

Immediately, I get started on the task he's assigned, although I do wonder why, there's plenty of vacant space as it is. A lot of the boxes have papers hanging out, I try to neatly fold them in without prying, I don't think he'd appreciate me eyeballing his notes. Most of the boxes are labelled, the first seven boxes I stack are all simply titled "Genomes", which seems like a lot of boxes for one topic to me. The rest it seems, are reserved for one box per topic, "Equipment Receipts" is the name of one box, "Scrapped" is another, but one catches my eye. One is much heavier than the rest, its name reads, "Dawson-Baskerville", what does that mean? I'll ask him if the chance presents itself.

'I'm glad you're as hard-wearing as you are scholarly' Locke laughs.

'Yeah' I laugh, 'My friend Dan and I, we do lots of hunting and fishing on his farm out of town, so I'm getting used to carrying heavy things around the place'

'Your friend from the… Pizza Place where you work?'

'One of them yeah, you should come in one night, our other friend Luke is an aspiring chef, best food you'll ever eat around here'

'Based on this arrangement I have here,' he waves his hands around the vacant room, 'Do I strike you as one who partakes in the finer things?'

I don't know if he wants an answer or not, with him it's impossible to tell. It's only when he finally laughs that I'm sure it was a joke. I laugh too, but this man is not normal. What did Wanda and Rhonda always say? The only people who come here are trying to hide away from the rest of the world?

'I'm not one for dining out at all I'm afraid, I much prefer to cook for myself'

'Fair enough' I say, trying not to sound uneasy, 'You don't know what you're missing out on though'

He forces his lips into a line and rests his hands in his lab coat pockets, thumbs sticking over the top.

'What holds humans back the most Warren?' he asks me.

It reminds me of how I felt when Ms Harper asked us about the most important adaptation, being placed on the spot like this.

'Our fears' I say, the first thing that comes to mind.

'Wrong' he says immediately, shutting me down, 'The thing that holds humans back, is ourselves'

'Isn't that kind of like fear? If we're afraid of trying something and doubt ourselves, we limit what we could do' I propose.

'No, fear does not hold anyone back Warren. When you're truly afraid, that is the only time when you are willing to do things you would normally never consider. Have you ever been truly afraid Warren?'

'No, never that afraid' I say.

For an instant, the vein across his temple swells, but dissipates as quickly as it came.

'I'm sure you will one day' he says as he stands to his feet, 'But let's not get off topic, when I say we hold ourselves back, I mean as a species. How cruel and covetous people can act, stomping down those beneath them in their avarice. That is the purest evil'

I suppose he is right, I have seen bad people, the sergeant who rounded up Dan's speeding fine, I don't think he's a good man. Elliot, whether he's a cultist or just a spoilt kid, definitely isn't a good person, not to me anyway, but I couldn't call him evil from what I've seen. I don't think I know what evil is.

'Unfortunately, there are bad people, sure' I respond, eager to see where he takes this.

'You've struck the issue my boy! But what no one seems to realise, is that the wicked aren't always hiding away in castles, twiddling their moustaches and playing a pipe organ, they live next door, and wave to you down the street. All people will corrupt if it means getting a step up on somebody else. Just crabs in a bucket, as they say'

He holds the corner of the curtain at the back of the room with both hands, the fabric threatening to tear even under his delicate grip.

'Well if it's so ingrained into us, how can you stop people from acting that way?'

'The same as you do with any issue, you find the cause and you dig it out root and stem' he smiles, 'Remember, you promised me you'd keep an open mind here'

Without breaking eye contact with me, he pulls the curtain away. There isn't a wall here at all, instead, there's an alcove housing something very bizarre. Several dialysis machines are wired up to a large mechanical base, the power cables running from it thicker in diameter than my arms. The base holds a glass cylinder vertically in place, full of a slightly green fluid and almost touching the roof of the niche, capped by a sort of metal closure. The fluid is viscous, I can tell by the way the bubbles struggle to ascend to the top. Suspended in the solution, is a sleeping... Thing

It has a long, furry body, kind of like a ferret, only the size of a large dog. From head to tail, I estimate it would be about a metre and a half long. About a third of its length is in its neck, which ends in a meaty skull with a flat face. The thing has its eyes closed, and the rest of its face is tucked under its forearm by hooking its long neck back around and into its chest. Each of its four feet have long claws on three wide-spread toes, and one jutting out backwards, like a bird of prey's.

'This is Lapdog, that is the name I assigned for it'

'What is it?' I ask, I can't pull my eyes from the container.

'It's a perfect creature that I made, perfectly obedient'

'I thought you said you were working on saving the planet?'

Locke Dawson avoids my question.

'In my time, I've seen countless injustices Warren, many to me, but most to other far more innocent people than I' he sighs.

I look at the razors on its feet again, if he made this, he made it for killing.

'How will Lapdog save the planet?' I ask, sceptically.

He pushes a square red button on one of the machines, and a low, mechanical whirring rings out. Through the fluid, there's a metal panel on the top of the tube sliding over, creating an opening. A futuristic doggy door for the world's most hideous hound. I step back.

'It's okay, don't be afraid' Locke holds up a hand to me.

He taps on the glass with his elbow. The creature's eye snaps open, it has no iris, only white with a pupil. It's body and tail uncoil, it notices the opening, and uses its tail to propel itself to the surface, flicking its body side to side like a crocodile. It sits on top of the tube, dripping with fluid, some spilling down the outside of its container, I watch the drops slowly race towards the floor while the Lapdog looks down at us.

'Come' Locke commands, and the beast leaps down and lands gracefully beside him, standing obediently, body low to the ground.

It's disgusting to look at. When open, it's mouth is perfectly circle, only it closes vertically instead of horizontally. Its face is unnaturally flat, with nostrils but no protruding nose at all. I don't think it can move its eyes, instead it has to carry its head with its long, thick neck to look around, because it just faces forward.

'Why is its mouth like that?' I ask him, unable to believe what I'm seeing.

'The short answer, is I don't know. None of its three precursors had this trait, but swivelled mouth aside, it's perfect. It isn't worth making another just to correct a superficial change'

Its three precursors? Superficial change? My head is burning with interrogations, this isn't at all what I expected to be down in this hole.

'How will this creature save the planet Mr Dawson?' I ask again.

'To be honest, it won't be Lapdog itself that saves this planet, certainly not single-handedly'

'Then what does it do?'

'Lapdog is more of an, induction for what's to come. The entrée, the springboard'

'What does that mean?'

'It's the first of my creations thus far to be perfectly obedient, as you can see'

He points down to the concrete and makes a clacking sound with his tongue, and in response the creature lays its long body motionless beside him on the floor. It's like a computer program that has stopped responding, like on Monster Masher when the game glitches out and the creature gets stuck in place. What does he mean by 'the *first* to be obedient'?

'So, you've made others then? That weren't obedient? What happened to them?'

'No one gets it right on their first try do they Warren?' he laughs, 'But only four attempts in a craft that no one has tried before is something worth being impressed with, at least I think so'

'That's not funny' I snap, 'What happened to the other three?'

'There have been... Complications in the past yes' he grows serious now.

'What complications?'

'Lapdog's three predecessors have issues with being more... chaotic. The first, the Progenitor was, uncontrollable, massive and deformed, it would follow reluctantly where I went but not much beyond that. I was so proud of it, but it was no good to me, so from it, I made a second which was a step in the right direction. Then a third, and then the fourth here, was exactly what I was looking for'

'Where are they now? The other three?'

He glares at me, disappointed in me for using such an urgent and judgemental tone with him.

'You promised me you wouldn't be overwhelmed Warren but you seem quite agitated'

He raises a brow only slightly, as though the situation only warrants a mild concern.

'Tell me what the fuck this is supposed to be!' I shout.

Locke's face twists in rage when I yell at him, the beast's claws dig into the concrete floor, and it takes a step backwards, it moves its head towards me. Locke clears his throat, and the beast faces forward again and steps back to, staring blankly ahead once more.

'Lapdog is marketable, that's essentially what it boils down to' Locke explains, 'Compliant and capable in every way, the perfect companion, the perfect work animal, the perfect guard dog, whatever people need it to be, it can do it'

I study it again, from its upright plane of a face all the way down its powerful dorsal side to the knives still dug into the concrete, I believe him. I really do believe that this thing could do anything.

'That's it? That's the noble crusade? You just want money? What about all the evil people that need to change?' I fire off at him.

Locke shuffles nervously in place.

'Now see Warren, this is the part that's going to be hard for you to swallow'

'And what's that?' I brace myself.

'You see, it's true that Lapdog is perfectly obedient, perfectly obedient to *me*'

'What...'

'It's complete, absolutely impeccable, so perfect that I'll never be able to create another one like it. But cloning an already existing creature is straight forward enough, that's where you would come in'

'You can clone?'

'We think of cloning as far off science fiction because we try to clone things that we didn't create with our own hands. Cloning something that I know inside and out is straight-forward enough'

I tremble in my place, my breaths becoming rapid and strained, this isn't real, none of this is happening.

'The cloning wasn't just to flex my intellectual muscle though, it was far more efficient to clone my first Lapdog attempt, making tweaks to its genome along the way, and again down the line until I arrived at this little one, rather than take a stab in the dark with a new genome every try'

I look down at the thing beside him.

'This can't be real' I say to it, wishing it would disappear.

Disappear.

'Try as I might, I cannot create creatures that can reproduce, at least not conventionally. Crafting a creature to be perfect and then cloning it is far more viable. We will leave this place once Lapdog is grown enough, and I will show you mass production, you would eventually take over that responsibility, while I make a start on the next step'

'You're going to sell these things to people as pets, so why do you need them to still obey you'

'Like all of us, and its three siblings before it, Lapdog has an underlying predisposition for violence' he focuses his cold eyes on me.

Like all of us. Violence. It's now that I start to truly feel afraid. The monster's claws are still embedded in the floor. Right through the stone.

'Once there are Lapdogs all over the world, we-' he says.

'What happened to the other creatures you made?' I ask again.

'Do not interrupt me boy' he snarls, 'Once there are Lapdogs all over the world, we'll start to introduce other species'

'Why? To kill all their owners? What the fuck for?' I shout.

'Well they will kill everybody eventually' Locke calmly tells me.

'What...' is all I can muster.

'Humans will ultimately be eliminated. Now, I've set up some things for the later stages, but as for the short term, that is, the cloning of Lapdog here, we-'

'You're insane' I whisper.

'Now Warren be logical. You must agree, there are people who don't deserve to live, no?' he tries to calm me.

'You're fucking insane!' I drown him out.

'Don't try to be righteous boy. Not that anyone seems to do anything about it, but everyone knows we are about to destroy the Earth with our greed anyway. Deforestation, air pollution, overfishing, overpopulation' he shouts back, 'How long do humans have left anyway? Hmm? I'll give you a hint Warren, you and your two friends won't be dying of old age. Evolution handed us this planet, and we spat in its face, we aren't worthy to be at the apex'

'And this thing is?' I point at Lapdog.

'There will be others. As many different varieties as I can create. Once they inherit the Earth, natural selection will take the reins again, and lead them to a new hierarchy, one much more responsible that the one we made'

Lapdog's talons are still dug deep into the floor, scratching the concrete like it's wet sand. I've seen stone sliced into before, once, and after I saw that, I heard that bloodcurdling sound.

'It was you, wasn't it?'

'Hmm?'

'Those people' I laugh, laughing is all I can do my current state, 'Those poor people, this thing killed them, didn't it? I actually thought it was Elliot... but it was you, right under everyone's nose'

'Well, not Lapdog itself, it came to this town as a single cell and has never even seen the outside of this room' he strokes his whiskery chin, 'But the other three most probably did kill those missing people, yes'

'What the fuck is wrong with you?' I shake.

He cocks his head and winds his hands over one another as though to prompt me to keep talking if I have more to say, but I don't. I really don't.

'Did you know those people Warren? You seem to care about all of them quite a bit. I'm sorry if they were close friends of yours but-'

'Shut your fucking mouth!' I snap, 'They were human beings'

Lapdog looks up at him, how a dog watches its master.

'They were human beings' he agrees, 'And that's why sooner or later, they had to go'

My utter horror turns into an unbridled rage with nowhere to channel it. What can I do right now? I've never felt as strong of an emotion towards anything that I do here, all the other things that have ever happened to me, good and bad, they are behind me now. Nothing will be the same after this afternoon, because I can't do anything.

'You won't get away with this' I say, more bravely than I actually feel.

He sighs, completely unintimidated, hardly even inconvenienced.

'I think it would be in your best interest to keep quiet about this when you leave now, if it really came down to it, my creatures could wipe this town away like the stain that it is'

157

He gives me a warped, feral grin. I spin on my heel and break for the door.

'So be it' he sighs, 'I'm sorry you couldn't understand'

I hear Locke grunt a command, and the beast's claws scratching against the floor as it leaps, but I don't look back. I dive through the door, and slam it behind me. I pick up my bag as I go up the stairs three at a time. At the top of the stairs, out on the street and people are walking and driving by, unaware of what's lurking underneath.

'Good to see you out enjoying the fresh air Warren!'

It's Ms Harper, walking across the other side of the road, arms full of groceries as she smiles at me. She carefully props the paper bags up to stop them from falling, she looks like she's in a hurry. My head turns by itself, numbly tracking her as she walks by. I hold up a feeble hand to wave as she passes, but I'm too slow, and she's already gone. That poor woman, unaware of what is sleeping and growing on the other side of the street behind me. This town is full of unknowing people, I was one of them until thirty minutes ago. Still holding my hand in the air, waving at nobody, I feel a tear roll down my cheek as the outside world becomes silent around me.

XIII
Paranoia

I haven't slept properly in five days, not since the paranoia crept in. I see it crawling everywhere I look, just watching me. Sometimes it's hidden in the shadows and sometimes it's standing right in front of me waiting for something to happen. When I lay down and try to sleep it crawls in through the window or up from underneath my bed, and when this happens I wonder if it would eat me or just kill me. This morning it was on the ceiling above my head. I don't think it's the creature itself that terrifies me, it was just like a dog sized ferret, mouth aside, it looked like something that could *maybe* exist. No, what horrifies me to my core, is the knowledge that at any moment, if Locke Dawson decides that I might say something, he could come after me, or my friends, or my family, or anyone in town. Or maybe he wouldn't bother, what would I know, I'm losing my mind after all. We had a chemistry test this week, for the first time in my life, I failed it.

'Come on Dan this isn't necessary' Luke groans.

'You asked for it' he answers sternly.

'That was when I was... You know...I don't even know what to get'

'That's why you've got us here, right Warren? Warren?'

My shoulder is gripped by Dan's strong hand, and my entire body wobbles from his shake. I remember where we are now. Outside the barber, it's after school, that's right, Luke wants a haircut and we told him we'd help him choose something. They look at me like they've seen a ghost, but it's not ghosts they should be worried about.

'Warren, you need some medicine or something' Luke says, looking at me with concern.

'Yeah you look like you might drop dead on us, what's wrong with you?'

159

The beast is behind the two of them, pacing around waiting to strike them from behind. I blink as hard as I can and it's gone.

'Yeah, nah, I feel pretty crook but I'm getting better' I lie, 'Come on Luke let Dan help, he sorted out my hair after all'

'Style advice is my new thing, I've decided' Dan takes a bow.

'I just want something trendy, I've never really chosen my own haircut before'

'Well you can choose today' Dan opens up the door and gestures for us to enter, 'It'll be fine mate I promise, just tell them what you're after'

'Hello, hello!' the barber greets us, I know him, but I can't think of his name right now.

What if Lapdog attacked us right now? What would I do? I'm sure it could if it wanted to, the lab isn't that far away from here. What would I do if it followed me here and attacked my friends? I gasp out loud.

'Warren?' Dan leans over to me, 'Seriously, what's the matter with you?'

We're sitting in the barber's waiting area. Dan is flipping through a gardening magazine. I see Luke in the chair, having his long hair hacked away at by the barber, by the amount that's been chopped away, we've been sitting for a while. Luke must like his haircut so far because he's smiling. No monster here. They're safe. Johnny, that's what the barber's name is.

'What's happening to you?' Dan asks, putting his magazine down in his lap.

'Nothing, why?'

'That's bullshit Warren, you think I can't tell that you're not just sick?'

'I am just sick'

160

'You told us that your meeting with that scientist guy went "okay" but I'm starting to think that's not the case. Tell me what happened?'

I don't think he'd believe me if I told him the truth, Luke might but Dan is far too pragmatic to believe in that sort of thing. Suppose he did though, what would he be able to do about it? I know exactly what he'd do, he'd tell me how he won't let three monsters live near his sister and mother and he'd march to that meadow with bow in hand. I close my eyes, and when I open them again, Lapdog is down by his feet. I'd give anything to go back and unsee what I saw, Dan would never put a burden on someone else, and I won't do it to him today.

'I've been a bit worried about something' I say.

'You're a complete zombie'

'I've been thinking about Elliot' I lie.

It feels terrible to lie to Dan, I feel like one of the people that need to be eliminated.

'You have?'

'Yeah about the whole cult thing' I say quietly.

'Me too mate, it's scary to think about hey?' Dan nods, fervent that I've seen reason, so he thinks.

Am I evil for not filling Dan in? For letting him continue thinking Elliot is the problem. He wants that to be the case so badly, he's so determined to blame the disappearances of three people on his hot-headed little pal. Did he really forget the roar we heard together out in the wilderness?

No, it's not fair for me to silently mock him for not knowing what I know. Locke Dawson and his Lapdog, I saw them, no one else, it's on me to do something. He showed me his lab and told me all his plans, and there wasn't anything I could do for everyone. Maybe I *should* let Dan know, and he can go out to the meadow and take care of them with arrows? Or, maybe I should stop being such a waste of an existence, always begging for purpose while making excuses for the things I couldn't do. I blink and the Lapdog is gone.

'Do you think I could borrow that machete?' I whisper after looking around the barbershop for eavesdroppers.

'What for?' he asks apprehensively, lowering his voice now too.

'I've just been thinking about what you said, about Elliot, I think you're right, it's gotta be him'

Now I'm lying. Dan nods with affirmation.

'So, I've been a bit… paranoid lately, worrying about if one day he or his cult or whoever decides to come after me you know? I'd like to keep something at home for protection'

This feels awful. I want to slap myself back to my senses and tell him I'm lying. He just keeps nodding with what I say.

'Okay, yeah sure'

'I know I won't need it. It's more for the peace of mind, I guess'

'Well if it helps you get back to normal then sure, I'll bring it in tonight for you at work, just keep it in the office'

'Thanks Dan' I fist bump him.

'Alright be honest' Luke says.

I jump at first, heart racing until I realise he's not talking to me. He blushes, as he walks over to us with his hands over his head, we both stand up and he drops his guard. His once long and wild hair is now much shorter and layered. It's such a change, it's going to take some getting used to. I look at it for a moment, and then realise he must have asked for a haircut like Dan's.

'Damn son' Dan studies him, 'We'll need to get you a stick to fend the ladies off I think'

'Shut up' Luke laughs.

'It suits you' I nod.

162

'Hey, you seem cured. You've got some colour in your face now at least' he says to me.

'Do I?'

'He was worried about the E situation, but I've got it sorted' Dan whispers to Luke.

'Ah right, I hope so' Luke says tentatively.

Luke tries to pay the barber when Dan suddenly steps in and hands the man a fifty-dollar note. The barber's name badge says *Jerry*. Jerry not Johnny. My memory is slipping, things are changing around here.

'What are you doing?' Luke asks.

'I've got this one mate'

'Come on stop, you don't have to'

'I know I don't' Dan smiles.

The bell on the door clangs as we step outside. The creature is waiting for us on the road, but I don't need to blink it away anymore, I won't waste any more days praying that it was dream that just doesn't exist. I know it's down there in that basement, I know exactly where it sleeps. Once it sees me looking at it, the thing scurries out of sight, and I let myself smile for the first time in days.

'Thanks for this you guys' Luke says, 'Especially for paying'

'Hey don't mention it, I've got money now' Dan says proudly, 'I'm glad you like it, your parents won't even recognise you'

Luke laughs nervously.

'Alright, I'm gonna walk home and face the music I think'

'Already?' Dan asks.

'Yeah, I'll see you guys at work though, I just want to do something by myself'

'Well okay, we'll see you then Slick' Dan winks. Luke rolls his eyes and turns to me.

'You're still a bit quiet Warren, you sure you're okay?'

'Yeah, I'm good yeah. I was worried about the... *E situation*' I look at Dan, 'But Dan's going to help me out'

'You guys better not be doing anything stupid'

'No, don't worry, Warren just wants to borrow a machete, you know just in case' Dan says, I wish he hadn't.

Luke frowns at us both.

'You know what I'm going to say. You know how I feel about violence'

'It's just for the peace of mind' I add.

'No violence' Dan holds his pinky finger in the air to Luke.

He shouldn't promise that, just in case.

'Oh, well alright then, I'll see you guys later' Luke turns on his heel, then rewinds, 'Unless, you guys want to come over?'

I stop thinking about Locke Dawson and his monster for the first time since I set foot in his lab the other afternoon. Lucas Kawamura inviting us into his home is historic, and I think I've earned a distraction.

'Sure, we've got time before work right Warren?' Dan says.

'Yeah of course, that would be cool Luke'

I think I know why he's doing this, he's afraid of how his dad will react to his new hairstyle, and wants some support there when he gets home today.

'Alright, well let's go' he sighs.

We pile into the Rustmobile and Luke gives Dan the directions to his humble abode. We weave through the neighbourhood for ages, but still he navigates, leading us all the way past the last houses, and further still. After a while of staring out the window at the vacant land, one final house is indeed out here. I guess it isn't that far, Luke's dad makes him walk to and from work after all, but when I get my first good look at the house, it might as well be on a different planet. The house is huge, at least three or four times the size of mine, spacious balconies hang outside the second floor, and a menacing, spiked fence secures the perimeter. Luke's dad must have been one hell of a chef to afford this. Dan parks on the road and the monster watches me from the front porch. I make myself blink it away.

'This is the place' Luke says nervously, hopping out of the car.

'Did we travel to the year three thousand?' Dan says.

I tap Dan on the shoulder when I see Luke turn red.

'I shouldn't be here, it's too rich for my blood, it's bigger than the Young's place' Dan says under his breath to me.

'Come on what are you waiting for?' Luke waves us out.

We follow him out and the automatic gate slides open, granting us passage onto the property. I wonder if it can do that on its own, or if someone inside has to press a button to let us in. The mailbox has a plaque that reads "R. Kullick" planted on the front, does no one else get mail? We remove our shoes at the door at Luke's request, and step into the palace, the ceiling is so high I'd have to stand on Dan's shoulders to touch the roof, the vestibule that we're in is bigger than the laboratory, I wonder how much it costs to set up a laboratory? I wonder how much it costs to own a house with a vestibule?

'I'm home' Luke calls, his voice echoing through the chambers.

'Hello my love' a woman's voice calls from somewhere deep within the house.

Luke leads us through the labyrinth of rooms to where the voice came from. I try not to look in any of the rooms, not wanting to be rude. One room we pass though has a hazy, electronic light coming from it. I steal a peek, and see what must be Robert, sitting in the dark, reclined in an expansive home theatre room, watching some sort of cooking show. The TV is about as big as my bedroom wall, and I can barely make them out, but they're definitely thick, red curtains behind it. They're not like the dirty brown ones that Lapdog hides behind, these are the kind I imagine falling down over a stage at the end of a play while the actors bow out. I can't see his face, or any of his body, he's sunken into a cosy looking arm chair, like the ones the villains have in old spy movies, his back to the rest of the house. All he has exposed is a strapping forearm hanging over the armrest, ending in a large hand gripping the TV remote so tight the plastic might splinter. The chef on the show pounds at a slab of meat with a tenderising mallet. Dan glances sideways at the back of the arm chair with nostrils flared, but we scuttle by before Robert can even notice our presence.

We come to the kitchen and Dan and I are bowled over immediately by the gleam of the chrome and marble. A long, island bench in the centre, with two metres of free space all the way around. Wide, beautiful benches all the way around, stoves, sinks, ovens, fridges. I've never seen something sheen so bright. A short, pretty woman is slicing an eggplant on the island, this must be Luke's mother, since she's in his house, they look almost identical, and she slices vegetables exactly the same way he does.

'Oh wow look at you!' she smiles.

He definitely inherited her smile. She wipes her hands and comes over and pinches his cheeks.

'So very handsome' she fusses.

'I brought some friends over Mum' he says quietly.

'You two must be my boy's friends from work?' she turns to us and hugs us both tight.

Dan's eyes widen and I hear him draw a sharp breath as this woman hugs him, he closes his eyes and hugs her back.

'Guys this is my mother, Katsumi' Luke says.

166

'Luke has told me so much about you! Especially you Warren, I hear you are very good at that silly game Luke always plays'

'Mum!' Luke peeps, embarrassed.

'And how is your poor boss? Send her my best wishes that her partner is found safe soon'

The three of us haven't had much work this week, Wanda has insisted on reopening for the sake of trying to maintain normalcy, but between her helping the police investigate and taking her time to grieve, we've only been in for an hour or two a day.

'We'll pass on the message tonight. It's very nice to meet you, I'm sorry we're unannounced' I say.

'No no, you boys have perfect timing! I was just making a stir fry' she places a hand in the middle of my back, and her other on Dan's in the same place.

Then guides us through to their large kitchen table in the dining room. Luke follows us in and smiles at Dan when he seems confused. Once we're seated, Katsumi leaves and then returns with three bowls balanced on her arm, she places one down in front of each of us and then leaves again, I assume to take some into the theatre room for Robert, but I don't hear him say anything. It has chicken and mushrooms in it, that much I can tell, but before I can ask her what else is in it, I notice she isn't eating any herself, I hope she didn't miss out for our sakes.

'That was incredible' Dan groans.

'Do you want something else? I can cook more, really. It would be no trouble'

'No thank you Mrs Kullick, I couldn't eat anymore even if I tried' I laugh.

She flicks her eyes towards the doorway, then looks down at the ground and smiles thinly.

'Please, you call me Katsumi' she says.

It takes some persuading, but eventually Dan and I managed to convince her to let us help with the dishes at least, although she is very insistent on retrieving Robert's from the theatre room herself though.

'It suits you' she says to Luke, as they dry the plates that Dan and I wash.

'I really like it too' Dan says.

'Your father though, you know he'll have something to say' she says softly, putting down a plate.

'Well, it's my head Mum' Luke scoffs, as he picks her plate back up.

Their resemblance is uncanny when they're side by side, they even stand at the same height. She seems proud of her son, but tentative about her lurking husband, instead she should really be worried about the other things that lurk in Southway. Katsumi looks at Dan and I, and then back at Luke.

'I know it is' she places her hands over his, 'But if he sees you with your new friends and-'

'For fucks sake let him see them!' Luke slams the plate down, but as far as I can tell it doesn't crack.

We all stand stunned in the kitchen, I didn't know Luke could physically be so loud. All four of us can tell that he's gone too far.

'Luke-' Katsumi begins, anxiously.

'I hope you aren't raising your voice at your mother'

The words reverberate through the house, the woken giant. The house falls silent again until his recliner chair clicks back into place. He's standing up. Luke flies out of the kitchen, around the corner and up the stairs, Dan looks at me for guidance, but a shadow falls over his face, and the bulky mass that is Luke's father is standing before us.

'Where is he?' he grunts, flicking his long hair out of his eyes.

'Are you ready to cook my love?' Katsumi clasps his hand, 'These are-'

'I've seen them before, their car almost touched my car' he stares Dan down, just as they did that night Rhonda was taken.

Rhonda was taken, Jesus, somehow, it's even worse to think about knowing the truth. As they say, ignorance is bliss, a luxury I no longer have.

'No, your car almost hit my car' Dan corrects him.

Katsumi grabs Robert's hands together in hers, she kisses them and pulls him to the doorway.

'Here Luke is' she quivers, still holding his hands.

Sure enough, there Luke is, looking up at his dad.

'Were you swearing at your mother?' the father talks down to his son.

'I'm sorry Dad' he says.

I don't like where this is going, Katsumi grabs my hand and tugs me away from him.

'Luke will only be a bit late to work' Katsumi tells me, she grabs Dan on her way past and drags us towards the front door.

'Hey wait!' he protests.

'Luke!' I call.

'Please tell your bosses, um, *boss*, that he will be there shortly and we apologise'

She shoves us out the front door, she goes to shut the door but we both turn and hold it open, tears roll down her face now.

'Mrs Kawamura is everything okay?' Dan begs.

She looks up at him and just shakes her head in dismay, she throws her arms around him and I place a hand on her shoulder.

'Thank you for worrying boys, I promise everything is okay, Robert just hates swearing'

Dan tries to push by her, rolling up his sleeves. I have to hold him back.

'Mrs Kawamura, we can call the police for you' I whisper, looking back into the house behind her.

'No! God no, it isn't like that' she waves her hands frantically and laughs.

We look at each other, both at a loss. There's nothing we can do, we nod together, agreeing to concede.

'Well if you're sure, okay, it was great meeting you Katsumi' I say.

'And thank you for having us, tell Luke we look forward to seeing him later at work'

I nod, although that's a lie, if all goes to plan I won't be at work tonight. She finally closes the door on us, we don't put up a fight, but Dan does suggest scratching Robert's car as we pass it on our way back to the Rustmobile. We sit, but we don't put seatbelts on, and Dan doesn't start the car, we still have half an hour until work. I'm reminded of when we sat in silence when Dan got the speeding fine.

'Nice house, very modest' Dan says, his expression as bland as his attempt at humour.

Locke Dawson's voice plays in my mind. *You must agree, there are people who don't deserve to live, no?*

'Jesus Christ' he holds his face in his hands, 'I know I'm the one telling you not to piss off Elliot, but... this is different mate, we need to... Everything is just getting out of control'

'Let's just get ready for work' I rest my head and close my eyes, 'He'll be alright'

Elliot, Robert, and Locke Dawson, swirl through my mind as the car bumps along, all of them circling around one another. When I open my eyes, we're at my house. I get out and go around to the driver's side window to talk to Dan.

'I'll text Luke' I say.

'Alright, I'll see you at work' he nods.

I turn to my house and walk away, but Dan speaks again.

'Warren, do you think we should have... done something back there?'

'He told us he doesn't hit him' I tell him.

'Did you really believe him when he said that?

'She wanted us to go, what else could we have done?'

'He said he doesn't believe in violence' Dan forcedly laughs.

'But he knows that it exists' I sigh.

We look at the sunset over Southway, the night drawing closer.

'Don't forget that machete tonight Dan'

I go inside to get ready for work. I didn't want to make the same mistake twice and run away from an evil again, but this evening it was out of my control, the other, greater evil sleeping underneath the town, well that ball is in my court now. For the first time in almost a week, Locke's pet isn't following me around, haunting me like a spectre. It's nowhere to be found, because I'm on the front foot, and I've decided that if Locke Dawson wanted to keep his beast protected until it was ready to clone, then he shouldn't have brought it here to me.

XIV
An Evil Place

The winter is well and truly underway now, the cold bringing the rain. As it drizzles down, I cough into my hands. It sounds very forced and quick, that won't cut it. I try again, aiming to make it longer and more painful sounding. This time it just sounds completely fake. I stand out the front of Wanda and Rhonda's and try again and again until I can fake a cough that I think is passable. I find that muffling the sound by covering my mouth helps too, I've told so many lies this week, I let Dan carry on believing that Elliot is a cultist, and now I'm about to call in sick to my grieving boss so I can go and break into a lab. Do we all corrupt in the end?

'Shut up' I say aloud to myself.

No, my little white lies to friends and petty crimes will stop Locke in his tracks, I'm doing this for everybody.

'Okay' I tell myself.

I practice the cough one more time, then rub my hands together and push the door open.

'Wait, how did he climb out of that ravine if he had a broken arm?' I hear Luke ask.

What the hell are they talking about? I head towards the back to see them. Luke stands at the bench, sleeves rolled up while kneading some dough with his hands. Dan sits on the bench behind him, the one with the sink. He should be doing something about the hoard of dishes next to him but instead he holds the large container of sliced olives, chewing on them unapologetically.

'No no, his arm was healed before he went to Antarctica' Dan explains, finishing his olive.

Luke stops kneading and turns around to me, I double-take when he reveals himself. He's perfectly fine. Huh? I'm relieved that he's okay of

172

course, but I had imagined his teeth to be missing and eyes to be blackened, perhaps Robert really isn't one of the monsters here in this town.

'I think if you broke an arm, you wouldn't be climbing out of any ravines for a long time' he says unconvinced, 'Especially not in Antarctica'

'How would you know? You've been to Antarctica, have you?' Dan retorts before throwing an olive up and catching it in his mouth.

'This about Maximillian Murphy?' I cut in, 'The time he explored Antarctica and fell into a ravine and had to climb his way out after not eating for a week?'

They notice me standing by the counter, Dan jumps down and tries to act busy, I just laugh.

'It was actually nine days' he says, mouth still full of olive cud.

'It does sound a bit... Embellished. Is Wanda coming in tonight? I ask them, and execute the perfect fake cough.

'Should be here soon' Luke looks up at the clock on the wall, 'She should just leave it to us'

'Look if she comes in, tell her I'm sorry but I can't work tonight' I say, looking away nervously as I do.

'How come?' Luke asks.

'I think I'm coming down with something' I say, clearing my throat again.

I think I've overdone the coughing, tried too hard. Dan looks at me, draped in doubt.

'Why'd you come in? Why not just call Wanda?' he asks.

I hold my ground, not willing to say anything that might raise any more questions.

173

'Because I had to get that thing from you. Did you bring it?'

'Couldn't it have just waited until after school tomorrow? Go home before you get us sick mate, I'll bring it around after work' he says, placing his olives down on the bench.

'Jesus Christ Daniel did you bring it or not?' I snap.

Luke drops his dough. I didn't mean to raise my voice, and I feel the blood rush to my face, realising my outburst. I've worked myself up for it, tonight's the night. It has to be tonight. I will not spend another night in paranoia and I will not allow that thing to live and be duplicated after what it's brethren have done to Rhonda and the others.

'Yeah mate' Dan nods, 'Yeah I brought it'

He almost looks afraid of me.

'Come on, it's in the car' he heads out the back and waves for me to follow.

Into the cold with the copious amount of moonlight doing nothing for the chill, it does reveal the scorched paint of the Rustmobile, he hasn't parked it very straight. He reaches into the tray and produces a towel. He unwraps it just enough to see the end of its black blade, where it curves into a point at the tip, before concealing it in the cloth again. He holds it out to me and I take it in my hand, I try to take it but I'm met with resistance. Dan looks at me with a grave seriousness I've never seen from him.

'I'm trusting you here' he tells me.

'Yeah, I know, thank you' I nod quickly.

I try to take the towel again but it still won't budge. His hand still holding in place.

'I know you're afraid' he continues, 'But I don't think you're afraid of Elliot'

He waits for me to say something.

174

'I really am' I lie.

We breath steam at each other, the clouds meeting in the middle over the machete as he tightens his grip on it.

'I followed you into the trees when you knew people had gone missing out that way. I don't think you're afraid of much, you want excitement, you're definitely not afraid of Elliot, so tell me the truth here'

I watch him while he accuses me, each of us still slightly pulling the machete towards himself and away from the other. I need to let Dan in on it, I could get him to believe me, I bet he'd even help. Yeah, of course he would. I'm about to open my mouth, when he lets go of the towel.

'Get going, we're about to open up. I'll tell Wanda you caught the plague'

It thumps into my chest without his pull to counteract mine. I hold it in both hands like it's some precious ancestral blade.

'Thank you' I say looking at it.

He turns away back inside.

'Be careful walking home with that, don't let Officer Dickhead see you with it'

'I don't plan on using this you know, I really don't' I tell him.

He stops and rests a hand on the doorframe. He looks back at me over his shoulder.

'I hope not Warren' he exhales, unconvinced.

'I promise you' I nod.

And that's the honest truth. I don't want to use it. I don't even think I'd know how to use it. He vanishes into the kitchen, leaving me with the weapon in the alley. I won't betray his trust. I just need it in case anything… goes wrong. At first, I thought of kicking the door in and slaying the beast, Monster Masher style. But then I stopped to think about just how badly that would go. I'm no fighter, Kevin doesn't count, I've never fought in my life. Even if I did know how to fight, if he found the beast diced to pieces, Locke Dawson would know exactly who was responsible. My plan now is to sneak in, I'll pick the lock like Luke told us how to, and then I'll mess with the machine. Shut it down or tamper with the nutrient levels of the fluid or something, anything to make that abomination choke to death in its jar. Locke will never be the wiser, tomorrow or maybe the next day, his beast will be floating belly up, and he'll just assume that he got the oxygen levels wrong or something. His precious creation gone before he can clone it and his plan foiled. He even said himself he could never make such an obedient creature again. How many lives will be saved by the end of tonight?

Dan clicks the door closed behind him, leaving me in the dingy alleyway with a weapon and an objective. I wish I could have spoken to them both more before leaving, but if I had made a big deal about it then they would have gotten suspicious, maybe that would have been a good thing. I double around from the alley and back around to the front of the restaurant, the lab isn't far away, but I take the long way by walking the way I usually would if I really was heading home, just in case my friends are watching from inside. When I see him next, I have to remember to ask Luke what happened this afternoon.

Detour completed, I make it to that staircase, packed tightly away, no chance of the moon's shimmers reaching down and lighting my way. The darkness is a good thing I suppose, it means Locke isn't inside. I look up and down the street, both ways three times each, checking for watchers, I try to gulp but my throat has become too dry. Should I just leave this one for someone else to handle? The army or something? No, I did nothing this afternoon, and now Luke is wearing my indecision on his face. For years now I've complained that nothing has ever happened to me, but never once have I stood up and made myself happen to something.

Nobody is watching, I drop down the first step and into the stairwell, I pull my phone out of my pocket just enough to use the backlit screen to guide my way. I have a text from Wanda.

Get well soon luv xx

Rhonda and Wanda, I wonder which one taught the other to text? But I ignore that one for now, those are the sorts of things I used to think about? Once there's no more steps left to descend and the door lies in front of me, my fingers peel back the towel and let it drop to the concrete. I hold the machete blade lightly in my hand, taking in a feel for its weight. The timeworn doorknob ticks unsuccessfully as I try to open it. It was worth a shot, but I anticipated as much.

Left to right, that's what he had said to do, it's not a spice cupboard, but I don't see why the principle wouldn't carry over. One hand on the handle and the other carefully on the blade, I slide the pointed tip in and scrape it against the striker plate. I've never done this before, but it's the type of thing you can just feel if you're on the right track, hot or cold. It's not too long until I've slid something inside something else and the door is open at my mercy.

I poke my head in and check all four corners of the room, for any glowing eyes, just in case Locke sleeps in one like a vampire. All clear. I remember where the pull chain that turns the lonely light globe hung from, and feel around for it in the black with my free hand. With the chain pulled, a hazy, ginger light strikes the room and I can confirm that nothing has changed. The curtain is back in place, concealing the monster jar, but other than that, same boxes of paper that I stacked and same old computers. I'm not wasting any more time, I strut across the room and reef that curtain across. Only, it's awake, floating in place, with its back to me, craning its thick neck all the way back over its spine, to look down on me with its round black eyes. Fuck it's terrifying.

'You know, you never will get to see the outside of this room' I tell it, though I'm not sure why.

Finally taking my eyes from it, I turn my attention to its machine. There's all sorts of dangerous looking buttons, none of which have labels. Maybe Locke made this so that nobody but him could use it. The pod isn't quite all the way up against the back wall, and so I pull out my phone light again, and check the back. It's a jungle of thick cords, some plugged into a dozen different wall outlets, and some just plugged into other cords, I don't even know where to begin. The creature slowly swings its neck through the viscous fluid to watch what I'm doing to its electronic tangles. We stare at each other again, as hideous as it is, it doesn't seem angry, it seems worried that I'm a stranger messing with its home. But, that's the design at work I suppose, a placid enough looking creature, until it's dragging you away to eat alive. I look into its black, lifeless eyes, I look until all I know is vengeance for both this thing and its master. Hideous or placid, three lives were snuffed out before they could make their own judgement, and for that it has to die.

Although, this one didn't do anything, Locke said it had never even left this room. Looking at its face, I honestly don't want to do this, it's death will probably be slow and painful, but ending this one now, will be easier than dealing with one in every household in the future.

'I'm sorry' I tell it.

I start tearing at the cords, yanking fistfuls at a time, grunting with the effort and met only with electrical whirs and sparking. From the corner of my eye, I catch it calmly watching me at work, as though it understands why I have to do this. I try not to think about it. Fuck what have I done? These cords need to look like they weren't tampered with. Shit.

Okay, shit. I'll just plug them back in but in the wrong places, surely that will fuck something up, and Locke will probably never check behind here, I hope. Hastily, I click plugs back into sockets, trying my best to insert them wherever looks the least right. The machine begins to buzz and the beast finally looks up. We've both heard this buzz before.

'No' I beg, 'No... No!'

The beast waits at the meniscus of its fluid, the top slowly but surely grinding open. It's like a dog hearing its leash being jingled up the other end of the house. It knows.

'Please' I breathe, shoving cords back into the outlets.

It's too late, the hatch is open and Lapdog crawls up the inside of the glass and slides down the outside. It places a claw on the control panel where red, angry looking lights flash at me, leaving goo over the switches and knobs. I grip the machete tight. No. Looser, like Dan had said that time. Yeah.

It looks lost without its father, bewildered of being let out without Master's approval, scouting around like a periscope. And then it sees me, blade in hand, trying not to cower. I wonder if it recognises me from before, or am I just the same meat as everybody else? It hisses, and then it's on me. I'm on the ground, hurled backwards by its weight. I remember being knocked over by that kid, Kevin? Was that his name? I don't have Dan to bail me out this time.

I stand to my feet, the beast ready to go again already. I hold the machete up across my body, like a knight ready to duel. I have no idea what I'm doing, while this thing was born a killing machine. It leaps again, I hop backwards and then feebly slash at it and miss, making a weak grunt as I do. Lapdog paces towards me so I back away, leading it in circles around the room. Every now and then it lunges and takes a swing with its front feet, and when it does I step back and swipe at its face. This machete and the thing's legs are about the same length, so all we are able to do is keep one another at bay. I need to think.

It hisses, as though growing impatient, as though it expected more of a challenge. You got it. It lunges once again, but this time I don't leap backwards out of its path, I step to the side. Lapdog lands right where I had been standing, right beside where I am now. I grip the machete, and rip it across its hide as hard as I can. I can feel the roughness through the blade as it slices through the fur and into the skin, because though the machete is quite sharp, the hide is leathery under the fleece. Blood flicks off the blade as thin, pale red rain. Lapdog hisses with agony, before it can recover I bring my knee up, and push kick its body away from me as hard as I can. Its weight is immense, especially for the thing's size, and so the kick sends us both flying in opposite directions. I land in the pile of cardboard boxes I had stacked, crushing them, sending loose pages flying throughout the room.

It all happens so fast as the papers shower down around us. Lapdog springs up and lashes out again, all it knows is to frenzy. As it leaps, I aim the tip right at its face. The vile thing weaves its long neck to the side, the tip of the blade passing harmlessly past its head. It slams into me, knocking us both back with its momentum, we slide along the floor together, until I'm underneath it on my back, and it thrashes about with its paws on my chest. My hands grip at its throat just behind its jaw, and instinctively try to strangle. The solid ligaments in its neck pulsate as it bites, never easing up for even a second to let me close its throat, but I continue to hold, if anything just to keep its gnashing teeth off of my face. Long, spindly teeth, they are, I haven't had a chance to study them until now.

Growing frustrated, and desperate for me to give in, Lapdog takes its foot and drills down with its hallux piecing into my left shoulder. The pain shoots from the flesh and down my body, then back up into my brain and out my mouth. Burning throughout my body, my arms staying up God knows how, and then my screaming stops, the pain plateaus, not getting any severer, I've taken its worst. It's still there, the pain, but it's torn its path through my body already, and it can't do any more than that. I let it wash over me. Clear. I still have a weapon somewhere.

I let my right arm drop, leaving only my punctured shoulder to pillar the weight of the beast, the fingers on my good hand feel for the handle on the floor, pulling it from the concrete and into my palm. Just as the weight becomes too much, I bring the machete up across my body as its throat falls onto it. The edge digs into its exposed neck just near the hilt of my tool, the skin much thinner here than on its back, and the blood oozes out in rhythm with what must be its slowing heart. As it pulls its head back to get away from the metal, I run the entire length of the blade across its gullet, sending blood hosing around the lab when it leaps backwards, tearing my flesh as it extracts its claw.

Falling to its back, on the blood-spattered paper and cold concrete, the beast is defeated. It whines and curls itself away, blood still pouring from the wound, I take a moment to sit and keep an eye on it, and let my mind and body rest a moment. Then I vomit.

I feel sorry for the beast, dying trying to execute the duty it was farmed to perform, before it even got a taste of fresh air. Born to serve a mad man, to be cloned until it had an identical baby brother in every household, all waiting for the click of the tongue. This one was surviving off nutrient solution, but it's three relatives must be eating livestock and wild animals, there's no way three things larger than this have survived off of only three humans since Locke migrated here with them. I've just admitted it to myself, haven't I? Those people were eaten.

'I'm sorry' I tell it, 'It had to be this way for you'

I don't know why I'm speaking to this fading abomination.

'But my purpose was to kill you'

I flex my fingers around the machete one more time, I suppose this is much less cruel than what I had planned for it, letting it suffocate and starve in its jar. I ram the tip into the top of its skull. Blood dribbles down my shoulder, the stream wrapping around my bicep and forearm before leaping from my fingertips to the floor. It's bad. Something is burning.

The papers on the ground begin to crumple as though under an immense heat. They crinkle upon themselves until the crimson specks begin to ignite.

'What the fuck?'

Page after page catches fire around me, flames turning them to ash. Eventually, the Lapdog's body combusts, steam hissing out when it escapes from its pores. The pale pool of blood it had died in now coagulated into a thick jam, until the body too, begins to crackle and burn. I turn on my heels as the room begins to ignite around me, the walls and floor about engulf themselves with me inside. I rip the door open, and leap three stairs at a time as the smoke chases me up. When I reach the top and spill out onto the street with my blood-soaked clothes and dozens of questions, Locke Dawson stands waiting for me.

'You've been busy tonight Warren' he says calmly.

He looks past me at the basement, with hands in his pockets, watching the orange glow light up his stairwell as the flames lick through the door below. I don't say anything to him, the fight still pumps through my body though, I completely forget about the blood spilling from my shoulder.

'What do you feel? Right now, tell me' he asks, no trace of anger as he watches it burn.

I squint at him.

'Do you feel proud? Do you feel like you've done something?'

'Yes' I say.

'Well you shouldn't' he sighs, 'You may have locked humanity into the cycle of suffering that I was trying to free us from'

'Killing everyone just because a few people are bad doesn't count as ending suffering, you bastard'

'A few people? Alright then Warren, what proportion of people would have to meet your definition of "bad" for you to agree with me that the world is an evil place?'

He raises his eyebrows waiting for my answer, but I don't have one.

'Ten percent? No, it would have to be much higher than that for the honourable Warren Avery! How about a quarter, what if one in four people in your life met your definition of evil? Would humanity still be salvageable?'

'Yes' I seethe.

'A third? Half? Two thirds? How many bad apples does it take to spoil this bunch?'

Two out of three people... Luke, Dan and I, what if two of us were evil? Who would be the one who was still good I wonder, I don't think it would be me, not anymore. No, it would have to be more than two thirds, it would have to be... Wait, what am I even doing considering this? He smiles from ear to ear, the first genuine smile I've ever seen from him. He knows he's got me thinking.

'I've been on many laps around the Sun Warren, almost seventy of them now. The things I've seen people do to one another, the things they've done to me and I've done to them, there isn't a soul alive that isn't rotten at its core. I didn't decide this overnight, I'm no mad scientist, I've been to so many places and met so many people, and every single one has let their fellow man down'

'You do what you do because you're *disappointed* with the world?' I ask quietly.

He blinks, just once.

'That's right'

'Then you're a pathetic old man, and I'm glad I stopped you tonight. What are you going to do with no Lapdog' I point down the stairs, almost arrogantly.

'Well, this is the first time one has died, so you have my thanks for confirming that they do indeed burn as intended' he says, still calm.

'What does that mean? Why did it catch fire?' I demand.

'I made them in such a way that their blood combusts when it isn't circulating, so their remains would burn along with the surroundings if one was to die, leaving no evidence for vermin to pick at'

'I don't need evidence for the small fry' I growl back, 'I'll just tell everyone about the other three'

His mouth is agape and his eyes are lost in the fading firelight, everything inside his lab almost completely burnt away.

'You saw this tame little thing living in a nutrient solution, and decided it was too scary, you tried to kill it in its sleep and almost lost an arm for your troubles. Do you really think, for even one second, that you could leave a scratch on its three big brothers that I let roam about?'

My face drops, and along with my features, the blade drops from my hands to the bricks too. He's right, it took everything I had physically and mentally, to defeat his most docile of creations.

'You've proven yourself to be twice as brave as I first judged you, but half as intelligent' he takes a step towards me now, 'But you should always take intelligence'

I watch him advance on me but I'm too shaken to move. When he's close enough, he rests a hand on my shoulder, and smiles assuredly.

'The human extinction will carry on without question, albeit we will skip the gentle introduction, the metaphorical toe in the water that was my Lapdog. I don't know what type of man you think I am, but I would have loved to do this quickly, fill the world with wonderful new pets, and then end everything painlessly before we even realise what was happening, honestly, I would have. However, only a fool assumes a plan will go smoothly, and so, I have... certain things in place that can commence the Second Selection'

No, it can't have been for nothing tonight. I finally managed to take a step away from him, duck down to the machete and raise it to his face in one motion, aiming the tip right between his eyes. He ignores the edge and raises an eyebrow at me.

'You are an insane piece of filth, and I can't believe you thought you could convince someone else to help you with this'

'Do you enjoy seeing people at each other's throats over resources? Because that's the world you will inherit. What makes those hopes worth more than those of the maggots and the fleas?'

'Nobody deserves to be eaten alive before they even get chance to change'

He laughs at the sentiment.

'People have had centuries to change Warren, what's going to make them start now? You?'

I take a look at myself. Not standing at six and a half feet tall, no muscles so to speak of, I don't even have eyes that match one another. Far from your movie hero.

'Yes' I say, well aware that it's a lie.

'Well, now who's insane?' he chuckles.

'Three or three hundred, however many you send my way, I'll kill them. I'd love to kill another one' I lie, making an effort to get in his head like he's done to me ever since I met him.

My comment wriggles its way under his skin, mocking his simmering pet down there in the coals he called a lab only fifteen minutes ago, makes his ligaments seize and his mind race. He runs his fingers through his slick hair and breathes with deep frustration, when he removes his hands, his hair falls in shambolic, silver strands over his brow. Taking a deep breath to compose himself, he taps the blade away from his face with his bony knuckles before he steps closer to me again.

'You can rest your arm now, we both know you won't cut me down, not yet. I'm not a spiteful man usually, but tonight you raised a hand against someone who should have been your partner if only you had the stomach to take a look at the world. It's tragic that your potential is going to be wasted because you have delusions of heroes and evils that compel you to side with the cockroaches that we call our species. But I suppose that's my own fault for expecting an open mind to come out of a small town, I should know better by now'

'Holy shit you waste a lot of oxygen' I tell him, refusing to put the blade down.

He grabs the machete suddenly, and my first thought is that he's trying to turn it on me, but the scientist takes the blade gently in his palm and guides it back towards himself, resting it again between his eyes.

'That's clever Warren, good one. I wonder if you'll be making these sorts of remarks when I take everything from you'

And the terrible, emotionless smile he gives in this moment, it turns me immobile once again.

'Now I have a busy night ahead of me, so if you've got the jokes out of your system and said what you needed to say, I suggest that you…'

He cranes his neck down, until his evil face is right in front of mine.

'Run'

And I run.

XV

Into the Night

I tear through the streets, faster than a person has ever moved before, I clutch my cut shoulder and don't dare look back. My heart bounces around between my desperate lungs, but even when they feel like they need to burst to relieve the pressure, I don't stop. My legs carry me away from that lab and into the night, cutting every corner that I can, putting as many turns between me and Locke Dawson as geographically possible. Something hisses at me from an alley, my head whips towards it out of reflex and my legs keep moving forward, tangling and finally giving way. Tearing skin from my elbow and wrist as I skim along the concrete. I can't run any further, I roll over and face the backstreet. It's only a stray cat and it's watching me.

My injuries sting as I probe at them with my hand. My shoulder has bled well into my work shirt, the wound wasn't as deep as it had felt at the time, and it has stopped for the most part. I can't remember a time I've ever bled like this before, a scratch here or there growing up while no doubt doing something stupid with Dan, and even in the recent weeks we've been fishing in the creeks, but nothing like tonight, finally, something that's worth a scar.

A dirty, orange thing, this cat is, it taunts at me again and darts into the gaping mouth of the alley and into the darkness. I'm about to call the cat a name for heckling me, but in the silence of the town, I can hear the footsteps from close by. Instantly, I spring to my feet and run again, and when I get far enough away, I stop to tune in once more, the feet are gone.

'There you are' I hear from behind me.

Spinning around, I'm greeted by the owner of the footsteps. This is the happiest I've ever been to see those woollen tassel things on that damn hat. The zips on Luke's backpack clink against each other when I throw my arms around him, he has to struggle to hold us both upright.

'What are you doing here?' we ask simultaneously.

'Looking for you' he says, 'Holy shit you're all cut up! Is that all blood?'

'It isn't safe here, he'll be coming' I wheeze.

'Who? What's going on? I've been walking around for about an hour and haven't seen anybody, where have you been?'

'You won't believe me'

'You can only try me' he says sitting down and gesturing for me to do the same.

I tell him everything, rattled as I relive it through the words, I describe every detail about Locke and the lab, every curve in the beast's long neck and every move we made as we danced. I list off the events until I catch up to where we are and the words are dried up, and without any more words, Luke and I are just sitting together in an alleyway.

'Alright' he nods, 'I believe you'

I look up, taken aback, and stare into his eyes with gratitude.

'You do? Really?'

'I mean, I'd like to say that stranger things have happened, but… for how strange you've been acting for a while now, it would have to be something *that* strange to make it all add up, you know'

'That strange huh?'

'That's right' he laughs, 'Come on, let's make a move'

He gets up first, then helps me, making sure to raise me by my good arm.

'You're my first real friend Warren, of course I believe you. I have absolutely no idea how to help, but I'm here for you, you know? I think you should stay at my house tonight. I don't know if you should be left alone'

I can't give him my full attention because movement behind him catches my eye. A spider, crawling across an open exhaust vent at the back of one of the shops, desperate to restring its web before the sun rises and the air shreds it apart again. Does it do this every night? Working tirelessly until the dawn comes and everything gets blown away and leaves little eight-legged Sisyphus with nothing to show for it? That's Southway though, one step forward and one step back, but not me, not anymore.

'Okay' I say to Luke.

It's all I *can* say, I'm still out of words for the moment.

'Do your parents think you're at work?' Luke asks once we're walking, 'Don't forget to let them know you won't be home, I don't want them to worry'

'Will when we get to your house' I grunt.

I insist we make a slight detour along the way, the park, the same one Dan and I had sat in when I bought Monster Masher. The three of us have been here before, spending afternoons laying on the grass, smoking a joint if there was no one around, tonight I'm only here briefly, to quickly bury the machete in the reeds by the creek that runs through here. It's not a foolproof hiding place, meaning Officer Dickhead could find it, but it only needs to stay hidden until after school tomorrow, when I can get rid of it properly. Evidence concealed, we reach Luke's magnificent home, there's still light coming from inside.

'Are your folks up?' I ask.

'No'

'But I think I see the TV on in there'

'No one will be awake Warren, trust me'

He takes a small key from between a gap in the bricks, then presses his index finger to his lips. I nod in understanding and he unlocks the door, he thrusts the door open, with a hint of anger it seems. He pushes inside and I follow him, but only after looking around outside one last time for Locke. Hearing the whinging drone of a late-night talk show coming from inside somewhere, I look to Luke for assurance. The sound of the TV is coming from that theatre room. Luke can tell that I'm thinking about it.

'Come on' he whispers.

I do as he says but not before stealing a look inside the room. Sure enough, Robert is asleep, faintly snoring in front of the TV. On the screen one man in a suit talks to another man in a suit, one waves his hands around and the other laughs. Christ, and I thought my life was boring. I can't blame him for getting bored to sleep by that studio swill, but I get the feeling that he spends more nights out here than in a bedroom.

Luke's room is up the stairs, we go through the lavish kitchen I saw earlier today and traverse to the centre of this labyrinth. I pass many closed doors in the corridors, all the same door with the same coloured paint, somehow, I can tell that a lot of them are kept locked. Luke's bedroom is easily twice the size of mine, his bed is probably three times the size of mine and his computer setup is immeasurably bigger than mine. He has three screens, they're curved slightly, arranged in a semi-circle shape. The edges are so thin that you could mistake it for one long curved display. The computer itself looks like a bar fridge, an angular, mechanical looking strongbox, and while I sit in an old creaky office chair, his seat looks like something out of a spaceship, or at least a race car.

'It must be something spectacular, to play Monster Masher on this' I gesture at it all.

I think I've had enough monsters for one lifetime as of tonight. Even though it's off, the equipment flashes with dim lights, they must indicate sleep mode or something, they add a nice light to the room. I'm thankful for it too, I don't think I'd be able to sleep in the dark.

'Do you want to watch something?' Luke asks, 'Might help you sleep?'

He points to a huge TV he has at the foot of his bed, I hadn't even noticed it when I stepped in. I groan as I sit down on the bed, my body aching and my shoulder stinging as I bend. Luke throws the remote down next to me.

'Chuck something on while I get something for that' he points at my shoulder as he steps over me.

The TV blares to life once I hit the power button, the noise sends me into a panic and I scramble to locate the volume down button. Even when the TV is hushed, my heart still races, from the shock of the sound, the loud noise enough to take me back down into the lab. Once things have calmed down for me, I have a look at what's on the screen in front. It's some old movie, a guy with a chiselled jaw and a woman with big breasts and long blonde hair are chained to a rock. Some sort of sorcerer floats over them with glowing hands and a billowing robe, cackling, and with a wave of his hands the room they're in begins to flood. How will they get out of this one? I just turn it off. I quickly text Dad telling him I'll be home after school tomorrow, I know he won't reply this late though.

'Here' Luke steps back inside the room and shakes a bottle at me.

The bottle and some tufts of cotton wool in one hand, and under his other arm he drags a huge mattress along the ground that must weigh more than both of us, he lets it tip over and land flat beside his bed for me.

'Thanks, I'll do it' I say, reaching out for the bottle.

'No, you won't' he scoffs, 'You can't even see where it is'

He dabs the alcohol onto a cotton wool ball, and gestures for me to pull my shirt up to expose the gash.

'This will sting, like, a whole lot'

'Get on with it' I brace.

And it does sting, it burns the wound even worse than it when it was torn open now that I don't have the endorphins coursing through me. But I don't react like I did then, I just let the pain seep in and sit, and then wait for it to pass, now that I know I can handle it.

'Nothing on TV?' he asks as he patches me up.

'No'

'Nothing at all? Not even some soap opera repeats?' he laughs.

I don't laugh though, I look down at the carpet.

190

'I could have killed him tonight Luke' I say.

Luke stops dabbing.

'Probably, but would you?'

'I don't think so'

'That's good then'

He starts to press the cotton wool on my shoulder again.

'But if someone wants to kill other people, they deserve to be killed, don't they?

'Depends what you believe, I don't think so. I don't believe in an eye for an eye, and I don't believe in an eye for seven billion eyes' he laughs.

'Wouldn't it be fourteen billion eyes?' I correct.

He laughs a hearty laugh, then remembers how late in the night it is.

'Glad to see you're feeling like yourself again, smart ass'

'Come on tell me, don't you think there's some people out there who don't deserve to live?' I ask, 'If someone wanted to kill *everybody,* and you had the chance to kill them, wouldn't it be eviller to let them live?'

He stops working on my lesion.

'What do you want me to say Warren? Do you want me to tell you that you would have been right to kill him?'

'No' I scoff.

'*Did* you want to kill him?'

No, of course I didn't, I don't want to take a life, especially not an old man underneath the streetlights. But, Locke Dawson shouldn't be

191

allowed to live that much is certain to me, and that means something has to give, maybe I should have sacrificed my soul to take him down?

'Of course, not' I say, 'I just want to know how to tell who is and isn't. I don't want him to be…right'

Luke stops again, for good this time. He scrunches up the cotton wool and puts it down, then places a patch over my shoulder.

'I guess you can just tell' he smiles, smoothing the patch, 'All done'

I roll my shoulder a few times, it feels better already, or maybe I'm too full of adrenaline to know.

'This is a really good job, where did you learn to do this?'

'Mum' he shrugs.

'I don't know what I'd have done otherwise'

'I mean I'm no doctor, you probably should still go to the hospital, just to get it looked at'

'What would I tell them? I'll just see how it heals for now'

Luke lays down on the bed.

'At least you got that scar you wanted' he chuckles.

'I might have more to come' I sigh.

'Hmm?' Luke sits up slightly.

'He said the extinction will carry on'

'I wouldn't worry about it' he sighs.

'You wouldn't worry about the extinction of the human race?' I choke.

'No, I mean… Look tomorrow there's probably going to be lots of fire fighters and police asking him questions, but think about it, he's not going to tell them anything about you because it would expose what he was up to, and he's not going to come after you as long as you're in public because I'd bet he's going to be extra careful with these other three pets now'

Shit, I had forgotten we still have school tomorrow, I'd left my bag at work the day before.

'Just try to get some sleep Warren, and we'll take each day as it comes and try to keep it as normal as possible'

'Starting with tomorrow'

'Yeah starting tomorrow'

'Thanks, for finding me and you know, patching me up'

'Instead of thanking me, you should be worrying about you're going to tell Dan'

Fuck.

'Try to get some sleep Warren'

And I do sleep. Never for very long, a half hour here and twenty minutes there, spending the time in between just blinking at the ceiling, not feeling afraid, but proud. I have no idea what to tell Dan, but I did it. I did something tonight. I saw the danger and I didn't run away, I saw this town's problem and placed it on my own shoulders. I don't know what will happen to me next but I do know I did the right thing, for everyone, even if it cost me myself. I open my eyes after finally settling into a decent slumber, and instead of the dark, I'm met with the warm sun. A shirt is folded on top of my chest, it's my work uniform, much less red than it was five or so hours ago.

'Good morning' Luke says.

He stands in his wardrobe, already dressed for school, looking for something else.

'Did you wash these for me?'

'Yeah, it's better than what it was at least. Luckily the uniform is dark so you can't see the… you know'

'When did you have time to do this?'

'I saw you finally get to sleep, so I got up and soaked it for you'

'Wow, Luke, you didn't have to do that' I smile.

'Yeah, I did' he laughs, 'What else were you going to wear downstairs? None of my shirts would fit you'

'I guess I didn't think of that' I sigh.

'Wow, usually you think of everything' he pulls a thick coat from the wardrobe and throws it at me, 'But you have had a lot on your mind, here put that on too'

'Why?'

'It wasn't just the blood, there was blood and some uh… Burn holes, on your shirt. Wear that to cover it up. We'll tell Mum and Dad you got the flu or something and were cold and couldn't walk home, and that's why you had to stay here. I don't know, at least it will hide the burns'

I get up from the floor, my arm throbbing at the motion, and pull the shirt on. I can feel the sharp scorch marks scrape against my skin. I pull the winter coat over it, it's a small size, but it's the type you'd wear in the snow, with plenty of other layers underneath, so it fits me fine. I've never seen the snow.

'My bag is at work, I've got my clothes for school in there'

'Alright, go clean up in the bathroom on the left there, and then…' he rolls his eyes, 'Let's get breakfast over and done with'

And he really does need to specify which bathroom. The house is so vacuous, with so many rooms off-shooting from those grand, marble hallways, they could bury a pharaoh somewhere in here and no historian would ever dig them up. On the right, that's what he had said, I slip the handle down and gently push the door and let it swing away from me, but I haven't got the right room.

This room doesn't have any floor furniture, perhaps this is the trend of late. Nothing on the carpet, but three walls are lined with shelves, and carefully arranged on them are framed photographs and certificates. The fourth wall hardly exists, one glass pane, curtained just like the one in the room downstairs, facing out to the east and letting in the sunrise. I step towards the window, I can see it all from up here, all the people and places that I've ever known, together in my field of view from upstairs here, save for Daniel, the Steele farm behind me somewhere. I turn my back on my house and my school to look at these photos. I walk by, hands behind my back taking in each one, I imagine this is what people do in art museums. With each step, Robert shakes the hand of another man in a suit in exchange for another certificate, in each portrait, he's in the same position in front of the same building. As the years go on, the camera quality increases and the colours spring out as though alive, but Robert seems to grow frustrated, or bored. He stops bothering to smile, and the suits he wears become creased like his face is in the present. I reach the corner of this wall, and now his grip on his certificate for the year seems weak, if there was another photo to come, I worry he might drop it altogether, but there is not. There is just another wall, and those same certificates begin, I wonder if he just got bored with it, they're all exactly the same, "Excellence" written in gold, loopy connected letters, only the number of the year changing. I don't think I blame you for wanting a change of pace Robert, but I still blame you for being a dickhead.

'I said on the left, this is the right' Luke says behind me.

I jump when he speaks.

'Uh yeah, no I realised the mistake as soon as I made it'

Luke looks at his dad in the most recent photo, I wonder if he does this often?

'He was popular in Melbourne, your dad'

'He was' Luke agrees.

'Seemed a lot happier back then as well, just quietly'

'He wasn't. Anyway, it's the room across' Luke turns away, 'I'll wait for you at the stairs'

I know better than to make another observation about Robert. I quickly scrub my hands in the sink and splash water over my face. In the mirror, I look like I've aged ten years overnight, creases in my face that were never there, and black bags under my eyes that look somehow even heavier than when I hadn't slept at all. We trudge down the stairs together, listening to the radio whining from the kitchen.

'How's your arm?' he whispers, touching his shoulder to gesture.

I give him the thumbs up before we turn the hall and see Katsumi at the stove top while Robert is reading the paper at the table.

'Good morning Dad, Mum. Warren stayed here tonight I hope that's okay'

'I'm sorry for being unannounced, I was sick after work and I live on the other side of town so…'

'You work at that pizza place, I remember you. What else do you do?' he asks.

'I study' I say, caught off guard.

'Warren is very smart, he recently got a flawless score on their biology exam Dad' Luke says.

He does me the honour of lifting an inquisitive brow at me from across the table.

'Is that true?'

'Yes'

I stare at nothing on the table, I'm so tired that I have to exert force to hold my head up to look at him, he's nodding approvingly at me.

'It's lovely to see you again Warren' Katsumi waddles over in her apron and gives me a hug, 'Sit please, I'll make more'

Luke and I sit at the table, I try not to twist as the pain in my shoulder shoots down my body with every bump.

'You're a sensible one, right? Warren, was it?' Robert watches me over the paper.

'That's right' I extend a hand over the table to shake.

I'm agreeing to what my name is, not that I am in any way sensible. He takes it, though only very reluctantly. Oh yeah, I think you're meant to shake hands standing. Katsumi brings over the food. The strangest looking omelette I've ever seen rests folded over itself before me. At least I think it's an omelette, although it's been rolled and spiralled over itself, all I know is that I want to eat it. Although, I'm so exhausted after the night I had, I'd eat just about anything. She must notice me looking down into the food.

'Tamagoyaki' she smiles.

'Okay wait, don't tell me, "tama" means "egg" and...'

I rack my brain, focussing back to all the nights Luke and I spent scrubbing dishes, but it won't come to me.

'Christ it just means cooked egg' Robert interrupts, 'The other boy though, he your friend?'

I stare back at him.

'Yeah, he is'

'The one with no respect'

We clash over the table without moving or saying anything more. If he thinks I'm going to agree with him, blacken Dan's name and be intimidated from across the table then he's more insane than Locke Dawson. I've decided that the Warren Avery who was afraid to act is gone, scorched away last night, I swear he won't back away when he's needed ever again.

'Wait everyone, what is this?' Katsumi stammers.

She turns the radio up.

'That's right Soph I was indeed on the scene earlier this morning, and the man, only very new to town mind you, uh sixty-seven-year-old Locke Dawson, who had bought the long forgotten downstairs lot agreed to speak with me briefly. Can we play that recording please?'

My insides fight each other for the spot in my throat. The radio clicks as they play it.

'I'm here in the town this morning, the sun has barely come up, and Mr Dawson thank you so much for speaking to us, I understand this has been a heartbreaking morning for you'

'Yes, yes that's right. You know I came to this quiet little town for the change of pace and you never expect anything like this to happen to you, I suppose until it does'

'Now I imagine it's far too early for estimates of the cost of the damage, but as anyone walking by this morning will tell you it appears to be quite extensive?'

'Yes, when I was coming in this morning I was shocked to see the firefighters already there. They did allow me down to have a look but it is safe to say that yes, there is nothing left, the place is gutted'

'Tragic stuff, now what did you have in mind for the place before the disaster struck?'

'I was planning to start my own business and run it from there'

'May we ask what sort of business?'

'Well, it doesn't matter anymore now does it?'

'Now if that wasn't bad enough, tell the viewers Mr Dawson, what happened last night before the fire?'

'I was attacked yes, out on the street right here. I was walking, just enjoying the cool fresh air after being down there all night and all of a sudden I have a blade aimed at my neck'

Luke looks at me with questions, and Robert notices his son's eyes move.

198

'Unbelievable, my deepest condolences, you escaped without injury though correct? Physical at least'

'That's right thank God. No injuries but I was threatened with, oh I'm not sure, some sort of blade? It had an orange handle I could see that much'

'Could you see the assailant's face?'

I hold my breath. I want to pray, but I wouldn't even know where to start with that sort of thing. Someone get me some rosary or holy water or anything. About average height and build, brown hair, one blue eye and the other green. There's no doubt about it, one Warren Kenneth Avery, hoodlum and assailant.

'No. Unfortunately it was far too dark to see'

What?

'Did they rob you? Did they say anything at all?'

'Nothing other than they were unhappy with my being here, that much they made crystal clear'

'Is there any chance that this goon came back in the early hours and set fire to your shop?'

'Like I said. It's all very hazy. That will be up to the authorities to deduce, far smarter men than I'

'Fair enough Mr Dawson I'd hate to pry any more in your moment of shock, but have said authorities determined the cause of the fire as of this time at least?'

'Not that they've told me yet no, but the cause isn't important as far as I'm concerned. It's happened and now I just need to spend today taking my next steps forward to moving on'

'A very wise and mature perspective Mr Dawson and I'd hate to take up any more of your time this morning with so much on your mind. Thank you very much for speaking to us'

'And the same to you, thank you very much'

The line crackles back to the studio.

'Absolutely heartbreaking Jim'

'I tell you what, it was Sophie. Such a dignified man, and this happens to him'

'Well I just hope it wasn't deliberate'

'With everything going on in this town these days Soph who knows. If you ask my opinion, I'd say it's a safe bet that whoever attacked Mr Dawson here also attacked those others. It's plain as day, put it in the books as far as I'm concerned'

'While we wait for an update on that one, we remind everyone to stay safe, and if anyone has any information to please-'

Robert gets up and turns it off himself.

'And there you have it' he throws the newspaper down on the table.

We all look at him confused.

'Well that was your friend' he lets me know.

Rage and guilt build inside me.

'How do you know that?'

'Because he's trouble. I notice he didn't tag along here... *This time*' he sneers at Luke, no doubt nodding to yesterday afternoon, 'That makes four people attacked now, Jesus Christ why did I have to pick this God forsaken place?'

'If this was the same person who kidnapped the first three people, why did this old man get off with a warning? Surely a sixty-seven-year-old wouldn't be a problem'

He relaxes his fingers to tilt the paper down and look at me over the top of the pages.

'Well aren't you sharp'

He flicks his paper back up, still speaking but without looking.

> 'Just a word of advice, feel free to leave it. But a certain type of people just draw trouble in and spit it back out at everybody else. You seem to have your head screwed on, you don't want to be with people like that'

He's right, a certain type of people *do* draw in trouble.

> 'Go on, don't be late for school, you two' he nods sideways at the doorway.

> 'I left my bag at work, we have to get it on the way' I tell them, 'We should go'

> 'Alright, see you later, Mum, Dad' Luke nods, unable to leave the table quick enough.

> 'Thank you for letting me stay the night' I tell his parents.

> 'Anytime Warren' Katsumi bows, 'Oh my God I can't believe you walked home last night. You boys just be careful for me on the way'

> 'It's broad daylight for Christ's sake' Robert grunts, 'And there will be cops all over the place. Whoever it was, they won't be a problem today. Although attacking the elderly like that, you're hardly a person at all. They'll be locked up soon, hopefully worse'

He picks the paper back up and aggressively turns the page, hiding his face from mine. I feel like he was talking at me. No, I must be imagining that.

XVI
The Breaking of
Elliot Young

Although I scrubbed as hard as I could, I was unable to remove all the grime from under my fingernails, all ten still encrusted with a thick layer of filth, I have to cross my arms to hide them. Luke and I sit in the courtyard, in the same spot I was sitting that day, slimy bricks underneath the shady tree, away from the students talking in their packs under the sun before the first bell. This day is just beginning, I can tell.

'How are you feeling?'

'Like shit'

Luke pulls a wrapped-up slice of pizza from his bag, must have been from work last night.

'You want it?'

'I'm not hungry Luke, thanks though'

'I made it' he tries to tempt me, 'It's...'

I don't have to decline again because he doesn't finish speaking. We both see the vehemence in human form that is Daniel Steele, walking towards us from the other side of the courtyard, no doubt with more than a few choice words for me.

'You heard the news then?' I ask when he's close enough.

But instead of using his words to respond, he uses his hands to slam me back into the tree.

'What the fuck did you do Warren!?' Dan spits under his breath.

A few people notice us, Elliot included, he springs up from his bench to follow Dan, excited I'm sure, at the thought of me being beaten.

'Dan calm down, people are listening' I hush.

'Do you think this is a joke? Because it fucking isn't'

'I need you to listen, let's go somewhere else and we'll fill you in'

'You don't believe this shit, do you?' Dan turns to him.

'You need to hear this out' he says quietly, looking up at him.

'For fuck's sake Warren, I knew I shouldn't have trusted you'

And that hurts more than having a claw slice into my muscles and having ethanol drizzled into the open puncture. Elliot catches up to us just in time to see my eyes grow moist at Dan's disappointment in me. He looks at me from behind Dan, his supercilious grin visible to me over my friend's shoulder.

'You know what Dan?' I stand up, 'Fuck you then'

I must say it loudly because people in the courtyard turn to us.

'What did you say?' he scowls.

'Fuck you. You were so fucking sure that this prick was a cultist' I point at Elliot, 'Now you turn on me?'

'Warren calm down' Luke stands up.

'Don't interfere, let them have at it!' Elliot grabs Luke's arm.

I grab Elliot's other arm.

'Don't you touch him' I command.

The tension now festering between all four of us, Dan being the only one willing to break it.

'Was it you, Warren?' he asks calmly.

'Are you joking?' I chide.

'Did you kill those people?'

'No, I didn't kill those fucking people! Nice of you to accuse someone you called your brother'

'But you attacked that old man last night' he says

'I didn't attack any old man!'

Furious and frustrated, I let go of Elliot and push Dan in the chest. The crowd's communal voice shifts its pitch up, their surprised song fluctuating, secretly hoping we come to blows, I know it. People can't help but stare at conflict, that's just how people are. He shoves me back, I forgot he's much stronger.

'Wait you guys' Luke says, Elliot still holding him back.

Down on the floor where he sent me, I pull my collar back to show Dan the bandage on my shoulder, where the Lapdog had sunk its fingers into my flesh.

'Do you think I'm lying?' I start to peel the bandage away.

'Guys, can you hear that?' Luke breaks away from Elliot.

A familiar howl bellows around the corridors.

'What the fuck?' says Elliot.

'That's it… The one we heard' Dan looks around.

I flick my eyes around too, a girl screams and points to the rooftop, she screams and points because a beast is perched on the roof tiles. It's big, bigger than the Lapdog, about waist height to a person I estimate from down here on the earth. A shorter neck, and shaggier fur, especially around its legs, but otherwise very similar to the wretched thing from last night. One of the three others, it has to be, the way it's claws dig into the shingles causing them to crack, it's identical to how the little one had etched the laboratory floor. People begin to shove at each other around the hallway entrances like penned cattle, this shouldn't be happening, Locke shouldn't have sent another one so soon, Luke had assured me he wouldn't. Although, that's forgetting that Locke is the most intelligent and ruthless person I've ever heard of, and he would know that I'd be exhausted, traumatised, and defenceless. At least it's still early, so not everyone is here.

'That's the noise…' Dan repeats to himself.

He doesn't look surprised or even scared, he just stares vacantly at the fiend. It looks down into the courtyard at everybody, searching, no doubt searching for me. It steps forward, loosening the tiles under its feet and sending them sliding down the slope and catching in the gutter, until they fall to the ground when the beast rests a foot on the tin and the whole thing collapses. It tumbles to the floor with the guttering and the bricks, the fall into the courtyard doesn't faze it in the slightest, it rolls to its feet and stretches it neck up high so its hollow eyes can scan the area for me.

The four of us can only stare at it, Luke has had a quick rundown, but only I really understand why this is happening to our school. The screaming around us has ceased now, everyone has either shuffled away discretely, or are in shock and unable to flee, everyone afraid to speak and risk drawing attention to themselves.

'Let's try to get out of here' Luke says quietly, not taking his eyes off it.

I'm not going anywhere, this is my fault. I have to do something. I shake my head at him.

'Warren' Luke says, 'Then let me help you'

'No' I say immediately, 'This is my problem, you guys get everyone out'

'Trust me' he says as he backs away.

Luke keeps his eyes up at the roof and pivots carefully into the corridor and out of its sight, I try to grab his wrist but he slips away from me. The beast doesn't pounce on him, it doesn't even notice him leave. Whatever he's doing, I hope he's thought it through.

'Dan? Dan!' I whisper and shake him gently.

He doesn't respond. I slap him across the face, hard enough to bring him back, soft enough to not alert anything.

'You were right' he whispers.

'I need you to get everyone out of the courtyard' I tell him.

'You were telling the truth and I didn't believe you' tears form in his eyes.

'Yeah don't worry about it' I click my fingers in front of his face 'It doesn't matter now, just get all these people out of here, move slowly'

'What are you going to do?'

'Just go, I trust you, I know you can do it, you always protect people remember?' I nod at him, 'You help everyone'

He nods back, and slowly backs away towards a group of younger students who are staring up in horror. Elliot has been fixated on the rooftop this whole time, almost impressed.

'What were you guys talking about?' he asks.

'You get out of here as well' I tell him.

'No, tell me what you three know'

'Elliot shut up, now!' I hiss under my breath at him.

'I just heard you! You told the Asian kid that it was your problem!'

I look back at the beast to make sure, it's found me. Time to think. It lowers its head and takes a careful first few steps toward us, the section of guttering crumpled around one of its hind legs from where the creature landed on it. Frustrated, the creature shakes its leg, and when the clanging metal strip won't easily release, it bucks through a window pane behind it. The glass blaring as it splinters, the sound causes several people to scream. I finally take my eyes away just to check how Dan is going, he's almost finished guiding everyone away. I knew he would.

'Hey!' Elliot nudges me.

When I turn back, the brute charges at us to pounce. Lapdog ferreted about its small home, but this one has enough muscle and space between us to stride up into a sort of gallop. I shove Elliot back as hard as I can, sending us both falling down in opposite directions, myself towards the bricks where we were this morning, and him towards the heart of the courtyard. The beast rams harmlessly through the space where we were standing half a second ago.

'Leave!' I call to him.

It looks between us, unable to decide or maybe unable to tell which one of us is me. Actually, how could it even know which one is me? It growls at Elliot out in the open, seemingly having made its decision. I don't think it was sent here to take vengeance on me anymore, I think it was sent here to start tearing people limb from limb, and begin the, what was it… The Second Selection?

The brick. I know exactly which one it is, I wobble it loose and clutch it in my hand, green lichens and worms drip down my hand as I raise it, ready to fight. By the time I turn back around, it has Elliot pinned to the floor just like Lapdog did to me, that technique must have been passed down the generations. Stand over their victim, dig the claws in to lock them down, helpless to the craning jaws that can then bite down. I have your number.

I lunge toward the monster and bring the block down across its head as hard as I can. It skips away to recuperate, giving Elliot a chance to get to his feet, it looks like it didn't get to pierce him luckily, Lapdog was enough to almost make me black out from the pain, the weight of this one would make your nerve endings explode.

Dan has done it, everybody has disappeared now, either hiding in classrooms or fled the school completely, opening up the battlefield nicely for us. The mongrel watches Elliot and I, standing side by side, processing who is who, which one was about to be its next meal and which one clubbed it over the skull. I prod Elliot with the brick.

'When it goes for me, hit it as hard as you can' I whisper to him.

'What?'

'Take the brick' I press it against his hand. He accepts it.

'Why are you whispering?' he asks.

'In case it can understand people'

'Why would you think it can understand people? You know more than you're letting on Fuck Eyes, did you bring this here?'

'This, really isn't the time, ready?' I ask.

I run to the right, but I'm tripped over, by Elliot's extended leg. I fall face down into the lawn, and roll over as quickly as I can, but it's on top of me. Its hulking frame pinning me down, it lightly drags its index finger over my stomach, until it locates my shoulder wound from last night, and I swear, I can see its vertical mouth smile. Much bigger than Lapdog's, this nail tears the old wound wider and deeper. I scream out in pain. Elliot stands behind the beast, watching. He tosses the brick aside, and hurries away. My body is on fire, burning up and down, no screaming is enough to release the pressure this time. I can't see or hear anything through the pain, until a familiar voice breaks though to me.

'Warren!' Luke calls.

The claw leaves my flesh, the beast withdrawing as Luke stabs its hide with a long kitchen knife, then with both hands on the handle, yanks it back with enough force to pull Locke's creation off of me. Am I hallucinating? No, he pulls me up and hands me a knife of my own.

'Told you I'd be back' he says, 'I just had to pick up a few things from cooking'

'Thank you' I say, 'Did you see Elliot?'

'No, why? Come on, we have to do this now!'

208

Armed with a dagger each, we square up to the lacerated beast, the blow to the head mustn't have done much, and Luke's slice isn't deep because it isn't discharging much blood. Lapdog bled like a pig, this one is so much more durable. Locke Dawson truly can make killing machines. But we can out think them.

'Stabbing was good. And stay in close to it' I grimace.

'Alright' Luke breathes, 'Okay'

It springs, but instead of shoving us both back like I did with Elliot, I step back at the last second. It swipes downward, claws sinking deep into the soft dirt, I plunge the knife down on its exposed neck. It hisses in pain, and pulls away to thrash in pain, knife still implanted. In its rampage, it charges into Luke, throwing him back. It follows up with its go-to move, its bread and butter, and pins him down. Luke slides his knife along the wet grass towards me. I see what he's going for.

I grab the knife and charge towards them. With great effort, I bring my leg up, and stomp the embedded knife further down into the fiend's neck. The knife slides in deeper until the handle is inside its throat. It howls and keels over to its back, scratching urgently at its haemorrhaging neck, the underside of the head wide open for me to bring Luke's knife down, through the tongue, roof of the mouth, and what I assume, is a brain. Dead. Grabbing Luke's wrists, I sit him upright and pat his thumping chest with respect for my little brother.

'We got him Luke, just like Monster Masher hey?' I laugh.

He nods at me, the colour returning to his face, and together we sit and stare what we've done until the burning starts. The damp lawn refusing to let the corpse combust like it did last night, instead it sizzles as it evaporates, eventually smouldering the flesh and bone away, until two knives can be seen, glinting in mess.

The silence brings petrified but curious students and staff out from their foxholes, they circle around us, giving the burning beast an audience. Once they realise the sizzling heap of charred meat is the same thing that mounted the school just minutes ago, the crowd then checks on the two of us. Dan bursts through the mob and drops to his knees beside us, hugging us both. It hurts my shoulder when he presses himself against it, and when he does release us, he's wearing my blood like an apron.

'You did it' he says, 'You guys really did it'

   The school cheers for us, every single person here is animated, rallying for the two of us. Have they put it together? Missing people and giant quadruped with blades for hands? Do they think this is the end of it? This is the first day of the rest of my life.

   'Stop!'

Parting the crowd with his hands, Elliot, the spineless rat, has crawled back out from his hovel.

   'Stop! Stop it!' he bellows at them waving his arms and making his way into the centre.

Everyone else falls silent for him.

   'Don't applaud this, it was his fault!' he points at me, 'I heard him say that it was his problem'

He isn't wrong.

   'Are you for real? They saved your miserable life' Dan steps forward.

   'These two as well! All three of them worked for that lady who went missing!' he says, desperate.

   'Don't start mate' Dan stares him down ruthlessly.

   'Don't *you* even start' Elliot turns and faces him, red in the face, 'After everything that I've done for you'

Dan narrows his eyes.

   'You can shut up now Elliot'

   'No, I gave you everything, and you spend a few weeks with these losers and you throw it away. He already had a bandage on, I saw it, what would *he* have a bandage from? He's involved, I'm telling you'

210

'Don't talk about them, talk about me, what exactly have you done for me?'

'Oh, I'm sorry' Elliot says sarcastically, 'I forgot how much you love Fuck Eyes and this little Chinese kid now'

When he says this, Dan stands to face him, so close that their foreheads must be touching. The audience wouldn't be able to hear him, because now he sibilates into Elliot's face.

'If you open your mouth again' Dan tells him plainly, 'I'll break your teeth from your mouth'

And his mouth does open.

'Your parents-'

But it doesn't get to open all the way. Elliot's nose cracks under the force exerted by the fist. He stumbles back, but manages to barely stay standing on his feet. He wipes the blood from his nose, onto his wrist, and looks at it for quite some time.

'I see, that's how it will be' he says to himself, deranged.

Dan advances towards him. I get up to grab him, but pain shoots through my body and brings me back down. Dan belts him again, this time knocking him to the ground. He kneels down over him and takes hold of his scarf, and beats him again. Years of ire teeming from his hands, finally being released at their source. Over and over, his fists collide with Elliot's face, everybody watches but no one speaks a word, not even the teachers, no one can look away. I thought this would be something I'd love to see, someone getting their just desserts, tasting their own medicine, but I don't like watching the blood flick from his fists when they swing. Why are we all like this?

'Please stop' Elliot begs through his swollen, split lips.

I cast the pain to the side and stand up to stop him.

'He's had enough man' I say, pulling Dan back.

Dan falls onto his back and brings me down with him. Elliot stands up like a newborn foal and runs his fingers over his mutilated face. His profile that was handsome when he woke up now beaten purple, covered in his own blood drawn by his most loyal servant. Surrounded by a horde of people that are either glad to see him crushed, or just don't care, he begins to laugh, broken.

'You've done it now Danny' blood spills from his mouth as he cackles, 'All three of you will regret it, you will. You'll regret everything Fuck Eyes'

He clutches at his hair as if it's on fire, unhinged.

'Calm down son, we're all shaken right now'

It's McGovern, his usually stern voice is soft this morning. He's scared, maybe from the beast we all just saw.

'Don't you touch me either' Elliot screams.

'We all have a lot to take in' McGovern steps towards him.

Elliot cowers away, blue scarf flowing like ribbon behind him, speckled with red from the blood it's soaked up.

'Can you really not see that this is Warren's fault?' he laughs, 'Are you all really that dumb?'

'Someone grab him, he needs help' McGovern says.

This makes Elliot run. He runs back past Luke, Dan and I, and out through the school. From down the hallway I hear his voice echoing as he hoots.

'I'll be back to get you Warren! I'll get you back' the voice mimics with glee.

The echo subsides, he's long gone. I don't know where he's running to, maybe he's going to get a weapon and come back? Finally having a chance to rest my arms down, blood immediately trickles down past my elbow and off the end of my fingertips. I'm feeling dizzy.

212

'Lord help us' I hear McGovern say, 'Alright, school is cancelled. Until further notice. I... Jesus, I need time to think'

McGovern retreats, I suppose to his office, no doubt he has some phone calls to make. Dan stands up to speak to everyone. He looks like a new man, fresh-faced and optimistic, like I remember him being as a child, a weight off his shoulders.

'It's over, the cause of the disappearances, was that thing' he looks at the smouldering pile, 'I don't think anyone doubts that. But it's over now, thanks to my friends here'

He turns to face us, Luke stands to join him, and gives me a hand up on his way over to Dan.

'Thanks to their quick thinking, we're all safe now'

Everyone cheers and applauds. I'm too woozy to speak up. Dan puts my arm around his shoulder to help me stand up.

'Warren and I, we actually heard that thing, and I was quick to brush it off, but he-'

'Dan' I groan, blood running down my arm.

'Shit dude you're bleeding bad' Dan props me up, 'You need to get to the hospital. Hey!'

I try to tell Dan that there's still two more out there, but my mouth releases no sound. My knees give way, and I'm out before my body even hits the grass.

XVII
Recovery

When I open my eyes I'm in a hospital bed, Luke and Dan sitting beside me on green plastic chairs, looking incredibly out of place in the sterile whiteness of this box. Luke reads a magazine while playing with the hangings of his hat, Dan taps on his phone, and rhythmically shakes his foot bent over his knee.

'Don't you guys have anything better to do?' I ask, pulling the stiff, tight hospital blanket sheet off me so I can breathe.

My voice catches them off guard, causing them to both look up from whatever they were reading.

'Good evening' Luke smiles, 'How do you feel?'

'Fine, shoulder hurts but otherwise fine'

I'm in a baggy black shirt that I definitely don't own.

'Is this yours?' I ask Dan.

'Yeah I brought you some shirts'

'He went overboard, considering you're only here for one afternoon' Luke laughs.

'What time is it?' I ask.

'About six, you slept all day' Luke checks the time on his phone.

'Did I need a blood transfusion?'

'No, you just passed out from the pain they said, you got stitched up and they let you rest' Luke explains.

I tap my shoulder, now professionally dressed and itchy now that I'm aware of the stitches.

'Yeah turns out you didn't actually lose too much blood, no arteries, something about capillaries, I don't know' Dan sighs.

'People are here to see you' Luke says.

'Who?'

'I'll get your mum and dad first' Luke suggests, leaving the room.

'They're here?' I ask.

'What kind of question is that?' he asks, 'What kind of parents wouldn't be here?'

Luke comes back with my mother and father. Mum has been crying. They run over to me and give me a hug.

'Hey Dad, hey Mum' I say.

'Warren, thank God' Dad says.

Mum grabs me by the face and looks into my mismatched eyes, checking deep into each one, making sure I'm still inside.

'It wasn't that bad, just stitches' I tell them, 'Oh, you guys know Dan but you haven't met Luke'

'We've gotten to know him quite well today' Mum smiles.

'We met here when we got the call, all of us went out for lunch once the doctors said you were just sleeping' Dad explains.

'That's good'

'Jesus, I can't believe it, that a wild dog appeared at the school, they say it was huge' Dad sits down on the end of my bed.

A wild dog, was it? It sure didn't look that way up close, but what else can you expect people to call that.

'They're calling it a feral dog until they can work out what animal it was' Luke add quickly.

'Ah, I see' I nod knowingly at him.

'And our boy fought it off!' Mum hugs me again.

'It was mostly Luke' I say, 'Wait, where are your parents?'

'They were here, they came to lunch with us' he explains, 'Mum wanted me to come home, but I wanted to be here when you woke up'

'Warren is very lucky to have friends looking out for him like you two' Dad nods at Luke.

I don't understand why they're acting like this is over and we saved the day, I still have so many questions.

'So, what's happening?' I ask, looking at each of them.

'What do you mean?' Dad asks.

'I mean, what's everyone saying? What are they doing?' I look outside the window, already twilight.

'Well Sophie and Jim wanted to get you on The Chatter, but we told them you could do it tomorrow when you're awake'

'Ugh I hate those two' I groan, 'I think I'd rather be dead'

'Warren! You… You shouldn't joke about things like that' Dad scorns.

'As for the townsfolk, I don't know' Mum shakes her head, 'School has been indefinitely cancelled, understandably, I feel for your poor principal. No one else was hurt physically, but mentally…'

'Police officers running around like crazy, that arson and a man attacked last night and now another missing person to worry about' Dad sighs.

'What happened to…him?' I ask, specifically at Dan.

He's been quiet this whole time, and he doesn't start up yet, chained to his phone and caged away in his mind.

'They're looking, but no luck, they expect him to turn up by tomorrow though' Mum says.

'They're saying he had some sort of breakdown from the sight of the… dog, and then the altercation with this brawler here' Dad laughs, placing a hand on Dan's shoulder.

'Dan?' I demand his attention, 'Are you in trouble? You beat him pretty bad…'

'No one's asked me about it yet, I don't imagine anyone will kick up a fuss' he shrugs.

That's not good enough of an answer for me, but I want to talk to him in private about this, remind him who he is.

'There's some other people out here who want to see you, your boss is out here and some other people who didn't have much to say' Mum says, 'We'll wait outside and after you're done we can get you released'

I never noticed it until now, maybe it's only because I've seen some not-so-caring parents lately, but my mum and dad are pretty cool, I'm lucky to have them, and I feel terrible that I've ever thought for a second that they didn't care about me.

'Hey Mum you guys don't need to hang around, is it alright if the three of us walk after I get discharged? I just want to stretch my legs and get some air'

Mum and Dad look at each other, unsure at first, but then they look at the other two boys in the room, and accept that I'm in good hands.

'Sure Warren' Dad smiles, 'We'll get some food started at home then so don't be long. Daniel, Lucas, you'll both join us, won't you?'

'Sure, Ken' Dan nods.

'Yes please' Luke smiles.

'See you then boys, don't be late!'

They stand and walk towards the door.

'I love you guys' I call to them.

It feels odd, I haven't said that in a long time. They look at each other again, this time in surprise, then turn back to me.

'And we love you too' Mum says.

'And we're proud of you son' Dad adds.

They gently push the door closed behind them, it doesn't click closed and slides ajar immediately.

'Wholesome' Luke says.

'I'll go get Wanda I guess' Dan stands up and stretches.

I stare at his back as he walks to the door, I can't help but look at him in a new light now, who was he helping by hammering down on someone begging for mercy I wonder?

'And you're all good?' I ask Luke.

'Not a scratch on me' he beams.

Dan reappears in the door frame with a crying Wanda, she's a wreck. He soothingly holds her arm, guiding her when suddenly, a man and woman push by them into my room, both with long trench coats and expensive looking sunglasses hiding their faces, despite being indoors.

'You wait' the man stares down to Dan and Wanda.

'Leave, we won't be long' the woman orders Luke.

After studying them, these people aren't dangerous, they're troubled, I nod for Luke to oblige, there's no reason for fear. Once it's just the three of us in the room, the man closes the door.

'Hi' I say coldly.

'Hello Warren' the man says.

'Who are you?'

'Arthur Young' he offers a handshake. I reluctantly accept.

'Caroline Young' the woman does the same.

Aristocratic language, designer shades, black hair, talking to others like gravel, wouldn't need a DNA test to work out that these are Elliot's parents.

'What can I help you with?' although I know why they're here, to accuse me of making Elliot run away.

They both remove their sunglasses to reveal four red, bloodshot eyes, sunken deep into creased hollows in their faces.

'Please' Caroline says, 'Tell us anything you know about where our Elliot might have gone'

I'm not sure what I feel. Not quite guilt, I didn't send their son away, that same son who threw his leg out and left met to die, even after that, I didn't hold him to the ground and beat him like an ape. I just feel heavy.

'I'm sorry, I honestly don't know where he went'

'Do you have any idea? No matter how farfetched? Please' Arthur begs.

I debate with myself whether to tell them how their son left me to be eaten alive. A cruel part of me wants to let them know that their son is a ruthless coward, but I think of my parents, and suddenly I don't see a high born, arrogant family anymore, I see two desperate parents looking for their child.

'The... wild dog appeared and jumped at Elliot and I, we fought it off and killed it, but your son had some sort of breakdown, and got into a fight with Daniel, he lost and ran away. Our Principal tried talking to him but he didn't say where he was going' I say, almost the entire truth.

I don't have the heart to tell them how their son ran away cackling about revenge like a maniac.

'I see' Caroline says, she begins to weep fresh tears, Arthur holds her tight.

'It's okay dear, the police are searching' he says, then turns to me, 'Thank you Warren'

'I wish I could help more, I'm really sorry' I hold out my palms.

'We appreciate that' Caroline says, calming down in Arthur's chest.

'But I don't know why you think I might know something about where he went, your son and I don't speak much'

They look at me like I've started to speak in tongues.

'Elliot often spoke highly of you' Arthur says.

What?

'He did?' I say out loud, I try not to sound audibly shocked.

'All the time. He spoke about how intelligent you were, how dedicated'

'We have had success investing in several scientific firms' Caroline says.

That explains the gross wealth, but why do I care where they pulled the riches from?

> 'It's the way of the future as you know' Arthur says, 'We always wanted our sons to find success in the sciences. Our first born, Arthur Jr… he didn't have much interest, he found success in other paths, and we haven't seen him for almost four years now'

> 'Five' Caroline corrects, misty eyed.

> 'Is it five years now since Arthur moved away?

She has to hold up the digits on her hand, unable to repeat herself. Five years is a long time to not see your kid, even if he'd be well into his twenties now, I wonder why he hasn't come back from wherever he went to see them. Arthur holds his fingers charily to his mouth, trying not to sob.

> 'Would you blame us Warren? The pressure we put our boy under, did we do this to him? The stress would make him angry, but do you know what I'd tell myself to get to sleep at night? I'd tell myself, "We're not chaining him down and forcing him to work so hard", but I knew exactly what we were doing to him. Constantly comparing him to our first-born, making seven figures by age twenty-three, rising above any peer that stated to even get close to him. We'd never tell Elliot he had to be like that, but we would make sure he was aware of his brother's success, and that we expected nothing less. Did we do it Warren? Did we break our own son?'

In the last week or so, I've had more to take in than the first seventeen years of my whole life. I used to think life was uncertain, Locke Dawson told me it wasn't worth living, but now I know it's just… So fucking complicated.

> 'You didn't mean for this to happen, when he turns up, maybe just make sure he knows that you're proud of him. I don't know, I'm not a parent'

> 'Elliot would study so hard, he would always say how badly he wanted to out do you' Arthur smiles, a tear rolling down his cheekbone.

'If nothing else, thank you for being a positive influence on him, you two must be quite the pair of friendly rivals' Caroline adds.

If he wanted to be rivals, he sure has never made it feel that way.

'I'm sorry' is all I can say, I won't lie to them.

'Well in any case, we apologise for intruding, we just...'

'No, I understand' I assure them.

'Come along Arthur, let's let Warren see the lady now. It's been a pleasure Warren'

Caroline smiles, and the two hold each other close as they walk out of my hospital room. Once they've gone, Dan brings Wanda in, she seems to have composed herself better now.

'Hey boss' I smile.

'It's good to see you awake Warren' her voice breaks and she has to cough it clear.

Dan guides her over to the side of my bed, then sticks his head outside into the hall and waves Luke back in.

'I won't take up much of your time' she says, 'I just had to thank you'

'Thank me?'

'The thing you killed today, it was the thing that took those people, that took Rhonda from me. Don't you think so?'

All three of them look at me, awaiting an answer but honestly, I'm not sure. There are still two out of four out there and today's main event wasn't *that* much bigger than Lapdog. If this was the fourth and third, I won't be able to survive the second and the progenitor. Not if it's going to be like these, not a chance.

'It could have been, yeah' I tell her.

Wanda takes a deep breath and lets one tear roll from each of her puffy eyes.

> 'Of course, it was that thing' she says, smiling, 'And you got rid of it for her'

I think I understand how she feels, to finally be given an explanation for her friend's disappearance. An insane, unbelievable explanation, but an explanation nonetheless. If nothing else today, I'm glad I could give this to her.

> 'When they find Rhonda and the others' Luke says, but I don't even think he knows where he's going to take that sentence.

> 'Oh Luke' Wanda laughs softly, 'Rhonda is gone, you all must know that'

We don't say anything back.

> 'I've accepted it, and I think you should too. I'm sorry, I didn't come here to be a downer, but Rhonda would have hated to see everyone moping around'

> 'She'd be telling me to stop complaining and sweep the hospital floor' I say.

Luke and Wanda laugh.

> 'I've thought about it since Rhonda went. No, hell, I've thought about it longer than that. I think it's time for a fresh start' Wanda sighs.

> 'You want to leave?' I ask.

> 'Well I thought, while I'm still young' she laughs, and once the laugh runs its course, she turns sombre, 'This town is bad news boys. Now more than ever'

> 'What do you mean? That thing is gone' Dan asks.

'What if there's more though? I don't know what the hell it was, you kids were the ones who saw it, but I don't want to hang around for a look'

'I think you're right' I agree, 'If you can leave, I think you should'

'I could sell the shop faster than you can blink' she retorts.

The three of us look at her sceptically.

'Alright maybe not that quickly' she laughs.

'So, we're all out of jobs hey?' Dan asks.

'Looks that way, I'll just tell people that you three were so useless that you made the business go under'

'I don't blame you, I was thinking about a career change anyway' I joke.

We all laugh, then fall silent, then Wanda lets fresh tears fall.

'I have a feeling things are going to get pretty crazy around town from here on out' she says, 'In case I don't get a chance to see you before I'm gone, I'll say goodbye now'

She waves all three of us in for a hug, Luke is trying not to cry. I might too. I owe Wanda a lot. She brought the three of us together after all.

'Thanks Wanda' I say aloud.

'Thanks boss' the other two boys repeat.

'And thank you boys' Wanda nods.

She releases us and stands up.

'So where are you going to go?' Luke asks, wiping his face with his collar.

'Not sure, over east I reckon' she scratches her nose, 'Somewhere hot, where it isn't so miserable all the time'

'There's plenty of desert out there' I say dryly.

'When you boys sort your lives out, finish school, and go travelling, you'll visit won't you?'

'We'd like that' Luke says.

'Can't promise we'll ever sort our lives out though' Dan adds.

She stands up as she laughs, and carries herself towards the door. She places a caring hand on the frame, and looks back to us one last time.

'Stay out of trouble, you hear?'

'You aren't the boss of us anymore, you can't tell us what to do' I laugh, 'But we'll try'

'Oh Warren' she trails.

She turns away and steps out of the room.

'There's just something about you' she laughs to herself from the hallway.

After her footsteps have faded and no one else comes into the room to take her place, the three of us are just left to twiddle our thumbs. I was hoping some more people would come to see me to be honest, especially Ms Harper, she would be worried about me, right? Maybe Ava could have come to check on Dan and stopped in? I understand though, after today I'm sure Wanda is right, things around here will be crazy, I'm sure everyone has put two and two together and blamed today's beast for the disappearances, but that just leaves more questions in its place.

'Well, that was sad' Luke exhales.

'Is that everybody?' I ask, trying not to think about it.

'Yeah that's everyone that was out there' Luke nods.

'Hurry up and get checked out Warren' Dan says unusually sternly, 'We need to talk'

'We do' I match his tone.

We get me signed off, it's not as complicated as I imagined, but it takes some insisting to let the hospital staff let me walk home. It's funny how rules sort of drop off in times of crisis, but they eventually give in and send me out into Southway. All of us eager to get back to my house, but Luke insists we go back to the spot in the park, next to the creek where I had stashed the fated machete last night, by the way he talks it sounds like he and Dan have already discussed what they wish to talk to me about while I was unconscious.

'You go first' I tell Dan, sitting down on the grass.

'As you wish' he crosses his arms, 'I saw how you looked at me in there, but I'm not going to apologise for what I did to Elliot'

'You don't need to apologise to me for that anyway, you need to apologise to his parents'

'Yeah no, I'm not going to be doing that either' he blows a raspberry.

'I don't think you understand their family'

'But you do?' he laughs in his mouth.

'I understand that you shouldn't bash people's teeth in when they're surrendering to you'

I retort.

'What if they deserve it?'

'You don't choose that for him Dan!'

Luke respires loudly and holds a hand up to each of us, begging us not to start.

226

'What's done is done' he looks at us both in turn, 'Yeah?'

Dan and I look away from each other.

'Anyway, what I will apologise for is going off at you without hearing you out this morning, and insisting with the cult theory, even when you were basically telling me it was wrong'

'You were right to not believe me, the cult theory was way more believable' I laugh.

'I shouldn't have doubted my friends' he hangs his head in shame, 'But I need to hear it, what happened with the old man?'

For the second time, I tell the story of how I entered that place hoping to just pull a plug, and left covered in blood and a blaze behind me. The heroics earning me nothing but an anonymous story on the local news in the morning, and an encore performance at school.

'So then, the question becomes' Dan mulls, now caught up to speed, 'Why didn't he just mention you by name and have you taken away?'

'To be honest I don't know'

He looks up to the sky and laughs softly.

'This town's finally earning a name for itself that's for sure'

'I think he's taken these other two and ran' Luke chimes.

'You reckon?'

'I think today was the second weakest one, and he threw it out as like a last stand, then he took the strongest two and he's fled somewhere to start anew'

I don't know if I buy this theory from Luke, I don't think Locke Dawson would waste one like that, not without some sort of a plan. He wouldn't do anything without being ten steps ahead.

'It's my turn to ask a question now, I can tell that you guys have discussed something without me, what is it?'

The two of them stare across at each other, silently nudging each other to be the one to speak.

'I'm against this by the way' Luke warns.

'Spill'

'The two of us were talking, and we were tossing around the idea that...' Luke passes it off to Dan.

'Just get on with it, someone!'

'The idea that you should be the one to protect Southway, from these things' Dan concludes.

As if following a cue, the winds die down, and I just have to laugh at them both.

'Do we not have police for this sort of thing?' I rub my jaw.

'Officer Dickhead and his goons? They must have put you on some wicked painkillers if you think the cops around here could do anything against that' Dan laughs.

'Even if we had the most capable police officers here' Luke continues, 'What do they know about fighting these things?'

'I don't know anything about fighting either!'

'Exactly, you've never been in a fight in your life remember? And look how well you've done' Dan nods at me with steely eyes, 'You have the observation, you have the reflexes, and you have the instinct'

Both wearing me down with their gaze, I have nothing to do but throw my hands up.

'For what?' I ask.

'To lead… Well, us' Luke finishes for him.

'Yes, we are serious' Dan says before I can complain again, 'And I know you want this Warren'

'I…'

'If you're really so worried about these things, you'd jump at this opportunity. We'll train, combat and reflexes, and then *if* anything pops up, and I don't believe that it will, we'll be ready to deal with it. Save people'

'What do you think about this?' I ask Luke.

He crosses his arms now too.

'I don't know how much use I'll be, but I agree with him'

I can't believe we're actually discussing this. I'm quickly growing frustrated with this conversation chasing me around in circles, Dan grows serious and direct, clearly he's had enough too.

'You always carry on about purpose and all that bullshit, and now you don't want it?'

'Mate, I was thinking more like, I don't know, a nice job or something. Not this shit' I say.

'Well sorry buddy but I don't think life gives a shit about what you had planned'

'Why me? Don't give me the reflexes shit either, there's other people out there I'm sure' I moan.

'You won't be alone, we decided today that you can count us in'

'That's very nice that you decided that, but I'm not your leader'

'Well who else? I'm not cut out for it' Luke says.

'You're two for two with the beasts right now' Dan says, '*If* there is more to come, we could do a whole lot worse than you'

I'm ganged up on, two against one, I can't fight them. A sparkle catches my eye, in the creek and underneath the reeds, that damn blade. In our haste last night, it seems I didn't cover it as well as I thought I had. The tip that I had used to pick the lock and open up my destiny, now points up through the water's surface right at me. I did say, even swore to myself, that I wouldn't back down anymore. Is this it? The purpose I was hunting after? So be it then.

'Alright then, let's get stuck into it then' I announce.

'Huh?'

I wonder if they knew I'd agree to this? But of course, they know me better than I know myself. I stoop down, body aching as my knees bend, and pull the machete out of the muck.

'Tomorrow, we've got training to do then' I stand up.

They both rub their hands together with vigour, I don't know what they expect of me, but if the time comes where another creation raises its long neck up at this town, I'll do everything I can to lead the three of us to surpass it. With help from the police or not, I know that with the two of them helping me, the second and even the first of these demons can try their best, but they won't lay another claw on this town.

'The Rusty is parked at your place, quick, let's get there and shove that thing away before someone sees it' Dan says.

'If we don't have school for a while, and we don't have jobs anymore, at least we have a good excuse to do all this training' Luke muses.

'As my first act as leader, I have decided that we'll spend this time training day and night, so that we'll be ready for anything' I point ahead as we walk.

'We're not on duty yet!' Dan sighs.

'If we're doing this, then we're always on duty' I tell them.

Where did Elliot go after today? Why didn't Locke Dawson give me to the police, he knew exactly who I am? The image of the scratch in the rock burnt into my mind, the creatures don't seem like they'd care to meaninglessly carve stones. There are some stranger beasts out there yet, that's for sure.

XVIII
Talk of the Town

'Hit me again' Luke says, fiercely determined.

'Follow it with your eyes' Dan instructs.

He ditches the pinecone at Luke, as hard as he can even though they're only about ten metres apart. It seems unfair, but that's how training is. It spins towards Luke's head, he brings the hatchet that Dan gave him up and across, the veins in his forearm wrapping around his newly accumulated muscle. The pinecone barely misses the wedge, instead it thumps against his knuckles and splits apart, sending woody flecks in all directions.

'Better' I say, placing more pinecones I've gathered down next to Dan.

I keep one for myself to toss up and down like a ball. Somewhere on the Steele family farm, the three of us and the Rustmobile are parked near where the pine trees begin, for a training exercise that I came up with, one that I think has worked well for us. It's a Friday evening and Spring is in the air, Southway is unusually warm, but not warm enough to make me shed the brown jacket that I've come to love. The same one I hated until Dan told me that it was cool. Although the new pinecones are only just starting to emerge, there's plenty around from this year's Autumn for us to hack at.

'Remember, from what we've seen, these… Do we have to keep calling them "things"?'

'I've been trying to think of something better for weeks' Luke laughs.

'Anyway, from what we've seen, they're big and dumb, so if you can get anywhere close to slashing a pinecone coming at you a million miles an hour, you can slash one of them'

'Speaking of slashing pinecones' Dan says.

From the corner of my eye I see one leave his hand, I slide the machete from the makeshift scabbard I've made, and swat the projectile away from my face. The pinecone hits the sharp edge and harmlessly falls to the ground. He won't expect this, not a second after I block it, I hurl mine at Dan in return. I should know my friends better though, he's ready, and he need only tilt his head slightly to avoid it.

'You're getting good now mate' he laughs.

'You too' I put the machete away.

He's right, over these last couple of months I've really tried to hone my knack for observation. While I've always been able to pick up on minute details, I was never under any great pressure and they were only ever the most meaningless things, but then again, I used to have a meaningless life.

Luke and I are getting muscles where they never used to be, Dan makes sure of that, when I'm not sharpening our reflexes with pinecones and such, Dan is strengthening our bodies, boiling us alive in the furnace of a tin shed at the back of his farm where he's set up weights and chains for us to sling around. This entire operation is of course fuelled almost exclusively on Luke's cooking, all three of these cogs meshing with the other two perfectly, until I'm sure in saying we can take on anything, if and when Locke Dawson decides to show his face again.

School eventually did go back to normal, it took them a long time but they got us back in the classrooms, albeit with a few new twists. The first being the pack of psychiatrists roaming the halls, you can hear someone being asked "How are you feeling?" every ten minutes or so. Luke and I get asked more than most people, I guess because we had a more hands-on experience, so to speak. They mean well, and I'm sure some people find them helpful, but it reminds me of how people would say "Good luck" to me all the time leading up to an exam, without actually caring what you responded with. Unintentionally condescending.

The second difference, is that Dan has lifted Luke and I up from the broken brickwork and into the Spring sunshine. It's me sitting on the table at lunch and recess now, people looking up to me as I make them laugh. Dan sure has done a lot for me, it's hard to believe not even six months ago or so, I sat alone on my slimy concrete and fantasised about being part of this crowd, and now I am the crowd. I'd be lying if I said I didn't enjoy it, but the heroics that carried me here, were only me trying to defend myself from something I started in the first place.

'I've been thinking' I say to Dan.

'That's dangerous' he lobs another at Luke, who dodges this one without issue.

Something else is happening here. I went into that lab, and the *very* next day, not even twelve hours later, he sent another one to attack me at school. Since then, it's been what, three months nearly, and nothing'

'Maybe he just knows when to quit?' Dan laughs.

'It was so bold to attack me in public, revealing the monster in daylight in front of a whole school. I remember it caught me off guard, everyone there would have been dead if it wasn't for Luke'

'Just doing my part Captain' Luke salutes, having heard us.

'In hindsight, it was the right move for Locke to keep going while he had the momentum, but then he just pulled right back. Biding his time, or waiting for something. I'm not sure exactly, but it's weird, right?'

'Hey they can't be *that* easy to create, he's probably decided it's not worth risking losing the two he has left'

'There's something else' I tug at my lip with my fingers.

'When aren't you thinking' Dan laughs.

He stops throwing pinecones and waves Luke over.

'What are you guys saying?' Luke asks.

'I've been wondering just how big these other two could be'

'You spoke to him' Luke puts his hands on his hips, 'Remember him giving anything away?'

I shake my head.

'Only that the original was "too wild" and he cloned it down, making it smaller and friendlier, and then twice more until he got the Lapdog he wanted'

'You're the only one who saw the Lapdog in the lab, how small was it compared to the one at school?'

'They were pretty close in size, relatively, I mean. I'm positive that they were the two youngest' I cross my arms.

'So, we want to know just *how* wild was *too* wild for old Lockey' Dan hums, 'Who's to say he even really came here with all four anyway?'

'He also told me that they could wipe Southway out if they had to, which makes me worry that these things might be too massive, even for us'

'Oi have some faith in your men! That's if he's even still here at all' Dan stops suddenly.

It's Isabelle, wading through the blades of grass, the three of us drop our weapons into the grass to not show them in front of her.

'Izzy what are you doing here?' Dan asks.

'What are *you* guys doing here?' she sneers.

'Secret stuff' I say, 'Sorry we can't tell you about it'

I try to be friendly, I hope she doesn't get upset. I don't know how kids work.

'How come?' she asks.

'Have you got your stuff ready yet? Are you excited to see Nanna and Grandad?'

'Yes, but why aren't you coming with us?'

235

Dan drawls for a second, thinking of what to say.

'Because… I went to visit them not long ago, they told me they can't wait to see you'

'Did they?' she asks, absolutely beaming, 'I wish I could stay with them forever'

'They did, come on we'll take you back home, we're going into town tonight' he ruffles her hair.

'Okay' she says, dejected.

We load up the gear and the four of us head back to the rickety homestead. Dan puts his sister inside and then comes back to unload with us, and when she's out of earshot, we finally start talking again.

'When did you go and see your grandparents? I thought they lived two hours away?' Luke asks naively.

I have to try not to laugh.

'I haven't seen my grandparents in years' Dan sighs, 'They go to stay with them pretty often, but mostly she doesn't even tell me that they're going'

'I'm… sorry man' Luke puts a hand on his shoulder.

'Don't worry about it, it's a good thing, it frees the place up for the party tomorrow'

'Which I still think is a bad idea' I cross my arms.

'Mate chill out' Dan says, 'We've had this planned for weeks now and you're only just deciding to whinge? I bet we won't hear a peep from you once you're with you-know-who hey?'

He nudges Luke suggestively, who has to turn away to hide his sniggering.

'Shut up' I say, embarrassed, 'I'm not whinging, I'm telling you, the three of us, are on high alert okay? And I mean it, no necking beers and no blazing up, got it?'

'Yes Chief' Dan groans sarcastically.

All the time the three of us have spent together now has made us extremely efficient, without saying a word we can finish training and be packed up and ready to go in a minute flat. Together we lower the stuff inside through Dan's bedroom window at the front of the house. We do this to avoid the attention of Faye, although I can't imagine her even acknowledging our presence. When the time comes to put my trusty machete inside, I ask Dan the same question I ask every time we train.

'You sure you want to keep it here? I should be the one to keep it'

'Absolutely not' Dan says.

'Come on, it should be me' I argue.

He runs a hand through his hair with frustration.

'What if this Locke decides to name drop you to the cops one day? And they pay you a little visit and find it in your room? No way mate, it stays here'

'I thought as the leader I have final say?' I laugh, he's given me this lecture so many times.

'Yeah well, it's my job to advise against such stupid calls'

'Guys, are we still going? It's almost six' Luke checks his phone.

'Shit is that the time? Let's get the show on the road then'

Tonight, we have a social event. The park is already abuzz when the three of us arrive, people I've come to know all sit and laugh on the lawn, sharing bottles and stories, safely hidden by the trees blocking the light of the streetlights. I see the orange dots swell and dim with each drag, floating around like fireflies as people pass their cigarettes and joints to their neighbours. The moonlight is more than enough to show us the landscape, it must be almost full.

'Heeey boys!' the crowd drawls when they see us approaching.

So many faces acknowledging that I exist, bothering to turn their heads when I appear, even after so many weeks the novelty still hasn't worn off for me, I don't think it ever will.

'What's up?' I ask everyone, most stand to greet us and we take the time to shake hands and pat backs.

Ava comes up and hugs Dan from behind, he only has time to give her a quick kiss, we're here to talk to one person in particular, and Dan has spotted him. One Todd Derry, local marijuana connoisseur and once friend of Dan and Elliot. I've met him a few times when buying pot with Dan, he seems to always be donning a thick hoodie and tonight is no exception. He's a bigger sort of bloke so his hoodies are huge with pockets that hold seemingly limitless numbers of lighters.

Once we're assimilated, everyone resumes chatting, we follow Todd when he pulls us off to the side slightly, to a seesaw out of the way. Dan and I sit on one end each while Luke and Todd sit on the bar in the middle.

'Drink fellas?' Todd holds up a brown paper bag at each of us.

The contents glug and splash against the glass inside.

'Can't, driving' Dan spins his keys around his index finger.

'Pacing myself for tomorrow night mate' I say.

'Fuck yeah' Luke says, accepting the bottle.

He unscrews the lid and chugs back, the smell burns my nose and eyes, but he does it without flinching. They're both more than a bit impressed, but I'm worried, the more time we spend doing these sorts of activities, the less reserved Luke becomes. Not a bad thing by any means, but I've always felt like Dan and I need him to help keep us grounded, especially moving forward into the unknown.

'Outdone by the young blood hey Danny?' Todd teases, taking the bottle back from Luke and clapping him on the shoulder.

'He's just too young to be afraid of that stuff yet, let him get a few hangovers under his belt then talk to me' Dan retorts.

'Hey pace yourself' I warn Luke, 'We aren't going to be here long anyway'

A few people must have overheard me because they boo loudly, I notice Celeste amongst those jeering, I'm glad it's too dark for anyone to see me blush.

'What did you want to see me about anyway?' Todd asks.

Dan stops rocking the seesaw and checks that no one is listening, when he's sure, he waves Todd closer to him.

'I heard you saw him' Dan says.

'Who?' Todd asks, taking a drink.

'Elliot' Dan whispers, and I can tell it hurts him to say that name.

Todd finishes his swig and cringes the liquor down.

'Who told you that? How'd that get around? Well, anyway, wasn't me who saw him, it was my cousin, you know him? Jason?'

'No' Dan says, 'I don't know him'

Luke and I shake our heads too.

'Shit, biggest stoner you'll ever see'

The three of us can't help but laugh, might be some family rivalry there between the cousins.

'Fuck off don't look at me like that! He talks a lot of shit so don't put too much stock in it, but yeah he told me he saw him'

The three of us sit up a little straighter.

'What did he tell you?' I ask.

'That he was out in the bush checking on… his plants' Todd uses air quotes.

'Of course, he was' I laugh.

'Reckons Elliot approached him, come walking out of the bush like a bunyip, looking and smelling like absolute shit. Anyway, handed him three hundred dollars, told him to get him some food and shit, and he could keep the rest'

'Sounds like old Moneybags' Dan rolls his eyes.

'So, what happened?' I ask, not wanting to get side tracked.

'Easiest money you'll ever make, he got him his stuff, met him at the same place the next day and gave it to him' Todd concludes, taking another mouthful.

'What else did they talk about?' I press.

Todd drops his eyes to the ground.

'Nothing man, I don't know' he mumbles.

'All he wanted was food? Alright, well where did they meet?'

Todd chuckles a sham laugh.

'Lads if I knew where Jason's weed plants were, well I wouldn't have to drink this cheap shit' he takes yet another long drink, then eyes me down, 'What's the fuss anyway? He must be living on the outskirts of town somewhere, the weather will get bad or he'll start missing Mummy and Daddy's money and day now and he'll come back'

'That or the police will find him' says a new voice.

We all look up and around for the owner of the female voice. Standing in the moonlight, is Celeste.

'Exactly' Todd points at her.

I've spent a considerable amount of time with Celeste these last few months. Not as much time as I spend training with the guys, but let's just say I haven't been wasting my time with textbooks anymore. She's so gorgeous, with curly, black ringlets and full lips. The two of us do like each other a lot, I think, and Dan keeps pressuring me to take things to the *next level*, but I can't help but wonder if it would be a distraction from the mission. She takes a seat in between Luke and Todd in the middle of the seesaw.

'I was sent over here to see what secret you boys were discussing. Unfortunately, not the big scoop I was hoping for'

'Please help me convince these guys to just let Elliot go and enjoy their night Cel. This weekend is going to be wicked, and these detectives here are worried about that rich kid who treated everybody like shit? Man, I'm almost glad he's out of our hair…'

'I think Danny might hold a bit of nostalgia towards his old pal' Celeste tuts.

'And I thought those clowns on the radio were the worst journalists in town' he scoffs,

'Trust me, I don't hold any nostalgia for him'

He stands up on the seat and leaps from the seesaw, causing Luke, Celeste, and Todd to jostle and stand up in panic, while I thump into the ground hard without his weight. He folds his arms and clenches his jaw, clearly already tired of talking to her. She can be a bit overbearing though sometimes, she wants to be a journalist once we graduate, she's always working an angle, trying to take in everything at once. I think that's why we get along so well, I do the exact same thing, just without speaking my thoughts afterwards.

'Then why do you want to know where he is so badly?' she asks him.

'Todd's right' I say, hoping to defuse any potential arguments, 'We should just enjoy the moment, sorry for the interrogation Todd'

'See Warren this is why they call you the smart one' He moves over to me and bumps my fist, 'All three of you need to chill, chips fall where they may or whatever'

'And I'm sorry for being forward Daniel' Celeste says, although I feel it's insincere, 'But before you celebrate, I think you need to go and see a certain someone'

She points subtly towards the main crowd, and sure enough, even in the dark it's unmistakeable that it's Ava staring daggers at this little group.

'Shit' Dan groans.

'Good luck with that' Celeste laughs.

He trudges away begrudgingly, like a man to the gallows.

'He's so dead' Todd laughs with her.

Luke and I don't join in, he shouldn't have ignored her earlier.

'Come on big fella' Todd calls Luke, 'If you're drinking there's some people you've got to meet'

I want to tell Luke to be careful, but I hold my tongue, he's proven he can look after himself, and I have faith in him. While I can feel Dan becoming indurated, obsessed with making sure we all sweat out every piece of weakness we have, Luke is loosening up and enjoying these moments he has to speak to new people and laugh with them. I know he'll look after himself. The pair looks to set off, but Celeste stops them.

'Todd if you're going back over there, any chance Warren and I can keep that over here?' She points to his bottle.

Todd blinks at her, and then looks at me, then back to her and back to me, before closing his eyes and smiling. He hands it to her.

'Thank you kindly'

'No worries Cel, you two have fun' Todd throws an arm around Luke and they turn away.

242

'Catch up later' I call to Luke.

But they're already dissolved and stirred with the rest of them, undergone endosymbiosis with the gathering. Someone is now playing music through a portable speaker that's materialised, I swear two dozen more people have showed up in the last few minutes.

'So, Elliot huh?' Celeste asks, sitting down on the other end of the seesaw, causing me to rise up from the sand.

'Can I decline to comment?'

'This isn't an official interview Warren, strictly off the record' she winks.

'He's a missing person, it's just interesting to think about what he's been doing all this time'

'He went missing and yet you, are still the talk of the town' she touches her lips, 'What's more interesting still, is why the three of you care so much about his whereabouts'

'He didn't go missing, he ran away, and we don't *care*, we just heard that someone Todd knew saw Elliot, just curious where he is and all' I shrug, gently rocking the seesaw back and forth.

'Did you at least hear what you expected?' she asks, then takes a drink.

I stare at her, I stare at the way the moonlight gleams through the glass and then the liquid before falling on her eyes.

'I'm not sure, but I'm glad we came here to ask him' I smile.

'And now that you're here, what are your plans?' She asks, picking up on my rhythm and going with it.

'Well, Ava might kill Dan in a minute, and I don't know if I'll ever see Luke again now that Todd's got hold of him, so I'm just…hanging I guess'

'Eh' she laughs, unimpressed.

'What?' I scoff.

'You just don't really... *hang*' she laughs.

'Why not?'

'Prior to six months ago, no one here even knew what your voice sounded like'

'And now it isn't six months ago anymore'

'Given my understanding of linear time, I think you're right'

'Oh, shut up' I roll my eyes at her.

She punches me in the arm.

'See this is what I mean, *hanging* implies relaxing, which you never do'

My face burns despite the cold night air.

'But you've come far kid' she adds quickly, 'Looks like those two really brought you out of your shell'

I look for Luke and Dan, but the crowd is far too dense now to possibly pick out a face.

'The three of you sure are close huh, closer than I've ever seen three non-related people' she ponders.

'As far as I'm concerned, they might as well be my brothers' I smile at the crowd, knowing they're in there somewhere.

'What do you guys even do together? I can't imagine you have many shared interests'

'More than you'd think' I shrug.

'Ooh very cryptic!' she adds, 'I love a man of mystery'

She theatrically leans into me, imitating swooning, she wraps her arms around my bicep and squeezes it with her hand.

'Do the three of you do much training together? What could the three of you be training for I wonder? You've never told me about any sports that you play'

I can feel her words picking me apart, trying to chip away at me, I don't like it, being prodded and poked like this.

'I thought you weren't a journalist tonight?' I cut her off.

She bites her cheek and looks away, taking time to compose her words.

'You know what? You're right Warren, I'm sorry for trying to pry'

She scoots her body closer in to me, and places a hand on my thigh.

'Dan and Luke' I say quickly, defensively, 'They're staying at my house tonight'

I don't know why I said this, I don't think they're sleeping at my house, not as far as we planned anyway. She laughs and takes the hand from my leg, then grabs my hand instead. She nestles her head in my neck and looks up at me.

'There's always tomorrow night'

Suddenly her lips are on mine, warm and soft. But we're only together for an instant before it's interrupted by the silence. In the movies, people kiss and rub their faces together and the music swells for the happy couple, but our music shuts off, and then there's chaos.

'Dude just ditch the fuckin' weed!' someone yells.

Celeste and I look away from one another and over to the voice. Towards the edge of the park, red and blue lights flash, near one of the entrances, and then torch lights flick our way. Dozens of shadows cast as everyone darts in various directions, a school of fish with a rock dropped into their pond.

'I bet this is your first time for this, isn't it Warren?' Celeste kisses me on the cheek, 'Best of luck to you'

Then she's gone, she rolls backwards off our see saw and into the dark.

'Here we go' I breathe.

As everyone scrambles, I keep an eye out for Luke, I've at least had the pleasure of meeting Sergeant Dickhead, but he hasn't seen how cruel he can be. I'd hate for him to be caught street drinking, Robert would just about have an aneurysm I reckon.

'Warren!' Dan grabs my shoulder in the anarchy.

'Where's Luke and Todd? And Ava?' I ask.

'I don't know. Gone'

Most people have fled now, but I see a few horror-struck faces peeping out of bushes and rapidly raising chests pressed behind tree trunks. None of them are Luke though. I swear if Todd has abandoned him somewhere I'm gonna belt him one. No, no I'm not, I mean, Todd wouldn't do that anyway.

'Well, well, what do we have here?' the voice booms.

We turn around, Sergeant Dillon stands before us, hands on his belt, scanning the darkness. He has a woman that I've never seen before kept just behind him, also in a uniform. She's tall and beautiful, with a round face and long burgundy hair, even tied back it reaches down to her elbows. She must be closer to us in age than she is to him, late twenties, if I had to take a guess.

'Having fun at the park? Just the two of you?' he sneers.

'Just looking for our friend' I say.

'And what, pray tell, were you doing that made you lose your friend?'

'Walking' Dan grumbles.

'Constable, breath test these boys, I can smell the booze on them'

'Really? I don't smell anything. They seem fine Sir, are you sure?'

'Just do it Constable, Jesus Christ I shouldn't even have to ask'

The woman takes the breathalyser out, slots a plastic piece into the end and presents it to me.

'One long breath please, until you hear the beep' she says reluctantly.

I inhale and blow into the machine, I've seen mum and dad get breath tested while driving before, it takes a moment for the results to appear.

'I don't know how they did things wherever they called you in from Constable, but a superior shouldn't have to be worrying about being undermined'

'Of course, Sir, I apologise' she bows to him

The device chimes and the Constable shakes her head at my results, then puts a new plastic piece on the end for Dan to do the same. Again, she shakes her head.

'They're both all zeroes Sir' she tells her Sergeant.

Dan twirls his keys around his fingertip.

'I'm driving' he smiles at him.

'I don't partake, too young' I add, pursing my lips sarcastically.

Dillon seethes. Tonight, he doesn't seem the same as he was that night he caught us speeding. He's still painfully aware of the authority he holds over everyone here, only now he doesn't swagger and gloat, now he's just stressed. He may be a dickhead through and through, but I understand the pressure he must be under with the investigations. Oh yeah, they said they were getting new police officers in, that must be why I haven't seen this lady around before. She seems very capable, but also very cautious of slipping up under his watch.

'Start looking for the other kids, these pricks aren't alone out here' he waves his hand at us.

'You got it Sir' she nods unwillingly.

'We'll be seeing you boys' Dillon waves.

His hand rocks side to side flamboyantly, while the Sergeant stretches the creases of his face into what I think is a smile. What a strange thing to do. Their torches come out from their belts as they brush past us, Dillon making no effort to avoid shining his right in our eyes, before swinging and aiming them around the park. The light catches some kids darting from cover to cover, fleeing when the torch hits them.

'Oh for fucks sake. Hey!' Dillon calls after them.

'Come on' I pull Dan, 'We need to find Luke before they do'

'Fucking Todd' Dan grunts.

We're at the entrance furthest away from the two police officers, the border of trees no doubt a good hiding place.

'Luke was enjoying himself, it's not Todd's fault the cops showed up' I say.

'Yeah whatever, you start that way' he points me left, in a grump all of a sudden.

'Sure, you got it'

I start spinning around trees, checking every side from every position to no avail. Everyone has gone now as far as I can tell, either run on home or been caught by the police. I wonder if Celeste made it. I look back and see their torches still swaying across the park, it doesn't look like they're walking. I think they're talking to someone that they've captured. We need to find Luke quickly.

I don't have to go far before I discover Luke's limp body on the grass. He lies against the trunk of a thick willow, propped up at the neck, he smells terrible. Vomit spattered onto his shirt and into a puddle beside his head.

'Here!' I call Dan over, still well within earshot, 'How you doing mate?'

He grunts, I think he was asleep this whole time.

'Hey it's Warren, you're all good Luke' I shake him gently.

'Where's Todd?' Dan asks, kneeling down.

'Idnno' Luke groans.

'Let's get him up' Dan grabs one of his arms, the side with the vomit.

Luke groans louder when we lift him up over the curb, starting our pilgrimage through the streets.

'Hold on you guys' he stirs.

'Need to spew?' Dan asks.

'No, no' he shakes his head, 'I need to tell you something'

We stop lugging him for a minute

'What's up?'

'I asked him, Todd, more about Elliot'

'Did he have anything to say?'

'He told me. He said that Elliot was interested in any parties happening'

I almost drop Luke.

'Did he tell him? Luke? Did he tell Elliot about it?'

'Yeah, he said that he did'

'What the fuck Todd' Dan sighs, 'Why didn't he tell us'

'He said, he said that he didn't tell you because you'd cancel'

'We are cancelling it. Now' I tell him.

'Hang on boys put me down' Luke moans, holding his stomach.

We set him down upright on the curb, but he immediately hunches back over to vomit.

'I'm not doing that Warren' Dan tells me.

'You need to. Elliot knows, why would he ask for information about that? He's planning something'

'What could he be planning? He's alone, running around out in the bush somewhere. Watch, all he's gonna do is call the cops on us to ruin it, Officer Dickhead will show up and we'll tell him we'll keep the noise down. Easy'

'You don't hide out around the outskirts of town for months just to ruin someone's party' I protest.

Luke vomits again. Dan crosses his arms and taps his fingers on his forearm.

'Don't take this the wrong way Warren, but you don't understand what it's like to have a girlfriend who's expecting you to throw a party'

'What does that have to do with anything? Do you think I'm wrong? About Elliot?'

'Yeah Warren, I do, because I think I made it clear to him what happens if he fucks with me!'

Once he starts raising his voice, I lower mine to try and bring him back down to Earth.

'Why risk it Dan? Ava will understand'

Dan looks solemn, he sighs to himself.

250

'No, she won't'

Luke wipes his mouth and spits.

'Fuck her then man'

Dan and I are both shocked, he usually tries his best to avoid swearing. I guess a lot of the time, he tries his best to avoid speaking at all.

'Sorry' he says, 'But it won't kill her'

'Luke, come on' I pat him on the back.

Leaving Todd in charge of him was a bad idea, I knew it, alcohol doesn't sit right with this one. Besides, I feel sorry for Dan, after spending time with Ava or even just after speaking to her, he never seems like himself, he just seems so drained.

'If it really means that much to you then' I nod at him.

'Thank you, Warren'

Strangely enough, I'm not sure that it does mean that much to him anymore, at least not really. Does he just want that normalcy to return, even for just one night?

'But the three of us, are on high alert, understand?' I look at them both, 'No drinking or smoking for us'

'No more drinking' Luke quickly agrees, 'No more'

While we help him back up, we can't help but laugh.

'Lukey you smell like shit, take that shirt off' Dan pinches his nose closed.

'Here put my jacket on'

Dan takes the other half of Luke's weight from me while I slip my arms out of my coat for him. Dan offers to help pull Luke's reeking, vomit-soaked shirt off, but Luke shoves him away when he tries to touch him.

'No no no no don't touch me!' Luke stumbles, pulling his shirt back down.

Dan looks at me for guidance.

'Okay Luke, it's cool, we were just trying to help' I hold my open palms up to him.

'Don't tell me you're a violent drunk' Dan laughs it off.

When Dan says this to him, Luke looks as though he could begin to cry, and both of us are unsure if we should approach him, is this a reaction to the alcohol? He buries his face into his own hands.

'Sorry, I just want to walk myself, I don't need to be carried'

'I... think you should stay at my house, maybe for a while' I tell him.

'I'd like that' he nods.

'Come on, you can have a shower when we get there'

Due to either the intoxication wearing off, or just the poison now being out of his stomach, Luke is indeed able to walk himself the rest of the way to my house. Bout of irritability aside, I think the kid handled himself well, but we need to be looking at tomorrow night. I won't make Dan call off his party tomorrow if it means so much to him, but if the three of us are to be Southway's shields, there will be no drinking until we vomit for me and my men. Now I know Elliot is out there waiting for me, ready to come back like he'd promised, and I can't help but wonder if there's anything bigger and hungrier out there too.

XIX
Heathens

'Are you kidding me?' Dan groans.

He picks up his cup and plucks the ping pong ball from it, then throws his head back and sends the drink down his gullet. Everyone roars as one and begins to applaud, but what they don't know is that tonight he's drinking straight lemonade.

'Mate, can you aim please?' Luke begs his partner, as Todd and Ava high five.

'This is the one' Dan wipes his mouth and then lines it up.

He slings the ball forward and it plops straight into the front cup on Todd and Ava's side, bobbing up and down in the dark liquid.

'An eye for an eye' I tell them as I spring to my feet, 'I'll be back soon'

I pat Luke and Dan on the back while I pass them, tonight the three of us are on high alert. They've been on a hot streak at the beer pong table, drinking down their mysterious mix. Only the three of us privy to the fact that it isn't really the secret mix that Luke told everyone that it is.

The party is in full swing, the most people I've ever seen in one place. Faces both familiar and unfamiliar, fill throughout the Steele house, sprawling over the furniture, down the halls and outside, music pounding at everyone's eardrums no matter where they decide to loiter.

'Hey Warren'

'Warren'

People call my name out as I brush past them, it's almost overwhelming. I thought I always wanted the adoration of others, but I'm not sure that I wanted this, they're not my friends, I wouldn't say that, I can count my friends on one hand twice over, and still have a finger to spare. Another guy stumbling ahead collides arms with me, I let him bounce off me, but he staggers into the wall and we both immediately pat each other on the shoulder in apology. Very briefly, his hand was over my scar, and that's all they know me for. These people, they'll wave at me when I pass, and they'll raise a glass or a mug at me, but I don't know any of them, I couldn't list a single thing about most of them. We carry on our opposite ways down the corridor. I've never been claustrophobic, but the thump of the music, clinks of the glass and the babble of the crowd make me feel uneasy, and even worse, distracts me from the mission.

It's my turn. Every fifteen minutes or so the three of us alternate going outside and having a look around, a few laps of the house with a torch, just to make sure nothing lurks nearby. We leave a torch by the back door to take and then leave for the next person. I push through the crowd and towards the back end of the house, but before I can reach the door, I'm spun around by the arm.

'Party's this way' Celeste laughs.

I try not to look down at the revealing dress she's wearing, my greatest challenge so far, apparently, and she absolutely notices.

'What could be worth such a hurry?' she charms.

'No, nothing, I just need to check something' I stumble through my sentence.

She slips her hand into mine, and wraps the other around my arm.

'Let's go and see if Daniel can take care of whatever it is, yeah? Come on' she leads me back where I came from.

She carves our way through the sea of faces, I don't need to bustle and weave past anyone this time, with her leading, they all make way for us. She smells really nice. Back at the table, even more spectators have become invested in their game, it looks like Luke and Dan are even making a comeback.

'Danny' Celeste interrupts, causing Luke to miss his throw, 'Warren says there's something that needs checking?'

Dan looks past her to me, confused, after all, it is my turn after all. *"I don't know"* I mouth to him. He eyes down my arm and sees us holding hands, and then looks quickly across the table at his opponent, Ava. I had almost forgotten they were a couple. Dan nods at me and smiles proudly, like a father looks at a son.

'Yeah, don't worry about that, I'll get it after this rematch' he smiles.

He bounces the ball on the table a few times, then casts it down the other end, cleanly into Todd and Ava's final cup. Her jaw drops while the rest of the house cheers.

'Sorry, love' Dan shrugs at her.

While the rest of the living area erupts around us, Celeste turns us around.

'Come on'

Most of the attendees are around the table now as they set the cups back up for their rematch, letting us make our way through the house, hands still locked. She takes me down the main corridor, and into Dan's bedroom.

'This is Dan's room' I tell her, stopping outside the door.

She laughs, and rests her other hand on the door frame.

'You don't know much about much, do you?'

'I'm sorry?'

'Come on' she takes her hand from the door frame and plants it on my chest, 'Even you must be able to tell, he won't be using this room tonight, but we can'

My heart thrashes against my chest.

'Okay'

I step into the room and she locks the door behind me with her free hand. She finally releases me, only to turn the bedside lamp on and angle it down and away, casting a dim glow over the room. It's romantic, I think. It's definitely something anyway. She sits on the foot of his bed and pats the spot beside her, insisting I do the same. I do it, and immediately her mouth is pressed against mine. I press back, concentrating hard on keeping the same rhythm and pressure as her. I mustn't be very good.

'I've seen you in action' she laughs, 'You operate better when you let your instincts do the work I think. Don't think too far in advance'

She pushes me onto my back.

'Okay' I say again.

She jumps on top of me, and begins to slide the straps of her dress away from her shoulders. The moonlight I've come to associate her with, splashes onto her beautiful face just like it did at the park. But the moon's beam also washes past her though, and looking around her hip, I can see a familiar bow leaning against the cabinet opposite the bed. She grabs my face and aims it back up at hers, but I resist and look at the bow. Beside it is a familiar machete, the one that's caused me so much grief. The one I slayed that thing with, all by myself. The one I allegedly threatened Locke Dawson with, the very one Dan insisted on keeping. If she saw it she'd know, she's too smart, she'll know it's the same one. I sit back up.

'Warren?' she asks, irritated and topless.

'Nothing' I smile.

I grab her jaw gently and pull her lips down to mine, she smiles as I bring her closer. I have absolutely no idea what I'm doing. We kiss forever, the occasional cheers and laughter from the rest of the house eventually becoming nothing to me as I get into the rhythm. I'm not thinking too far in advance now, I'm pretty sure I'm not thinking at all.

Suddenly, there's a collective gasp throughout the house and a few seconds later the music shuts off. Celeste and I both stand up.

'What's happening?' she asks.

256

I pull my shirt and jeans back on and put an ear up to the door. Someone is talking.

'Let's go and find out' I throw her dress to her.

She quickly wriggles into it, and together, we open the door and step out into the corridor.

'Get the fuck out of here. Now!' a voice growls as we move up the hall, it's Dan.

We turn the corner.

'No Danny, I don't think I will just yet'

Elliot stands near the open front door, dirty and unshaven. His once ever-styled hair now hanging down in long strands and flowing into the beginnings of a beard, the hair almost as dark are the heavy rings around his eyes. Everybody else watching him from across the living area and the kitchen. Everyone notices Celeste and I though, especially Elliot.

'Here's the man! And what do we have here?' he asks theatrically, looking at the both of us, 'You've done well for yourself since that day at school Warren, I'll give you that'

Dan steps forward, putting himself between Elliot and the crowd, they stare each other down.

'Even Warren is doing better than you these days mate' Elliot laughs.

He nods over in my direction and crosses his arms, I'm only just noticing it now, but he has thick, leather gloves on.

'Get out of here, go and see your fucking family for Christ's sake' Dan hisses at him.

'Mother and Father? Don't make me sick. Besides, I just got here! For so long I had to watch from afar, until you stopped checking outside every two minutes for me'

Elliot produces a large hunting knife from his belt, the room gasps in shock. No one dares breathe it out, let alone move. He paces the room now, doing laps around Dan as he stands alone, weighing the knife in his gloved palms to intimidate him. Luke looks to me, weighing up our options. If we went together, one of us could get behind him, but that blade is extremely close to our friend, and I have no doubt that this madman would make use of it. I stand Luke down with a subtle shake of my head.

'I heard some noises out there' Elliot continues as he paces, 'Horrible noises really, roars and all sorts, and I know you've heard them too'

Everyone is watching him circle Dan, although now everyone seems interested in what he has to say.

'Now why is it, that I heard roaring when I was out there on your farm? Could it be roars from the same thing we saw at school that morning? Why would something like that be here, where you and Fuck Eyes so often play together?'

He asks it to everybody, they glare at each other as he reaches Dan's facing side during his lap.

'I wish I beat you worse that day, you still have teeth left' Dan spits.

Elliot gently pokes him in the chest with the tip of the knife, everybody gasps, but Dan refuses to flinch.

'You don't deny knowing that something is out there though' Elliot smiles.

Suddenly, he puts the knife away, and backs away to the still open door.

'Maybe I should just get out of here, maybe you're just far more trouble than your worth old friend. Everyone else has worked that out'

The veins running up Dan's forearms start working in overdrive, churning hot blood through the valves.

258

'Ava there has worked that out, she's told me about it before' Elliot adds.

I can almost hear Dan's teeth grind in the silence.

'Your parents worked it out' he continues.

Dan takes a step towards him now.

'Even Warren will work it out one day. You know where to find me' he finishes.

Elliot steps out and slams the door behind him. The crowd erupts into chatter.

'What the hell was that about? What noises? Warren, has he told you about this?' Celeste asks, but I ignore her and make my way to Dan.

People are starting to move, irritated, confused and no longer willing to politely acknowledge me on their way past. Celeste and these other fickle people will blame the three of us for this, I know they will. Luke grabs my arm.

'What's the plan?' he asks.

'You're in charge here Lukey, keep everyone calm' Dan joins us, 'Warren, are you with me?'

I should have put my foot down, I knew this was a bad idea, and I knew Elliot would show up. I can see the emotions burning through Dan's body, and I have to remember that this isn't his fault. This was me, it was my turn to keep watch, and I let myself be distracted, I failed him, so I won't deny him this chance.

'Of course' I nod, 'They don't know you're involved in this Luke, you keep everyone busy, and we'll hop out your bedroom window, Dan'

'The gear's ready to go' he nods, and heads for his room 'Let's go'

'Yeah, I saw the gear' I sigh, but he's already pulled away.

'I can't do this Warren' Luke panics.

'Of course you can, you've helped me fight a monster, and I've seen you drink your weight in alcohol, you can talk in front of a few people for a while'

'What if you need me out there?'

'We might, but someone has to stay here' I look at Dan, 'And it's sure as hell not going to be him'

He watches Dan shove the frightened people out of his way as he marches to his bedroom.

'Keep an eye on him okay?' Luke says, now looking at him, 'Everything is, I don't know, it's chipping away at him. I just hope he doesn't break'

'He won't, trust me. I've known him my whole life, he won't break'

'Stay safe out there' he tells me, 'Whatever happens'

'You can count on us' I shake his hand.

I'm grabbed by Celeste again and pulled away from Luke before he can say his piece.

'Warren? Tell me, what is going on? Where is Dan going?'

I pluck her hand off me, and nudge her towards Luke and the rest of the crowd.

'I just need to see him for a minute, sorry' I pass her by.

'Are you kidding me? You need to explain what Elliot was talking about' I hear her scoff as I do.

I find him in his room, quiver already on his back and bow in hand, he also has a knife on his belt, like Elliot had. In his other hand is my machete, he passes it to me.

'Ready?' he asks.

'Dan, before we go-'

'We don't have time for-'

'Elliot asked Todd's cousin about the party!' I cut him off, 'He knows about the roar we heard, he wanted to cause a scene in front of everyone and get a reaction I'm telling you!'

'He'll get his reaction' Dan ignores me and slides the window open.

'He said, we know where to find him, you know what that means?' I plead.

'That meadow' he grunts'

'And why would he be there?'

'Bastard's probably been living there' Dan throws his leg over the window frame, 'Are you coming or not?'

I storm over to him.

'I need to know, that you're *good*' I tell him to his face.

'What's that supposed to mean Warren?'

'How often do you think about Elliot?' I ask.

'Jesus Christ' he pinches the bridge of his nose, exasperated.

'Do you think about hurting him?' I demand, 'Dan?'

With one leg outside and one in, split down the middle, he looks straight up so that the moonlight catches in his exposed eye.

'Only when I'm awake' he sighs.

'I'm worried about you'

261

'Would *you* let the old man live, if you saw him again?' he challenges.

This is completely different, isn't it? I don't know, who am I to tell him his judgement is wrong.

'If it comes to it, and I mean right down to it, I'll let you do what you have to. But, if you have the choice, just remember who you are, alright?'

He's still looking up and not at me, obviously unimpressed with the time we are wasting by philosophising.

'He's getting away' Dan pulls himself all the way outside.

I sigh, and without a choice and machete in hand, I'm pulled back in. I follow him out the window, dragged away from Celeste's adoring eyes and the dozens of friends I thought I'd never have, and into the unknown darkness all to help my oldest friend chase a shadow back to that place that we swore we'd never go near again.

XX

Where It Isn't So Miserable

The Rusty revs as Dan speeds down the dirt road, although it's all just gravel in the headlights to me, Dan swears he can see where Elliot has run.

'You think he'll actually be there' I ask.

'Yep' Dan says bluntly.

'I still think it's a trick. He wanted this exact reaction Dan, he wants to be followed. He told us about the roar, and told us exactly where he'd be. He could have just slashed the tyres if he didn't want to be chased'

'I'm not as smart as you Warren, but even I thought about that. I don't care if it's a trick'

'I'm just saying, we're giving him what he wants'

'Well that's his thing, Elliot always gets what he wants'

He's blinded by his rage. The further from the house we get, the more I want to lay down the law and insist we don't follow him, but as his friend, I know that's not what he wants to hear. Before I can decide, Dan's erratic driving brings us to the entrance. It's not as far as I remember, hell, Elliot just ran here from the house. Dan's already out of the vehicle and examining the ground.

'He would have gone in here' he nods.

The entrance we had hacked all those months ago has overgrown significantly since then, but there are some fresh, green breaks in the ferns and sticks. Dan's right, this has been used recently.

'We're doing this then?' I ask.

'We are' he nods.

'And what are we doing?'

'This, the two of us can take him, easily'

'It's not him I'm worried about' I sigh.

'There's nothing else, there's been nothing else since school that day Warren. If there was any more, then more people would have been disappearing'

'Something's changed, I'm telling you. I'm not stopping you, we just need to be ready for, you know...' I taper off, he knows what I mean.

He steps into the scrub with an arrow already poised.

'If you aren't stopping me, then why are we still here?' he asks, walking forward, before I can answer.

Marching back into the wilds, like we did that day, after the roar we heard I never wanted to be in these trees again especially not under tonight's circumstances. Although, since that day, I've seen worse than just the roars, I've trained myself to react fast, and I've got a comrade who I've seen to be deadly with his bow. A comrade I let down tonight.

'Dan?'

'Yeah?'

'This is my fault'

'What do you mean?'

'I should have been checking the perimeter. But I... Let myself get distracted'

Dan stops walking, and turns around. A cheeky grin.

'No one thinks straight in that situation, not even you. It's not your fault, it's just growing up. But if we make it out of here, I want to hear all about that'

'Right, maybe' I laugh.

I laugh, but I am embarrassed, maybe I'll get lucky and be torn apart tonight so I can avoid answering Dan's questions later. We don't speak again until we reach that meadow. Elliot sits atop one of the white rocks, knees up wrapped in his arms, he holds his knife in his gloved hands and whistles to himself as though we've kept him waiting. It's the rock with the scratch on it. Far less mystery surrounding it now than when I first saw it, the things that growl out here now given forms to imagine. When Dan and I last stood here, the howl sent us bolting, but tonight, I don't think anything could make him move.

'You took your time fellas. Far out you brought a lot of gear'

He eyes us up and down, for some reason he looks at me more, even though I only have the one blade.

'Did you think I'd come alone? You fucked up here' Dan pulls the bowstring back.

Elliot laughs at him.

'Did you think *I* would come alone?'

Dan and I finally look away from him, only to look at each other. Then suddenly, we hear a roar. Elliot smiles.

'Yeah I hate to tell you this Danny, but I couldn't give a shit about you'

'The feeling is mutual' Dan scoffs.

'No' Elliot shakes his head, 'It isn't. You hate me, you can't stand anything about me, I wonder how many hours you've spent thinking about me? But I don't care what happens to you, whether you live or die, doesn't upset me one way or the other'

Dan bares his teeth.

265

'You are nothing Daniel' Elliot then points at me, 'I'm much more interested in Warren here'

Another roar echoes out from the trees, closer now.

'Why don't you attend to that while Warren and I talk?' he asks Dan, nodding in the direction of the sound.

'Go on' I tell Dan, without looking away from Elliot.

'Warren?' Dan says.

'I'm two up on you, it's your turn' I say dryly.

'You sure?' he whispers.

'I'll catch up soon, this won't take me long' I ready the machete, 'Don't forget that they burn'

He nods back without saying more, it's hard for him to do it, but he lowers the bow away from Elliot and heads in the direction of the roar, sharing an icy stare with him as he passes him on the rock.

'Strangle him with that fucking scarf for me'

When the crunching of Dan's footsteps no longer reaches us, Elliot leaps down from his boulder, knife in hand. He stretches up, and then down to touch his toes. I grip the machete tight.

'So here we are' he says.

'What are you doing here Elliot?' I ask.

'Looking for you' he shrugs.

'Why?'

'I want to finally see which of us is better, now that Danny can't step in'

'No one has to be better' I say, 'We don't have any scores to settle, you can just come back'

He laughs hysterically.

'Really? You of all people think things can just go back to normal?'

'Look I'm really not interested in fighting, we all have bigger problems to worry about. What exactly do you want to get out of this?'

'I want you to suffer' he hums, 'That's all I want'

There's no escaping it, it seems, because Elliot always gets what he wants.

'Settle your score then' I breathe, 'Come on!'

He sprints at me immediately, knife forward. It's simple and obvious. I step to the side, as I did to Lapdog that night, then I slash at the blade in his hand, not wanting to cut him, just hoping to knock it away, but his grip on it is strong. He steps away, and I wait for him to follow up, or say something snide again, but instead I hear another roar, and Elliot laughs.

'It sounds like something doesn't like it when people get too close'

'We need to go and help him' I say.

Elliot throws his knife to his other hand and then back again. It thuds against his thick gloves.

'I'm sure he's fine' Elliot takes a step towards me, I take one back.

'We don't need to fight. You can come back. People are worried about you. I spoke to your parents' I tell him.

He stops stepping, and for the first time possibly ever, he lets his features soften.

'You did?'

'I did, the day that you ran away, they were heartbroken' I tell him.

'They were?'

'Honest' I smile, 'They were so proud of you, they didn't blame you for anything, shit man, they actually blamed themselves for putting too much pressure on you'

Tears well in his eyes, I can tell by the way the moonlight brightens as his eyes glass over. He lets the knife slip from his hands and into the grass, before he slums to his knees and holds his head in his face. I take a step towards him, with a hand outstretched.

'They weren't disappointed in me?'

'No, not at all' I tell him.

I take another step towards him, I throw the machete down into the grass. He observes it very carefully, he watches it leave my hand and hit the ground like a feather, without making a sound. I'm close enough now to see his fists buried into the soil, he clutches at the dirt as he hangs his head.

'You just need to come home' I say, I kneel down next to him.

He looks up at me and smiles. He wasn't crying. The dirt flies into my face, directly into my eyes and mouth, sending me backwards as I flinch away. Before I can even bring my hands to wipe my eyes, my jaw crunches closed as Elliot swings his boot into my face. Blinded and in pain, I hock the blood and grit from my mouth, already awaiting the next hit. But it doesn't come.

'You always knew everything, didn't you? I wonder if you know what's about to happen next' I hear him say over me.

Nothing happens next though, he doesn't taunt me more or impale me with his blade. I finally blink the sand away, and take a look around. He's gone. I rub my jaw and get to my feet. He wanted a fight and then he just flees? Maybe he didn't think he could win? No, Elliot Young always thinks he can win.

I feel around in the grass for the machete, but my fingers find nothing in the field. He's taken it, to strand me out here with no weapon. Fucking Elliot. I wanted to help him, I wanted to bring him home to his parents.

I never should have spoken out in class that day. Listening for a few minutes, I hear no roars in the distance, and since I heard no screams, Dan must have done his part, even when I failed to do mine.

Caressing my swollen chin and still blinking the muck from my eyes, I head deeper, trying my best to follow where Dan went, where we refused to go that day. The path Dan has pushed through is straight, he didn't let anything get in his way for what must be half a mile at least, it's hard to tell, the thick, leafy branches don't exactly allow for the same magical luminescence as the open meadow had. Eventually, I do see light up ahead. Not the moon's pale glow from above, but a warm orange from within the trees.

'Dan!' I call, picking up my pace.

I stop stroking my jawline in order to use my hands to push branches away as I sprint towards the light, until finally, the trees open, into yet another clearing. This one is larger, with more of the same, quartz boulders, only much bigger, and instead of long, spindly blades of grass, this clearing has the odd patch of slimy moss, but is barren dirt other than that. Small fires are strewn around the area, dotted around one massive, burning heap. Something far larger than a van, is blackened and crisped in the inferno, it seems I arrived too late to see what it looked like. In the bonfire, are at least a dozen short sticks jutting out from the corpse, burning away, blackened arrow shafts sticking upright, until they split and join the crackling. On the opposite side of the field, at least fifty metres away, some of the boulders are so large, and arranged in such a way that they form an overhang, a huge shelter, almost like a cave. Just in front of this natural edifice, Dan lies on the ground, bow and quiver cast aside.

'Hey!' I yell, running to his side.

When I reach him, he isn't dead, he isn't even unconscious. His eyes are open, round and bronze staring up into the sky. They don't react even when I come into his vision.

'Dan?' I kneel, 'Talk to me, what happened?'

'Nothing' he croaks.

'Are you okay?'

'Yeah'

'Are you hurt?'

'Not really'

There is blood though, barely seeping from a scratch on his leg and another on the side of his head, neither seem to be causing him any pain. I look around again, at the fires in the field.

'Holy shit' I sit down from the shock, 'How many?'

Dan holds up his index finger.

'You're still one up on me' he laughs humourlessly.

I run my hands through my hair. We both turn to the blaze, the smaller spot fires must have been where it bled, he stung it full of arrows, that's for sure.

'How big was it?' I ask.

'Big enough' he laughs again, 'What happened to you?'

'I tried to get him to calm down, and I thought I did it too, but he escaped. Threw dirt in my face and ran away'

Dan finally shows some expression and looks at me.

'He just left?' he asks, 'He let you go? Why?'

'I don't know' I tell him.

Finally, he sits up.

'There's something you have to see'

He rises to his feet and gestures for me to do the same. Limping slightly on his cut leg, he takes me over to the stony outcrop and we duck our heads underneath.

270

'It's kind of dark but, well, you can't miss it' he sighs.

The cave doesn't run deep at all, yet I still have to squint, not only to see in the gloom, but also to shield my eyes from the stench under here. There's sticks and leaves, arranged into some sort of nest that would be big enough to park a car on, and there's blood, and there's bones.

Most of the bones seem to be from animals, half a skull of what must have been a horse, some sort of hooved leg over there, eventually I find what he meant for me to see. Shimmering in the glint of the moon, are a set of unmistakable gold rings on a severed hand and forearm.

'Jesus' I choke.

'Yeah' he replies.

'That's her' I say quietly, reality sinking in even though I've known for weeks, 'That's Rhonda'

'So, this is where those people ended up? Under a rock' Dan says.

'It looks that way'

'You know, I actually only met her the once' Dan nods, 'That evening, when I marched myself down there and applied for that job to pay you back'

'I'd forgotten about that'

'I basically invited myself in and begged for a job, at first they were annoyed, but when I told them I had my own vehicle, Rhonda threw her hand out at me and said "Welcome aboard" before they even asked my name. I'll never forget how fucking loud her jewellery was when she shook my hand'

I don't have anything to add, these rings escaped being devoured, but what good do they do her now? Wherever she is now, she couldn't take them with her, but there's someone out there somewhere who might finally find her solace, a shame we have no idea where she is. She's somewhere hot, where it isn't so miserable all the time.

'Let's get these rings off' he says, having the same though as me.

271

I nod, and he kneels to slide each ring off the fingers, and collects them into his pocket. I collect his bow and all the salvageable arrows I can find while he does, perfectly content with not touching the detached hand.

'We should go back' I say, 'Luke's been entertaining for a while'

'I'm... Just gonna send everyone home I think' Dan sighs.

'Really?'

'I can't explain any of this to them' he holds his arms wide, encircling the cave, the bones and the fire, 'Even if I could, I don't want to, I'm just so sick of it'

'If it makes a difference Dan, I'm grateful for what you did'

'Hmm?'

'I know you would have loved to have a crack at Elliot, but if we had traded places, I wouldn't have been able to beat that thing, not on my own. So, thank you for that'

'You think I don't see you and Luke look at me like I'm a killing machine? You don't have to worry, I'm still me, and I do what has to be done to help people, not what I want'

He gives me a thumbs-up as we begin kick dirt over the fires, until all of them are extinguished, leaving us in the dark again. We drag our bloody bodies back through the tangles, slower this time, the sound of the metal clashing in Dan's pockets rings with each step, but otherwise the night is quiet.

'Hey where's that machete?' he asks.

'Gone' I sigh.

'Gone how?'

'Gone as in Elliot took it. I guess he wanted to leave me defenceless. Maybe he didn't count on you surviving out there'

'Maybe' he grumbles.

'It's lucky that thing was in that clearing, if you had got the blood in amongst the trees they would have gone up in flames around you' I say, making new conversation.

But Dan only grunts in agreement. He moves like a soldier, I think whatever he saw out there will have taken a toll on him, even though he'll be stalwart to never let it show. Due to his hobbling on a sliced leg, it takes us forever to reach the first meadow, and almost double that to get back to the car. Crunching down the gravel road, we see two familiar blue and white vehicles with red and blue lights on their roofs. It seems tonight just won't end for me.

'Jesus Christ'

'Officer fucking Friendly' Dan slaps the steering wheel in frustration as roll into the driveway.

He removes the rings from his pockets and hides them in the glovebox, then reaches back to make sure his bow and arrows are tucked away well behind the back seat. We hop out of the car once everything is hidden out of sight.

'Elliot, surely'

'Oi wait' I stop him, 'How did he know about that place Dan?'

'Who knows, probably saw the track we made that time and used it'

I hate to accuse, but I have to ask.

'Did you tell him? About what we heard that afternoon out here?'

'What? No, of course I didn't!' he snaps.

'I'm just asking, how else could he have known that place?'

'We promised we wouldn't tell anyone, and I didn't' he says.

'Actually, I told Luke' I murmur.

'Well there you go, maybe Luke told him?'

'Fuck no Luke didn't tell him!' I say, offended.

'It was only a joke Warren. Come on, let's see what this bullshit is about'

We approach the house, the female officer we saw last night is stationed at the door, looking as rigid as she was at the park.

'Can I help you?' Dan asks her sarcastically.

She's caught off guard, it's like she was zoned out, Dan's words snap her to attention. She's very surprised to see two dirty and bloody boys appearing, but she makes every effort possible to keep professional.

'Sergeant Dillon and I received a noise complaint, and are just here to settle things down' she announces.

She reminds me of those Buckingham Palace guards you read about, how they have to stay serious at all times no matter what. I've only seen her twice but I can tell she takes her job very seriously, I suppose that makes her a good cop.

'Who complained?' Dan asks, 'The closest neighbours, if you can call them that, are miles away'

She's caught unaware again, and clears her throat quickly.

'We don't give out that information, it was anonymous'

'Right' Dan drones.

'Where is the Sergeant?' I ask now.

'Inside' she nods, 'Waiting for the host I imagine'

'Well here I am' Dan waves sarcastically at her.

He shouldn't antagonise this lady, she's just doing her job, and I can tell she has a better heart than Dan is giving her credit for, or what this town allows her to have.

'Doesn't sound like he tells you much' I laugh.

'Only what I need to know' she says, trying not to scowl.

'You *know* there was no noise complaint, don't you?' Dan asks her.

'I-' she begins.

'Just like last night when you knew the two of us weren't drinking. Is it because he's your superior then? Is that why you go along with what you know isn't fair?'

She doesn't answer his question, but she does at least listen. Dan is keen to push past the Constable without exchanging anymore words, but something in my mind says I can help offer something to this woman.

'Excuse my friend, we don't mean to be rude' I say, 'But if you don't think this is right, you should say something'

She's at a loss at first, but I think I have her worked out.

'And I don't mean to be rude, but what could you possibly know about that? In all your, what, sixteen years of wisdom?' she laughs.

She's not being snide or condescending, her voice is soft and downtrodden.

'Seventeen' I correct.

'Apologies, seventeen' she rolls her eyes and laughs.

She cocks an eyebrow at me. Dan nudges me in the ribs, gesturing to hurry up.

'How does that work out for you?' she asks.

'I'm not sure yet, but I think I'm going to make the world a bit less of an evil place'

'You're Warren, right?'

Dan looks at me as if to tell me to shut up now, but I nod at the policewoman, I don't know why, but I can tell she's good news for this town.

'Yeah, but how did you...'

She points at her own eyes.

'Oh right, of course' I laugh.

I forgot what it was like to have someone find the novelty in my eyes, it's only when a person first moves here that they get to stare and look between them. The last person before her was Luke, Jesus that was a long time ago. Dan elbows me again, harder and with more intent now, no doubt eager to confront the Sergeant.

'He seems to have taken a liking to you, the Sergeant, treats you like his right-hand man... well woman' I misstep.

'I've always tried my best to do what's right, even before I got transferred here' she nods stoically.

'You'll have your work cut out for you' Dan half smiles, arms locked crossed.

'You sure you can't tell me more about your philosophies? Because I wonder if it has anything to do with where the two of you just were and why you're so beat up?' she smiles wryly.

'Yeah it has everything to do with that Constable'

I don't think she expected me to be honest, but I don't think you become Sergeant Dillon's sidekick unless your capable, as cruel as he is, he wouldn't stand weakness in a second in command. I can tell she's adept, clever and most important, she's just, and I don't mind if people like that figure me out. She smiles and steps aside for us, I like this lady, she's actually good fun.

276

'Constable Marigold' she extends a hand.

'Warren Avery' I shake.

'Look you guys' she puts her hands behind her head and exhales, 'To be honest, I have no idea what we're here for. I don't know what the Sergeant is playing at, just go and ask, he's been glued to his phone all night'

'Thank you, Constable' Dan adds impatiently, stepping past her.

"Finally" Dan mouths to me when we turn away from her, I shake my head at him. Sure enough, Sergeant Dillon is inside, sitting atop a stool in the kitchen, tapping his fingers on the benchtop while our friends all stand around awkwardly and nervously. His eyes widen when he notices we've stepped inside.

'Sergeant Dillon' he says standing.

'Yeah, we know, we've met before' Dan notes, 'A few times now, unfortunately. The Constable outside said there was a noise complaint'

'Just making sure things aren't getting too out of hand out here'

'Doesn't look out of hand to me' Dan looks around sarcastically, 'Everyone looks afraid, actually'

'Well, I see a few familiar faces from last night at the park' Dillon looks around too, 'I can't help but wonder if there's an underage drinking epidemic in our little town'

Dillon steps towards Dan and looks down at him.

'It's my understanding that it is not illegal for someone under eighteen to drink on private property, only illegal to buy it for minors, is that right?'

Dillon turns his attention to me, his face twisting. As he paces menacingly towards me, a voice from the door stops him. It's Constable Marigold, standing in the doorway behind us, she looks scared, but determined. The room holds its collective breath, waiting for what will come next, and from who's mouth. Buzzing. A mobile phone alert, rattling as it vibrates across the laminate. The Sergeant spins around and leaps back to the bench top and picks his phone up to look at the screen. He studies it for a time, then slips it into his pocket.

'Thank you, Constable' he announces, 'You are correct'

'No, thank you Sir' she bows slightly, I can see her breathe with relief.

'I'm sorry for any inconvenience, Daniel, was it?' he turns to him.

'You know it is' he grunts.

The Sergeant then spins to me.

'And you?'

But I don't answer, he waits and leans his head and silently tells me

'I apologise for any distress I have caused, we'll be on our way, Enjoy the rest of your night everybody, apologies again'

He waves behind him as he makes for the door, he even has a slight spring in his step.

'Sir is everything okay?' Constable Marigold asks.

'Yes, Arianne, of course it is' he beams at her, 'Come along'

He steps by her, leaving her as stunned as Dan and I at his change of personality. Her mouth moves slightly but no words come out, she wants to say something but can't.

'Constable?' Dillon calls from outside.

She closes her eyes and calls back.

'If it's all the same, I'd like to offer some of these kids a ride back into town, as long as that's alright. Some of them seem like they might need it'

278

She braces for his response.

'Excellent idea Marigold' he calls back, 'I'll see you tomorrow then, remember, we're on early'

'I remember, you told me' she salutes.

'Good luck'

His car can be heard champing across the gravel and into the distance, as the Constable steps further inside to address the crowd.

'Okay, um. Sorry about that everyone, I really am. Is there anyone who needs a way back home?' she claps her hands together enthusiastically.

No one responds immediately.

'You're not in trouble or anything, I promise' She raises her hand, 'I'm just trying to help, that's all I want to do'

A few, particularly groggy people lift their hands, one of them I see is Todd. His beanie resting crooked on his head and some vomit residue on his chin. It looks like Luke managed to keep the party going before the police showed up.

'Okay, okay cool' Constable Marigold smiles, counting out four people, 'Now I can do more trips if we need okay? Or I can call some other officers. Don't worry, they won't be the Sergeant. Don't tell him I said that though'

Everyone laughs, and she laughs too. She's nervous and unsure of herself, but her presence is very warm, she radiates a feeling of safety. I knew I liked her. More and more people warm up to her, she smiles with pride. As she takes Todd and the other first three partygoers to the car, they stare at Dan and I like we're devils. It's not just them, everybody studies my swollen jaw and Dan's cuts. With utter disgust they eye us down, blaming us for being held hostage by the police. I catch Dan looking at Ava, who only glares back with contempt from the other side of the room, she can only glower at him for an instant before she has to look away. Dan doesn't even waste the time trying to talk to her, he just hangs his head in shame, I don't know much about much, but I know what this means for them. Constable Marigold rests a hand on his shoulder on her way out, causing him to look back up.

'It's okay' she tells him, her cheeks are red but she wears an uncontrollable smile.

Soon enough, another three cars come to whisk people back to their homes, and every person that leaves curses us on their way out, some with their words, some just with their eyes. Ava can't shuffle past Dan quick enough.

'Sick party man' they scoff mockingly.

'What the fuck?' they ask.

Mostly, they just look confused. Do they think we killed Elliot or something? Eventually, only Luke remains, sitting alone on a couch, resting his head on his knuckles. I didn't even see Celeste go, and that makes me sad.

'So' I ask, lifting my arms and looking around the room, 'What did we miss?'

Dan slumps down on the other couch and lets his body sag so he ends up with his head hanging upside down off the side of the cushion.

'Things were going well until the cops showed up' Luke blows a raspberry.

'Where did they come from?' I ask, 'Did anyone call the cops?'

He shakes his head.

'Not that I saw, but…'

'But what?' Dan groans, still upside down.

'Everyone was pretty bummed' he sighs, then looks to Dan, 'Especially Ava'

Dan sits upright.

'Oh well'

'Oh well?' I repeat.

'She asked me if the three of us had been in contact with Elliot since he went missing, I told her no, and she just said that she knows you've been up to something' Luke says.

'That's her problem then' he stands up, 'We've hardly spoken for ages anyway, if she'd turn on me like that without even confronting me, then I don't want anything to do with her. You know, for ages now all I've ever done is try to help people, that's what I did tonight, and that's what I'll do for the rest of my life. But why should I bother with someone like that?'

'Dan, you have spent a lot of time with us, training I mean' Luke says sheepishly, 'Maybe you should have made more time for her'

'Maybe' he shrugs, then looks at the cut on his leg, 'But then maybe I wouldn't have been strong enough tonight. I don't regret anything'

'What the hell happened out there? Luke asks.

And we tell the story, well mostly it's just me, doing the telling, Dan still refuses to go into detail about what he did in that second clearing. But I tell Luke about Elliot and how he escaped, and then I found Dan, and then we break the news about Rhonda.

'That's them' he sighs as Dan spills the rings onto the coffee table.

'Yeah' I nod.

'We decided to give them to Wanda' Dan tells him.

'She'd like that' Luke smiles, 'But how are we going to get them to her? Did she tell you guys where she was going?'

We shake our heads and stare at the rings on the table until Dan and I have to lay down. We laze about for some time, we don't turn on the TV or even speak. I have to ask Luke.

'Did Celeste say anything about me?'

He looks surprised.

'No, she didn't. Actually, as soon as you left I didn't see her again'

'She went home?' I ask.

'Must have' Luke shrugs.

'That's good, I'm glad she didn't have to see Sergeant Dickhead'

'Sounds to me like she just came to see you Warren' Dan flexes his eyebrows suggestively.

'Fuck off' I blush as Luke laughs.

'What did you get up to?' He asks when he stops laughing.

I stand up and turn away to hide my red cheeks.

'Stop wasting time and help me clean this place up' I bark.

Dan leaps to his feet, almost tipping on his wounded leg.

'I was hoping you'd offer, no doubt Mum will find out about the cops and kill me, do you guys mind helping me clean up? Just so the house is tidy for when she kills me tomorrow night when she gets home?'

'You sit' Luke orders, 'Let me look at your cuts and then we'll clean'

Luke scrounges some old, suspicious bandages and antiseptic cream from the laundry room cupboard, it looks older than all three of us, combined. While he attends to Dan, I scoop the cups, bottles and bongs into a black rubbish bag. Eventually, they grab a bag each too and help me.

'How do you know how to dress wounds so well?' Dan asks Luke, shaking his leg.

'Just picked it up I guess' Luke says quickly.

'Well you've done a good job, I'm ready for more' Dan laughs.

'Don't joke about that, please, no more' I sigh.

'What was it like? Tonight, out there I mean' Luke asks.

Dan stays silent, he rotates the empty beer bottle in his hand, then throws it into his bag.

'Big' he says gravely, 'Bigger than the one at school'

'Jesus' I massage my head, 'I don't know if we can do this'

'What are you talking about?' Dan asks, he seems genuine.

'I don't know how long we can keep this up, not if they're going to keep getting bigger'

Dan slams his rubbish bag on the floor, the cans and bottles inside clink on the tiles, startling me.

'If they get bigger Warren, then you just have to get stronger. If they get further away you have to go further to hunt them down. If they learn to multiply, you have to inspire more people to fight' he tells me.

He's got two fists up, and speaks triumphantly. It's unlike him to be so profound. Wait, multiply? Wait, I hadn't thought of that. Locke wanted to clone Lapdog at first, but if he wanted to overrun the human race, they'd have to reproduce somehow, he's not exactly getting younger. If he wants this to work out for him long term, they need to learn to multiply, he never brought that up, and I failed to even consider it.

'Hey thanks' I say.

'Sure' Dan gives me a thumbs-up, 'But can we keep cleaning please? This place looks like a bomb's hit it'

'Right now, I just wish I could have inspired some people to help clean up before they left'

Luke and Dan look at each other, then begin to chuckle. It's infectious, I laugh with them, until the three of us are leaning on furniture, bent over in conniptions. And even though, I threw a party, moved a cop to defy her superior, spent the night with a girl, and finally brought at least some closure to the disappearances that started it all, I can't force myself to be excited. I know that after we clean this house tonight and lick our wounds tomorrow, the sun will come up on Monday morning and nothing will ever be the same again.

XXI
Lysosome

I can't see the creatures in the jars today, it seems they've been dusted and pushed back deeper into their shelves, hidden away from the fluorescent lights above. Harper has cleaned recently, perhaps this morning even, unusual for her. I remember her once telling us that she refused to dust because we are all made of dust, and she doesn't want to accidentally clean anybody. Maybe the winds are changing around here after all, hell, nothing is the same, not anymore. My fingers tap at the back of my phone in my jeans, growing impatient, they pull it from my pocket just enough for me to see the screen.

Did you make it home alright on Saturday?

Celeste?

Are you at school today?

Still no reply from her. I swear under my breath.

'Is something the matter Warren?' Harper snaps.

She spins from the board, arms folded in an instant. She looks sour, has she heard about the weekend? Who would have told her? It seems today that everyone's opinion of me has dropped. The whole class spins with her to face me, the army of critics taking aim, the very same faces that drank and laughed with me not even three days ago, now forgotten my heroics and thrown me into disesteem. If only they knew what I'd done for their sakes, Daniel as well, but as they say, everyone is a critic.

'Sorry' I pretend to clear my throat, 'Go on'

Harper rolls her eyes behind her glasses and twists back to the board, she was drawing a cell. Splashes of colour held within a wonky circle, a splodge for all the different organelles floating throughout, and in the centre, an ugly red splotch of a nucleus at the core, everything else swirling around it. It's drawn in an old, raggedy red marker, one that's been run over much darker colours, dirtying its rosiness. Is that me? Ugly and alone at the centre of everything while the other pieces dance around me? Maybe instead I'm the lysosome, ready to burst and dissolve everything around me, nasty or not. I do a quick check, she hasn't drawn any lysosomes.

The seat in front of me, once filled with such a mounting arrogance that I struggled to see the board, now empty, and I don't even want to look ahead. Harper continues to teach, in between her shady glances she keeps throwing me, her and everyone else.

There's talking and feet clumping up towards us from the hallway. The class looks away from me at last, only to focus their ears on the commotion. Vaguely familiar voices bounce down the empty hallways and carry right to us.

'No, I understand' one says to the other.

That's Principal McGovern. There's two other voices, a man and a woman. I don't need to recognise them to know who they are. They stomp closer and closer, until I can hear the Sergeant's voice clearly.

'Up here? Which one?' he asks.

Harper steps down from the front and closer to the door to listen, several others do the same and she makes no effort to stop them. Eventually everybody except me is crowded together, climbing over one another to press an ear to the door.

I close my eyes and wait for it to come. My fingerprints were found at the lab, or maybe Elliot finally showed himself and reported me, or handed the machete in and they got my fingerprints from that? I think about the thick gloves he wore the other night, and then I accept my sealed fate.

The footsteps and voices swell, getting faster and louder as they reach our room. I keep my eyes scrunched closed, unsure of why, maybe my body wants to get in some final moments of peace before they open and the police are towering over my desk. I wait and wait, but the police never come. The sound crescendos outside our door, and then without skipping a beat, it diminishes as they continue disappearing down the hallway past us. Everyone is confused, especially me. I think maybe everyone wanted them to step into our room. What is happening?

'Well that was our tension for the day' she laughs, as everyone trudges back to their chairs, 'Now we-'

'Get the fuck off me!' echoes up the hallway at us.

Daniel.

'Don't you touch me!'

Rage boils out from my skin, as in the same instant it all comes together. It's me alone who leaps to their feet this time, desk catching on my knee and being thrown over, but I won't daintily hold my ear to the door and beg for hints like these cowards. I yank the door right open and throw myself out into the corridor, and my wrath is instantly diluted with a drop of guilt.

Sergeant Dillon and another large officer each hold Daniel Steele by under one of his shoulders. He's well above the ground, swinging his legs and kicking out like a caged animal, the handcuffs clinking behind his back as he writhes and gnashes his teeth. McGovern, ever stern, hikes behind them, I can't imagine what's going through his head. The woman, with the long hair, Arianne, follows behind them, and by far, she looks the saddest of all.

'What the fuck is this?' I spit as they march towards me.

'Just asking your friend some questions' Dillon grunts, he doesn't look at me.

'Step aside please Warren, I mean it' McGovern warns.

'Why do I have handcuffs on if I'm being questioned?' Dan lashes.

'Because you're being unreasonable' Dillon says.

'Fuck off you grub!' Dan yells.

As they approach, he manages to get a toe on the ground, and instantly pushes off of it. He boots a nearby bin, sending the aluminium clanging down the hall when it skittles along the concrete. Dillon and the other officer rip him backwards immediately. While the echo rings out up and down the school, the escort reaches me and they push me to the side. As my friend passes by in chains, he mouths words to me.

'It's not your fault' he tells me.

My heart breaks.

'No! I scream.

I start to give chase and take him back from them, but McGovern stops following the police and grabs me by the arm.

'Constable! Hey!' I call to her, 'What is this?'

'Get back inside right now' McGovern barks, flecks of spit flying from his mouth.

He shoves me back towards the door, the rest of the class is back up and watching.

'Not one more word' he points at me, before storming off.

I don't hate the Principal for this, it must be hard for him, his school has had some strange happenings as of late, an arrest, or questioning or whatever they just did to Dan, it can't look good. All I hear for the rest of the day is my own heartbeat, I feel so trapped and alone, Luke didn't come into school today so I had nothing and no one. At the end of the day, I tried to talk to Harper, not about anything in particular, just to talk to somebody.

'Ms Harper?' I say, once the room has emptied.

'Yes Warren?'

Completely unenthusiastic, she doesn't even stop wiping down the whiteboard to look at me.

'Is there something you needed?' she asks impatiently.

She's never cared about keeping the board clean before.

'No' I give up and turn to the door, 'Don't worry about it'

There was a time, where I'd talk to her after almost every class, and she'd seem grateful for the enthusiasm, but now she's just another person who can't stand to look at me. Trying not to let show how hurt I am, I slide the door open, she finally puts her cloth down.

'I'm just busy is all' she lies, apparently feeling guilty now.

'Sure' I roll my eyes and step outside.

'What happened to you?' she asks.

'I'm sorry?' I reply from the corridor.

'You used to be so disciplined, until you… Started doing whatever you're doing with that boy. I just hope you aren't throwing everything away Warren'

What a strange thing for her to worry about. If I told her how Dan poked arrows into something ten times his size until it dropped dead, alone and in the dark, would she imply he's trouble? If I told her about the things Locke Dawson wanted to do to the world, would she be so gung-ho about science still? She was like a second mother to me in a way, she inspired me to study hard to carry science forward. I did that for her and look what I have to show for it, wounds and scars and blood on my hands.

'Don't worry about me'

I walk away from her. What even is there to throw away? This life of what? Luke's absence worries *me* though, I imagine his parents must have found out about the party we threw and the police showing up, Robert must have grounded him or something. Shit, I wonder how Dan's mum will react about today, if she would care at all, probably not. I don't think Dan will be in jail or anything, that's not how it works right? I should have asked the Constable, but she wasn't doing anything to stop the Sergeant today, maybe I was wrong about her.

I walk through the empty town towards my house, I think the community has felt the ripples of Locke Dawson's work ever since he arrived here, even if most will probably never even know who he is.

Are you home? Dan got arrested at school

I don't have to wait long before Luke replies.

I've got the flu don't come over

That was quick.

We can talk about Dan later, cant talk right now

He adds the second text quickly, how does he type so fast, especially if he's so busy? It's unusual for him to not care about something like that either. I thrust it out of my mind, it doesn't even crack the top three weirdest things that have happened.

My front door creaks open and no one answers when I call out, Mum and Dad aren't home yet. Good, I think I'm finished with trying to talk to people for a while. I slink over to my room, dragging my school bag lazily down the hall, it's not as heavy as it used to be, not because I've grown stronger, but because I stopped bringing all those textbooks to school. In my room, the first thing I notice is the copy of Maximillian Murphy's autobiography that Dan had lent me, and I had never bothered to read even though I told him I would, now he's gone. I grip the strap of my bag as tight as I gripped the machete that night, and I scream. I swing my bag against the walls, papers raining down as my note books tear at their spines, the zips and clips picking away paint with each thrash. I yell until I cry, and then I cry until I collapse on my bed and fall asleep.

'Warren? Warren it's almost eight, love'

My eyelids snap open and I sit up. Mum and Dad sit on the foot of my bed. Mum rests a hand on mine while Dad straightens up the papers he must have picked up from around the room.

'We didn't want to let you sleep through the night without eating something mate' Dad tells me.

He puts the papers down on my desk, and he brings up a dinner plate from the floor. It has mashed potatoes and some kind of meat, I think pork.

'Thanks' I grunt.

'Oh Warren, I know this must be hard for you' Mum says.

Behind her, I can see scratches on the wall where I slammed the bag.

'What's hard?' I ask, unsure of how much they know.

'Your friend' Mum sighs, 'They talked about him on the news'

'What did they say?' I ask, dad placing the plate on my lap.

'That he was arrested at school, and had to be dragged kicking and screaming' Dad says disapprovingly.

'Because they grabbed him' I stare Dad down, 'The Sergeant is the biggest dickhead'

'You shouldn't disrespect the police like that' Dad scolds, 'They just have a job to do'

'You shouldn't lick their boots' I chuckle, 'Two cops dragging that kid out of school by his arms for throwing a party, the true peacekeepers'

'Your friend is suspected to have burnt down that shop, and attacked the old man who owned it' Mum says loudly and firmly, before me and Dad can get into it.

'Wait, what do you mean?' I ask.

'They found the blade the attacker used to threaten that poor man, it said it matches the description perfectly' Mum sighs apologetically.

'How did they *find* that?' I ask, knuckles already white.

Elliot.

'Your friend also matches the description of the attacker that the man gave to the police after it happened' Dad adds.

'He doesn't match any description. That's not right, I listened to the news the next morning and Locke said he didn't get a good look at the attacker, how can there be a description?' I ask.

'Look, to be honest mate, I always had a feeling he was trouble, even when the two of you were kids' Dad nods sadly.

What the fuck Dad?

'How can you say that about him?' I snap, 'Don't you understand something is wrong, the police are lying!'

'Warren love, I know it's shocking for you, it's shocking for us too'

'What would you know about shocking? There was no fucking description of the "*attacker*" at all!' I sneer.

I take the plate off my lap and swing my legs out of bed.

'Warren, part of growing up is realising that people aren't always what you think' Dad says.

You got that right. Since that day I bumped into Locke Dawson on the street, Daniel and Lucas have been just about the only people who turned out to be what they seemed. Everyone in this town seems to be either a rat or a snake, no, rats and snakes at least have spines.

'To be honest, I always thought he was a bit of a loser too, never going to go anywhere' Mum adds to Dad's insult.

'Life is full of these moments Son, but you get through them. What you to do...' he places a caring hand on my shoulder.

'What?' I ask.

'Is try to move past it. If you focus on school you can get your grades back up by the end of the year and...'

I don't hear a word he says after he starts talking about my fucking school grades right now. This doesn't just tip me over the edge, it shoves me into the chasm. I slap his hand away and leap to my feet. Picking up the dinner plate, and as hard as I can, I ditch it against the wall, sending porcelain around the room. Mum shrieks in horror.

'Warren!' Dad stands up and yells, 'I know this is hard for you but you-'

'Do you want to know about the fucking "shop" that was burnt down? I can tell you all about it because I did it' I tell them.

Dad drops his sentence halfway, then he looks at Mum.

'No, you didn't' she says confidently.

'I did' I laugh, 'Not deliberately, and nobody attacked any fucking old man. Do you want me to tell you about that old man? Do you want to really be *shocked*?'

I'm getting aggressive now, hatred emerging through my voice when I have to talk about Locke. I don't mean to, I really don't.

'Because I sure was shocked when that old man told me he planned to end the human race. When he admitted that he had made these... these fucking things that had made those people disappear. The big scary dog at the school, it came there because I slit its brother's throat the night before!'

Both my parents shake at the knees.

'W- Warren? Listen to me buddy' Dad smiles nervously, 'I think we need to get you to the hospital okay? I think you're in some sort of shock or something. It's not your fault, we'll get you help'

'No, I think you're in shock, I don't think... your star pupil little boy would do anything out of line, could he?' I fake gasp.

'You didn't' Dad shakes his head, 'You didn't, that doesn't make sense'

'Whatever, I'm going out' I tell them, picking up my coat from the back of the chair.

'No wait!' Mum begs, 'Whatever you think happened we can talk about it'

'I know exactly what happened' I slide my shoes on, 'Those fucks on the radio you listen to everyday don't, and you definitely don't. Dan is the bravest and most selfless person in the world, and because the maggots at the police station told you that he's bad, you decide you've always hated him?'

I push past them, shrugging their hands away as they grab at me. They both call to me as I march down the hall, again I block them out, but when I reach the front door and the time comes to open it, I hesitate. What will I do, what am I even doing? Where am I going?

'Warren please, let me ask one question' Mum says behind me.

'No, I'm so sick of no one ever doing anything except spew back what they're told to, and everyone that does kick back gets cut down. Why is everyone so... Just so fucking complacent?'

Is it because everybody is evil?

'Warren, I'll believe you' she starts.

'What?' Dad asks, 'He doesn't know what he's saying, he's not in his right mind!'

'If it really wasn't that boy, sorry, Daniel' she corrects herself, at least having the respect to use his name, 'Why would the police lie?'

That's... actually a really good question Mum.

'I'm going to find out, thank you' I say, closing the door quietly behind me.

'Warren pl-'

The rest of their sentence is left trapped inside that house. I jog down the street at first, eager to put some distance between us in case they come looking for me. Quickly it turns into a sprint, even when I'm sure they've decided to let me have my space, I just need to run, I want to get away.

Lights behind me, I have nowhere to turn, I've run out of side streets to dive down, Fuck. Pointlessly, I try to speed my stride up, my parents gain on me until the lights are so bright behind me, my shadow ahead grows long down the road. When it stops beside me, the car looks different to how I remember. Mainly because it isn't my parent's car. Daniel rolls down a window and sticks his arm out to me, smiling as always.

'Weird day huh?'

XXII

A Different Beast

'What the hell? I thought you were gonna be locked up?'

'That's...Not really how it works' he laughs, 'Come on get in, you look like you've run a marathon'

I do what he says and join him in the car, I notice he has a lot of clothes in the back seat.

'I'm just, running, I don't really know'

'That's unlike you, to not know things' he laughs and turns the key.

'I kind of flew off the handle at Mum and Dad' I admit.

'What about?'

'It doesn't matter, and you're just... Driving around?' I ask.

'Seemed like a pretty good choice considering that I'm, well, let's say, no longer welcome at home'

'What even happened? Today I mean' I ask.

'The feds took me downtown' he says in his best cop voice, 'They wanted to know about a certain machete that was found on my property'

'Elliot' I grind my teeth.

'They said I matched the description this Locke guy had given them'

'Which is bullshit' I interrupt, 'Go on'

'The whole thing was bullshit mate. I told them that night I was at work, they said they couldn't verify that because the business had since closed and the boss had moved away. After that I refused to answer any more questions, you know like how the crims in the shows demand to speak to a lawyer? They wanted to know if the machete was mine, what I used it for, all that shit. I think they got pissed off when I wouldn't answer, they just took my finger prints then let me go'

'Is that even proper procedure? Was it the Sergeant?' I ask.

'Of course it was the fucking Sergeant! Him, the lady we met before, and the other guy who got me at school. Arianne and Brad their names are, I think he said'

'Who gives a shit what their names are, they're fucking with us, majorly' I snarl.

'Hey you were pretty sure the lady was a saint the other night, but she wasn't sticking her hand up to say anything today'

'Anyone in cahoots with Elliot Young, is no saint to me'

'Shit Warren, I didn't know anyone actually used the word "cahoots" anymore'

'This is fucking serious' I snap at him, but I instantly regret it.

'Yeah, you're right' he laughs, 'Sorry'

'No, I'm sorry, I'm sorry I did this whole thing to you. I'll explain it all to your mum'

'Don't bother, I don't want to go back there again anyway'

'Going to stay with Ava for a while or something?'

'That would be a bit weird, considering that as of this morning we aren't together anymore' he jokes.

'Fuck man'

'Yeah, "too much trouble" apparently' he sighs.

We both stare ahead through the glass, he doesn't seem upset though, he looks forward like someone who's seen everything. Ever since the day he bashed Elliot's face into the ground, Luke and I would worry about him, but this man doesn't break, he does the breaking.

'So, they just took your fingerprints and let you go?' I ask him, changing the topic.

'Well, yeah, sort of'

'What does "sort of" mean?'

'It felt like they were in a rush to get me out the door, one minute the Sergeant's asking me questions like he's got me dead to rights, then the Constable, she came in talking to him about something urgent sounding. So, he started stressing the hell out, so he told me I had to give them my fingerprints, then after that they let me go home'

'What was the urgent thing? What did they say?'

'Come on, do you think they'd let it slip around me? Anyway, then I went home and Mum was already there and she was screaming, "failure" this and "Wish I never had you" that'

I don't know if the reality has truly set in for him yet, or if he's just doing his best to avoid looking at it, making jokes and acting like he doesn't mind that his life fell apart today. And it's my fault.

'I'm going to make this right for you. I don't understand what's going on at Southway Police, but I'll fix it' I promise him.

'So, what's the plan chief? What's our move?' he claps his hands together.

'If Luke is being fucked with too… He wasn't at school today remember?'

'Is that what we're doing?' he asks.

298

And I need only nod for him to turn us in the direction of Luke's house. Time seems to pass, or maybe I doze off for five minutes, either way, before I can try to process anything that's happened, we're out the front and Dan is pounding his knuckles on the grand wooden door of the Kullick or Kawamura or whichever household it is. I slap my own cheeks to wake up.

'Hey listen, maybe you should let me do the talking' I say quietly.

'Why?' he keeps knocking.

'Luke's old man has never exactly been a fan of yours, they talked about you on The Chatter, and if he heard it then he definitely won't be happy to hear you at his door'

'Man, fuck The Chatter. Fine, go on then' he steps aside for me.

I rap my knuckles on the imposing door now.

'Hey Luke it's us, we need to see you' I call, trying fruitlessly to look through the stained-glass panel on the door and see within.

I move around from the front porch to peer through a window.

'Any luck around there?' Dan asks, standing in the garden to try another window.

I'm only greeted by the back of those velvet curtains, this room must be Robert's den that we saw him resting in that day.

'Nothing, knock again for me'

He slams his fist into the wood again, only faster and more forcefully with each repetition.

'Hello?' I call louder now.

'Fuck off!' we get in return.

My ears prick up. It was muffled and came from deep within the house, but it was definitely Robert, there's no mistaking it.

'Prick. What do we do?' Dan asks me.

'We're not leaving!' I shout back at him.

'Warren what are you doing?' Dan asks me, whispering now.

'Fuck. Off. Now' Robert growls back.

'Check if it's locked' I tell Dan.

He tries spinning the handle but it refuses to turn, I hop around from the window and rejoin him on the porch.

'Locked'

'Alright you ready?' I ask.

'Ready for what?'

'To kick the door in'

'What? Why? We'll just text him to sneak out later' Dan shrugs.

Dan tries to walk back down the driveway, but I think about when I tried to text him earlier.

'We don't have later, you know that' I tell him gravely.

He looks up and around, licking his lips nervously.

'Yeah I guess everything is pretty fucked for us hey' he laughs weakly.

'And you know Luke might not have *later* either, not if we leave him in there'

Dan looks back at the house. He knows I'm right.

'Let's get this over with then' he readies himself.

We both knock on the door one last time, but don't wait for an answer.

'We're coming in one way or another' I announce.

'Jesus Christ for the last time. Fuck off you criminals!' Robert roars.

'No please no!' Katsumi shrieks.

'Three... Two... One' I count.

Our heels slam into the wood beside the lock, and the door flies in and slams into the wall inside, Katsumi's crying is audible now.

'What's going on, are you okay?' I call, 'Luke?'

We sprint through the house, no lights are on, we push ourselves off walls as we bump into them to keep speed, desperately trying to remember the layout of the mansion, we navigate the hallways like bats in a cave.

'These fucking delinquents, you let them into my house!'

'No!' Katsumi cries.

'Stop!' Luke groans.

'Sounds like the kitchen' I tell Dan.

I can tell by the way the voices echo, the kitchen was the vastest looking room of the house by far.

'Right' he pants.

Sure enough, a lone light from the kitchen comes into view.

'Stop' I command, bursting through the doorway.

'Boys no!' Katsumi cries.

Dan and I turn the corner and rocket into the kitchen. Blinded by the light bouncing off all the chrome, I'm barely able to make out Luke and Katsumi kneeling on the floor by the central island, her arms over him while Luke clutches his face. I've barely taken it all in, when I'm grabbed from behind and thrown to the floor. Robert puts a knee into my chest and a hand around my throat.

'Criminals, coming into my house. Trying to corrupt my boy!' he makes a fist with his free hand.

He's unshaven and wild with rage. As I'm studying his face, Dan brings a fist across his jaw, only to be met with a powerful backhand that sends him stumbling rearward.

'You won't take him from me, you understand Monster Boy? You won't take this family down with you!' he closes his grip on my neck.

I try to tell him that he's a piece of shit, and that I should have known he was like this, but I have no air left in my lungs to say even a single word.

'My son finally makes some friends, and they're the dirtiest scum I've ever seen. The one who burnt down that old man's shop, and *you*' he strikes me in the face with his other hand.

There are some people out there who don't deserve to live, no? Locke asks me as I feel my consciousness slipping away. He releases his grip on me all of a sudden and I fall to the floor to breathe. Dan claws at Robert from behind, desperate to trap him in a headlock, but it only takes Robert one powerful elbow to put Dan back down on the kitchen floor. With blurred vision from the lack of blood flow, I watch Dan spin in place after Robert's strike before falling to the floor. Before he can get back to strangling me, a wooden sounding thump echoes around the kitchen, and Robert is clutching the back of his head.

'You little shit!' he yowls, turning away from me and revealing blood streaming down the nape of his neck.

Another thump, and Robert's head jerks around to face me again, and when his massive frame collapses on the floor, I can see Luke breathing heavily with a blackened eye, but standing. He brings the rolling pin down over his father's unconscious body over and over, thrashing it into his back while he lays face down on the tiles. He kicks him onto his back, and then starts working on his ribs. The thumping only stops when I reach over and catch his wrist mid-swing.

'It's alright now' I place an arm around his shoulder.

He drops the rolling pin to the ground, it clinks and trundles away along the kitchen floor. Robert is out cold but still breathing, so Luke and I turn our attention to his mother. She looks at her husband laying on the floor, I swear I can see her smile. I lift Dan to his feet, bleeding from the nose, he wipes it on his sleeves, red war paint for his face and arms.

'You need to leave boys' Katsumi says, surprising us all.

'Wait what are you doing Mum?' Luke yells.

I spin around to see Katsumi with the kitchen phone in her hand.

'Calling the police' she starts to sob.

'I think he needs an ambulance for now more than anything' Dan says, rubbing his face.

'No' she sighs, 'Calling the police on you'

'What?!' all three of us exclaim.

'You three need to hide for a while. Just until he calms down. Okay, let me think'

'Mum are you out of your mind?!' Luke takes her hand.

'You know how bad it will be for me if he finds out I didn't call the police'

'Then just go!' Dan steps up, 'You could leave right now!'

'He'd find me. I have nothing without him, everything you see, it's all his' she weeps.

'Then call the police on him and they'll take him away! Just tell them what happened' Luke begs.

'You sure have a lot of faith in this town's police all of a sudden' Dan sighs, 'I understand where you're coming from Mrs

Kawamura, we'll look after your son until he can come back, you have my word'

'Yeah but... What if we all ran...' Luke says, exasperated.

He'll come to understand eventually, I turn to Katsumi, she's extremely frantic.

'I won't mention you by name boys, tell me where you'll be going and I'll point them in the opposite direction'

'Guys don't listen to this shit' Luke spits.

'You need to understand that this is for your safety' she assures him.

'*My* safety? Bullshit! You're a coward!' Luke screams at her.

'You don't know your father like I do' she forces a chuckle, 'I remember once, he-'

'I don't want to hear it' Luke turns his back on her, 'After all these years we finally have a chance to be free of him and you won't do it?'

'Luke...' I try to calm him to no avail.

'She's just trying to send me away! Are you insane Mum? Where do you expect me to go? Do know what's out there?' he points.

'You know what's in here' she points down at her husband's limp form, 'It won't be for long, just until he calms down'

'Will he calm down though?' I ask sombrely.

'I'll give you some time to get some things together' she tells him, ignoring my question.

'How very *generous* of you Mum' Luke sneers, then storms out of the room.

'Do you think I want to send you away Luke? Do you think I want to be alone with him? Your father would kill us both if you stayed. This way, at least you'll be far away' she tries to explain, but he's already left the kitchen.

While Luke gathers his things in his room, we sit with his mother awkwardly. She clutches the phone, afraid that we might try to confiscate it. We could do it, very easily. But I've felt Southway slowly closing in on me for days now, her calling the police telling them we broke in and assaulted her husband will damn us sure, but some things are just inevitable, like Elliot getting what he wants. I'm still not sure how the pieces fit together though.

'Look I understand what you're doing' Dan tells her 'But can't you just lie and tell him you called the police without actually doing it?'

'He's a different beast Daniel, powerful. If I lied and he found out, I'd be as good as dead' she cries.

I used to believe that living without purpose was the greatest curse, but I only ever felt that way because my life was so bland to know anything else. I can't imagine living so trapped. Dan hugs her, he understands it too, it's just cruel that Luke can't see why she made this choice. In its own way, she's being the braver than the three of us combined, and I can't help but wonder why this life was so punishing to not give Dan a mother like her. Or, was it not life that made Robert like this, was it me, the criminal, that tipped him over the edge? Luke told us that he was never violent to him, but I don't buy that for one second, but if it was me that made Robert violent, then I may as well have hit him myself. I won't let them carry my burdens.

'One of the officers, I think she may be able to help you Katsumi' I say.

'You do?' she asks, ecstatic for another option.

'No no no' Dan shakes his head, 'Fuck all of them, I know you have this thing about the Constable, but trust me, none of the cops in this town are trust worthy, I'd know. Katsumi knows this piece of shit the best, whatever she thinks is the safest option, that's what we're doing'

I can't argue with him about that, but I really do think Constable Marigold would at least try to help this situation if we explained it to her, but if it really did make it worse and Robert took it out on her... Well, what's the next step up from this?

'I don't think I have much reason to stay in town either, but it's not me that you need to convince' I point up at the ceiling.

Neither of them say anything for some time, we just stand and listen to Luke moving around in his room, until the door closes. I can see Dan gearing up to argue, but Luke reappears in the doorway, woollen hat planted on his head and a bursting backpack over one shoulder. He stares his mother down, I wish he could understand her.

'Hey mate, you've gotta realise where she's coming from' Dan reasons.

Luke ignores him, steps over Robert's body and starts picking things from the cupboard and forcing them into the backpack.

'Please I-' Katsumi pleads.

'I don't care what you have to say' his voice breaks, still facing the cupboard.

He's wearing a black, expensive looking windbreaker, and the material scratches as he pulls away from her when she tries to touch him.

'Hear her out' I tell him, putting on my best leader voice.

Still reaching into the cupboard, he tentatively holds a tin of figs in his hand.

'This is the hardest thing I'll ever have to do' she tells him straight.

The tin slips from his fingers and bounces along the tiles, clanging over to Dan and I. I stop it with my foot, silencing the room. Luke's shoulders bounce as he sobs until he falls to his knees. His mother falls with him, and they just hold each other and let it out.

'Then don't do it' he whispers to her.

306

'I love you, my sweet boy' she kisses his head, 'You won't be gone long. You have strong friends, they'll protect you if anything happens'

Dan and I look at each other, even the socially savvy Daniel Steele is at a loss for what to do here. I can tell he's proud of Luke, and I am too. Suddenly, he rises and stands tall over his mother.

'We look out for each other, I'll get strong enough to protect them back, I'm not a coward'

He says it as though it's directed at her, she sighs and picks up the tin of figs. Luke's face unwrinkles and his scowl disperses.

'If you're still here when your father wakes up, he'll probably kill you. And if he finds out you ran and I didn't call the police, he'll probably kill me. You need to leave, at least for a while until everything calms down around here. That's just what it is. It's the way it has to be, for us both to be safe'

'Yeah well, you have to understand something too' he says immediately, I don't think any of us expected him to be so composed.

'I'll do what you say, I don't agree but I get it. But when I see you next' he points at his father, 'It better not be here'

'Luke…' she looks up at him.

He reaches out a hand, takes hers and pulls her close into his chest.

'I understand why you can't leave tonight or tomorrow, but whether it's weeks, months or years, when we next meet, you better not still be here'

'Yes, you have a deal' she says simply, nodding into his chest.

And the two of them smile at each other. The "Kawamura Smile" I've come to think of it as. Their faces radiate and the tears fade, Dan and I eventually join them in a group hug.

'We'll all look after each other' I say.

Robert stirs, his arm twitches and I brace, just in case he's ready to jump up and fight again.

'It looks like it's time boys' she sighs.

We all stand, the three of us taking a second to catch our breath, then I nod for her to do it. She punches the three buttons on the phone and then holds it up to her ear. I can hear the line ring a couple of times, then she speaks.

'Yes? Hello yes, my husband has been assaulted'

She speaks as though she's distraught, although I know this is pretend, I have a feeling that a life with Robert has got her used to faking emotions.

'Yes. Yes, he is breathing. No, I didn't recognise them, they're gone now. Yes, Southway. No? Wait what? What do you mean occupied? What major incident? Call back later?! You're the police? How are all the officers- Hello?'

She looks at the phone in confusion, before setting it down on the marble.

'What was that about?' Luke asks.

'They said... That there was a major incident on the North side of town and no officers are available' she stares at the phone perplexed.

'Yes! Now you can say you made every effort to call the cops but they wouldn't help, he can't hold that against you now!' Dan cheers.

'Hang on, this doesn't make sense' I scratch my chin, still sore from where Elliot kicked it, 'This must be what they were talking about when you were there today Dan'

'You think its *him*?' Dan asks.

I don't answer straight away, and I don't need to ask him to elaborate.

'There should be one left after all' Luke half smiles.

Dan rubs his hands between one another.

'This is what we trained for boys! Since the police sure aren't capable enough to do anything right' Dan claps us both on the back.

'If that's the case, we'll need some gear' I sigh.

'Great, a trip back home' he turns up his nose.

'I'm afraid so' I nod us towards the doorway, 'Luke, we'll give you a minute'

'I can never repay you' Katsumi says as we're walking away.

I don't know if she's talking about bursting in to fight Robert, or promising to look after her son, but either way, she doesn't need to thank us.

'Until we meet again' I wave to her, 'Oh, and we'll be going North'

XXIII
The Blood and the Water

Dan yanks the hand brake upwards abruptly, and we snake across the gravel until he brings us to a stop. Then ever so slowly, he rolls down the driveway, until we're close enough to the family home.

'We going to walk all the way from here?' Luke asks.

It's true, we're still a while away from the old Steele house, we've parked in the driveway.

'Not us, just me' Dan tells him, 'What time is it?'

I check my phone for the time, I have a lot of missed texts and calls from mum and dad, I ignore them.

'Ten thirty, just about' I tell him.

He lowers the handbrake and starts to turn the car around, carefully and quietly, letting it roll idle as much as he can.

'That's good yeah, she'll be asleep' he says to himself.

After our vehicle is turned, facing the way we came in, Dan twists the key back towards him and slides it out. I'm about to commend him on forward thinking and securing our escape route, but Luke speaks out.

'Let me come with you'

'Absolutely not' Dan scoffs.

'You helped me with my Dad' Luke argues.

Dan opens his door and hangs his long legs outside to stretch.

310

'Yeah but fighting is easy' he looks out to his home, 'This won't be'

'Dan-'

'Just stay here' he hops out and cracks his neck before turning to me in the passenger seat, 'Make sure he stays put Warren, I'll be back'

Luke hops out too, I make no effort to stop him.

'We could carry more stuff if I came' he hisses quietly, but Dan is already out of earshot.

Luke and I look out towards the house, easily seen by the smoke coming from the chimney waving across the dark blue night sky. I bet Dan lit the fire place, even after getting taken in for questioning by the police, I bet he still made time to light the fire for them.

'We should, uh' I begin, 'Make sure we're ready to go quickly'

Leaning against the doors, we watch him dart along the ground, like a ninja from a movie sneaking past guards in a palace. He reaches his bedroom window, and jiggles the frame out of place, sets the glass panel gentle against the wall, and hoists himself inside.

'Hey Luke?' I say.

'Yeah?'

'It's kind of fucked up but, thank you for saving me, you know, from your dad. I really think I was close to dying there'

'It had to be done' he sighs.

'How do you feel?' I ask.

'Worried, about this big incident' he says, intentionally avoiding it.

'You know what I'm talking about Luke'

He tightens his eyes fiercely, watching the house.

'I feel proud Warren, and I feel strong. I just hope Mum gets out of there'

'I know she will, because you inspired her tonight' I rest a hand on his shoulder.

'Isn't it fucked for feeling proud for beating up my dad?' he sighs.

'I don't think I'm smart enough to answer that' I laugh nervously.

I really don't know what to tell him, I think he was right to do what he did, if that's what he wants to hear.

'When you told us he never hit you, was that the truth?' I ask.

'Are you asking me if he's evil?'

'No, I know he's evil, you can just tell' I quote him.

Luke nods down with a wry smile.

'It's no secret that dad has money, as evil as he is, he was always happy to spend it on me and Mum. But now, I realise that was only to keep us too busy to rebel. Shiny new things that kept us down on our knees. Computer games to shut me up. He did buy me Monster Masher though, and without that I don't know if we would be friends, so thanks Dad, for that at least'

I don't think he's even talking to me, I don't think he's talking to anyone, the swelling of his black eye seems to be going down, and I can see that his eyes aren't full of scorn.

'Although, we've played Monster Masher in real life now haven't we Warren?' he laughs.

I'm glad he's lightened up, he didn't seem like himself for a moment there.

'True, how do you rate it compared to the computer version?' I ask

'It's a lot harder' he shrugs, 'Look!'

Dan's hand gently lowers two backpacks, three sleeping bags, and finally his bow and the remaining arrows out of the window.

'Should we help him?' Luke asks.

I don't get to answer Luke however, because I notice movement in the house. A shadow flicks across the light of the fire place. I hop out of my seat and hiss at him.

'Dan!' I wave him over.

He looks at me, then at the front door, I see him swear under his breath. He slings the gear onto his back quickly, and then makes his way over to us. The front door swings inwards when he's about halfway between us and the house.

'Daniel?' Isabelle asks, rubbing sleep from her eyes.

She steps out of the doorway, still in her school uniform, and runs barefoot on the rough gravel until she reaches him.

'Hey Izzy' Dan's voice breaks.

He drops the bags to the ground, no longer caring about the noise level. They're close enough for us to hear.

'Fuck's sake' I drop my head into my hands.

'I can't watch this' Luke says, doing the same.

Dan approaches her, and kneels down to talk to her.

'What are you doing up silly? You have school tomorrow' he laughs and brushes a strand of hair from her eyes.

'Where did you go today?' she asks.

'I was just visiting Lucas and Warren' he tells her.

'You didn't tell me' she says annoyed.

'I know I didn't, I'm sorry' he tells her.

My heart breaks for him.

'Actually Izzy, I think I'm going to stay with them for a while, okay?'

'For how long?' she asks, upset.

'I'm not sure' he exhales.

'Well, can I come? You never let me do anything with you guys' she groans.

'I...' he stammers.

Then he begins to cry, he hugs her close, one hand gently on the back of her head.

'I think I might be gone for a long time Izzy. But I promise I'll take you somewhere really cool when I get back'

'Where?' she asks excited.

'It's a secret' he tells her, 'I can't tell you about it just yet'

'Alright but you've promised' she tells him strictly.

They smile at each other. When I look away from them to check on Luke, the front door slams against its frame.

'What the fuck are you doing here? Get away from her?' Faye screams at him.

Fuck.

'Isabelle get over here, now!'

Izzy looks back at their mother, then back at Dan, her face washed with confusion, before running back to the house.

'Get inside' Faye orders.

She thrusts Isabelle inside the door, so quickly that the girl almost trips on the doorstep.

'Don't shove her' Dan growls.

'Don't you try to tell me what to do with my child' she barks.

'Since when do you give a fuck about your children? Because you didn't this afternoon when you kicked me out of home'

'I won't have a dirty criminal in my house, and you're no child of mine'

It cuts me, I can't imagine how Dan feels. He is a criminal sure, I've seen him do double the speed limit and buy and sell marijuana, but he's not the criminal for what she thinks he is. I want to say something, I have to, but Luke grabs my wrist when I try to move.

'What?' I mouth.

'Let him' Luke whispers.

'I've felt that way for a long time' Dan continues, 'It doesn't matter to me what you think I've done. I know I grew up to be a good person, and I know I didn't get that from you'

'Oh, grow up and stop acting like you had it so bad' she shrieks.

Even with only the minimal light coming from the front porch, I can see the red in her face now.

'I'm leaving now' he tells her, picking up the gear again.

'Like father like son, they say' she laughs.

'You know what, I can't say I blame him anymore' Dan laughs back.

'You arrogant little shit!' she spits.

Furious as he says this, she marches off the porch towards him, while his back is turned as he loads the gear onto the back. However, when her bare feet reach the gravel she yelps in pain, and has to take a step back. Dan looks back at her and laughs.

'I hope you know that I'll be calling the police for your trespassing. Enjoy your second arrest within the same day'

'Knock yourself out, I have a feeling they won't do anything. Oh yeah, and I wasn't arrested today, only questioned. Not that you wanted to hear me out' he slides into the driver's seat.

I think it's at this point that she notices Luke and I, we get into the car before they can resume the shouting.

'Wh-' she stammers, lost for words.

Dan jerks the key and springs our trusty ride to life, he rolls down his window and sticks his neck out.

'Oh yeah one more thing, there was a giant monster living out this way. I took care of it, just like everything else around here, but there's at least one more around. You should look into that'

He rolls us forward to turn the ute around, but when his window is closest to his mother, he stops mid turn. Closer to her now, I can see that that fierce redness is gone from her face entirely, only a ghastly white.

'No wait, one more thing' he laughs, 'I don't know how, but I'm going to make sure Isabelle gets out of here, and gets raised by someone who actually gives a shit. Goodbye'

'Worthless, just like your father! Get back here!' she starts.

And he finishes the turn, spewing exhaust smoke in her face and leaving her screaming behind us in the night. We stay silent until her voice is well and truly gone and we're on our way back towards town.

316

'You okay?' Luke asks him.

'Of course' he nods strongly, 'She just needs to be brave for tonight'

The trees and the gravel eventually blur into buildings and asphalt, my mind hardly registers the change, I don't know what I register anymore.

'Alright Warren, what are we doing?' Luke asks from the back seat, he sounds weary.

'Heading North' I tell him.

'Are you sure about this?' Dan asks, 'We could just leave?'

'If the old man is involved, I have to know'

'Come on we have a long drive ahead as it is' Dan sighs, 'We've been through enough shit tonight'

I can't believe what I'm hearing from him.

'You'd trust Southway with Sergeant Dickhead now, would you?'

'Man, fuck Southway, all it's done is give us signs that it doesn't want us!'

'Would you trust Isabelle with them?' I jab.

'Warren' Dan grits his teeth, 'Don't go there'

Luke sticks his head in between us from the back seat like a parent annoyed at our bickering.

'Guys, we got the gear, and we promised ourselves we'd protect Southway'

'I'm not backing out' Dan exhales, 'But I'm not doing this for Southway anymore, I want to tie up our loose ends and get out of here'

'If this "major incident" really is the last of the four Lapdogs, we just have to make sure it burns and then I'd say Southway is quite protected'

'And if we run into the police and Elliot is with them' Dan nods, 'I'll strangle him with that scarf'

We cruise through town, entirely silent, eventually past Wanda and Rhonda's and down the main street. I try my best to take in the familiarity, this should be the last time I see this place. It's pleasant, breathing it all in, until we pass the lab, closed off with police tape.

'It's going to be dangerous you guys' I say, 'Real dangerous. You don't have to come with me'

'Of course we do' Luke begins, 'If it wasn't for you, we-'

'Holy shit' Dan slams the brakes on again.

I turn back to Dan to see his face coated in red and blue light. We've reached the north exit of Southway, the giant "Welcome" archway that stands over the road, and up ahead are about half a dozen police cars with their lights blaring. Officers wander around and chatter, I can't see anything past them.

'Let's have a look' I say.

Dan nods and pulls us off the road, parking in behind some nearby trees. The three of us spill out, and collect our weapons from the back as the drizzle begins, typical Southway. Dan taking his bow and Luke taking his hatchet, my usual machete gone, so I opt for the second biggest one in Dan's collection. This one is far smaller and plainer looking, no striking orange handle like the other, this one's handle is worn, uncomfortable brown leather. No razor thin blade that looks like fine steel, only painted black with cheap paint.

'Sorry about your other one' Dan says, noticing me holding it.

'I'll make it work' I say, 'Let's get closer'

Scuttling forward, we take up position crouched behind one of the police cars, the furthest one away from the commotion. Droplets ping off

318

the roof of the car, getting heavier now. Dan peers around the headlights at the front while Luke and I look up through the window and out the one on the other side.

Something is happening on the road. The police cars have been arranged two on our side parked horizontal across both sides of the road, and another two arranged the same at the other end to block any traffic. There's a few other vehicles parked haphazardly in the middle, about ten police men and women are in between, they all wear long rain jackets over their uniforms, some have hospital masks and rubber gloves on. Officers closest to the centre are having the most powerful reactions, some kneel beside their cars, it initially looks like they're praying, until they start to gag.

We snap our heads down as one comes close to us to vomit. He spits a few times and wipes his mouth. Is he a new recruit? What has he seen? When he raises his head into the light, I can see that it's Sergeant Dillon. He stands up straight and runs his hands back through his hair, then strokes his stubble.

'This isn't real' I see him mouth.

He slaps himself across the cheek and shakes his head.

'Come on, come on!' he says aloud, before turning to the other officers, 'Alright gather around!'

When his back is turned, I wave Dan and Luke to move. We scurry away from the car we're behind, moving in closer still, careful to keep behind the officers while they get up to hear what the Sergeant has to say. Luke and I obscure ourselves behind one of the most central cars, Dan stays one further back, bow drawn, so he doesn't have to see what we do. There's blood, lots of blood. The whole section of bitumen is washed through with gore, slowly mixing with the rain and flowing away. It's coming from a car, not a police car, a family sized car, just off to the side of the road, front end crushed in so badly that I can't tell much about it except that I think it had white paint underneath the red. Luke grips my wrist and points over his shoulder. With not a drop of colour in his face, and trembling lips he shows me where to look. I follow where his finger is directing my eyes, over the bonnet of the car and onto the road, where a severed leg in a plastic bag, rests with its stump facing us.

XXIV
Extinction

I don't look at the limb for more than a millisecond before ducking back down and cup my hand over Luke's mouth, afraid he might scream. I forgot he hadn't seen Rhonda's arm in the meadow like we did. Maybe Dan and I should count ourselves lucky to have been eased into the horror a bit.

'Listen up' Dillon addresses everybody else.

I see a light coming from his hand, at first, I think it's a torch but when my eyes adjust I can tell it's his phone.

'I want this road clear. Forensics, collect everything, meanwhile my guys, start moving the vehicles'

My ears prick up when he says this.

'Move' I direct my friends away.

Dan moves immediately but I have to pull Luke by his collar to get him out of his trance. The three of us dive and slide into the brush off to the side. No one notices us, I can tell because they keep talking.

'We've done what we can tonight. I want everyone to recover and regroup before we start the investigation in the morning'

'What will you do Sir?' a man's voice asks.

We can easily hear them from our hiding place, they're yelling to get their voice over the rain.

'I'd like to stay on scene for a moment. See if there's anything we missed in our... Shock'

That's suspicious.

'I'd like to stay too if I may, Sir' a woman says.

I see her step forward, although they face away from us, I can tell by the long, burgundy hair falling down the back of her raincoat that it's the Constable.

'Arianne, no. This is your first major scene, you've done your job tonight'

'I've got the stomach for it' she argues.

'You all have your orders' Dillon finishes.

And with that, everyone begins to move. They tread through the blood and get into their cars. The guys with gloves and masks carry the plastic bags, with what I can only assume must be more body parts, to the northernmost cars. It's efficient the way they move the cars, coordinating in such a way that no one boxes anyone else in. This is going to be a massive police operation, and a huge story for Southway, those tapeworms that speak on the radio every night must be salivating right now. Disappearances in a tiny town can be swept under the rug away from outsiders, but these forensics guys aren't locals, and I'm sure they'll go back to wherever they came from and talk about what they've seen. I keep an eye on the Constable, she hides in the very spot we were just in, until all the others have left. That must be the Sergeant's car.

Dillon stands in the rain with his head down at his phone. Texting? He looks around the area, and then pockets his phone and walks off the road and into the trees on the opposite side to us.

'Where did he go?' Dan whispers, struggling to see past some leaves.

The Constable is watching him as well, it takes her no time at all to decide to open the car and pull out a pistol from the back, as well as what must be bullets, and give chase to her superior.

'Come on!' I wave them.

Into the trees we go, but try as we might, the three of us can't find her. She's too far ahead and it's too dark to try to follow any path she may have taken. I lead them through, hacking a straight line for us to march down. In our struggle, we come to where the trees end and the leaf litter is replaced with fine stones, a gravel pit surrounding what seems to be an abandoned saw mill, just how far did we go? I had no idea this was even here. Probably fifty metres in towards the centre of this, is a massive, hulking metal building, standing caked in rust at around roof height, this must be, or, *have been*, the main building. From the top most point of that, a horribly rusted conveyor belt runs down to a sort of trough on the ground. An assortment of metal frames and dead machines are strewn around, the rust is so bad it's hard to tell what any of them were, or if they were even all once part of the same thing. Against the main structure, an all too familiar old man leans, while the black-haired boy who I saw in the meadow perches on an old electrical box beside him.

When I see them both together, Locke Dawson and Elliot Young, I want to go berserk. Is this where Locke was living? Is this where they both have been? My first instinct is to check for any saw blades that may be around, but it seems they were all removed from this place. I have to force myself to be calm, at least for now, and it's only when I do, that I notice Sergeant Dillon standing ten metres away from them.

'That's Locke?' Dan asks me.

I know him well enough to know he's really got his eyes on Elliot, and that he's trying to stifle the rage in his voice. I hope he can stay in control here. Luke points over to our left, Constable Marigold is doing the same thing we are, hiding and listening, with a million questions to ask.

'He's so weak looking' Dan says, looking back at Locke.

I shush him for now when they start to speak to one another.

'You got here so fast Sergeant!' Locke says to him.

'I was able to get here so fast because I was called just out of town, a family, four dead, one unaccounted for. Looks like their car hit something' Dillon says, unimpressed.

'A shame. Was alcohol involved?' Locke asks.

'They hit something' Dillon cracks his knuckles, 'Then that something tore apart whatever was left of them'

Locke widens his eyes, silently asking Dillon if he has more to say.

'Are you accusing me of something?' he asks.

'I know it was one of your demons' he snaps.

Elliot looks between them, a child caught between his quarrelling parents. A child, that's what he is. Dillon unholsters his pistol from underneath his rain coat and aims it at Locke, who doesn't react at all. A heavy, silver revolver, unnecessarily powerful looking for a small-town cop to carry. Elliot ducks behind the metal piece he was sitting on when Dillon clicks the hammer back.

'We had a deal, and you went back on your end' Dillon says.

'I didn't do anything at all' Locke tells him calmly, 'And I didn't command anything to do anything either'

Dillon takes steps towards him with the gun raised to the old man's face.

'Which one was it? It destroyed their car, killed the parents instantly, but I know it survived. Show it to me!'

Locke doesn't answer until the gun is touching his forehead, at which point he finally nods at Elliot. The boy makes a vaguely familiar clicking noise with his mouth, it takes him a few times before he gets I right, and I recognise the sound. The same one Locke used to command Lapdog in his lab.

'Well done, that was good' Locke congratulates.

There's metallic clanging from within what looks like the main building. The Sergeant watches the building shake, dust floating down as something hits against the metal.

'They don't much like being woken up Sergeant' Locke sighs, 'Especially not when they're injured'

Finally, the clanging stops, and yet another Lapdog appears to me from around the side of the mill. There's no doubt what it is, same vertical running mouth, same concrete pipe of a neck, but this one almost walks upright on two feet. The bulk of its standing weight being on the hind legs, its front legs resembling arms more than anything else. The knuckles on its hands reach the ground and drag like a gorilla's, the claws overgrown, they curl up and almost reach into its own wrists.

'Regarding your car crash, it most likely was this one that they hit, yes' Locke admits as it sits obediently between Elliot and himself, 'The last one of its kind, the two that were lost to young Avery were-'

Dillon fires his gun, bullet after bullet until I count six, he unloads them into the thing's skull. Elliot flinches further away with each bang, Locke only makes enough effort to shield his face from the blood that spatters outwards. Chunks are torn from its head and neck and without a noise, it tips over dead.

'And now they're extinct' Dillon announces, reloading the gun with bullets from his belt.

Neither of the three say anything for some time. Dillon keeps the gun on Locke while Elliot peers over his box. I can't see the Constable anymore, shit, where did she move to? The corpse finally combusts, this one taking longer than the other two that I saw, this must be because it's bigger. Pieces of its decimated head have been strewn so wide, that small fires have started in a few places, giving us much more light to work with, and it's only with this new light, that I can see how furious Locke is, a fury that I saw myself firsthand that day. He watches his precious thing burn, losing all four now, he mourns.

'You gave me your word that you would take these things and leave, I kept my end of the bargain' Dillon snaps.

'I lost all four' Locke weeps.

'Just shut up' Dillon tells him, gun raised once more, 'I gave you a chance but that was a mistake I won't make twice'

'*Did* you do what we asked though?' Elliot asks.

'Yes! The fingerprints will just take time' Dillon stammers.

'Well I don't have time!' Locke yells at him, 'Avery singlehandedly almost brought me to a halt, I don't have time to *wait* for the fingerprints. I want Avery now'

'Then fuck it, at this point I'll just bring you Avery, why fuck around with this other shit at all?'

'Because I want to hurt him' Elliot finally says.

I see Dan stretching his fingers for an arrow, I grab his wrist and shake my head.

'I'll kill all three of them, I could do it right now'

Locke makes two whistling noises, causing Dillon to alert. Elliot seems the most concerned of all, when the metal clanging starts again. Whatever is happening, Elliot knows what it is.

'You shouldn't have come here Sergeant' Elliot grimly tells him.

He's much more confident that he was a moment ago. This isn't right, that's all there is, that's all four.

'It *could* have been this one that that car hit tonight' he gestures at the flames, still unable to look at it, 'Or, it could just have easily been one of these two'

Locke cackles from around the side, and a new beast trots around to face him. This one is completely different to the ones that I've seen, not a secret fifth Lapdog relative. A boar as large as a bull, with two white upward curled tusks coming from each side of its mouth and two fighting horns along the ridge of its nose, they're so large together that they almost cover its whole head like armour. A thick, shaggy orange mane draped over its bulging shoulders, I can't believe those legs can hold all of its weight up. It sniffs and snorts at the flames, scratching at the ground around it with its tusk, I wonder if it can sense the death. Locke clicks again and it forgets about its brother, and faces up to Dillon.

The saw mill has not finished groaning yet, the steel continues to creak along, the rust flaking from the upper most beams. Up above, the conveyor belt begins to wobble, releasing trapped woodchips that slide all the way down to the bottom. A long arm with curled claws hooks into the worn tread on the belt and pulls itself out from the opening. Not as large as the boar, but not small by any means, this creature quickly slinks upside down along the underside of conveyor belt by digging it's claws in, before dropping down to join its allies. This one is the most unnerving of all. A sloth with two long, spindly arms ending in razor sharp fingers, the fur on its face is so dark I can't even see if it has eyes or not, it glides so low to the ground like a shadow. The Sergeant collapses to his knees, unable to hold the gun at arm's length for any longer.

'What do you think?' Locke asks, 'These are two of my favourite genomes to use. These are only young still, I took my assistant here and gave him a crash course in cloning, not bad for his first attempt, no? I lost quite a few planned genomes in the fire that night, but these two are tried and true, perfect for the treetops and plains of the world'

Elliot is his assistant then? I see, he fell for the trap.

'What the fuck are these ones?' Luke mouths.

In comparison, Lapdog and the... well, Pre-Lapdogs, were domestic looking, but these things are other worldly. Imagining Locke presenting the world with the dopey looking Lapdog, everyone's new favourite household pet, ushering in the new era of science, only for him to then escalate to these things. Humanity wouldn't have a chance.

'Let's not be hasty' Dillon begs, 'I can bring you Steele, I'll bring you Avery himself!'

'I'll get Avery, don't you worry. We- wait, someone is there' Locke stops everything.

My heart stops. There's no way we've been seen or heard from this far away. Dillon looks behind himself, but it's not at us. I nod at Luke and Dan to get themselves ready, but we don't get to act, the Constable rushes from the trees to join her superior, firing her gun into the air a single time.

'Stop this right now! This is insane!' she screams.

'Oh? I believe we told you to come alone?' Locke says to Dillon.

'I did! I swear I did!' Dillon quivers, 'Get the hell out of here'

'What the hell is happening between the three of you?' she demands.

'Nothing anymore, this alliance is done, but the two of you won't be leaving here alive' Locke tells them.

He clicks his tongue.

'Now!' I yell.

Dan looses a thoughtless arrow as soon as we pop up, it clinks against metal causing everyone to turn in shock and the beasts stop in their tracks, now unsure of their target. We leap out of the trees and join the confused police officers.

'What the fuck are you doing here?' Dillon asks.

'Don't worry I have plenty of questions for you too, you germ' Dan says.

'Stop, we are all allies' Luke tells them.

All five of us eye up the two beasts with no idea what to expect.

'For now' Dan agrees, eyeing the Sergeant.

Elliot and Locke do the math in their minds, I can see the gears turning. Two beasts that we haven't seen before, and five of us. How confident is the old man? Locke clicks his tongue again, deciding that he likes the odds, and hell breaks loose.

XXV
The Violent Science

Elliot lends Locke a hand, helping the frail man away from the machinery while we're pinned down by the new creatures. Luke immediately joins the two officers, Dan and I detached from them slightly.

'Alright, get ready for this, we don't know what they can do' I tell everyone.

'You've got the most hands-on experience kid, what do we do?' Dillon calls to me.

'Those guns work, don't they?' Dan yells back.

'Yes, they work'

'Should we leave these things to those two then?' Dan asks me.

I see him, watching Elliot and Locke, watching with the hatred steaming from his mouth in the cold while he taps his hands on the shaft of his next arrow.

'Dan'

'What?'

'Are you with us?' I ask.

'I... I could get them Warren, I could catch the two of them so easily'

'I don't doubt that you could, but we need you here'

'No, you don't, let me finish this'

'I might not, but what if Luke does?'

Dan looks over at him, nervous as hell, he grips his hatchet and stands slightly behind the two adults and their guns.

'Don't forget who you are my friend' I tell him.

'You're right' he admits, 'Let's make this quick, then they're next'

The boar scrapes its foot into the dirt and the sloth's claws rap together as though its snapping its fingers. The five of us tighten up the formation. The sloth to our left and the boar to the right. The boar seems physically stronger and harder to take down, I should have to tackle that.

'Uh okay, can someone with a gun help me with the pig, and the other three can take... whatever that is'

'I'm with you' the Constable decides.

She slowly swaps places with Dan, neither taking their eyes off the beasts until she's beside me and Dan has, begrudgingly, joined the Sergeant that has always given him so much grief. The sloth moves in, clinking its claws together towards them, seeming to drift while it's circling them, effectively separating them from us. I realise it may not be a sloth at all, when I see how quick it moves.

'Get back kid!' Dillon calls.

He rips Luke backwards by his shirt just as the sloth stabs forward with its fingers pointed together like a spear. The Sergeant throws Luke out of the stab's reach and responds with a bullet at the sloth, I don't think it lands, I see no blood spray, and no chunk of its head go flying, but it causes it to scuttle around the back of the mill and inside, the two of them chase after it.

'Follow them' I point Dan after them.

Constable Arianne and I face up with the boar, I think the sound of Dillon's gun makes her fire too, she puts two quick shots into the beast but they're harmlessly sponged by its thick hide and buried into its shoulder.

'Save them, we have to work this out' I tell her.

In response, it drags its hoof on the dirt like a bull then charges at us, tusks and horns ready to pierce. It gets close enough to show off how sharp its appendages are, but we both manage to roll to either side, then back up together.

'You can just call me Ari' she says.

The beast charges again, it's so fast to gear up for another. The lapdogs that I fought were dim-witted enough to blindly leap at you, but being baited into that was their weakness. I look over this thing's rippling leg muscles and strong, toothed head. It was designed for endurance, to ram things over and over until there's nothing left. We roll away again, letting it pass through, but we can't do it forever.

'Please, it's much quicker to say' she laughs.

'Okay, this way Ari'

I point us towards the machinery, and we crouch behind the metal box Elliot had sat on. I can hear the grunts and gunshots from within the mill, as the three of them chase the dancing sloth around inside. It sounds like it's giving them trouble, but at least they're alive.

'What do you-' I start.

But the beast rams into the box, sending us falling forward into the dirt, we fly so far forward that we're almost under the conveyor belt now. The electrical box is destroyed, chunks of rusted metal splinter off, our cover destroyed. I make an effort to recover as quick as I can, but Ari is already up, she helps me off the ground.

One of the pig's tusks has a chunk of metal lodged on its tip. I hate to think what it could do to a human body. It doesn't ready its next charge straight away this time, has it stunned even itself? For once, I try not to spend too much time analysing it, and slash at its nose.

330

My swipes ding off the tusk and horns without so much as causing them a notch, but eventually, I manage one nick on its snout, and even with this beaten, second grade machete, it slices through its nose like it's butter. It's not deep, I don't think it even noticed, but it tells me what I need to do. It drags hooves again.

'Good job' Ari says.

'It's face, it seems pretty soft' I tell her, out of breath from the flurry of slashes, 'The skin on its back could take bullets, but I cut the skin on its nose with this old thing'

'Hey that's clever' she says, 'Is that why it has the horns do you think?'

Before I can look for long, the beast charges again, but I can't play matador anymore. Being beaten by Robert, then thrown around by this pig is starting to take a toll on my body it seems, instead I have to just throw myself out of the attack. Again, Ari is ready to pick me up, she fires another bullet at it as it finishes its follow through under the conveyor belt but this one isn't even acknowledged by our opponent.

'If only it didn't have the, you know' she gestures at her own face.

'Tusks?' I say.

'Right, I can try to shoot them out I guess?' she suggests.

'It can keep its teeth, but can you bring this down?' I point up at the belt.

She looks up and smiles, realising what I'm thinking.

'I'll leave the timing up to you' I tell her.

'I've got it, you won't have to roll this time, kid'

She fires shots at all the joints in the metal above us that she can see until the gun clicks emptily. I don't know how accurate she was, but it will have to do now. The boar gets ready to rush at us, it's superstitious hoof drag complete, Ari watches it, her mouth moving as she counts to herself, we rest our hands on the metal frame.

'Say when' I remind her.

'Now!' she yells, and we begin to shake the conveyor belt.

The corroded metal moans from a dozen places as we rock it back and forth. In the half of a second that we're quaking the metal, I somehow have time to worry that we've left it too late, but the belt doesn't just fall, it snaps in the middle, and just like that, we're too early. The lower half of the belt, the half that we're holding, gives way and falls in between us and the boar just before it reaches us with its explosive force. Unlike the electrical box though, the half of the belt doesn't crumble when it bashes its skull, this is thick steel, its front most horn cracks against the belt and the hog squeals at the impact. I jolt backwards reflexively, while I feel like I could collapse, Ari has the spatial awareness that we need. She takes one step forward and leaps off her toes, grabbing onto the top half of the belt and pulling it down as hard as she can. Under her weight, it finally gives way, collapsing down right onto the stunned beasts back. At first it thrashes, desperate to buck the metal off its spine, but soon it lies still, succumbing to the weight and accepting what's to come next.

'Is that what you had in mind?' Ari asks as she wipes the rust from her hands.

'More or less' I laugh, taking her hand and being hoisted up for what feels like the dozenth time tonight, 'Maybe I shouldn't have tried something that needed such precise timing, lucky you're switched on'

Tusks and mane poke through the belt in places, the shrapnel rising and falling over its belly lets me know it still lives. I hand her the machete.

'What's this?' she asks, taking it tentatively.

'This is your victory, and you have no bullets left, right?'

'Oh, right' she says slowly, looking at it.

She's hesitant to end its life.

'And then help those guys inside'

I start to walk away, when she calls me.

332

'Warren?'

'Yeah?'

She looks at the weapon in her hand, then holds it back out to me.

'Whatever you're doing, are you going to need this?' she asks quietly.

I look down at my hands.

'No' I say.

I jog this time, fresh with adrenaline, darting into the trees, pressing off the ones that are in my way with my hands, only stopping to listen every so often. They can't have gotten far. Once I'm far enough away from the battle behind, I can hear him.

'Curses!' Locke grunts.

I sprint towards the voice, bouncing off the trees until I see the back of his white lab coat ahead. Elliot holds both his hands, he seems to be stuck.

'Damn this old body. Always holding me back!'

He kicks at the brushwood, his thin legs not strong enough to tear through the tangles on his own. Elliot looks up to see me charging at them first, and opens his mouth to speak. Before he can say anything, I grab Locke by the back of his coat and yank him backwards, making special effort to slam him down on the ground, he squeaks when his back meets the floor. Elliot can't believe it, and I don't give him enough time to think too hard. With the strongest fist I can clench, I sling my arm forward and bury my knuckles in his cheekbone. His whole body leaves the ground for an instant before thudding when it meets the earth again. He doesn't make a noise. Now I can deal with you.

I turn back to the old man and kneel over him, fearful, he throws his hands up in front of his face. I wrap my hands around his neck, and knock his head against the ground, I hope there's a particularly hard rock under there. This night has taken most of my strength, but I don't need much more to end this old man. I slam his skull again and again, I do it for Bert,

Joy, Rhonda and each of the family members from tonight. Once they've each had a blow, I keep going, for myself, until I need to rest my hands.

'Warren, my boy, Warren listen. Don't you see?' he chokes, 'Don't you see my point now? Look at yourself'

I do what he says. I'm kneeling over a man in his sixties with both hands around his throat.

'This life hasn't been very kind to you and your friends has it Warren? But that's not your fault, you didn't choose things to be this way. We're all just born to suffer one way or another, the only way to free us all is-'

I dig my fingers harder into his neck. He gasps.

'It's not too late to join me, my boy. This hate is just what you needed' he stammers, 'You needed to feel it. You can have Elliot. Do with him what you please. I know you've always hated him, he's told me so. He couldn't hold a candle to you'

I ease the pressure off again, then I take one hand and instead grab him by the scruff of his shirt. He inhales with relief once he can swallow air again.

'You really have no idea' I spit.

He looks up at me afraid, his feeble timeworn hands clasping at my wrist now, begging me with his eyes to let go. He fooled everyone with his performance on the radio, but he's no helpless old man to me, he's hardly a person anymore, he gave up the right to call himself that.

'You know Locke, I used to pray for something like this. That a reason for living would just appear to me. I used to think science has all the answers but maybe that's only because it has all the problems too. I don't want any more answers or purposes, I don't care if we crawled from the ocean or were made from the dirt, I don't even care if aliens put us here just to laugh, we're here now, and I won't let you carry on'

'So...' he croaks.

He grows weaker, I tighten my grip.

> 'I don't know how you became this pathetic, what the universe did to you to make you so empty inside, but I don't care. Life isn't perfect and sometimes it doesn't even make sense, but it is precious, and it's worth living. I won't let you choose to take it away from everybody, I personally promise you that'

I don't mean to sound so melodramatic, is this his influence on me? He manages to squeeze in another breath.

> 'So, kill me. Kill me right now' he wheezes.

My hand instantly lets off when he says this, my body afraid it might obey. What am I doing? I couldn't kill somebody. I wouldn't. I pull my hands up to my chest, Locke rubs his throat where I had my fingers pressed.

> 'No' I say simply.

I don't say it to him, I say it as a command to myself.

> 'Why not?' he asks, his voice recovered slightly, 'Do you think I deserve to live in your eyes Warren?'

He's taunting now.

> 'Or do you think that deep down you're all talk? Why? I think you could do it'

> 'I wouldn't' I snap.

I let him scuttle backwards slightly, but not further than an arm's distance.

> 'But you could' he nods, 'Do you want to know why you won't?'

I stare over at him, he rises to his knees to match my pose.

> 'Let me guess, because then I would be the same as you, deciding for someone to die?'

Locke Dawson laughs. He howls at me until his bruised throat stings and he has to cough.

'The same as me? No, I think you know that killing me would make you *worse* than me'

'Fuck up' I hiss.

'The people, here in this town. The old man who lived alone, the woman who owned the... tailor, was it?'

'It was a shoe shop' I seethe as he mentions them.

'Apologies, Elliot didn't explain very well. Your friend, the restaurant manager, and this family tonight. I did not *choose* them to die Warren'

'You made the things!' I scream in his face, he slides backwards again, now up against a thick tree.

'They are absolutely unbiased, they just feed on whoever they happen to come across. The only one of my creations that has ever hounded somebody in particular was the one I sent to your school. I forced your scent on it from the remains of the laboratory because you had stolen from me, but even then, I knew you would survive, I only needed to jostle you, show you that you stood no chance'

'Consider me jostled' I raise my hand to him.

'But I did not have your boss killed just to spite you' he holds his hands up.

'You did so!' I shout, but there's no conviction in it, 'Because I wouldn't go along with it'

'I don't claim to be a judge or a saint Warren. I'm not as delusional as you like to think, and I certainly don't think I have the right to pick and choose who lives'

He chuckles to himself.

'Nobody will be spared Warren. Not you and your friends, and once everything is in place, not Elliot, or even myself. I don't want to rule this world with my creations, I want to gift it to them, in hopes that they are more responsible with it than we ever were. Unfortunately, some people will go sooner and some will go with more violence, but we will go all the same, without prejudice. I don't decide, if you choke me to death, could you say the same?'

For once, I ignore what he has to say, he's spent enough time in my head. Before I make my move, Locke's eyes dart upwards, looking behind me. I finally look away from the scientist, turning back to investigate, but before my head even gets halfway, a boot's heel slams into the side of my face.

Through the flashes fading in and out of my vision, I can make out Elliot helping Locke to his feet. I roll onto my knees to watch them while I nurse the side of my head. A torch's beam shines through the trees and flickers over their faces, or do I have a concussion? I'm only just now noticing that the commotion behind us has stopped, this is the others approaching.

'Quick, let's go!' Elliot says franticly.

But Locke shrugs Elliot's hands away, and drags his pathetically thin legs back over towards me, they crack as he kneels down to me on the floor. I can't pull one hand away from my temple, the pain is too great, Elliot has kicked me twice in the same place in just a few days. I throw my free hand around beside me, looking for my blade or a rock or a stick or anything. I recall what Elliot did to me in the meadow, and scratch at the ground, digging up some dirt to throw in Locke's face, but before I get enough, he places a gentle hand on mine.

'I like you Warren, I really do. More than anything I wanted you for my own, I just needed you to suffer and see. You were very close, weren't you? I hope I've shown you how cruel this world is tonight'

'Hey!' I shout to the others, 'Over here!'

'Whenever you see injustice, I hope you remember me, and remember that this world will be an evil place as long as humans

337

exist. But, if I know you like I think I do… Well, I wish you all the best in your efforts to come'

With great determination, he rises and joins Elliot, who props his master's arm around his shoulder and helps him hobble. On the ground like a worm, I clutch at their ankles as they move further and further out of my reach. The two of them, the two people I hate the most, escape together into the darkness, until they're long gone, leaving me face down and battered in the dirt.

'Warren? Hey!' they call, that's Luke, I think.

'I'm here!' I call back.

My head still pulsating, I bring it up to call out to my friends again.

'Here!'

The lights grow closer, bringing crunching of the leaf litter, until Ari, then Dillon, then Luke, and then Dan, appear before me. Ari pulls me up with great force and thrusts the torch light on my face to see my injuries. Dan has an arrow drawn and Dillon his gun, together they scope ahead.

'Where did they go?' Dillon asks me.

I point ahead, where I saw them dissolve away a minute ago, or was it an hour ago?

'Let them go' Ari tells him.

'Excuse you?' he scoffs.

Ari passes me over to Luke, freeing her up to stand up to her superior.

'What will you do? We're exhausted, we don't even know where we are. Let's help these kids, for now, we can regroup with the other officers, and tell them what happened'

He doesn't seem convinced, and he eyes her up and down, apparently taking offense.

'We will look for them, but first we need to help these boys' she concludes.

'As you wish' he grunts, holstering his gun, 'The road was back this way'

I'm glad to see him finally listen to reason, and I don't think there's a person better suited to put him in his place than her. Dillon marches us back the way we came from, Ari following closely behind.

'You guys okay with Warren?' she asks.

Dan takes one of my arms from Luke and props me up.

'Yeah, we got him' he nods.

Luke and Dan carry my shoulders behind the officers.

'How are you?' Luke asks me.

'I'm going to kill him' I groan.

'Hey! Don't forget we've got some questions for you!' Dan barks at the Sergeant at the same time.

'Say again?' Luke says, 'Sorry I couldn't hear over old foghorn here'

'I'm going to *stop* him. I said I'm going to stop him'

XXVI
Set in Motion

It's only when the five of us file out from the trees and onto the moonlit road that I notice how badly the others are beaten. To my right, the side of Luke's face is grazed, dirt pressed into the blood, to my left is Dan's arm, the arm he's used to support me all this way, with two parallel cuts near his elbow. Did he raise that arm to shield his face from claw perhaps? He also sports a cut near his nose, although that split could be courtesy of Robert. I cannot remember.

Ari seems to be the most unscathed, tonight only branding her with an array of scratches and messy hair. Dillon is bleeding from the mouth, he hunches over and spits flecks of red into his hand before wiping it onto his rain jacket. I imagine that when the sun comes up, all of us will have bruises that we can't even feel for now. I can wait for my body to heal though, I could rest and let someone stitch me up, but they got what they wanted tonight, I have no spirit, I don't even know who I am or what I'm capable of. Elliot always gets what he wants. Always.

I watched my friend beat his father unconscious tonight, it was self-defence sure, but it was only because of me that Robert was driven to that point. I watched a boy I grew up with be labelled a waste of skin by his own mother. I saw him have to break into his own home to get weapons to help me, and then have to turn his back on his sister because of the war I thrust onto him. I ran from my own parents, I ran after telling them about me and my monsters, will that be how they remember me? I used to see snow and sand and ocean when I closed my eyes to dream, now I only see red.

'Alright Avery, it's time' the Sergeant announces.

I look towards him only to be greeted by a gun barrel aimed down at my face.

'Get up Avery. If you come peacefully, you have my word that we'll pretend your mates had nothing to do with this'

He waves the gun lazily at Luke and Dan.

'You won't touch him' Dan staunches over him.

Ari takes a step towards him as well and he becomes rattled when they close in, turning the gun between them.

'You're the only one who needs to be taken in' Ari grabs his wrist.

Dan moves in to help her.

'Stop!'

'Hey!'

We all jump as the shot rings out. I look around at everyone. Ari. Luke. Dan. Myself. All fine, the round shooting harmlessly away into the night. We all breathe out collectively.

'Now back off. Everyone. Back off!' Dillon snarls.

His greasy hair now falling in glossy threads down his temples. He pulls back the hammer with his thumb and points it back at me.

'He's the centre of it all' Dillon thrusts the gun at me, 'All they wanted was him, if he gets taken in, everything here can just go back to normal, see?'

'Who told you that? The insane old man or the sidekick?' Ari asks.

'I was saving lives God damn it!' he shrieks and points the gun at Ari, 'They told me all they needed was him' Dillon gnashes.

'Did he tell you anything else while you worked with him? Did he tell you how he wants those things to eat everyone until there's nobody left on Earth?' I ask, numbly.

His jaw clenches and his fingers tighten around the gun.

'I didn't work with them you fuc-'

Daniel cannons into the Sergeant, sending them both tumbling. The gun slides from his hand, harmlessly away onto the pavement. Dan picks himself up, Luke and I stand as well, and together with Ari, we all stand over him watching him cry.

'I only did what I was told' he sobs, 'I didn't ask questions, I just did my part of the deal'

'What deal?' asks Ari.

'The boy, the boy who was missing, Elliot, he contacted me one night, and told me to meet him at the sawmill. The old bloke was there and they showed me that thing, he told me they would make the disappearances end if I helped them'

The four of us watch as he weeps on the ground, he's telling the truth I can tell. I can see that Luke and Ari see it too.

'That's the truth I swear. I just wanted to make it stop'

'What did they ask you to do?' she asks, less callously now.

'All he said I had to do… All Elliot said they…'

'Speak. Clearly' Dan grunts.

'Look they didn't tell me shit. The kid told me there would be a party, and he gave me an address. Your house' he points to Dan, 'They just wanted that machete, all I had to do was keep watch, make sure no one tried anything funny until Elliot gave me the sign that he'd got it. The next day he handed it in, and all I had to do was make sure that you got the blame for the lab. That's all they wanted me to do, make sure no one interfered while he got that damn machete, then I just had to make sure we found Daniel Steele's fingerprints on it'

The way he repeats himself, he's distraught. Has this night taken its toll on him? Is he weak of will or are the rest of us just the strong? I don't feel strong, I feel like I've been inflicted with a lifetime's worth of injuries in one night.

'You mean you were asked to ruin my life, and you were happy to do it without asking questions. That's what you mean to say' Dan hisses.

'You attacked the old man with it in the first place' the Sergeant says.

'No' I interrupt, 'I did'

'What Warren?' Ari says, 'Why?'

'Well I didn't *attack* him' I'm sick of going back to this, 'There was this one, it was perfectly obedient, he showed me. He wanted to, I don't know, mass produce it and sell it, and then let them turn on everybody. I couldn't take what I saw. Everywhere I looked I would see it. I knew straight away it was him and his monsters taking those people. So, I borrowed that machete, and I broke into the lab and killed it. He caught me and promised to put me through hell, and that his plan would carry on'

'And then I found you' Luke speaks for the first time in ages, 'And the next day, at school. After we killed the one that came for you, Elliot ran away'

'And while he was crying out here in the bush, he must have met up with the old man, and they what, bonded?' Dan asks.

'Yes' Dillon says, 'That's basically what they told me, yeah'

'So, Sergeant, then Elliot contacted you' Ari takes over from him, 'And he told you to make sure that Daniel here was blamed for everything?'

'That's the truth' he nods.

'That's the dumbest thing I've ever heard' Dan laughs, 'As if the old prick wouldn't just ask you to blame Warren, how does framing me help him?'

'The way they explained it, it sounded like it was the boy's idea, not his'

'Bullshit' Dan laughs at him.

I wanted you for my own, I just needed you to suffer and see.

'Sergeant' I address him, 'You truly did believe you were doing the right thing?'

'Yes Avery, uh Warren, sorry. I know I was. They told me that if I did what they asked, they would take the devils and leave'

That's all you can ask of anybody.

'Very well' I say, 'Look if you need someone to blame or whatever, you can say that the monsters were my fault if you'd like. I'm leaving tonight anyway, so if I disappeared and suddenly the disappearances stopped too, I think that would wrap everything up nicely hey?'

I chuckle and sigh.

'Hang on' Dan stops me, 'We don't have to go anywhere anymore! Ari, if we really can trust you more than this maggot, we need the police to help us with a couple of things around here'

'Of course, Daniel. You're not going anywhere Warren, you did everything you could to fight, this worm was only ever trying to save himself'

She takes her gun now, and aims it at him.

'No, I wasn't!' he wails, 'On my life, I only did what they told me so they would leave'

'And what's your life worth now?' she smirks.

'Don't do it Miss'

It's Luke speaking up, he steps over to her and puts his hand over the gun.

'I beat my father pretty badly tonight' he tells her, 'He would hit me all the time, and my mum. For so long I imagined what that would be like to fight back. These guys, they gave me that chance, but it doesn't feel good, I don't feel fulfilled'

'He put so many lives in danger by working with that old man, he can't be trusted' she maintains.

'Not as a police officer, fuck no, but you can let him live' I add, 'He didn't know how manipulative Locke is, he doesn't deserve to die'

'I'll step down as Sergeant, immediately!' he begs.

Dan paces back and forth, tapping his bow on the ground beside him.

'Locke and Elliot are gone, he can do no more harm here without them' he agrees with us.

'Well, "Sergeant", I think you're lucky that I'm outvoted' Ari puts the gun away.

Although that's what she says, I don't think she would have killed him, I think it was all for show. She was shipped here in the most hectic time, and set under someone far less kind and capable, I think she's just been waiting for a moment like this. I wonder what she will do with the town that she's inheriting? It's a shame that I won't be staying here to see it.

'Thank you' he grovels, 'Just let me live'

Ari closes her eyes and exhales.

'The Southway Police is now under my command, and I won't ever let this sort of thing go unpunished around here again' she announces.

Dillon gets to his feet, his shaky knees barely able to hold up his weight.

'I will make things right, Arianne'

A few days ago, Ari would have done anything this man told her without question, but now she eyes him like a hawk, doubting that his words mean anything at all.

'Twice now I've had them, but I let those devils stand in my way, it won't happen a third time'

She nods with respect, but only slightly.

'See to it that you do, but until then I don't want to see you'

He turns and runs, further and further until he's nothing but a grey smudge in the night air out to the South.

'You weren't really going to kill him, were you?' I laugh.

'Used all my rounds back there remember?' Ari clicks the gun harmlessly, 'Alright, I've got work to do, this is going to be a long night'

'Hell yeah, congratulations on your promotion' Dan says dryly.

The three of us applaud her, mostly as a joke, but it is truly relieving to know the police are in more capable hands now.

'Thank you' she laughs, 'I have some explaining to do tonight, but first thing tomorrow, I'll work on clearing your names, somehow'

'Just tell everyone that the Sergeant was helping with the… what did he call them, demons? Devils? And they all ran away together?' Dan suggests.

'No' Ari says immediately, 'We established that he only cooperated because they assured him that they would leave. You guys were right, as misguided as he was, Chuck was only doing what he thought would help. I want to end injustice, not spread it by lying about him. I won't throw him under the bus like that'

'Throw me under the bus then, I don't care since I'm leaving anyway' I say.

'Don't be an idiot' Dan says, 'We don't need to run away anymore'

'No, I don't, but I need to chase' I tell him, 'It was us, but how long until it's somebody else? Which lazy little town will he hang his hat in next?'

'Hold up Warren' Luke asks on the verge of tears, 'Where would you start looking?'

'I don't know yet, north somewhere' I shrug.

'If you're going after them' Dan says, arms crossed, as is becoming a common occurrence when he speaks 'Then good luck keeping me away'

'I'd like that, more than anything, but I can't ask that of you. You both have things to sort out here, and Ari will actually help you with them, I'm sure'

'What do you need?' she hits her fist in her palm, 'I'm in your debt, anything at all, I'll do my best to help you'

'Thank you, these guys can explain what's going on'

And then I turn to them.

'So, this is it then? Catch you later?' Dan scoffs.

'Thanks for sticking by me the whole way. Luke, Dan' I smile at them.

'Don't do this' Luke begs.

'You guys have work to do here, but there's nothing left for me'

I hug Luke tight.

'Trust Ari alright, she'll help your mum out' I tell him.

'You're a fucking idiot' Dan says, before wrapping his arms around both of us.

'Isabelle too, you're gonna get her somewhere happier, aren't you?' I nod.

'Once Izzy and Katsumi are safer, we could come with you Warren, if you just wait' Dan requests.

'I don't know how long that will take, and I'm not going to let them get too far away' I shake my head 'Thank you, for showing me how to make my own purpose. I hope I helped you both get free enough to make yours'

After some time, a tearful Ari speaks.

'I uh' she clears her throat, 'I can probably give the two of you a place to stay, at least until we sort everything out with your families'

'You guys will take care of the place while I'm away yeah?' I raise an eyebrow.

'Fuck this place' Luke says.

We all laugh, for what could be the last time, the same way we would laugh stoned out of our minds or when we'd fish and one of us would fall in. God, things were simple.

'Hey uh Dan is it alright if I hang on to this?' I pick up the machete, that Ari had left on the road, 'Just in case'

'Of course. Just in case, remember what happened last time you said that? You still owe me for the one you lost by the way' he smiles through his tears.

'It's time for me to go, you guys' I smile and pat them both on the back, ending our embrace.

They move over to Arianne and she puts a caring arm over each of them.

'How long do I have? Before you declare me missing or whatever?'

'Within twenty-four hours is the standard, but I'll leave it as late as I can'

'I'd appreciate it. Guys, is it okay if I take some food from the Rusty?'

'Take whatever you need' Dan says, 'We'll leave it parked there and get it in the morning'

'Ari, please take good care of them' I point at them.

'Don't worry about us' she gives me the thumbs up.

'Until we can all see you again' Luke smiles.

'Until then' I nod.

It takes some time due to the resistance their feet put up, but eventually she turns them away, an arm around each of their shoulders to stop them from looking back. The last police car, the one that was the Sergeant's, is the one that whisks them away from me, until I'm alone on the road, with nothing and no one.

XXVII
Summer Rain

The wet gravel crunches underneath my soaked, aching feet. It takes all my strength each time I drag one foot in front of the other, but even so I haul myself down the highway and towards the unknown. Puddles on the road throw the moonlight back up at me, I can see them on the asphalt as far as I can see ahead, the road as straight as an arrow. The egg on the side of my head twangs as a cool, southerly breeze weaves through from behind me, and I have to rub it with my hand.

I've taken one of the sleeping bags and a backpack of supplies from the Rusty, I don't know where I'll sleep tonight, fuck, I don't even know how much longer I'll be alive. But, because Locke Dawson, that brilliant devil, deemed humans too wicked to be left to our own devices, I won't come back until I've seen this through, cleansed the country of his creations and seen him brought to justice. In a way I think he's right about humanity, it did create him after all, so how virtuous can it really be? No one could be born into the world already filled with hate, so I have to wonder what it was that broke his faith in his fellow man?

I pick up my pace now, striding instead of plodding. He took everything from me, but I will take it back. I was a fool to think there was a set destiny for anyone in this world, people are just too unpredictable to act on divine purpose, but it's that complexity of people that sets us apart from the beasts. I thank you for that much Mr Dawson, this is the most alive I've felt in my life, but I won't allow you to snuff out the countless hopes and dreams, even those of the maggots and cockroaches. I speed up even more.

A bright light appears from behind me, casting a long shadow of myself ahead of me, a car. My dark silhouette stretches North along the highway, telling me to get moving, but as the mechanical rumbling approaches, I turn away from myself and look back. It's closer than I thought, not so close to see it clearly yet but the tears have already brimmed in my sockets, I should have known. I laugh to myself, it's all I can do. I'm angry at them for coming, but I'm not strong enough to pretend I'm not relieved. The vermilion panels, ugly and dented, roll to a stop behind me, the lights flicker out and they both hop out at the same time, Luke pulls his woollen hat on and Dan goes around the back and pulls out a fuel can.

'Sorry to keep you waiting' Luke beams.

'Just had to get some fuel' Dan shakes the canister at me, the liquid inside sloshing around.

They both have had their injuries dressed, no doubt by Ari.

'What are you two doing here?' I ask, out of breath.

'You didn't think we'd let you go alone do you?' Dan says after looking at Luke.

'You should go back' I tell them.

'Didn't I tell you he'd say that?' Dan laughs, approaching me and giving me a hug.

'We have nothing left here either remember? It's not like either of us can go home right now' Luke says.

'You've got family that need help' I say.

'Well, we told Ari all about it, and she promised she'd start to sort those things out for us tomorrow' Dan says, 'You were right to trust her Warren, she's the best, so we feel pretty good about leaving Izzy and Katsumi for her to take care of'

'We gave her those rings too' Luke says mournfully, 'She said she's get them to Wanda, where they ought to be'

'Did you also tell her that you're leaving?' I ask.

'Yeah' Luke sighs, 'We told her that we need to look after you'

'I think she understands' Dan nods and smiles.

My eyes overflow, the tears run down my face.

'There's no changing your minds, is there?' I ask.

'Nah' Luke says.

'No chance' Dan says at the same time.

'Then what are we doing standing on the road like dickheads? My feet are killing me' I slap them on the back.

I step past them towards the vehicle but Luke speaks again.

'Wait, I just thought of something'

'Yeah?'

'You know how they can track your phone, through the GPS or whatever it is?'

'That's not real!' Dan groans.

'It is' Luke affirms, 'I read about it online! We can't take them'

'That's like those people who think birds are all spy cameras set up by the government' Dan laughs, 'Warren tell him it's not true, you're a scientist'

'I'm not sure, fuck science, it's brought me nothing but grief' I grunt, crossing my arms, 'Let's destroy them'

'Fine, it's not like we need them now. If there's any final messages you need to send boys, now's the time' Dan declares, taking his phone from his pocket.

I think about it for a moment, composing something nice in my mind, then I pull my phone out. Even more missed calls from mum and dad. I pull up a new text message.

I love you both, and I'm sorry for everything, don't worry about me, I'll see you again, I promise

Sent. I pull my phone battery out and hurl it into the trees. Then I stamp down on my phone until its nothing but silicon splinters and circuit board shards. Luke does the same.

'Send anything?' I ask him.

'Yeah, I just told mum I love her and to remember our promise you know?'

'That's nice Luke, you'll see her again soon, once we wrap this thing up'

'Do you really think they're going to slip up and let us find them' Luke asks.

'That means more training then?' Luke groans.

Dan hurls his phone back down the road, after several seconds it clinks along the road.

'Who did you message?' I ask.

'No one' he says, 'I was just waiting for you guys'

'So, we're done here?' Luke exhales with finality.

'Yep, come on' Dan hops in the driver's seat.

Luke in the front passenger seat and I get into the back. The supplies take up all the foot room, so I lay down across the back seats. The seatbelt clips dig into my back and the seats are hard, but it feels nice to be able to lay down after tonight.

'You right to navigate?' Dan asks Luke.

'Sure' Luke pulls out a map book from Dan's stash, 'Where are we going, Captain?'

'North' I say, 'North for as long as you can stay awake Dan, then we find somewhere to camp and we plan our next move from there'

'Hope you guys know some songs and games because it's going to be a long night. Luke, get me one of those energy drinks Ari gave us'

Luke laughs and rummages through a bag, but I'm already dozing off. The car sputters to life and we roll forward. North.

'Oh yeah' Dan says between swigs, 'When we were at the police station, Ari gave us something for you! Under my seat, careful though'

Apprehensive, I reach my hand under there, and in amongst the rubbish, is a familiar feeling handle.

'No way' I pull out the machete, it's definitely the one.

'She took a look at it and said there wasn't any fingerprints on it after all, how strange is that?' Luke laughs.

'Said we may as well take it in case we knew anyone who might need it, know anyone?' Dan asks, looking at me in the mirror.

'Yeah, I know somebody, thanks Ari' I say back down the road.

Sliding it back under, I have to lay down when my head starts throbbing again, I wonder if the bruise around my throat has risen yet?

'This is the furthest out of Southway I've ever been' I yawn, stretching my arms.

'Really?' Luke asks, 'Wow, does it feel any different?'

I tilt my head back and look out the window. Upside down, the stars race away, getting left behind as the three of us skyrocket onwards into the unknown. I can see them all so clearly as we leave them, clearer than I ever have before. Until I looked up at the stars outside, I had hardly even noticed that the sky ahead is clear, the Southway rain is nowhere to be found.

'Yeah' I tell him, 'It does'

'And off we went'

From humble beginnings

'I was on my way. I had my friends and my mission, it was everything I wanted, in a way'

Well, don't stop, then what happened?

'After that, my world expanded. When we set out that night, it led to me meeting more people than I ever would have if my life had stayed on course'

Was that for better or for worse, do you think?

'Let me keep going and you can decide for yourself'

So, where did the three of you end up?

'Let's not get too far ahead, we had a whole lot of driving to do yet. I definitely don't miss that'

You can skip over most of the driving, if you'd rather.

'Then get comfortable, because things had only just gotten started'

ABOUT THE AUTHOR

Aaron Hughes was born and raised in the timber town of Manjimup in the south-west of Western Australia. Pursuing a fascination with science, he left the karri trees of his home town to study genetics in Perth, but the course ended up killing his passion for the subject.

Remembering the blistering remark of an English teacher that 'no one except Aaron should ever attempt creative writing again', he returned to Manjimup to write the book that had been swimming around in his head for years. *Nucleus: The Violent Science* is the first in a series of thrilling young adult sci-fi novels that follow the real-world and moral journeys of Warren Avery.

Lightning Source UK Ltd.
Milton Keynes UK
UKHW010644190520
363466UK00001B/49